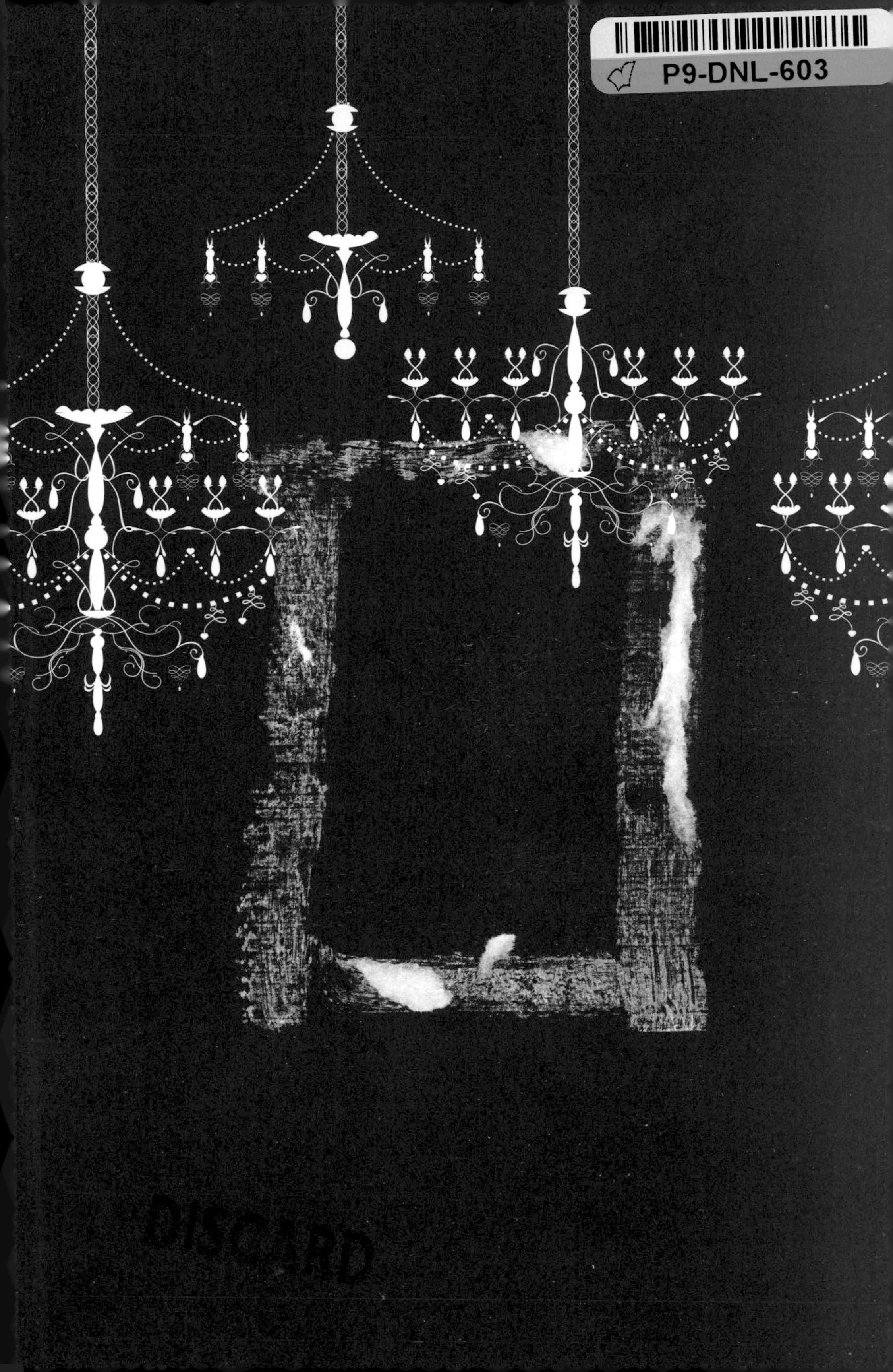

First Star I See Tonight

SUSAN ELIZABETH PHILLIPS

WILLIAM MORROW
An Imprint of HarperCollins*Publishers*

This book is a work of fiction. References to real people, events, establishments, organizations, or locales are intended only to provide a sense of authenticity, and are used fictitiously. All other characters, and all incidents and dialogue, are drawn from the author's imagination and are not to be construed as real.

HarperCollins books may be purchased for educational, business, or sales promotional use. For information please e-mail the Special Markets Department at SPsales@harpercollins.com.

FIRST EDITION

Designed by Bonni Leon-Berman

Library of Congress Cataloging-in-Publication Data has been applied for.

ISBN 978-0-06-240561-6 (hardcover)
ISBN 978-0-06-256025-4 (international edition)
ISBN 978-0-06-264187-8 (Barnes & Noble signed edition)
ISBN 978-0-06-264188-5 (Books-A-Million signed edition)
ISBN 978-0-06-264189-2 (Target signed edition)

16 17 18 19 20 RRD 10 9 8 7 6 5 4 3 2 1

In memory of Cathie Linz:

lover of cats, the Beatles, red boots, birthdays, librarians, friends, and good books. As Paul sang, "You and I have memories longer than the road that stretches out ahead." Thank you for the enthusiasm and the endless encouragement you gave your fellow writers. And from those closest to you, most of all, we thank you for giving us De.

First Star I See Tonight

1

The city was his. Cooper Graham owned this town, and all was right with his world. That's what he told himself.

A kitten-voiced brunette knelt before him, her long, dark hair brushing his bare thigh. "This is so you won't forget me," she purred.

The felt point of her Sharpie tickled his inner thigh. He looked down at the top of her head. "How could I forget a beautiful woman like you?"

"You'd better not." She pressed her lips to the phone number she'd written in black marker on his leg. It would take forever for that ink to wear off, but he appreciated his fans, and he hadn't pushed her away.

"Sure wish I could stay and chat with you," he said as he politely drew her to her feet, "but I have to get my run in."

She hugged the places his hands had touched. "You can text me anytime, day or night."

He gave her his automatic grin and set off on the paved path that ran along the Lake Michigan shore beneath Chicago's magnificent skyline. He was the luckiest guy in the world, right? Sure he was. Everybody wanted to be his friend, his confidant, his lover. Even the foreign tourists knew who he was. Berlin, Delhi, Osaka—made no difference. The whole world knew Cooper Graham.

Burnham Harbor slipped by on his right. It was September, so the boats would be coming out of the lake soon, but for now, they bobbed at anchor. He picked up his pace, making sure his running shoes hit the Lakefront Trail in perfect rhythm. A woman's blond ponytail bobbed ahead of him on the running path. Strong legs. Great ass. No challenge. He passed her without altering his easy pace.

It was a good day to be Cooper Graham, but then every day was. Ask anybody. The colony of seagulls circling the Chicago shoreline dipped their wings to honor him. The leaves of the giant oaks that shaded the path rustled with frenzied applause. Even the horns of the taxi drivers racing by on Lake Shore Drive cheered him on. He loved this city, and the city loved him right back.

The man up ahead had an athlete's build, and he was fast.

But not fast enough.

Coop passed him. The guy didn't even look thirty. Coop was thirty-seven and banged up from a long football career, but not banged up enough to let anybody get past him. Cooper Graham: drafted out of Oklahoma State by Houston; eight seasons as the starting quarterback for the Miami Dolphins; a final trade to the powerhouse Chicago Stars, where, after three seasons, he'd gifted the team with diamond-encrusted Super Bowl rings. Once that ring was on his finger, he'd done the smart thing and retired while he was on top. Damn right he had. He got out of the game before he became one of those pathetic old-man jocks trying desperately to hold on to his glory days.

"Hey, Coop!" A runner coming from the opposite direction called out to him. "The Stars are going to miss you this year."

Coop gave the guy a thumbs-up.

The three years he'd spent with the Stars had been the best of his life. His roots might be buried in the Oklahoma dirt, Miami might have matured him, but it was Chicago that had ultimately tested him. And the rest was football history.

"Coop!" The pretty brunette heading in his direction barely kept from stumbling as she recognized him.

He gave her his patented female-fan smile. "Hey, sweetheart. You're lookin' real good."

"Not as good as you!"

His body had taken a beating over the years, but he was still strong, with the same quick reflexes and winning attitude that had brought him national attention during his college days. That attention had only grown hotter as the years had passed. He might have retired from pro ball, but that didn't mean he wasn't still at the top of his game—except now, the game had shifted to a new playing field, one he was determined to conquer.

Another mile sped by. Then two. Only the bicyclists were faster. They were his courtiers, clearing the way for him on this September afternoon. No one could catch him—not the young Turks who manned the pits at the Board of Trade or the tattooed gym rats showing off their pumped-up biceps.

Coop hit the three-mile mark, and a runner finally passed him. Young. Maybe a college kid. Coop had been slacking, and he kicked it back up. Nobody beat him. That's the way he was made.

The kid glanced over. He saw right away who was beside him,

and his eyes nearly bugged out of their sockets. Coop nodded and ran on, leaving the kid behind. *Old man? Forget that.*

He heard feet coming up behind him. The kid again. Now he was next to Coop, looking for bragging rights. *"I ran with Coop Graham today, and I kicked his ass."*

Not gonna happen, baby boy.

Coop sped up. He wasn't one of those asshole players who believed he'd won that Super Bowl ring by himself, but he also knew the Stars couldn't have done it without him because, more than anything, Coop had to win.

There was the kid again. Pulling up. He was scrawny, with toothpick legs and arms too long for his body. Coop must have him by fifteen years, but he didn't believe in making excuses, and he dug in. Anybody who said winning wasn't everything was full of it. Winning was all that counted, and every loss he'd suffered had been toxic. But no matter how much he'd seethed inside, he was always the sportsman: self-deprecating, gallant in his praise of the opposition, never complaining about bad calls, inept teammates, or injuries. No matter how bitter his thoughts, how poisonous each word tasted in his mouth, he never let it show. Whining made losers into bigger losers. But, goddam, he hated to lose. And he wasn't going to lose today.

The kid had a long, steady stride. Too long. Coop understood the science of running in a way the kid didn't, and he reined in his tendency to overstride. He wasn't stupid. Stupid runners got hurt.

Okay, he was stupid. A searing pain crucified his right shin, he was breathing too hard, and his bad hip throbbed. His brain told him he had nothing left to prove, but he couldn't let the kid pass. He wasn't made that way.

The run turned into a sprint. He'd played through pain his whole career, and he wouldn't cave in to it now. Not in the first September of his retirement, while his former teammates were busting their asses running drills to get ready for another Sunday. Not like other retired players content to get fat and lazy living off their money.

Five miles. Lincoln Park. They were side by side again. His lungs burned, his hip screamed, and his shins were on fire. Medial tibial stress syndrome. Ordinary shin splints, but there was nothing ordinary about this kind of pain.

The kid fell back and caught up. Fell back. Caught up again. He was saying something. Coop ignored it. Blocked out the pain as he always did. Focused on his pumping legs, on grasping whatever molecule of air his lungs could suck in. Focused on winning.

"Coop! Mr. Graham!"

What the hell?

"Could I . . . have a . . . selfie . . . with you?" the kid gasped. "For . . . my dad?"

All he wanted was a *selfie*? Sweat dripped from every pore of Coop's body. His lungs were an inferno. He slowed, and so did the kid, until they both came to a stop. Coop wanted to drop to the ground and curl up, but the kid was still upright, and Coop would rather shoot himself in the head.

A drop of sweat trickled down the little shithead's neck. "I guess I shouldn't . . . interrupt your workout . . . but . . . it'd mean a lot . . . to my dad."

The kid wasn't breathing nearly as hard as Coop, but with the discipline of fifteen years in the NFL, Coop mustered a smile. "Sure. Be happy to."

The kid pulled out a cell and fussed with it, talking the whole time about how he and his dad were Coop's biggest fans. Coop struggled to keep his lungs working. The kid turned out to be a

Division I sprinter, which made Coop feel a little better. Sure, he'd have to keep his hip iced for the next couple of days, but so what? Being a champion was his birthright.

All in all, it was still a good day to be Cooper Graham.

Except for one pesky woman.

He spotted her on the Museum Campus right after he'd cabbed it back to get his car. There she was, sitting on a bench, pretending to read a book.

Yesterday, she'd been dressed like a homeless person with scraggly gray hair. Today her black shorts, leggings, and long T-shirt made her look like a student at the Art Institute. He couldn't see her car, but he had no doubt it was parked somewhere close. If he hadn't happened to notice a dark green Hyundai Sonata with a broken taillight parked near him one too many times in the last four days, he might not have realized he was being followed. He'd had enough of it.

But as he headed toward her, a city bus pulled up. Maybe she had ESP, because she jumped on, and he missed his chance. That didn't bother him much, since he was fairly certain he'd see her again.

And he did. Two nights later.

✶

Piper crossed the street to the entrance of Spiral, the nightclub Cooper Graham had opened in July, six months after his retirement from the Chicago Stars. The light September breeze feathered her bare legs and blew up under the skirt of her short black sleeveless dress. Beneath it, she wore her next-to-last pair of clean underwear. Sooner or later, she'd have to do laundry, but for now, all she cared about was recording Cooper Graham's every move.

Her scalp itched from where she'd tucked her short, chopped hair under the long brunette wig she'd picked up at a resale shop. She prayed the hair, along with the scoop-neck dress, cat's-eye liner, scarlet lipstick, and push-up bra would finally get her past the primitive life-form who passed for Spiral's door manager, an obstacle she hadn't been able to overcome on her past two attempts.

The same doorman was on duty tonight. He was shaped like a nineteenth-century torpedo: fat warhead, thick tank, feet splayed like fins. The first time, he'd grunted his dismissal of her at the same time that he waved a pair of swishy-haired blondes through the club's brass double doors. She, of course, had challenged him. "What do you mean, you're full? You're letting them in."

He'd taken in her cropped dark hair, best white blouse, and jeans with his squinty little eyes. "Just what I said."

That had been last Saturday night. Piper couldn't do her job unless she was inside Spiral, but since the club was open only four nights a week, she hadn't been able to make her next attempt until yesterday. Even though she'd combed her hair and put on a skirt and blouse, he hadn't been impressed, and that meant upping her game. She'd picked up this dress at H&M, traded in her comfortable boots for a torturous pair of strappy stilettos, and borrowed an evening clutch from her friend Jen. The clutch wasn't big enough to hold more than her cell, fake ID, and a couple of twenty-dollar bills. The rest—everything that correctly identified her as Piper Dove—was stashed in the trunk of her car: laptop computer; a duffel containing the hats, sunglasses, jackets, and scarves she used as disguises; and a semiobscene-looking device called a Tinkle Belle.

Spiral, named after Cooper Graham's long and deadly accurate spiral passes, was Chicago's hottest club, and a line had predictably formed at the velvet rope. As she approached Torpedo Head, she held her breath and drew her shoulders back to push up her breasts. "You're busy tonight, gov," she sort of cooed in the fake British accent she'd been practicing.

Torpedo Head noticed her breasts, then her face, then dropped his chin to take in her legs. The man was a pig. Good. She cocked her head and gave him a smile that revealed the straight white teeth her father had spent thousands of dollars on when she'd been twelve, even though she'd begged him to use the money to buy her a horse. Now that she was thirty-three, the horse still struck her as the better deal.

"I cawn't get over how big American men are." With the tip of her index finger, she pushed up the bridge of the retro-trendy eyeglasses she'd added at the last minute to further disguise her appearance.

He leered. "I work out."

"*Obb*-viously." She wished she could choke the son of a bitch with his Spiral lanyard.

He waved her through into the club's luxurious black-and-bronze interior.

She'd never liked the club scene, not even when she was in her early twenties. All that purposeful merriment made her feel somehow apart, disconnected. But this was business, and Spiral, with its megacelebrity owner, was no ordinary dance club. Two levels of smart design allowed for a great dance floor but also places to talk or troll for hookups without having to scream over the music. The movable leather banquettes and the more private nooks with their softly illuminated, cube-shaped cocktail tables were already filled with the Thursday-night crowd. Tonight's DJ spun from a booth perched above a dance floor where muted colors blended and re-formed like horny amoebae.

She bought her one drink of the night, a six-dollar Sprite, at the central bar. Over it, a suspended ceiling of LED rods hovered like a golden UFO. She watched the bartender for a while, then made her way through the crowd to a recess between a pair of icicle-shaped bronze wall sconces, where she planned to observe the host as soon as he appeared.

A skinny guy with waxed hair and a bottle of Miller Lite stepped in front of her and blocked her view. "I'm not feeling good. I think I'm missing some vitamin U."

"Get lost."

He looked so hurt.

"Hold on," she said with a sigh.

His expression was pathetically hopeful. She adjusted her glasses and said, more kindly, "Most of the pickup lines you find on the Internet are cheesy. You'd do better if you'd just say hi."

"You for real?"

"Only a suggestion."

He curled his lip at her. "Bitch."

So much for trying to be nice.

The guy went off in search of easier prey. She took a sip of Sprite. Torpedo Head had exchanged his door manager position for bouncer duty. His specialty seemed to be chatting up leggy blondes.

The club's VIP lounge was located in an open mezzanine. She scanned what she could see of it for her quarry, but he wasn't visible among the guests sitting near the bronze railing. She needed to get up there, but a blond bulldog of a bouncer had been stationed at the bottom to keep out the riffraff, which, unfortunately, included her. Frustrated, she worked her way through the well-heeled throng to the other side. And that's when she spotted him.

Even in a crowd, Cooper Graham stood out like a beacon in a candle factory. He was ridiculously masculine. Beyond ridiculous. He was the Holy Grail of men, with thick brown hair the color of burnt toast drizzled in honey. He had a square jaw, broad shoulders, and a cleft in his chin that was such a cliché he should have been embarrassed. He wore his customary uniform: perfectly fitted button-down shirt, jeans, and cowboy boots. On most people, cowboy boots in Chicago were an affectation, but he'd been born and raised on an Oklahoma ranch. Still, she didn't like the boots; the long, muscular legs rising above them; or—as a lifelong Chicago Bears fan—the team he'd played for. Piper had to work hard for every penny, unlike this arrogant, egotistical, overly privileged ex-Stars quarterback and his stable of movie star girlfriends.

She'd been following him for nearly a week, and he'd been on the floor of his nightclub every night it was open, but she doubted that would last for long. Celebrity nightclub owners tended to fade away under the grind of real work.

Graham was doing the rounds—slapping men on the back and flirting with the women who were lined up around him like jets on the runways at O'Hare. She didn't like judging other members of her sex, but that was part of her job now, and none of these girls looked as though they were future CEOs—too much hair swinging, eye batting, and boob thrusting. Watching them made her grateful that she had zero desire to hook up with anyone right now. All she cared about was her job.

The crowd surrounding him was growing. She looked around for a bouncer, but the only ones she spotted were busily engaged in deep conversations with the female guests. So far, no client had hired her as a bodyguard, but she'd taken a lengthy training course, and she could see that Graham's lack of security was irresponsible, although it might let her get closer to him.

Graham seemed at ease despite the crush, but she noticed him occasionally scanning the crowd, as if he were looking for a pass receiver. His gaze flicked in her direction, then moved on.

As the crowd around him approached a dangerous level, he somehow managed to work himself free and head up the stairs toward the mezzanine and the VIP lounge. Now that she was inside the club, her inability to follow him there was maddening.

She made her way to the ladies' room, where she heard nothing more interesting than gossip about who'd made it as far as the fur-covered bed he reportedly kept in his office. Someone touched her shoulder as she came out. *Torpedo Head.*

Like the other bouncers, he wore dark pants and a white dress shirt that must have been specially tailored to fit the thick neck that marked both him and his fellow goons as former football players. "You have to come with me."

Other than offering Miller Lite Boy some much-needed advice on improving his pickup game, she hadn't done anything to draw attention to herself, and she didn't like this. Rearing back on her unwieldy heels, she brought out her fake accent. "Oh, gawd. Why?"

"ID check."

"Crikey! I already showed it at the bloody door. And I very much appreciate the compliment, but I'm thirty-three years old."

"Spot-check."

This was no spot-check. Something was up. She was about to refuse more forcefully when he jerked his big head toward the steps that led to the mezzanine, inadvertently giving her the chance she'd been waiting for to get closer to the VIP lounge. She gave him a blazing smile. "Right, then. Let's move along and settle this."

He grunted.

At the top of the mezzanine steps, a pair of bronzed pillars marked the entrance to VIP, but as they got close, he grabbed her arm and herded her around a corner and through a plain door off to the left.

It was an unimpressive office where folding wooden shutters covered the lower half of a pair of windows, and a wall-mounted television silently broadcast ESPN. An iMac sat on a streamlined desk across from a two-cushion couch. Above it was a framed Chicago Stars jersey with the name Graham on the back. The Stars aqua-and-gold team colors had always looked girly to her in comparison to her beloved Chicago Bears no-nonsense navy blue and orange.

"Wait here." The goon stepped out and closed the door behind him.

VIP was only a few steps away. She counted to twenty and reached for the doorknob.

The door swung open in her face. She tripped backward, focusing so hard on keeping her balance that the door shut again before she realized who'd walked in. A whoosh roared through her ears.

Cooper Graham himself.

She felt as if she'd been struck by a supernova, and she hated that. After following him for six days, she should have been better prepared. But seeing him from a distance and being ten feet away were completely different experiences.

He'd sucked up all the air in the room, and the good ol' boy grin he turned on his customers was nowhere in sight. This was his face at the line of scrimmage. One thing was certain. If Graham wanted to see her, this wasn't about a simple ID check.

She mentally ticked off the possible reasons she'd been detained and decided she hated every one of them. But she told herself Graham wasn't the only one in the room who knew how to fake a play, and unlike him, she had everything at stake.

Even though her heart was pounding so hard she was afraid he'd see, she tried to look as if this was the thrill of her lifetime. "Brilliant! I say, I'm quite gobsmacked."

His eyes, a shade darker than his burnt-toast hair, swept over her, taking in her long wig, pushed-up breasts, and okay legs. She wasn't a beauty, but she wasn't a dog, either, and if she had a shred of vanity, she would have been demoralized by his obvious disdain. But she didn't, and she wasn't.

She dug her toe-numbing heels into the carpet as he came farther into the office. His thick brown hair was a little disheveled. Not fashionably rumpled—more the dishevelment of a man who couldn't be bothered with bimonthly haircuts or a shelf full of grooming products.

Stay calm. Keep your focus.

Without warning, he snatched her clutch away, and she gave a little hiss of dismay. "Bugger!" she cried, a few beats too late.

She stared at his oversize hands—ten inches from thumb to little finger. She knew this because she did her homework. Just as she knew those big hands had thrown more than three hundred touchdowns. The same hands digging in her clutch and pulling out her fake green card.

"Esmerelda Crocker?"

A good investigator had to improvise, and the more detail she could give, the more convincing she'd be. "I go by Esme. Lady Esme, actually. Esmerelda is a family name."

"Is that so." His voice rolled from his lips like deep water over a parched Oklahoma prairie.

She gave a shaky nod. "Passed down through the generations to honor the second wife of the fifth Earl of Conundrum. Died in childbirth, the poor cow."

"My condolences." He looked inside again. "No credit cards?"

"They're so vulgar, don't you think?"

"Money's never vulgar," the cowboy drawled.

"How very American of you."

He began rummaging in her clutch again, something that didn't take long, since she'd left her wallet safely stashed in her car—a wallet that held her fresh new private investigator's license as well as half a dozen business cards.

DOVE INVESTIGATIONS

Est. 1958

Truth Brings Peace

The original business cards had read: "Truth Brings Piece." Her grandfather had been a brilliant investigator, but a lousy speller.

Graham smelled like money and fame, not that she could exactly describe what either one smelled like, but she knew it when she sniffed it, the same way she knew that the future of her business depended on what happened next. She pulled in the few molecules of air his presence hadn't already burned up. "I don't really mind you mucking about in there like that, but I am curious what you're looking for."

He shoved the clutch back at her. "Something that'll explain why you've been following me."

She'd been so careful! Her mind raced. How had she given herself away? What rookie mistake had she made that had sunk her? All her hard work was for nothing—sleeping in her car, living on junk food, peeing into the Tinkle Belle, and—worst of all—spending her life savings buying Dove Investigations from her cheating, detestable stepmother. Dove Investigations—the detective agency her grandfather had founded, her father had built, and the one that would have been hers from birth if her father hadn't been so bullheaded. Every sacrifice she'd made would be useless. She'd be forced back to life in a cubicle, right along with having to live with the knowledge that a pampered jock like Cooper Graham had gotten the best of her.

Acid churned in the pit of her stomach. She arranged her forehead in a confused frown. "Following you?"

He stood silhouetted against the framed Chicago Stars jersey displayed on the wall behind him. His blue, button-down shirt made his already formidable shoulders look even wider, and the rolled-up sleeves showcased the lean muscles of his lower arms. The expert fit of his dark jeans—neither too tight nor too loose—exhibited the long, powerful legs that had been designed by God to be steady, strong, and quick—much to the disadvantage of her Chicago Bears.

His gaze was as grim as an Illinois winter. "I've seen you parked outside my condo, following me to my gym, to here. And I want to know why."

She'd thought she was being so inventive with all her disguises. How had he managed to see through them? Denial would be futile. She sank onto the couch and tried to think.

He waited. Arms folded. Standing on the sidelines watching the enemy's offense fall apart.

"Well . . ." She swallowed. Looked up at him. "The fact is . . ." She released her breath in a whoosh. "I'm your stalker."

"Stalker?"

A rush of adrenaline spread through her. She wouldn't go down without a fight, and she shot up from the couch. "Not a dangerous one. Lord, no. Merely obsessed."

"With me." A statement, not a question. He'd been here before.

"I don't make a habit of stalking people. This . . . quite got away from me, you see." She didn't know exactly how this tactic could save her, but she plunged on. "I'm not full-out barmy, you understand. Just . . . mildly unhinged."

He cocked his head, but at least he was listening. And why not? Lunatics were always fascinating.

"I assure you, I'm only a bit of a nutter," she said breathlessly. "Absolutely harmless. You don't have to worry about violence."

"Only that I have a stalker."

"Not the first one, I daresay. A man like you . . ." She paused and tried not to choke. "A god."

The hard look in his eyes indicated he wasn't easily swayed by flattery. "I don't want to see you anywhere near me again. Got it?"

She got it. It was over. *Fini.* But still, she couldn't give up. "I'm afraid that will be impossible." She paused. "Until my new medication kicks in."

The cleft in his chin deepened as he set his jaw. "What you're doing is illegal."

"And mortifying. You can't imagine how humiliating it is to be in this position. Nothing is more painful than . . . unrequited love." The last two words came out as a croak she hoped he'd attribute to adoration, because everything about him got her hackles up. His size, his good looks, but most of all, the arrogance that came from a lifetime of people kissing his taut butt just because he'd been born with natural talent.

He didn't show even a flicker of sympathy. "If I catch sight of you again, I'm calling the cops."

"I—I understand." She was done. This had been a futile tactic from the beginning. Unless . . . She nodded at him with manufactured sympathy. "I understand how terrifying this must be to you."

He leaned back ever so slightly on the heels of his cowboy boots. "I wouldn't say that."

"Rubbish." Maybe she'd found the chink in his manly armor. "You're terrified I might suddenly pop out at you when you're walking down the street. That I'll be armed with one of those odious handguns you insane Americans insist on carrying around like chewing gum." And like the Glock in her car trunk. "I'd never do that. Good gracious, no! But you don't know that for certain, and how would you defend yourself?"

"I think I could handle you," he said dryly.

She managed to look puzzled. "If that's true, why would you be concerned about a harmless twit like myself following you around for a bit?"

He no longer seemed quite so laid-back. "Because I don't like it."

She tried to appear both sympathetic and adoring. "So terrifying for you."

"Stop saying that!"

"I understand. It's a dreadful dilemma."

His eyes flashed lethal golden sparks. "It's not a dilemma at all. Stay the hell away from me."

She forged on. "Yes, well, as I believe I mentioned, it's not that easy—not until my medication takes effect. The doctor has assured me it won't be much longer. But until then, I'm quite helpless. Perhaps a compromise?"

"No compromise."

"A week at the most. In the meantime, if you spot me, you'll simply pretend I'm not around." She brushed her hands together. "There. That's done."

No surprise. He wasn't buying it. "I meant what I said about the cops."

She twisted her hands, hoping the gesture didn't look as theatrical as it felt. "I've heard terrible things about Chicago jails . . ."

"You should have thought about that before you started your stalking gig."

It could be the stress of so many sleepless nights, or even a spike in her blood sugar from all the junk food. More likely it was the threat of losing everything she'd worked for. She dipped her head, slipped off her glasses, and dabbed at her dry cheeks with her knuckles, as if she'd started to cry, something she'd never do in a thousand years no matter how horrible things got. "I don't want to go to jail," she said on a sniff. "I've never even had a traffic ticket." Now *that* was a lie, but she was an excellent driver, and the speed limits on the city's expressways were moronically slow. "What do you think will happen to me there?"

"I don't know, and I don't care."

Despite his words, she detected a hesitation, and she dove for it. "Yes, well, you might as well call them now because no matter how hard I try, I know I won't be able to help myself."

"Don't say that."

Did he sound the slightest bit rattled? She managed another sniff and dabbed at her eyes with her index finger. "I wouldn't wish the pain of this kind of love on anyone."

"It's not love," he said with disgust. "It's craziness."

"I know. It's absurd." She swiped her perfectly dry nostrils with the back of her hand. "How can you possibly love someone whom you only met today?"

"You can't."

Until he threw her out, she wasn't giving up. "Couldn't you reconsider? Only for one week until the new pills restore my sanity?"

"No."

"Of course you couldn't. And I do want the best for you. I can't tolerate the idea of you cowering in fear, afraid to leave your condo because you're terrified you'll see me."

"I'm not going to be terrified—"

"I'm sure I'll be able to survive jail. How long do you think they'll keep me? Is there the slightest chance you would— Never mind. It's too much to ask you to visit me while I'm behind bars."

"You're completely nuts."

"Oh, yes. But harmless. And remember, it's only temporary." She'd gotten this far. She might as well go for broke. "If you were physically attracted to me . . . You're not, are you?"

"No!"

His outrage was reassuring. "Then I won't offer to . . . sexually satisfy you." *Gleckkk!* She was going to wash her mouth out with soap when this was over.

"Get some help," he snarled.

He went to the door and called in his goon. A few minutes later, she was on the street.

Now what?

2

Cooper had met a lot of loonies during his career, but that lady lived in a bat house all her own, complete with blacked-out windows and a big ol' hole in the roof. One thing he'd say for her, though . . . She was straightforward. She'd laid her crazy right out on the front lawn for all the world to see.

He needed to get back down to the club floor, but he stayed behind his desk. After two months in this business, his office still smelled strange—not of rubber and sweat—not of specially formulated pain compounds and chlorine-doused whirlpools. Instead, it carried the scent of paper and paint, of new upholstery and a computer printer cartridge. But as much as he missed those familiar smells, he wouldn't let himself hold on to the past. Opening Spiral was his announcement to the world that he'd never become one more washed-up jock with nothing better to do than seal himself in an announcer's booth and broadcast bullshit about plays he could no longer pull off himself. The nightclub business was his new turf, and Spiral was only the beginning. He intended to build himself an empire, and just like in football, failure wasn't an option.

He turned back to his computer and Googled "Esmerelda Crocker." Her green card had given her age as thirty-three, but she looked a lot younger. He flipped from one screen to the next and eventually found her name on an alumni list for London's Middlesex University. No other information. And no photo to show that crazy-wide mouth, firm jaw, or those wily eyes almost the exact color of a blueberry Pop-Tart—eyes that demanded he jump into her crackpot world right along with her.

If he hadn't been so pissed, he would have laughed at her offer to "sexually satisfy" him. He didn't need any more crazy in his life. Besides, after eight years of seeing his name plastered all over the tabloids, he was on temporary hiatus from women.

He hadn't intended to turn into a cliché—one more NFL quarterback with a beautiful Hollywood actress in his bed. He wouldn't have, either, if he'd stuck with a single actress. But after that first relationship had fizzled due to conflicting schedules, too much publicity, and infidelity—hers, not his—he'd met another beautiful A-lister. And then another. And then one more after that.

In his defense, all four of those relationships had been with stars who were brainy as well as beautiful. He liked whip-smart, successful women who also happened to be heart-stoppingly beautiful. What man didn't? And being an NFL quarterback gave him access to the cream of the crop. Now, however, all his laser-sharp attention was focused on growing a nightclub empire. Women brought too much drama, too much press, and too damned much perfume. If he was quarterback of the world, he'd outlaw the stuff. Women should smell like women.

Esmerelda hadn't worn perfume, and with all her disguises, who knew what her hair looked like? But there was that interesting face and those shapely legs. Still, the whole episode was making the back of his neck itch exactly the same way it did right before he got blindsided.

*

Piper jerked off her wig and drove home from Spiral with one desperate scheme after another churning through her head. A different approach. A better disguise. But it wouldn't take him long to see through both. If she didn't come up with something quickly, she'd be on a one-way street back to a computer job in a cubicle, something she couldn't abide thinking about. Her last job as a digital strategist for a local chain of auto parts stores had been interesting at first, but after the second year, boredom had begun to set in, and by the fifth year, she'd found herself dreaming of a zombie apocalypse.

Her father had denied her the career she was born for, working with him at Dove Investigations—or even working with one of his competitors, something he'd made certain didn't happen. Everybody in the country knew him, and Duke Dove had put out the word. *"Anybody who hires my little girl to do any investigating that doesn't involve stayin' at her computer is gonna have to deal with me."*

But Duke was dead, and she owned the business he hadn't wanted her to have—the business she'd paid far too much to buy from her stepmother only to discover too late that Duke's client list was woefully out-of-date, and her stepmother's bookkeeping practices were, if not outright fraudulent, the next closest thing. Piper had bought little more than a name, but the name was precious to her, and she wouldn't give up without the fight of her life.

By the time she fell asleep, she'd made up her mind. She was going to stick with barmy Esmerelda Crocker and hope for the best.

The next morning, she showered, slipped into jeans and a T-shirt, and ran her fingers through her wet hair—no need for a wig. After she'd grabbed her coffee and a slice of three-day-old pizza, she set out.

The second-story condo she couldn't afford to keep much longer was part of a five-unit brownstone in the city's Andersonville neighborhood and boasted its own private parking space. As she slung her bag into her car along with her travel mug and the cold pizza slice, she wondered whether she'd be in jail by the end of the day. It was a risk she had to take.

Graham occupied the top two floors of a converted, four-story former seminary on a tree-lined street in Lakeview. Lakeview wasn't Chicago's most expensive neighborhood, but it was one of its best with great shops, trendy restaurants, a stretch of shoreline, and Wrigley Field. She wedged her Sonata into a semi-parking spot across from a postage-stamp park and took a few bites of the pizza and a swig of coffee. Her days of treating herself to a morning Starbucks were gone.

She tugged on a blade of her real hair—short, choppy, the same chestnut brown Duke said her mother's had been, before she'd been murdered in a sidewalk robbery. Piper was four at the time and barely remembered her, but the effect of her mother's violent death had set the course of Piper's upbringing.

Duke had raised Piper to be tough. He'd enrolled her in one self-defense class after another, along with teaching her every trick he'd picked up over the years. He'd taught her to be strong, and even when she was very young, he'd freeze her out if she cried. He'd rewarded her toughness by teaching her to shoot and taking her to ball games, by letting her go with him on trips to the corner bar and laughing when she cussed. But no tears. No whining. And no visits to play at a friend's house until he'd run a background check.

That was the bewildering, contradictory part of her upbringing. At the same time he demanded strength from her, he was also maddeningly overprotective—a constant source of conflict between them as she'd grown older and he'd planted himself firmly between her and her ambitions. He'd raised her to be as tough as he was and then tried to wrap her in cotton.

She wadded up the rest of her pizza and shoved it in the overstuffed litterbag hanging from her dashboard. She'd begged Duke to let her join him, but he'd refused.

"This business is too dirty for a woman. I didn't spend a fortune on your education to see you staked out in a car photographing some asshole cheating on his wife."

Her throat tightened. She missed him. The disturbing combination of his harshness and his overprotection had caused years of raging arguments between them and left her feeling as if she was never quite enough. Still, she'd never doubted his love, and she kept expecting to hear his voice on the phone warning her not to be walking around the goddam city at night or getting into a goddam cab without making sure the driver had a legitimate license.

You drove me crazy, Dad. But I loved you.

She forced a sip of coffee down her tight throat and tried to concentrate on transferring the last of yesterday's handwritten notes to her laptop instead of thinking about her money-grubbing stepmother, who was now enjoying a town house in Bonita Springs bought with Piper's money. An hour went by. She wanted more coffee, but that would mean pulling out the Tinkle Belle.

Just as she'd begun to wonder if Graham would appear, his one-hundred-grand metallic-blue Tesla emerged from the alley that backed up to the building's garages. But instead of pulling into the street, he stopped. The sunlight reflecting off his windshield kept her from seeing much, but she'd parked in plain sight, and he had to have spotted her.

The moment of decision. Would he call the police or not?

She made herself put the window down and give him a cheery wave, along with a thumbs-up, that she hoped signified Esmerelda was loony, but not dangerous, and that he should ignore her and go about his business.

He still didn't pull out, and she couldn't tell if he was on his cell. If she drove away now, he wouldn't have her arrested, but she'd also be giving in, and that wasn't how she was made.

His car began to move. She started her Sonata and followed him toward Uptown, straining all the time to hear a siren. She kept three cars between them, not trying to hide her presence, but also not crowding him. The Tesla abruptly swung into the right lane and squealed around a tight corner onto a narrow residential street. She veered into the right lane and made the same turn.

Cars were parked on both sides of the street, and a man in an orange T-shirt pushed a hand mower across the wedge of grass that made up his front lawn. She drove another few blocks and spotted the Tesla on a cross street off to her right. Another quick turn and the car had disappeared. Graham wanted her to believe he could get away from her anytime he chose. Just as well he didn't know Piper had been taking rigorous courses in offensive, defensive, and high-speed driving—another strain on her budget, but skills she hoped she'd need. Too much aggression on Esmerelda's part would send the wrong message, and she backed off. Besides, she was fairly certain where he'd end up.

Sure enough, he arrived at his gym not much later. She waved to him from her perch across the street. He threw her a glare, and she responded with the peace sign. *Barmy, not dangerous.* He stalked into the building.

For the rest of the afternoon, she followed him. She gave him plenty of room so he wouldn't get too uptight. He stayed away from the rougher parts of the city where she'd twice seen him in intimate conversations with street corner drug dealers. Hard to believe he'd have to buy his drugs off the street, but she'd jotted down each encounter in her log for her client to see.

Late in the afternoon, he disappeared into a mirrored-glass building on North Wacker that housed a major investment group. She knew Graham was looking for financing to start a national franchise of high-end nightclubs with other famous athletes at the helm. Since he had more money than the Illinois treasury, he could probably finance a big chunk of it himself, but Graham wanted buy-in from the business community. She wished she knew more about what made him tick. Why didn't he take over an island somewhere and live the rest of his life smoking dope on the beach?

Eventually, he emerged. As he walked toward the parking lot, the sunlight played in his hair, and the building's mirrored surface reflected his long, sure stride. She didn't like noticing those things about a man with so many objectionable qualities: his smug self-confidence, his air of entitlement . . . his outrageous net worth.

Afternoon rush hour had picked up. He knew Chicago's short-cuts nearly as well as she did, and he took the side streets on his way back to Lakeview. For no apparent reason, his Tesla slowed to a crawl on a one-way street a few blocks from Ashland. His arm shot out through the driver's side window, and he hooked what looked like a small grenade over the roof of the car. It landed in a barren patch of land between a nail salon and a bail bonds office. Three more of the missiles followed, and then the Tesla drove on.

It had happened so quickly she might have imagined it if this weren't a repeat performance. She'd seen him do the same thing two days ago in Roscoe Village. She'd noted the incident in her log but hadn't known what to call it. Those pseudogrenades would go unnoticed unless someone was actively looking for them. What was he doing?

Just as she decided to drive back to investigate, she heard a siren behind her. She glanced in the rearview mirror and saw a squad car approaching. She moved over to let it pass. Instead, it settled behind her, lights flashing. The cop was after *her.*

Cursing under her breath, she swung into a strip mall. *That bastard!* He'd been playing cat and mouse with her. From the beginning, he'd intended to call in the police.

The squad car followed her into the parking lot, its flashing red lights smearing a path across the front windows of a Subway and a dentist's office. The reality of the situation hit home. It was over. Graham was going to file charges against her. Every penny of her savings was gone, and she had no safety net, no other wealthy client waiting in the wings to take the place of the one she was about to lose.

Using all the curses she'd learned at her father's knee, she retrieved her driver's license—her real one—from her wallet. Her fake IDs were safely stashed in her underwear drawer. Not her Glock, though. Concealed carry was legal in Illinois, but she still kicked it as far under the driver's seat as it would go, praying for a miracle.

While the cop ran her plates, she extracted her registration and insurance card from the glove box. When he finally approached, she saw that he was about her age, early thirties, one of those super buff guys who should have been Mr. January on a Naked Cops of Chicago calendar. She put down her window and worked on her friendliest, most innocent smile. "Is there a problem, officer?"

"Could I see your license, registration, and proof of insurance, ma'am?"

She handed over the papers. As he examined her license, the smell of his cologne drifted through the open window. She was clearly coming unhinged because "It's Raining Men" buzzed through her head. She wondered if his uniform was being held together with strips of Velcro.

"Are you aware that it's illegal to tape up a broken taillight?"

This was about her *taillight*? Graham hadn't turned her in? She went weak with relief.

"I saw you were cited with a defective equipment violation in August," he said, "but you didn't get it properly fixed."

The swishy-haired nightclub blondes at Spiral could probably talk their way out of this, but Piper was so grateful for the reprieve that she didn't even try. "I couldn't afford it, but I know that's no excuse. It's not my habit to ignore traffic safety." Except when it came to speed limits, but since he'd checked her plates, he'd already discovered her old transgressions, along with the fact that she had a Concealed Pistol License.

"Driving an unsafe vehicle is dangerous," he said, "not only to you but to . . ."

She didn't hear the rest of his lecture because a one-hundred-thousand-dollar metallic-blue Tesla had whipped into the strip mall. As the car parked in front of the dentist's office, fresh dread swept through her. The officer knew her real name, and what had turned out to be a simple traffic stop had escalated into a major disaster.

She wasn't the only one who noticed the ex-quarterback unfolding from the driver's seat like some kind of urban panther. The officer stopped talking. His chest expanded and his cop cool evaporated as Cooper approached, extending his arm, and introduced himself, as if such a thing were necessary. "Cooper Graham."

"Sure! I'm one of your biggest fans." The hunky cop pumped Graham's hand as if it were a backyard oil rig. "I can't believe you're not playing for the Stars this year."

"All good things come to an end." Cooper's drawl was straight out of the Oklahoma prairie. She half expected to see him poke a blade of switchgrass in the corner of his mouth to maintain the illusion that he was harmless.

"That was some game you played against the Patriots last year."

"Thanks. It was a good day."

The two of them talked blitzes and pass rushes as if she weren't there. For someone who was such a stickler about the rules of the road, Officer Hottie wasn't nearly as exacting when it came to following proper police procedure for a traffic stop.

Graham had his own agenda. He took in her short hair, which had been hidden by last night's wig. "What'd she do?"

"Didn't get a broken taillamp fixed. You know this lady?"

Graham nodded. "Sure do. She's my stalker."

The cop shot to attention. "Your stalker?"

Graham gave her a piercing look. "Annoying but harmless."

Suddenly, Officer Hottie was all business. "Step out of the car, ma'am."

A string of obscenities jammed against the back of her front teeth. Officer Hottie had heard her speak. He knew she didn't have a British accent, but if Graham heard her plain midwestern speech, whatever slim chance she had of seeing this through would be ruined.

"Lift your arms, please."

She clamped her jaw shut to keep all the words she couldn't say from spilling out. Hottie didn't order Graham to step back as he should. Famous football players could do whatever they wanted.

Fortunately, the cop only did a visual body search. Until he spotted a suspicious bulge in the pocket of her jeans. "Ma'am, I'm going to have to search you."

She couldn't say a word in her defense, not while Graham stood there taking this all in with sadistic satisfaction. She gritted her teeth as Hottie patted her down.

He was professional. He only used the backs of his hands. But it was still humiliating. Here she stood, at the mercy of two virile men—one of them touching her, while the other might as well have been, considering how closely he was watching.

The cop pulled the package of peanuts from her pocket, examined it, then handed it back to her.

"We sure appreciate the great job you officers do to keep us safe." Graham's cornpone sincerity made her want to puke.

"How long has she been stalking you?" Hottie asked.

"Hard to say. I didn't realize it until a couple of days ago. That taillight gave her away." While she gnashed her teeth at her own stupidity, Graham was tightening the vise around her. "She was a chatty little thing when I confronted her last night, but she doesn't seem to have much to say now."

Officer Hottie turned his attention back to her. "Do you mind if I have a look in your car?"

She knew the law. He couldn't search her car without probable cause, but Graham's accusation had given him that. And would Cooper continue to believe she was harmless if he knew about her Glock? She needed to disclose where it was before the officer began his search.

She started to cough, pounding her chest with her fist and doing her best to muffle her words so her lack of a British accent might go unnoticed. "Make him . . . go away . . . first." More coughing. "Then you can . . . look."

The fake coughing made her choke for real, and the cop took her words as permission to search, but he was enjoying rubbing shoulders with one of the city's most famous athletes too much to tell Graham to step away. Instead, Hottie ordered her into the back of his squad car.

She watched through the smudged window with mounting dread as Hottie opened the passenger door with Graham observing. It took the cop less than ten seconds to find the Glock. Graham turned toward the squad car, and even through the window, she could see his fury.

Hottie opened her trunk, exposing her tote bag bulging with disguises. Looking puzzled, he picked up her Tinkle Belle. A long conversation ensued between the two men. Finally, Graham shook hands with the cop and made his way to his Tesla without another glance in her direction.

✶

Hottie, whose name turned out to be Officer Eric Vargas, eventually confirmed Piper's employment, and after three hours at the police station and a second ticket for failing to repair the taillight, she was finally free to leave. Normally, she loved the homey comfort of her tiny condo with its high ceilings, bowed window, and hardwood floors, but today, she was beyond comfort. As she pulled a cold Goose Island from her refrigerator, she heard a knock at the door. "Piper! Piper, are you there, honey?"

Piper adored her downstairs neighbor, eighty-year-old "Berni" Berkovitz, but in the last few weeks, Berni had begun showing signs of dementia, and Piper was feeling too defeated right now to give her the attention she needed. Not that she had a choice. Berni was lonely, her eyes were still sharp, and she knew Piper was inside.

Piper trudged to open the door. "Hey, Berni."

Berni didn't wait for an invitation but came right in. Her neighbor's short, Day-Glo-orange hair was uncharacteristically showing its gray roots, and her trademark crimson lipstick had gone missing. Before her husband's death, Berni had worn exotic outfits, but now, instead of harem pants, a gondolier's shirt, or a poodle skirt, she'd wrapped herself in Howard's old cardigan with a pair of sweatpants.

Piper held up her beer. "Want one?"

"Not after Labor Day. But I wouldn't say no to a vodka on the rocks."

Piper had the remains of a bottle of Stoli Elit from her prosperous days, and she went to get it. "Your generation sure knows how to drink."

"A source of pride."

Piper forced a smile. In some ways Berni was the same person she'd been before her last cruise, when Howard had suffered a fatal heart attack off the coast of Italy. Piper wished everything could return to the way it used to be for Berni, but then Piper wished for a lot of things it didn't look as though she could have.

"You've been gone so much lately, I've hardly seen you," Berni complained.

"You'll be seeing a lot more of me." Piper tossed some ice into the glass of vodka and made herself say it out loud. "I bungled my big job." Although Berni didn't know the details of the case, she knew that Piper had an important client.

"Oh, honey, I'm sorry. But you're smart. You'll work it out."

Piper wanted to believe that, but the reality was that tomorrow she had to let her client know Graham had identified her, and by the time that unpleasant meeting was over, she'd be fired.

Another knock sounded on her door, a knock that was purely ceremonial because her neighbor Jen let herself in without waiting for an invitation. She was still dressed for work in a sleeveless emerald-green sheath that fit her slim body perfectly. Her dark hair swung to her shoulders, and her makeup hadn't moved since she'd applied it early that morning.

"Scattered showers tomorrow," she said glumly. "We need the rain, so that's good, but the ragweed count is going to be a bitch." She sniffed, as if she were already suffering. Nineteen years ago, Jennifer MacLeish had been Chicago's hot new television meteorologist, but she was forty-two now, no longer a fresh-faced girl, and she was convinced the recently appointed station manager was about to replace her with a younger model.

"Howard had a lot of trouble with ragweed," Berni said. "I wonder if he still does."

Jen exchanged a look with Piper, then made her way to the couch, her nude-colored pumps clicking on the hardwood floor. "Sweetie, Howard is gone. We understand how much you miss him, but—"

Berni shook her off. "I know you both think he's dead, but he's not. I told you. I saw him last week, right in the middle of Lincoln Square. He was wearing one of those foam cheeseheads. But Howard hated Green Bay, and I can't think why he'd be wearing a cheesehead."

Jen looked toward Piper for help. They'd heard the cheesehead story several times now, but since both of them had attended Howard Berkovitz's funeral, they were disinclined to believe he'd resurrected—let alone as a Green Bay Packers fan.

As Piper poured the last of the Stoli for Jen, there was another rap on the door, this one tentative. Berni sighed. "It's her."

"Come in, Amber," Piper called out. And why not? If her friends weren't here, all she'd do was brood.

Amber Kwan, her downstairs neighbor, entered the apartment tentatively. "Is it okay? I wasn't invited, but . . ."

"Neither were they," Piper pointed out. Amber was a slightly overweight twenty-seven-year-old with porcelain skin, shiny black hair, and an insecurity that vanished only when she took the stage as a permanent member of Chicago's Lyric Opera chorus. Most of Piper's childhood friends had moved out of the city, and she was grateful to have these three in her life.

"Hello, Mrs. Berkovitz. How are you feeling?"

Berni gave her a tight-lipped nod. Berni didn't like Amber because she was Korean, but since Amber believed Berni's age gave her a pass for racial prejudice, she wouldn't let Piper or Jen confront Berni about it.

"I'm out of vodka," Piper said. "Beer?"

Amber settled on the edge of the ottoman. "Nothing, thanks. I'll only stay for a minute." Amber had moved into the building more than a year ago, but she continued to behave as though she were an interloper in their group, even though Piper and Jen had welcomed her. "I stopped by to see if you're still thinking about subletting," she said apologetically.

"No!" Berni declared. "Piper, you're not going anywhere, and Amber, you shouldn't have brought this up."

"I don't want you to sublet," Amber said hastily. "But you said you were going to have to, and I have friend who's a visiting professor at DePaul. He's looking for a rental."

Leaving her cozy condo would be like stabbing herself in the heart. But unlike Berni, who wanted to bring her dead husband back to life, Piper was a realist. "Let me sleep on it. I'll give you an answer tomorrow."

There wasn't much to sleep on. She could no longer afford to pay the mortgage on the condo she'd scrimped for years to purchase, and she wouldn't impose on her friends, despite their offers to let her stay with them. By renting out her condo and moving into the basement of her awful cousin Diane's two-flat in Skokie, she'd be able to avoid selling this place for a while, and she'd also preserve her friendships.

"The last thing we need is a strange man living here," Berni said. "I won't have it."

Jen didn't voice an objection. She understood that this was a last resort for Piper. "He's a friend of Amber's," she said, "so he won't be a stranger."

"He was one of my professors at Eastman," Amber said. "A very nice man."

"I don't care," Berni said. "We don't need a man here."

Apparently, the gay newlyweds in the downstairs unit didn't count.

"Having Piper subletting is better than forcing her to sell,"

Jen said. "And you know she won't move in with any of us. It'll only be until she gets her business on its feet." She uncrossed her long legs. "Unfortunately, I'll be unemployed by then. It's me we should all be worried about, not Piper. She's tougher than I am. And younger."

This pronouncement wasn't as self-centered as it seemed. Jen was taking the heat off Piper. "I know broadcasting too well," Jen said. "The younger and the blonder, the more the powers that be want to hire them. And Dumb Ass is a sucker for twenty-one-year-olds." Jen had referred to the new station manager as Dumb Ass for so long that Piper had forgotten his real name.

Jen took a swig of vodka. "Studying meteorology is the new go-to major for every pretty girl who has even a passing interest in science. The colleges are turning them out in macrobursts."

"Talent is more important than looks," Amber said loyally, and then quickly added, "not that you aren't still beautiful."

Amber was used to being judged only by her agile coloratura-soprano voice, and that made her naive about the television industry. Piper tried to encourage Jen, but growing up as the daughter of Duke Dove had let her see every facet of male sexism. Jen was being held to a different standard than the men at the station were, and she had reason to worry.

Berni shot up from the couch. "I know what I'm going to do!"

"Put out a contract on Dumb Ass for me?" Jen said glumly.

"I'm going to hire Piper to find Howard!"

Piper regarded her with dismay. "Berni, that's not—"

"I'll pay you. I've been looking for something special to spend my income tax refund on. Nothing could be more special than this."

"Berni, I couldn't take your money. Howard had a—"

Another knock sounded on the door, this one more forceful than the others. No one had buzzed her condo, and her usual visitors were already here. She set down her beer, made her way across the carpet, and turned the knob.

He filled the doorway—all long muscles, big shoulders, and powerful chest.

"Hello, Esmerelda."

3

The barbarian was at her gate. Piper's stomach plummeted. "How did you get in the building?"

He regarded her with the golden-brown eyes of a wolf ready to devour his prey, not because the wolf was hungry, but just for the hell of it. "Your downstairs neighbors are Stars fans."

They weren't the only ones. Berni squawked as though she'd laid an egg. "Cooper Graham!" She jumped up from the couch, agile as a teenager. "Oh, I wish Howard was here! Oh, my goodness."

Cooper tipped his head to her. "Ma'am."

"Howard was a Bears fan like Piper," Berni told him, "but I was born in the western 'burbs in the days when hardly anybody lived out there. I'm Berni Berkovitz. Bernadette, really. I've been a Stars fan from the beginning. And Howard always rooted for the Stars. Unless they were playing the Bears," she amended.

"Understandable." He was all celebrity graciousness, waiting patiently as she rambled on. Jen, in the meantime, crossed her very shapely legs, dangled her pump from one toe, and swished her dark hair away from her face, waiting to be noticed. Amber, however, was mystified. She could name every obscure composer from the past four centuries, but she barely knew Chicago even had professional sports teams.

Berni was still gushing. "Oh, my, Piper. You said you had an important client, but I had no idea . . ."

"I'm not a client of *Ms. Dove's*." Cooper stomped on her name as if it were a cockroach. "I'm the person she was hired to investigate."

Thank you, Officer Hottie, for your big mouth.

Berni sputtered, then turned accusing eyes on Piper. "Really, Piper? Why were you investigating Cooper?"

While Piper tried to unlock her jaw, Jen rose gracefully from the couch. "Jennifer MacLeish. Channel Eight weather. We met at the Children's Charities Holly Ball last year, but I'm sure you don't remember."

"Of course, I do." His hand engulfed hers. "It's good to see you again, Ms. MacLeish. Although I can't say much for the company you keep."

Amber dashed toward the door. "I'll leave."

"Not you, Amber," Jen said. "He's talking about Piper."

Graham nodded. "That's true."

Piper took a slug of beer, wishing it were the Stoli.

Berni couldn't stand Amber's ignorance. "Amber, this is Cooper Graham. He's one of the most famous football players in the world. Even you have to have heard of him."

"Oh, I'm sure I have," Amber said, sure of no such thing.

"Amber sings with the Lyric," Jen explained. "She's both clueless and amazing."

"I'll bet I've heard you," Graham said.

Fat chance, Piper thought. Graham would no more darken the halls of the Lyric Opera than he would throw a deliberate interception.

"Ladies, as much as I've enjoyed meeting you, I need to talk to *Ms. Dove*"—another cockroach stomped into oblivion—"about a business matter."

Amber began to turn to the door, then stopped and moved next to Piper. Jen did the same thing. "Maybe we can help," she said firmly.

Girlfriends stuck together, and none of them were leaving until Piper gave the word. With the greatest reluctance, Berni joined them. They were a unit: a ballsy television meteorologist, a Korean opera singer with the voice of an angel, and the number one Stars football fangirl. How screwed up could Piper's life be when she had friends like this?

"It's okay," she said. "I can handle it."

"Are you sure?" This came from Amber, who suddenly looked as formidable as Wagner's Brünnhilde.

Not sure at all, but Piper nodded. "It's business."

"I'm certain this is a simple misunderstanding," Berni said, and then, in a pseudo-whisper, "I'll leave a retainer check in your mailbox, Piper. That's how it's done, right?"

"No check, Berni. We'll talk tomorrow." After today, what was one more challenge?

"Piper?" Jen said.

As much as Piper appreciated their concern, she couldn't let Graham see her as a weakling. She forced a lazy wave toward the door. "Later."

On her way out, Berni regarded Graham. "Piper is a very good person."

"It's been a pleasure meeting you, Mrs. Berkovitz," he said.

She touched his arm. "I make an excellent brisket. If you ever get hungry for brisket, you let me know."

He gave her his odious fan-smile. "I'll do that."

"Or my divinity fudge if you've got a sweet tooth."

He smiled, the door closed behind them, and his affability vanished. Piper's only defense was a strong offense. She set her shoulders and charged toward him. "My surveillance was legal. Yes, going into the club could be a gray area, but Spiral is a public space, and you'd have to prove that my presence caused you extreme emotional distress. Somehow I don't think a judge would buy that from a former MVP."

He loomed over her, six feet three to her five feet six. "Who hired you?"

She straightened her spine, trying to gain another inch of height. "I can't tell you that. But I will say that it's no one who wishes you harm."

"Why don't I find that comforting?"

"It's the truth."

"And you're an expert on the truth, Esmerelda?"

She struggled to keep her cool. "Nobody likes being duped. I understand that. But I had a job to do."

"Not impressed. Who are you working for?"

"Like I said: no one who's a threat to you."

"I'll decide that for myself."

"I have nothing else to say."

"Is that so?" He bored in on her. "Let me put it this way: you can either tell me now or you'll hear from my lawyers."

He had to know a lawsuit would destroy her. She tried to channel a wealthy CEO. "Lawsuits are such a time sink."

"Then give me what I want."

She couldn't do that, but she had to do something other than fall on her knees and beg him not to sue her. "I'll make a deal with you. If you back off, I'll tell you who your real enemy is. And it's not the person who hired me."

He gave her his iciest stare. Waiting. She fought the suffocating feeling that he was once again sucking the air out of the room. "That model you've been singling out," she said. "Blonde. Big boobs, tiny hips, and bizarrely long legs. I know—she's only one mouse at a cheese convention—but this mouse calls herself Vivian, and you've been having lots of cozy chats with her."

"What of it?"

"After a few snorts of funny stuff in the ladies' room, she's telling all her friends how she's going to trick you into getting her pregnant. You want someone who's a real threat to you? She's your gal."

"Nobody had better be snorting anything in the ladies' room," he declared. "That's why I have security."

"You're paying them way too much."

"And you're making this up."

"Am I? Has your so-called security picked up on the side business that at least one of your employees is running? At your expense."

"What kind of side business?"

"Don't call your legal eagles, and I'll tell you."

"I've already called 'em."

She gulped. "Suit yourself. But I strongly suggest you do your own liquor inventory instead of farming out the job. And when you come up short, remember this conversation."

"You're bluffing."

He was done with her, and as he turned to the door, she knew she had to give him something more. "Keep a closer eye on your red-haired bartender. Then call me and apologize."

That stopped him. His face toughened with anger. "Keith? That's bullshit. You picked the wrong guy to lie about." He drove a pointed finger in the general direction of her head. "You've got twenty-four hours to give me the name of the person who hired you or you'll hear from my lawyers."

The door slammed shut behind him.

✶

Cooper fumed all the way to the club. She was a liar ten times over. Keith Millage was one of his oldest friends. They'd played ball together all through college. Bartenders were notorious for skimming from club owners, and Cooper had brought Keith out from Tulsa just so he'd have someone he trusted watching his back. As for Vivian . . . Coop had no interest in any of his customers, but if he did . . . Unlike some of his stupider teammates, he'd never made himself vulnerable to those "accidental" pregnancies.

He pondered the most important question. Who'd hired a detective to follow him and why? He knew the Chicago nightclub business was cutthroat, but what could anyone hope to learn?

He arrived at the club and settled behind his desk. He didn't like mysteries, and he especially didn't like mysteries when he was trying to attract an investor. Not just any investor, either. The best in the city. The only one he wanted to work with.

It was time to get down to the floor. He was the card that drew in customers, and while other celebrity nightclub owners made only passing appearances, he played to win, even if it meant being accosted by overzealous fans and trapped by self-proclaimed football experts who only thought they understood the game.

To his disgust, he caught himself watching Keith that night, a guy he'd trust with his life. His hostility toward Piper Dove hardened. As he turned his attention to the group of women pressing up against him, he made up his mind. Nobody won a championship by letting his enemies walk free. He was taking her down, right along with her penny ante detective agency.

On Monday morning, Piper dressed in black for what was certain to be the most miserable meeting of her short-lived career as a business owner. Black sweater and black wool slacks. She polished her ancient black boots and unearthed a pair of jagged silver earrings. As long as she was going down in flames, she'd look tough while she did it.

Deidre Joss's right-hand man and senior VP met Piper in the reception area of the Joss Investment Group offices. Noah Parks was Piper's regular contact, the person she'd had to call with the ugly news that Cooper Graham had made her. Even though he was an East Coast Ivy Leaguer, his buzz cut, blunt nose, and square jaw made him look like a former Marine. He gave her a curt nod. "Deidre wants to talk to you herself."

Noah directed her through a set of glass doors into a light-flooded hallway where bands of cream-colored marble bordered the hardwood floors. At the end of the corridor, he opened a door into the office of the firm's president and CEO.

Tall windows and sleek designer furniture projected stripped-down elegance. But the whiteboard that took up most of the end wall testified that this was a workplace, not a showroom. Its CEO sat at an imposing desk beneath an oil painting of her father, Clarence Joss III. Like Piper, Deidre Joss was following in her father's footsteps, but unlike Piper, she hadn't been forced to buy the business from a jealous stepmother. At thirty-six, Deidre was only three years older than Piper, but she seemed a generation older in sophistication and experience.

Tall and thin, with small dark eyes that tilted up at the corners, a long, patrician nose, and mahogany-brown hair, she looked more like a prima ballerina than a CEO. She was dressed in black, as she'd been at their only other meeting, a jersey dress with ropes of pearls. She'd lost her husband in a snowmobile accident a year earlier, so Piper wasn't certain whether the black was a statement of mourning or an exceptionally flattering fashion choice.

Deidre came around the front of her desk and shook Piper's hand. "I hope the traffic wasn't too awful this morning." She gestured toward the arrangement of couch and chairs. "Have a seat."

Noah remained standing by the door while Piper took a gray leather conference chair and Deidre resettled in a chair nearby. This assignment had meant everything to Piper, and she'd been determined to do it so perfectly that Deidre would continue hiring her for future work. So much for determination. Now she was a loser kid called to the principal's office.

"Tell me what happened." Principal Deidre crossed legs long enough for a grand jeté.

Piper outlined the details, leaving out only the appearance of Esmerelda Crocker.

Deidre didn't believe in padding her words. "I'm disappointed."

Piper had no grounds to defend herself. "Not as disappointed as I am. I followed him too closely. It isn't a mistake I'll make again, but that doesn't change what happened."

She could have added that Deidre was the one who'd issued the order to stay close, but that would sound like an excuse.

"I want you outside his home," Deidre had said. *"Trail him during the day, and get into the club at night. Find out how much he drinks. What kind of women he's seeing, and how many there are. Before I consider a business partnership, I have to know exactly who I'm dealing with."*

Noah came over to stand beside Deidre's chair. "I'm sure Graham demanded to know who hired you," he said.

"He did, but I didn't tell him."

Noah didn't hide his skepticism. "He's an imposing guy. That's hard to believe."

"Under Illinois law, the only way I'd be forced to reveal a client's identity is with a subpoena." Piper didn't mention how likely that was to happen. She had enough real alligators to deal with before she started worrying about the ones still lurking in the swamp. At the same time, she wished Deidre would give her permission to volunteer the information. Since Deidre was considering going into partnership with him, he'd surely understand the wisdom of her having his personal and business life investigated beforehand.

But Deidre wasn't volunteering anything. "Let's hope it doesn't come to that."

"I'll take your report." Noah held out his hand, and since he'd moved to stand by the door, Piper had to get up to deliver it to him. She'd stayed awake most of the night checking every detail to make sure she hadn't missed anything. She'd also included a summary of the expenses she'd incurred, praying they wouldn't try to back out of paying her because she hadn't completed the job.

Deidre touched the pearls at her throat. "I hired you because your father did business with mine, and I believe in helping women who are starting their own businesses. I'm sorry this hasn't worked out."

She seemed genuinely regretful, and Piper's disgust with her own incompetence made it impossible for her to fight back. "I only wish I'd been able to meet your expectations."

Noah gestured toward the door, less sympathetic than his employer. As Piper followed him down the hallway, she could feel the ruins of her career crumbling beneath her feet.

✶

For the next few days, she had to force herself to go to the office instead of staying home with the covers pulled over her head. It was mid-September, and unless something drastically changed, she'd barely make it to Halloween before she'd run out of money and have to close her doors. But not yet. One way or the other, she had to drum up some business.

In her father's time, Dove Investigations had occupied the entire one-story brick building Duke had purchased in the eighties. Now, her stepmother owned the whole thing, and all Piper could afford to rent for herself was the former bookkeeper's office in the back.

When she'd moved in, the office had been as dingy as a fictional detective's office. She'd splurged on an olive-green rug with a black sunburst pattern to camouflage the vinyl floor tiles, then painted the walls off-white and hung some kitschy posters of old *True Detective* magazine covers. A secondhand store had yielded a library table she'd spruced up with flat black enamel paint to use as a desk. She'd added a good light and a pair of black steel-framed chairs for the clients she'd hoped she'd attract.

Her voice mail included another message from Graham's attorney demanding a meeting for the following week. She deleted it, as if that would make it go away forever, and switched on her computer. Out of habit, she did a quick search to see if there was anything new on Cooper Graham. Nothing.

She made herself cold-call more law firms, then followed up by sending them a copy of her brochure.

DOVE INVESTIGATIONS

Est. 1958

Truth Brings Peace

- Legal, Attorney, and Corporate Support
- Insurance and Domestic Investigations
- Hidden Assets Investigations
- Background Checks
- Missing Persons

She'd considered getting rid of the firm's old slogan, "Truth Brings Peace," but it was part of her family history, starting with her grandfather, and changing it would feel like wiping out her heritage.

A rap sounded on her office door. She jumped up. But instead of a new client coming in off the street, Berni barged in. She'd pulled herself together enough to tie a hippie headband around her Day-Glo-orange hair and wear a fringed vest over her sweatpants. "Now, Piper, before you say anything . . . I know you don't believe I saw Howard in Lincoln Square. I hardly believed it myself. But I lived with that man for fifty-eight years, and I should know." She brushed past Piper and settled in one of the chairs across from the desk. She opened her bag and pulled out an envelope. "Here's a one-hundred-dollar retainer." She slapped it on the desk.

"Berni, I can't take your money."

"This is business. I need an investigator, and you're the best there is."

"I appreciate your faith in me, but . . ." She tried a new tack. "I'm too involved personally. It would keep me from being objective. Another investigator would—"

"Another investigator would think I'm a crazy old woman." Her fierce glare dared Piper to agree.

Piper settled behind her desk, hoping she could use logic to persuade Berni to give up her delusions. "Let's look at the facts . . . You were in your stateroom with Howard when he had his heart attack."

"But I wasn't with him when he died. I told you. I'd slipped out of the ship's infirmary to use the toilet, and then I fainted when that quack of a doctor told me he'd passed. Who knows what was in that casket they shipped back."

If bureaucracy hadn't gotten in the way of Berni seeing Howard's body before he was cremated, none of this would be happening. "All right, Berni." Arguing with her was futile, and Piper reached for her yellow pad. "Let me ask you a few questions."

Berni gave her a smug smile. "You look very nice today, by the way. You should wear lipstick more often. And it almost looks like you combed your hair. You have beautiful, shiny hair, Piper. I know that eggbeater haircuts are fashionable now, but a nice pageboy would be more feminine."

"Seriously, Berni, have you ever known me to give a crap about being feminine?"

"Well, no. But men seem to like you anyway. Not that you pay much attention. I still can't believe you're thirty-three years old and you've never been in love."

"Freak of nature and waste of time."

"Love is never a waste of time," Berni asserted. "I've been wanting to ask . . . Are you a lesbian?"

"I wish."

"I understand. Women can be so much more interesting than men."

Piper nodded in agreement. She trusted her girlfriends a lot more than she'd ever trusted a boyfriend in the days when she'd still been interested in having a boyfriend. But this conversation wasn't helping Berni get past her delusion. "Exactly when did you see the cheesehead guy?"

"Howard! And it was September fourth. Exactly sixteen days ago. It was game day for the Packers. I'd come out of the bookstore, and there he was. Sitting on a bench in the plaza watching the pigeons."

"And wearing a foam cheesehead . . ."

Berni's smugness vanished. "That's what I can't understand. Why would a Bears fan like Howard wear a cheesehead? I could have understood if he was wearing a Stars hat. He liked the Stars almost as much as the Bears."

Considering the fact that Berni believed her husband had come back from the dead, his choice of headgear didn't seem as though it should be the primary question. "Did he see you?"

"He sure did. I called out his name. 'Howard!' He turned, and all the blood drained right from his face."

Piper clicked her pen. "You were close enough to see that?"

"Maybe it only seemed that way. But one thing I do know . . . He recognized me, because he got up right away and ran off. I tried to follow him, but with my hip, I couldn't catch up." Her face crumpled. "Why would he do that? Why would he run away from me like that?"

Piper dodged that question and posed another instead, one she would ask if this were a legitimate case. "Were you and Howard having any marital troubles while you were on the cruise?"

"We bickered. What couple doesn't? That man refused to take care of himself, and you should have seen him on the ship, loading up on bacon and bakery. He knew exactly how I felt about that. But we loved each other. That's why losing him has been so terrible."

Even though Piper wasn't a romantic herself, she didn't doubt the love Berni and Howard had. She also didn't envy it. Men were a lot of work, and when Piper's past relationships had burned out, she hadn't been all that bummed. Then her father had gotten sick, and she'd lost interest in everything but work. She had more than enough complications in her life without adding a man to it.

She asked Berni a few more questions and promised she'd investigate. Berni's gratitude made her feel like a fraud, and to ease her conscience, she took a detour past Lincoln Square on her way home.

The brick plaza held its customary assortment of kids, couples, young mothers pushing Maclaren strollers, and a few oldsters, none of them wearing a foam cheesehead and none of them bearing the slightest resemblance to Howard Berkovitz. She felt ridiculous even looking, but she wanted to face Berni with a clear conscience. As for Berni's one hundred dollars . . . She'd take her out for a great dinner.

✶

The next day, a friend of a friend of Jen's called. She thought her boyfriend might be cheating. Piper was glad to have a new client, but unfortunately, the boyfriend was stupid, and that same night Piper snapped a photo of him going into a motel with his other girlfriend. Case solved in less than twenty-four hours. Heartbroken client. Minimal money.

As she was locking up her office on Wednesday evening, six days after Graham had busted her, his legal eagles left another message for her to ignore. Who said denial was a bad thing?

She'd parked her car near the modest green-and-black sign for Dove Investigations that hung over her office door. A Dodge Challenger pulled into the space next to her. The door opened and a man got out. A very good-looking man wearing jeans and a T-shirt over a torso of rippling muscles. She didn't recognize him until he pulled off his sunglasses. Mirrored, naturally. "Hi, Piper."

It was Hottie. She eyed him warily. "Officer."

"Eric."

"Okay."

He rested his hips against the fender and crossed his arms over his too-sculpted chest. "Want to get some coffee or something?"

"Why?"

"Why not? I like you. You're interesting."

At least he didn't say she was cute. She hated that. "Nice to hear," she told him, "but I'm not too crazy about you."

"Hey. I was just doing my job."

"Sucking up to Cooper Graham?"

He grinned. "Yeah, that was pretty cool. Come on. Twenty minutes."

She thought about it. Unlike her father, she didn't have any close contacts in the police department, and if by some miracle she could stay in business, she'd need a few. She nodded abruptly. "Okay. Let's go. I'll follow in my car."

As it turned out, their coffee date lasted nearly an hour. She wasn't completely surprised by his interest. Good-looking guys had started coming on to her when she'd been a freshman in college. At first, she'd been confused by their attention, but she'd eventually figured out her lack of interest was what attracted them. One of her short-term boyfriends had told her that hanging with her was like hanging with the guys.

"You like sports, and you don't care if a dude brings you flowers and shit. Plus, you're a babe."

She wasn't a babe, and she hadn't come close to falling in love with any of them, maybe because every relationship she'd been in had eventually made her feel . . . almost empty, as if a hole she didn't understand had opened inside her. Right now, her aversion to relationships was a benefit. One less complication in a life that was complicated enough.

Hottie was a decent guy. His stories about life on the force were interesting, and his attention wandered only once, when a super-hot brunette in a tight sweater walked past their table, but since even Piper had noticed her, she couldn't fault him. He asked her out to dinner for the following weekend. Amber had given her a ticket to the Lyric for that night, and she told him she already had plans.

Being turned down for a night at the opera seemed to surprise him. "You're an unusual person," he said.

"And you're a nice guy, but it's really not a good time for me to date."

"All right. We won't date. We'll just hang out sometimes, okay?"

He had good stories, and she really did need a contact in the police department. "Okay. Pals. No dating." She paused. "And I'm not hooking up with you."

She could see he didn't believe her.

*

By the next night, Piper was doing the ultra-depressing job of trying to figure out what to pack and what to get rid of. Subleasing her apartment was no longer up for debate, and Amber's professor friend was moving in tomorrow. His rent would cover her mortgage and condo dues, temporarily postponing her need to sell. She kept telling herself she wouldn't have to live in her cousin Diane's tiny basement apartment forever—an apartment with no separate entrance, a moldy bathroom, and worst of all, her cousin Diane, who was a nonstop complainer. As for Diane's two bratty kids . . . Piper suspected her cousin was keeping the rent ridiculously cheap so she could be guaranteed a built-in babysitter, a prospect even more depressing than living in a basement.

Piper was leaving most of her things behind for Amber's professor, but she had a couple of boxes of personal items to pack up, including a grubby stuffed pink pig she'd rediscovered in her bottom drawer. Oinky. His seams were frayed, his plush fur bedraggled. He'd been her childhood lovey, a baby shower present to her mother.

When Piper had turned five, Duke had announced that Oinky had to go. "Only babies carry around crap like that. You want everybody to think you're a baby?" She'd told him she didn't care what people thought and that Oinky wasn't going anywhere.

Despite considerable pressure, she'd held her ground until she was seven. That's when the neighborhood bully had knocked her down and made her cry. Duke had been furious, not at the bully, but at her for crying. "We don't have sissies in this family. You get back out there and kick that kid's ass and don't let me goddam see you cry again."

She could no longer remember exactly what she'd done to Justin Termini, who'd later become her first boyfriend, but she did remember the awful knowledge that she'd failed Duke. That same night, she'd grabbed Oinky, thrust him in Duke's face, and then stomped outside to fling her pig in the trash. She'd been amply rewarded with a big hug, a trip to get ice cream, and praise for being tough as any boy in town. Duke had never discovered that she'd climbed out on the roof that night, shimmied down the porch post, and retrieved Oinky from the garbage can. She'd hidden her pig away for the rest of her childhood.

Oinky had long since outlived his usefulness, but she couldn't get rid of him, and she tucked him in the box with her sweatshirts. She took a break to make herself a sandwich and carried it to the bay window. As she looked down on the twilit street, she saw a metallic-blue Tesla pull into a parking space. Her sandwich stalled on its way to her mouth as the driver's door swung open and Cooper Graham got out. Her appetite vanished. She hadn't returned his attorney's calls, and he'd come after her himself.

The downstairs newlyweds were heading up the sidewalk. She'd seen one of the men in a Stars sweatshirt, so Graham wouldn't have any trouble getting them to let him in the building. In less than a minute, he'd be pounding on her door. She could either refuse to answer or meet the beast head on.

A no-brainer. She'd been through enough lately. She wasn't answering.

But cowering inside her apartment proved too much for her, and by his third knock, she'd stalked across the room and jerked open the door. "What do you *want*?"

4

He pushed into her living room, bringing a megablast of hostile energy right along with him. "Keith has been skimming me."

"Your red-haired bartender? Yeah, I know."

Six feet three inches of angry male entitlement planted himself in the middle of her carpet. "Why didn't you tell me?"

Her chin shot up. "What the hell? I did tell you!"

"Not in a way I could *believe*!"

She stared at him, exchanging glare for glare.

He looked away first, raking his fingers through his hair only to have it spring back into rumpled position. "So maybe I wasn't in the mood to listen."

She shoved the door closed before all her neighbors came running out to investigate. "I doubt you're ever in the mood to listen."

"What do you mean by that?"

Her frustration got the best of her. "You're so used to feeling superior that you've forgotten there are people who might know something you don't."

One of his big, competent hands landed on the blade of his hip. "What's your deal anyway? Do you feel like such a failure that you need to attack anybody who's successful?"

"No. Maybe. I don't know. Fuck you."

He laughed. A genuine jolt of amusement that seemed to shock him as much as her and quickly faded. "How did you figure it out?"

"Never let any guy believe he's superior to you," Duke used to say. *"Except your old man."*

"Simple powers of observation." She purposely reclaimed the sandwich she could no longer imagine eating. "Something I'm *good* at."

He cocked his head at her. "Educate me."

"Pay me," she retorted.

He shook his head, not as if he were denying her, more as if he were trying to shake off a concussion. He glanced around the condo, saw the open suitcase piled with clothes, the cardboard box she'd loaded up with nonperishables from her kitchen: cereal, canned soup, boxed mac and cheese. She knew how to cook but never seemed to get around to it.

"You're moving," he said. "Too bad. This is a nice place."

"It's okay." It was more than okay. And it would be hers to keep if she gave up and went back to her old job. But she didn't want to do online promotions for motor oil or deal with one-star reviews because a customer's replacement ignition coil failed. That kind of work had sucked out her soul.

He picked up Oinky. "Nice pig."

She fought the urge to snatch her pig away. "School mascot."

He took Oinky with him as he sat uninvited on her cocoa-colored sofa. Compared with Officer Hottie's pumped-up calendar-boy gorgeousness, Graham was rougher at the edges—the planes of his face more rugged, a battle scar on his forehead, another on the side of his jaw. That cleft chin. He was hard as nails, despite the hand clasping her pig. In times of war, Graham would be the commander men followed into battle. In peacetime, he led his team to glory. All in all, a man not to be trifled with.

"Keith and I've been friends since college," he said. "I trusted him as much as I've ever trusted anyone."

"Your mistake." But there was something about the slump in those big warrior's shoulders, the burnished shadow in his wolf's eyes that got to her.

"Don't let yourself get sucked in," Duke had said. *"Every jackass has a sad story."*

The sandwich had crumbled in her fingers. She dropped it untouched in the trash. "You're not the first employer who's been ripped off by a trusted employee. It happens all the time."

He curled his hand around the ankle he'd hooked over his knee. "I should have seen what was going on."

"Your so-called security people should have seen. That's why you hired them. But they're probably taking a cut."

His head came up, and he bristled with hostility. "My security people are top-notch."

She gave him a faintly pitying look. "So rich and yet so dumb." It felt good to see what he couldn't. "The reality is that you're so used to everybody bowing and scraping that you don't understand most people only show you their best side. You've forgotten how many creeps there are. All your fame has made you a babe in the woods when it comes to living in the real world."

She expected a hot dispute. Instead, he set her pig aside and drilled her with his eyes. "Who hired you to follow me?"

She steeled herself. "That's confidential. Don't ask me again."

He uncoiled from the couch. "Let me get this straight. Even though I have the best lawyers in the city on your ass, and even though your two-bit detective agency is barely surviving—yeah, I did some investigating of my own—you're still not giving me the name of your client, is that right?"

She had to hold her ground, no matter how much she wanted to cave. "What part of 'unethical' don't you understand?"

"Oh, I understand, all right. So let me put it another way. Turn over the name, and I'll hire you myself."

She gaped at him. "For what?"

"For your suspicious nature. I'm a fast learner. It's obvious I need another set of eyes in the club. Just for a couple of weeks. Someone who can see what I've been missing. Security to check on my security, if you will."

This was her dream job. Exactly what she needed right now—a client with deep pockets offering work that would be both interesting and challenging. Her head spun. There was only one catch. A big one. "And all I have to do is . . ."

"Turn over the name of your client."

At that moment, Piper hated Deidre Joss. Deidre's stubborn insistence on anonymity was going to ruin Piper. She should just tell him the truth.

But she couldn't. She stalked across the carpet to the door, fighting the ache in her chest. "Nice talking with you, Mr. Graham. Too bad you have to leave."

"You're not going to do it?"

The urge to give him the name he wanted was so strong she had to clench her teeth. "I don't have your money, or your power, or your fame, but I've got ethics." *Ethics.* She'd never hated a word more.

"Once you step over the line, you can never step back. Remember that."

Duke had probably been talking about sex, but the fact was, if she gave in on this, she'd be giving away her self-respect, and she wouldn't do that for anything or anyone.

Graham came closer, dangling the golden carrot. "Think of all the money you could make on this job . . ."

"Believe me, I am!" She flung open the door. "I did you a favor. Now do me a favor and get out of here so I can finish packing and move into my cousin's shitty basement and come up with another way to stay in business without selling my soul."

The sadistic bastard grinned. A big grin that took over his rugged face. "You're hired."

"Are you deaf? I told you! I'm not selling out my client."

"That's why you're hired. Meet me at my condo tomorrow morning at ten. I believe you know where it is."

And that was that.

*

Piper awoke at dawn the next morning, her mind still reeling from what had happened. After downing two cups of black coffee, she settled on wearing her khaki skirt, a short-sleeved army-green T-shirt printed with a red scorpion, and her scuffed brown ankle-high booties. Semiprofessional without looking as if she was trying to impress him.

She was ready too early, so she killed time by detouring to Lincoln Square and stopping in at the few places that were open. Not surprisingly, nobody recognized the photo of Howard that Berni had given her. *Because he was dead.*

As Jen had forecast, it was unseasonably warm for late September, and Piper kept the windows down on her way to Lakeview. At exactly two minutes before ten, she parked in one of the three allotted visitor spaces in the alley behind his residence.

Once part of a Catholic seminary, the brick building had sat empty for years before it was converted into three luxury condos. Graham owned the two-story penthouse, while a local real estate titan and a Hollywood actor with Chicago roots owned the other two units.

She walked along a fern-bordered brick pathway to the front entrance and into a small lobby with a high-tech video security system she'd like to know more about. A computer-generated voice directed her to a private elevator that rose automatically to the penthouse. The door opened, and she stepped out into an expansive living space with brick walls and big industrial windows. The two-story-high ceiling had exposed ductwork painted a flat charcoal. The bamboo floors lay in an oversize chevron pattern, giving the space a sleek edge, and the long bookshelves on one wall held a collection of books she'd bet anything he'd never opened.

Two men with their backs to her sat on a curved oyster-colored couch the size of three normal couches. One of the men—the one she'd come to see—wore a white terry cloth bathrobe, the other, a blue dress shirt and dark pants. He was the man who rose and walked around the end of the couch to shake her hand. "Heath Champion," he said.

Heath Champion, aka "the Python," was a Chicago legend and one of the most powerful sports agents in the country. He represented two of the Stars' great former quarterbacks, Kevin Tucker and Dean Robillard, as well as her own brand-new client. Despite his all-American good looks and courteous manner, she knew a snake when she saw one, and she didn't intend to drop her guard for a second.

"You must be the incorruptible Ms. Dove," Champion said.

"Piper."

Graham didn't bother to get up, merely jerked his head. "Coffee in the kitchen."

"I'm good," she said.

"You'd better be," he retorted.

Champion gestured toward the couch. "Have a seat."

She focused on the view through the windows so she didn't have to look at her employer right away. A shady courtyard three stories below nested inside ivy-covered brick walls where fat yellow mums made bright spots in the shade. The ferns had begun to brown at the tips, and the leaves floating in the basin of the stone fountain announced that fall was approaching.

She forced herself to turn toward the couch. Graham sat sprawled in the center, his crossed ankles propped on a wood-and-glass coffee table shaped like a flying saucer. His white robe had fallen open far enough to reveal bare calves and an angry scar on his right knee. Another smaller scar marred his ankle. How many others did he have? And what was he wearing underneath that robe?

The thrum of female awareness infuriated her. Too much caffeine.

She put down her gray messenger bag. The couch was deep-seated, designed for a large man instead of an average-size female. If she sank back into it, her legs would stick out in front of her like a kindergartner's, so she perched on the edge.

He took in the scorpion on her T-shirt. "Company logo?"

"Still trying to choose. Either this or a smiley face."

Graham's own face was tan against the stark white robe, and the open neck showed a little chest hair. She gave him a few begrudging points for not manscaping, then took them back just because she could.

He smiled, as if he'd read her mind. "What's your plan for improving my security? I know you have one."

She wouldn't let a barely clothed client ruffle her. "Before I reopened the agency, I worked as a reputation manager and digital strategist for a chain of Chicago auto stores."

"What the hell is a reputation manager?"

"An online watchdog. I monitored business sites and social media platforms for bad press. Pushed down negative search results. Put out Internet fires and fine-tuned the Web site."

Graham was quick to catch on. "And that'll be your cover?"

"It's the simplest. Although that ghoul you call a door manager might recognize me."

"Doubtful."

"I need to get going," Champion said. She caught the glint of a wedding band on his left hand and pictured his wife—an otherworldly buxom centerfold model with two-foot hair extensions and lips inflated like pool toys.

"You and Annabelle ditching the city for a lovers' getaway?" Graham asked.

Piper hoped Annabelle was the buxom centerfold wife and not an unauthorized sex partner.

"No idea what you're talking about," Champion said.

"Take some tomatoes with you." Graham tilted his head in the general direction of the open kitchen, an efficient arrangement of aluminum and steel. "And whatever else you see that you want."

"I won't turn you down." Champion crossed the kitchen and went out through a set of glass doors into what appeared to be another indulgence of the ultrarich—a rooftop garden. She wondered how much it cost Graham to have it tended.

Now that she was alone with him, the penthouse no longer felt so spacious. She needed to get down to business. "How did you figure out your ex-pal Keith had his hand in the till?"

"I followed your suggestion and did my own liquor inventory."

"And you came up short."

"For starters." He rose from the couch and made his way toward the kitchen. "The son of a bitch wasn't ringing up dozens of orders. He was also comping a crapload of drinks every night and getting big tips in return."

"Rookie management mistake," she said. "Letting employees decide who to comp. And keeping the tip drawer by the register makes it all too easy."

He set his mug in the sink and glanced out the glass doors toward the garden. She didn't like sitting while he was on his feet, and as she rose, she saw what she hadn't noticed before. An open metal staircase at the opposite end of the penthouse leading to a sizable bedroom loft. She wondered how many of his hookups had gotten their stilettos stuck in those metal slats.

The kitchen didn't look as though it was used for much more than brewing coffee, which made his rooftop garden even more of an indulgence. "From what I observed . . ." she said, ". . . and remember I was at Spiral to keep an eye on you, not your staff . . . Your pal Keith might have had a side deal going with a couple of the servers. Claiming a drink had been returned when it hadn't, then voiding the sale and pocketing the money. That kind of thing."

"Which servers?"

She wasn't throwing anyone under the bus without evidence. "That's what you're hiring me to find out."

Heath Champion came in from the garden carrying a grocery bag with green carrot fronds sticking out of the top. "You're the only guy I know who's growing brussels sprouts. Tomatoes I understand. Jalapeños, sure. But brussels sprouts?"

"Deal with it."

She'd forgotten to turn off her cell, and it blared out the theme from *Buffy the Vampire Slayer.*

Graham arched an eyebrow at her. "Very professional."

She grabbed the cell from her messenger bag. The call was from Officer Eric. She turned off the ringer and reached back inside. "I have an agency contract . . ."

Graham tilted his head toward his agent. "Give it to him while I put some clothes on." He headed toward the stairs, and for the barest moment she imagined standing under those open metal stair treads and looking up. She thrust the folder toward Champion.

He set down his garden produce and took it from her. She watched nervously as he studied the contract. Even though she'd resisted the urge to inflate her flat rate, he might still think she was too expensive.

Champion pulled a pen from his shirt pocket and clicked it. "He can afford a little more than you're charging."

She tried to absorb that. "Aren't you supposed to be protecting his best interests?"

Champion smiled, but didn't respond.

Graham appeared a few minutes later dressed in jeans and a chest-hugging Stars T-shirt that did an exceptional job of displaying his remarkable shoulders. His agent handed him the contract.

Graham studied it, raised an eyebrow at Champion, then looked at her. "Knock off five hundred," he said, "and you can have the apartment over the club instead of moving into that shitty basement apartment you mentioned."

"Cheap bastard," his agent said cheerfully.

"There's an apartment over the club?" Piper said.

"Two of them," Graham replied. "One's occupied, but the other's free. It's noisy when the club's open, but you can always buy earplugs."

"She'll knock off three hundred," Champion said. "That's as low as she goes."

Which put her right back where she'd begun, except she'd have a place to stay.

Graham squinted at his agent. "Remind me again why you're still working for me?"

"Because you need a conscience."

Graham didn't seem to take offense. Instead he turned his attention back to Piper. "Move in whenever you like, but I need you on duty tonight." He pulled a set of keys from a kitchen drawer and tossed them over. "I'll introduce you at the staff meeting. Eight o'clock sharp."

She had a job, and she had an apartment that wasn't in her cousin's basement. As she gathered up the contract, she wanted to kiss Heath Champion. But there was one more thing.

She gazed at a spot right between Graham's dark eyebrows. "This means you're not still suing me, right?"

She didn't like the quick flash of his crocodile's teeth. "I'll get back to you on that."

✶

"There's something I'm missing here," Heath said as the elevator doors shut behind Piper Dove.

Coop investigated the contents of Heath's produce bag with more concentration than it warranted. "What do you mean?"

"Why did you offer her that apartment?"

"The closer I keep her to the club, the more bang I get for my buck."

Heath retrieved his bag. "I hope your buck is the only thing you're thinking about banging. That woman is not one of your actresses."

"I've noticed. Besides, as you may have observed, I'm not too fond of her."

"I got that."

"And she flat-out despises me."

"Definitely not one of your fans."

"But the thing is, the woman's got guts and integrity."

"She's got more than that. Great eyes, an interesting face, and a very nice pair of legs."

"Not interested."

"No entourage?"

Coop was damned if he'd let Heath land any more digs about either his ex-girlfriends or Piper Dove. "Get the hell out of here and go see your wife."

"I'm on my way."

With Heath gone, Coop wandered through the kitchen into his garden, his favorite place on earth. He'd always liked growing things, and he hadn't seen why living in a city should change that. His big, multileveled wraparound terrace had brick walls high enough to protect the garden from the wind, making this an ideal growing place. He'd built the raised beds himself—hauling up every bag of dirt, every plant, and every pot.

During the football season, the green, earthy smells had taken his mind off the pain of his injuries. Whether he was amending the soil, deadheading flowers, or harvesting the vegetables he gave to the food pantry, out here he hadn't been able to hear the clash of helmets, the grunts of hard hits, the roar of the crowd that swept over the field like a rogue wave. Out here, he'd been able to forget the adrenaline rush of being in control of the whole savage ballet that made up an NFL game.

Now that he was no longer playing, he came out here to get away from himself—away from the constant churning in his head as he thought about the future. But today the peace of his garden wasn't working. A week had passed since his last meeting with Deidre Joss, and he hadn't heard a word. She'd said a decision would take time, but he wasn't good at waiting. In another few months, Spiral would break even, and he'd be ready to move on to the next phase of his new career—building a franchise of nightclubs around other big-name athletes who were too busy or not smart enough to set out on their own.

Piper Dove's appearance had been a welcome distraction, even though she rubbed him wrong in a dozen different directions. But she interested him, too. Despite the Esmerelda charade, there was a raw honesty about her that would serve him well, and he looked forward to seeing how she would reconcile her obvious dislike of him with the fact that she needed his business.

Unfortunately for her, his intrinsic politeness toward women seemed to vanish when she was around. Equally unfortunate, the day-to-day operations of a single nightclub had begun to bore him. He could use a diversion, and Piper Dove just might be it.

✶

Later that afternoon, Piper slipped the key Graham had given her into the metal door that opened off the alley behind Spiral. The small hallway had battleship-gray walls and smelled like French fries, but the floor had been swept clean. A door at the end appeared to lead to the club's service areas, while the staircase on her right led upstairs.

As she began the climb to the third floor, she was glad she didn't have much to haul. She reached the top and stepped onto the landing.

It happened fast.

A shadowy figure jumped out . . . A gun pointed right at her head . . . A sting to her temple . . .

"You're dead!"

5

Piper reacted instinctively. She grabbed the arm of her assailant, kicked out her leg, and brought him down with a loud thud. Only as she heard the woof of pain did she realize the voice that had declared her dead had come from a female instead of a male.

A teenage girl sprawled on the bare wooden floor clutching her arm. A bright yellow Nerf gun lay beside her, the hard foam bullet that had hit Piper coming to rest against the landing's painted baseboard.

The girl was one of America's ethnically ambiguous: with tawny skin; bright amber eyes; long, dark curly hair; and a promise of beauty when her adolescence was behind her. "Ohmygod, I'm sorry!" she cried, revealing a set of silver braces.

Piper went to her knees. "Are you okay?"

"I thought you were an assassin!"

"A lot of them around here?" Piper reached out to check the girl's arm.

"I'm okay." She pushed herself into a sitting position.

Piper was relieved to see the arm wasn't broken, but she was also pissed. "What did you think you were doing?"

"I thought you were someone else." The girl reached for her Nerf gun, which had been modified with red rubber bands to intensify the firing mechanism.

"You have a license to carry that thing?" Piper asked.

"I know. It's stupid. It was, like, kind of embarrassing buying them."

"Them?"

"You need more than one. It's kind of a game. But it's, like, serious." She scrambled up from the floor. She was nicely proportioned, although—being a teenage girl—she probably thought she was fat. "You must be the new neighbor. Coop told Mom somebody was moving in, but I, like, forgot about it. I'm Jada."

"Piper. So what's with the sneak attack on an innocent person?"

"I go to Pius now." Piper recognized the name of a city parochial high school. "I'm one of the Pius Assassins."

"Does the pope know about that?"

"You're funny." She said it seriously, as if she'd assessed Piper and now had a category to fit her into. "We only moved here from St. Louis right before school started, so it's kind of a way for me to, maybe, like, get to know kids."

And try to fit in, Piper thought.

"I'll show you your place," Jada said. "It's smaller than ours but it's okay." She pointed to one of the three doors that opened off the small, square hallway. "That door goes to the club. There used to be, like, an Italian restaurant where Spiral is now." She indicated the door in front of them. "Me and my mom live there. It's not as nice as our place was in St. Louis, but Mom wanted to leave, and Coop invited her to move in here. My dad died in a car wreck when I was nine. He was a private trainer for a while, and him and Coop were, like, best friends. Coop paid for his funeral and everything."

"That's tough. I lost my mom when I was young, too."

"So did Coop. This is your place." Nerf gun at her side, she headed toward the farthest door and twisted the knob. It was unlocked.

The space wasn't big, but it was decent, with mustard walls, parquet floors from the seventies, and a pair of small windows that looked down over the alley behind the club. A white Formica counter separated the modest kitchen from the living area, which had a matching moss-colored couch and recliner as well as a couple of oak end tables and lamps.

"The bedroom is the best part." Jada disappeared through the opposite door.

Was it ever. Piper stopped just inside to take it in. Most of the space was occupied by a king-size bed with a padded headboard and off-white duvet. The opposite wall held a large flat-screen TV. A state-of-the-art electronic charging station occupied a bedside table, and a pair of funnel-shaped pendant lights hung from the ceiling on each side of the bed.

"Wow."

"Coop sleeps here sometimes."

Not anymore, he doesn't, Piper thought.

"He likes to be comfortable," Jada explained.

"No kidding." Piper sat on the end of the bed and felt the cushy support of an expensive foam mattress.

Jada, picking at some already tortured black nail polish, gazed with longing at the iPad in the docking station. "Coop is really rich."

"Rich isn't all it's cracked up to be," Piper said, which was a total lie.

"I guess."

"Tell me about the Pius Assassins."

Jada pushed a long lock of hair behind her ear. "It started a couple of days ago. It's kind of like a class bonding exercise for all us sophomores."

"Those nuns get zanier every year."

"The teachers don't really like it, but as long as we don't bring Nerfs on school property there's nothing they can do about it. Everybody in the sophomore class who wanted to play had to pay, like, five dollars. We have a hundred twenty kids in our class and ninety-two signed up."

"And the goal is . . ."

"Be the last person standing."

Piper was starting to get the drift. "Like *The Hunger Games*."

"And win the four hundred and sixty dollars." Jada pulled her curly dark hair into a ponytail behind her head and then released it. "I really need the money because my phone is, like, embarrassing. I never say that to my mom, but she knows, and it makes her feel bad because we can't afford anything better." She dipped her chin. "I shouldn't have told you that. Mom said never to talk about money."

Piper's heart went out to her. "So how does the game work?"

"You can't kill anybody on school property or, like, at a school activity or if they're at work or from a moving car because kids get hurt that way."

"Comforting."

"No kills if you're on a bus or the El going to or from school, but any other time is okay."

"I can only imagine how the commuters feel about dodging Nerf bullets. Especially in Chicago. You're lucky nobody has shot real bullets at you."

"We're supposed to be respectful of other people."

"How's that working out?" she said, with only a little sarcasm.

Jada's forehead crumpled. "I'm really sorry about what happened. The thing is, you're not allowed to go into a person's house to kill them unless somebody invites you in. And, like, if any of the kids showed up downstairs and said they were one of my friends, one of the bouncers or the servers would probably let them in."

"You might want to talk to them about that."

"Mom won't let me. Since Coop lets us stay here for free, we kind of owe him everything, and Mom doesn't want to make any waves."

Free? Piper's suspicious nature made her wonder if altruism was Coop's only motive for providing free lodging. "If this happens again," she said, "I could seriously hurt you."

"That was pretty cool. You have really fast reflexes."

Now that Piper knew she hadn't broken the kid's arm, she had to admit she was happy with herself.

Jada was thoughtful. "Maybe we could have a code. You could, like, knock twice fast and once slow at the bottom of the stairs before you come up so I know it's you. I really need the four hundred and sixty bucks."

"Help me unload my car, and I'll think about it."

Jada led the way downstairs. She leveled her Nerf and took a quick survey of the alley before she stepped out.

Piper had stuffed everything into two suitcases and a couple of boxes. Jada took one of the suitcases, gun still raised, head swiveling. Piper pulled out the other. "Do you really think anybody's coming after you back here?"

Jada looked at her as if she were a moron. "You're kidding, right? This is a great place to ambush me. The third day of school, these kids named Daniel and Tasha hid behind Coop's car. They were working as a team."

"Cagey of them."

"They're dead now," Jada said with all kinds of satisfaction. "I tried to get Tasha to team up with me, but she's one of the popular kids. She also likes Daniel."

"Another woman being stupid over a man."

Jada gave a world-weary nod. "I know. I'm going to be a psychologist someday."

"Hard to imagine much of a future with Murder One on your rap sheet, but follow your dream."

Jada grinned, her wide mouth and silver braces so winning that Piper forgave her for the ambush.

Tony, the club manager, had a big voice, a bigger smile, and an effusive personality, but Piper vowed to keep her eye on him anyway, although, since Graham had told him exactly why she was in the club, that wouldn't be easy. At the staff meeting, Coop introduced her as the new digital strategist. She learned that Torpedo Head's name was Jonah. He was the head bouncer and a former Clemson linebacker. Even though he didn't seem to recognize her, his gaze was far from friendly—either because he had a naturally surly disposition or because he'd decided she wasn't hot enough to work at Spiral. The other six bouncers also looked like former football players, a theory it didn't take her long to confirm.

Tony briefed the servers on the premium brands they were pushing that evening. Piper found it interesting that Coop stepped in at the end to warn them about overserving guests. As the meeting broke up, she said, "You walk a fine line here."

"I want to build a business based on people having a good time, not killing themselves."

"Ever think about miniature golf?"

"Cute."

At nine o'clock, the guests began spilling into the club—long-haired women in short skirts, stretchy dresses, silk blouses, and incredible shoes. Guys in sports coats, open-collared shirts, or pricey T-shirts that showcased their pecs. All of them seemed to be vying for the attention of the Oklahoma cowboy who'd come to Chicago by way of Miami and brought glory to their city. They swarmed him like wasps, pushing and gesticulating. The bouncers let it happen.

A woman in fitted leather shorts and another rocking a scarlet dress with a cutout midriff passed by. Piper only had one dress in her closet suitable for the job—the innocuous black number she'd had on eight days ago, the night she'd been caught. The one good thing about having worked in a cubicle was that she could wear jeans. Dressing up for a job was a pain.

As she walked around the club, she saw that new bartending practices had already been put into place, but one of the servers, a slender brunette named Taylor, caught her attention. That first night in the club, Piper had observed that she seemed to have a particularly close relationship with bartender Keith.

When Taylor stopped at the bar to pick up a drink order, Piper introduced herself. "I'm thinking it might be interesting to post a regular feature profiling some of the servers on Spiral's Web site.

Put up a picture, a couple of fun facts. Do you think the staff would go for it?"

Most of the servers, Piper had already observed, seemed happy with their jobs. The pay was good, they got decent benefits, and none of them were expected to do lap dances to sell bottles, but maybe Taylor wasn't as happy as the rest. She set the drinks the bartender handed her on a black lacquer tray. "Sure. They'd do anything to make Coop happy."

Was there a slight edge to her answer? "They? But not you?"

"Oh, yeah. Me, too. It's a great job."

Her enthusiasm didn't quite ring true, and Piper made a mental note to keep a sharper eye on her.

Coop was being pressed for autographs, and none of the bouncers was stepping in to give him some room. She appreciated the wisdom of keeping the bouncers from looking like prison guards, but these guys had taken it too far. Everyone wanted to be Graham's friend, and even though tonight's crowd was benevolent, that could change. Still, it wasn't her job to watch out for him, and she stayed on the move, hanging out at the bar, drifting toward the dance floor, and making frequent checks of the ladies' room.

As midnight approached, she headed toward VIP. The odious Jonah stopped her at the bottom of the stairs. "You can't go up there."

She'd met these grown-up bullies before. He knew she was part of the staff, but he wanted to make sure she understood he was top dog here. Her heels gave her an extra couple of inches of height, and she utilized every bit of it. "I go where I want. If you have a problem with that, take it up with Mr. Graham. But don't cry when you talk to him. You'll only embarrass yourself."

She pushed past him and headed up to VIP. Her first night on the job, and she'd already made an enemy.

This lounge was decorated in bronze and black like the rest of the club, but with lacquered lattice screens separating conversation areas and a golden jewel of a bar at one end. The female servers' uniforms were identical to the ones on the main floor—suggestive but not trashy. Black slip dresses with twin spaghetti straps that crisscrossed at the back and a midthigh hem edged with an inch of black lingerie lace. Some of the women wore calf-hugging leather stiletto boots, others, gladiator sandals that laced up their calves but still looked more comfortable than the shoes Piper was wearing.

A man she recognized as the Stars' new running back sat with a couple of Bears players and a predictably gorgeous quartet of swishy-haired twenty-somethings. She wandered over to the bar and chatted with the bartenders while she observed her surroundings. Here, most of the guests tended to keep their attention on the people at their own tables instead of letting their eyes wander from group to group like the main floor clientele. The VIPs apparently assumed they were the most important people in the room.

She made her way to the small ladies' lounge at the back. As she stepped inside, she saw a dramatic-looking brunette she dimly recognized as an actress on one of the Chicago-based cop shows. The actress sat on a padded cube in front of an oval mirror, staring at her reflection as muddy mascara tears rolled down her cheeks.

Piper stopped inside the door. "Are you okay?"

"My life is shit," the actress said in a slurred voice, not taking her gaze from her own reflection.

Judging from the size of the diamonds in her ears, and her exquisite royal-blue one-shoulder dress, it couldn't be too shitty.

"Men are shit. It's all shit." The inky tears kept rolling.

Piper debated making a quick exit, but she'd been on her feet for hours, and her heels were killing her. She sat on the next cube and slipped them off. "Sounds like you're having a bad night."

"A bad life. It's shit."

"Kick him out. Just a suggestion."

The actress turned a pair of startled blue eyes at her. "But I love him."

Oh, lord . . . How many stupid women could one planet hold? Piper tried to sound compassionate. "Not to get all Zen on you, but maybe you should love yourself more."

The actress grabbed a tissue and dabbed at her mascara tears. "You don't understand. He can be so sweet. And he needs me. He has problems."

"Everybody has problems. Let him fix his own."

The actress's perfect nostrils flared with hostility. "You obviously have no idea what it's like to love from the very bottom of your soul."

"You're right. Unless you're talking about taco-flavored Doritos."

The actress was not amused, and she leaned closer, bringing the scent of her zillion-dollar perfume along. "Who are you?"

"Nobody. An employee. I'm doing social media for the club."

The woman took in Piper's less-than-memorable dress, so out of place in this rarefied air, then rose none too gracefully from the stool. "I feel sorry for you. You have no idea what you're missing."

"Misery?" Piper said as kindly as she could manage.

The actress stormed out.

Piper stared glumly at her reflection in the mirror. So much for a fallback career as a life coach.

She wasn't used to keeping nightclub hours, and she dampened one of the black guest towels with cold water. The door opened, and the prettiest of the swishy-haired blondes who'd been hanging out with the football players came in. "You, too?" she said as she saw Piper pressing the cool towel to the back of her neck. "I have to get out of here. I'm seriously sleep deprived, and I have my orals coming up in two weeks."

"Orals?"

The blonde leaned toward a mirror and wiped a lipstick smudge from her front tooth with her index finger. "I'm getting my doctorate in public health."

Swishy-haired, beautiful, and smart. "So not fair," Piper muttered.

"Sorry?" The woman cocked an inquisitive ear.

"It sounds challenging."

"Easier done on a full night's sleep, that's for sure." The woman made her way toward one of the three toilet cubicles.

As Piper headed back downstairs to be with the common folk, she reminded herself that a good detective didn't make assumptions like the ones she'd been making about the swishy-hairs.

✶

The theme from *Buffy* awakened her the next morning. Momentarily disoriented by her new surroundings, she fumbled for her phone, knocked it to the floor, and then hung upside down over the edge of the bed to get it. "'Lo."

"Open the door, Esmerelda. We have to talk."

"Now?"

"Now."

She groaned and flopped back onto the luxurious mattress. The bed was heaven, and she didn't ever want to leave it, especially now, when she wasn't nearly sharp enough to go one-on-one with her employer. She gazed at the time through bleary eyes—nine thirty.

But she hadn't gotten to sleep until after three. Thank God the club wasn't open every night. Four nights a week was more than enough.

She'd slept in a Chicago Bears T-shirt and underpants. She fumbled with her jeans and awkwardly zipped them as she crossed the living room on bare feet. She didn't look at him as she opened the door. "I don't even talk to myself until I've brushed my teeth." Turning away, she headed for the apartment's tiny bathroom, where she peed, brushed, and pulled herself together. When she came out, he was sitting on her couch, one ankle crossed over his knee, a Starbucks cup curled in his giant hand. She looked around hopefully for a second cup but didn't see one.

"You've spent one night on the job," he said, "and I've already had my first complaint about you."

She didn't have to think long to come up with the most likely source, but she played dumb. "No way."

"You pissed off Emily Trenton."

"Emily Trenton?"

"The actress on *Third Degree*."

"That's the worst show," she retorted. "I don't know about you, but I'm getting sick of seeing women's bodies with slit throats and bullet holes every time I turn on the TV. Whatever happened to letting audiences use their imagination? And don't get me started on the autopsy shots. I swear if I see another—"

"Your job is to watch the staff, not antagonize the customers."

She started to protest, then stopped herself. "You're right. It won't happen again."

He seemed surprised that she wasn't arguing with him, but she'd been out of line with the actress, and she saw no sense in defending herself.

He took a sip of coffee and studied her. "What did you say to her, anyway?"

"I told her she should dump the guy who was making her so miserable."

"One of the dirtiest players in the league," Graham said in disgust. "Late hits, facemasks, head butting. You name it, and the son of a bitch has done it. One of my MRIs has his name written all over it."

"Yet you let him in the club."

He shrugged. "If I excluded everybody who's pissed me off, I could be out of business."

"I don't get why you're doing this in the first place. It's a semi-seedy business—not that Spiral is sleazy, but the hours are crap, and you already have enough money to buy a small country. Or an island. That's what I'd do. Buy an island."

"They're a dime a dozen."

Lack of caffeine made her stupid. "I don't like you." She quickly amended her statement. "Let me clarify. Personally, I don't like your sense of entitlement, but as your employee, I am completely loyal to you. I'd even throw myself between you and a bullet."

"Good to know."

Considering the fact that he'd given her a job and offered her an apartment, she was being rude, even for her. He also didn't seem inclined to censure her for last night's incident with the actress. "Sorry. I have an attitude problem when I haven't had my morning coffee."

"Only then?"

"Other times, too. I'm kind of a guy that way."

"Really?" His gaze dropped to her breasts, and that brought her fully awake. She'd forgotten she wasn't wearing a bra under her

Bears T-shirt, and she automatically slouched. He smiled. Why not? He'd seen some of the most expensive breasts in the world, and hers were nothing more than ordinary. But still, he'd made her uncharacteristically self-conscious.

"The coffeemaker's on the counter," he said.

She started for the kitchen, then remembered she hadn't bought coffee. "Never mind. I haven't been to the grocery."

"There're beans and a grinder in the kitchen downstairs. I'll unlock the door for you."

"Let me get my shoes first."

Her shoes weren't all. She slipped on a bra. When she came out, he'd found Oinky, and he held it up. "Exactly what school has a pig for a mascot?"

"Community college. Farm country."

"Ah." He flicked the pig to her with a short underhand spiral that she doubted he expected her to catch. But she did.

She relished her small victory as he led her down the back stairs. Instead of turning toward the club's kitchen at the bottom, he opened the door into the alley. "Hold on a minute, will you?" He stepped outside.

She peered out and saw that the wind from last night's storm had strewn some sodden liquor cartons across the alley's cracked pavement and in its muddy craters. Graham wasn't happy. "This was supposed to have been cleaned up already." He grabbed a soggy box and tossed it in the Dumpster, then snatched up another. She gave him points for being willing to do the dirty work himself and went out to help.

As she gingerly pulled a waterlogged carton from a filthy puddle, she saw Jada coming down the alley. The grocery bag in her arms suggested she had responsibilities a lot of kids her age didn't. Jada waved and Piper waved back, then turned to pick up more sodden cardboard.

A teenage boy popped out from around the corner, Nerf gun in hand.

Piper stiffened, then spun around, calling out Jada's name.

Jada reached for the Nerf protruding from her jacket pocket, but the bag she was carrying got in her way. Her teenage assassin braced his gun hand like a TV cop. The girl was going to die. But not on Piper's watch.

She lunged forward and shoved the first thing she touched directly into the path of the bullet.

Cooper Graham.

6

Graham stumbled. Not from the bullet, which had bounced harmlessly off his arm, but from being thrown off balance without warning.

A second bullet whizzed past from the opposite direction as Jada took control. "You're dead!" she cried.

"Not fair," the kid protested.

"Totally fair!" Jada retorted.

Graham, in the meantime, had gone down in the middle of the alley, one hip landing in a pothole brimming with filthy water, a foot landing in another. "What the *hell*?" he exclaimed.

Defeated, Jada's murder victim disappeared around the corner. Jada gasped as she finally noticed what had happened to Graham. Piper raced to him. Rivulets of mucky water splattered his skin and clothes. A dab of mud had even lodged in that formidable cleft in his chin. His jeans were filthy, his hands grubby. She went to her knees next to him. "Oh, God . . . Are you okay?"

Jada charged down the alley. "Coop! Please don't tell Mom! Please!" She whipped toward Piper. "I would've been killed if it hadn't been for you!"

And now Graham was going to kill Piper. Not with a Nerf gun, but—if the look on his face was any indication—with his big, filthy hands.

Muddy water seeped through the knees of Piper's jeans as she leaned back on her ankles. "You'd . . . better go inside, Jada."

Jada didn't need prodding. With one backward, pleading glance at Graham, she, the grocery bag, and her Nerf disappeared into the building.

Piper was alone in the alley with a man who'd built his career on single-mindedly dismantling his opponents. As he shifted his weight from the pothole, a desiccated grapefruit rind slid off his shoe. She reached out. "Let me help you up."

"Do. Not. Touch. Me. *Ever.*" He came to his feet with both the grace and the deadly intent of a leopard. Who could blame her for stumbling a little as she stood up? Clenching his teeth, he ground out the words "*Never touch me again!* Do you understand?"

The murderous heat in his eyes was more than a little disconcerting. "Yes . . . sir."

His icy rage turned hot. "What the hell *is it* with you?"

"I'm a finely tuned fighting machine?" She'd made it a question instead of a statement, but either way, it was a big mistake because his expression grew even more thunderous.

"What I did was instinctive," she said quickly. "You were in the way, and I reacted automatically to protect Jada."

"From a fucking Nerf gun!"

"Yes . . . I know, but . . ." Now didn't seem like the most opportune time to explain about the Pius Assassins, so she settled on the abbreviated explanation. "It's a game. Money and peer acceptance for the new kid are at stake."

"In case you didn't get the memo, I am *not* one of the players."

"No. Absolutely not. If you hadn't been standing in the way, I'd have blocked the shot myself."

The muscles tightened at the corners of his eyes. "Barely ten minutes ago, you were bragging about taking a bullet for me. How's that working out?"

"Well . . ." She gulped. "Now you know exactly how fast my reflexes are. That has to be sort of comforting. How many humans on this planet are quick enough to sack you?"

Uh-oh. Wrong thing to say, because the steam boiled right out of his ears. "You didn't *sack* me! You *ambushed* me."

"Potato, poh-tah-to. But I get your point." He hadn't noticed the blood trickling from the heel of one of his multimillion-dollar hands, but she had. She rushed to hold the door open. "Let's go inside so you can get cleaned up and I can get that coffee you promised me." She tried to think of something that would appease him. "We can have a business meeting at the same time. I'll give you my first report."

Miraculously, that did seem to settle him a bit, although he grabbed the door from her and pushed her none too gently into the hallway. Only then did he notice his bloody hand. He blistered an obscenity.

"Just a scratch." She shot ahead of him to open the second door into the kitchen. "I'll patch you up in no time."

"Like hell you will."

"All I need is a first aid kid."

"And a license to kill." He stalked past her. "Or maybe you already have that?"

"Funny *and* smart. I'm so lucky to be working for you."

"Shut up." Still, his rancor was a little less heated.

The small, spotless kitchen had a stainless-steel counter, oven, deep fryer, and grill to prepare the club's limited food menu: minisliders, French fries with malt vinegar, and—at two in the morning—platters of complimentary bourbon fudge brownies. As Graham washed up at the sink, Piper found a first aid kit in the well-organized pantry, but he snatched it away from her. "Give me that thing. Call me greedy, but I want to keep this hand."

"So insulting."

When he flipped open the plastic lid, she saw specks of gravel in his palm. "I really am sorry." She was going to have to do more than apologize to appease him. "Here's some good news. From what I've observed so far, your VIP staff is exemplary. Considering the size of the tips they're getting, they should be, but it's reassuring to have that confirmed." He didn't look mollified. She needed more. It wasn't the right time to talk to him about his lazy bouncers, and she had no evidence to back her suspicions about Taylor, the server. That left her with only limited possibilities. "I know this will make you happy. I'm going to personally update your Internet fan club site."

He rummaged inside the first aid kit. "I already have someone doing that."

"Yes, but unlike them, I know the difference between a subject and a verb." A trickle of blood was running down his wrist. She grabbed a paper towel and gave it to him but decided not to mention the dab of mud still lodged in his chin cleft. "You're a big celebrity in Chicago now, but how long will that last if you don't keep pumping the social media machine? You only played for the Stars for three years, not like Bonner or Tucker or Robillard, who built their careers here. Fame fades, and if you want your business to grow, you have to keep your edge."

He didn't like that. "I always play at the top of my game, something you need to remember."

She was trying to pacify him, not insult him, and she steeled herself. "For the next few weeks, I'll also monitor and respond to the club's online reviews." This was exactly the kind of work she thought she'd escaped. "And that, my friend, is totally worth a few muddy potholes."

He pulled out a set of tweezers. "Keep talking."

"You want more?"

He shrugged.

"Give me those." She snatched the tweezers from him.

He didn't seem to believe in holding a grudge, and as he handed them over, he appeared more contemplative than angry. "You're pretty much a train wreck, you know that, right?"

"Only around you."

"Why is that?"

Because he controlled her future. "Because you're a legend."

"Try again, Esmerelda."

"I'm human." She swabbed the tweezers with one of the disinfectant pads. "You're . . . superhuman."

"You're not seriously going to give me that 'you're a god' bullshit again, are you?"

Exactly what she'd been about to do. "Of course not. I'm merely pointing out that I get nervous around you because I'm a regular person and you're larger than life."

"A viper pit wouldn't make you nervous." She brightened at the compliment, but he went on, oozing satisfaction. "You're sucking up to me because I sign your paycheck and because you need that paycheck to stay in business."

She set her teeth. "A bitter pill to swallow. Now hold still." She began to clean the gravel from his hand. It had to hurt like hell, but Captain America was built of vibranium, and he didn't wince, nor did he take his eyes off her.

"Tell me about yourself," he said, as if he really wanted to know. "The nonbullshit version."

She probed as gently as she could. "Only child. My mother was killed in an armed robbery when I was four, which left me with a father who alternated between treating me like the son he really wanted and being overprotective. Talk about schizophrenic."

"Explaining your personality disorder."

"Best not to insult the woman holding the tweezers." She extracted another bit of gravel. "I have combined degrees in computer science and sociology from U. of I. and eleven years working at desk jobs I grew to hate. I thought about giving my father a coronary and applying for the police force, but I didn't want to be a cop. I wanted to work for myself. Fast-forward . . . I bought Dove Investigations from my stepmother after my dad died." No way was she telling him how much she'd overpaid for what she'd ended up with.

"Bought it?"

One piece of gravel had gone deep, and she worked as gently as she could. "The alternative was murdering her. I thought about it, but they can put you in prison for that."

"Good point. Straight or gay?"

"Me or the Wicked Stepmother?"

"You."

The gravel was out, and she dabbed the wound with antiseptic. "Straight. Unfortunately."

"Why do you say that?"

She cleaned the tweezers and put them back in the kit. "In general—and there are exceptions—I like women more than men. They're more interesting. More complicated. And they're loyal. One of my biggest regrets is my lack of sexual attraction to members of my own sex."

He smiled. "Sounds like you've had one too many bad boyfriends."

"Says the man who's dated most of Hollywood. What's it like to go to the Oscars?"

"Boring as hell." He wiggled his fingers, as if he were checking to make sure she hadn't stolen one of them. "Current boyfriend?"

"Your cop pal is working on it, but no."

"Cop pal?"

"Eric Vargas. Officer Hottie?"

Graham laughed. "You're kidding, right? Not to be offensive, but"—the evil glow in his golden eyes indicated he intended to be very offensive—"isn't he a little out of your league?"

She grinned. "You'd think so, right? But I've never had much trouble attracting good-looking guys."

He frowned, not liking that his deliberate put-down hadn't made her curl up in the corner and cry. "You have a theory about that?"

"I do." She applied one of the large bandages to the heel of his hand. "They think I'm one of them, and that makes them comfortable around me. Until they figure out I'm using them. Not callously. I don't believe in that. But, really, how can you take most straight men seriously?"

He cocked his head, as if he wasn't hearing all that well. "You're using them for . . . ?"

"For—what do you think?"

She'd sacked him again, and he seemed temporarily at a loss. She loved her flippancy. He couldn't see how short-lived her bed-hopping days had been or how lonely they'd made her feel.

"So you're basically a man-eater?" Graham said.

"Oh, no. I'm not sexy enough."

He started to say something—almost as if he wanted to argue with her—then he backed off. She snapped the kit shut and got up to look for the coffee beans.

*

Coop watched as Piper disappeared into the pantry. She wasn't beautiful, but she was . . . what? He could only come up with one word. *Infuriating.* Maybe two words. *Infuriating* and *intriguing.* He looked down at his mud-splattered jeans. The tear in the arm of his jacket. His bandaged hand. Infuriating, intriguing, and . . . a little bit dangerous. Those quick reflexes; her dark hair, as jagged as old razor blades; those shrewd blue eyes, and thick slabs of eyebrows; that crazy-wide mouth; and a jaw nearly as solid as his own. Her body, too. There were no bones protruding. Her curves were right where they should be.

But . . . as soon as this gig was over, she was out. Now wasn't a good time to have anyone unpredictable around him, even though she gave him this odd—not exactly a rush—more a hyperawareness. She was unexpected, and that meant he had to keep up his guard.

No, that wasn't quite right, either.

He had to be attentive when he was with her, but not guarded. The opposite of guarded, really. He didn't pull his punches. Didn't even consider it. He was always polite, even to women who grated on him, but with her, he was like a junior high bully insulting a girl just to see if he could make her cry. But there were no tears from Mister Piper Dove. She could more than hold her own.

She came out of the pantry. Nobody who wasn't smart graduated from the University of Illinois with a double major, and he chalked up her intelligence as another irritant. Considering his own dismal academic record, his attraction to brainy women was ironic. But his lousy grades had been the result of too many hours on the practice field, not stupidity.

Piper got the coffeepot working without a tutorial. She was lying about her male conquests. Or maybe not, because there was definitely something about her. By the time she'd poured her coffee, he'd figured it out.

It was the challenge.

The way she carried herself, the way she charged after what she wanted. She was a woman who attacked life instead of waiting for it to unfold around her. And her general imperviousness to him had stirred up some kind of primitive bullshit need to conquer. Which was exactly what other men saw in her. A test of their masculinity.

He doubted she understood that, but even if she did, he couldn't see her playing the bitch card. She didn't care enough about attracting men to deliberately make herself difficult. Her life centered around her job, and men were nothing more to her than a necessary inconvenience. Because of that . . .

He was going to nail her.

The thought came out of nowhere . . . or maybe it had been lurking in his subconscious all along. He wanted to take her right now. Against the sink. On the counter. Strip her naked and reassert the natural order of things. Male over female.

The sting in his wounded hand restored his sanity. He was disgusted with himself. Where the hell had that come from?

She set down her coffee mug. "What did I do now?"

He realized he was scowling. "Breathe."

"Deepest apologies." She raised her mug toward him, unscathed by his rudeness. "You did a noble thing today, Mr. Graham, whether you wanted to or not. Saving Jada from an untimely death is good karma."

"Stop calling me Mr. Graham." He didn't mess with his female employees. Ever. Didn't need to. And he wouldn't mess with Esmerelda. Not yet. Not while she was working for him. But the minute her job ended, she was fair game. Before he saw the last of her, he intended to show her which one of them was the better man.

*

Piper yawned and stepped into the hallway, her travel mug in hand. Even though it was Sunday morning and she'd worked until three, she couldn't afford the luxury of sleeping in. She needed to get to her office.

The door to Jada's apartment opened, and a slender, dark-haired woman carrying a backpack emerged. "You're our new neighbor," the woman said as she spotted Piper.

"Piper Dove."

"I'm Karah Franklin."

This must be Jada's mother, although she looked more like an older sister. Dark, curly hair swirled to her shoulders, and her warm brown skin didn't require even a touch of makeup. The woman's beauty suggested Coop hadn't given her a free apartment simply because he'd been friends with her husband but because they were lovers. She looked enough like Kerry Washington to qualify as a movie star girlfriend.

Karah shifted her backpack to her shoulder. "Jada told me you'd moved in. If she bothers you, let me know."

Piper remembered the sight of Coop sprawled in the alley yesterday morning. "She's no bother. She seems like a terrific kid."

"Have you actually *met* her?"

Piper smiled. "We have an understanding."

"I'm working and going to school to get my accounting degree, so I can't keep track of her the way I should." Guilt oozed from every part of her. "Right now, I'm heading for the library."

Piper noticed the woman's tired eyes. Not Coop's current lover, then, because if she were, he wouldn't let her work so hard. "That sounds tough."

"It could be a lot worse. Anyway, nice to meet you."

"You, too."

When Piper reached her office, she finished her lukewarm coffee while she talked to Jen on the phone about Berni. Then she turned on her computer. Her job at Spiral was temporary, and she had to keep marketing herself. She'd been using her Web site to post tips on self-defense, credit card fraud, and personal security, putting to use everything she'd learned from her father and from the classes she'd taken in the past few years. Now she intended to take some of that information and put it in a flyer as an additional promotion for her business.

She wanted important clients—law firms, big insurance companies that investigated disability fraud. Until that happened, the fastest money she could make was based on suspicion. She typed away:

HOW DO YOU KNOW IF HE'S CHEATING?
IS SHE REALLY OUT WITH HER GIRLFRIENDS?

She began laying out the signs of a cheating partner—too many late nights at work, unexplained phone hang-ups, new interest in personal grooming. She'd hand-deliver the flyer to hair salons, sports bars, coffeehouses—whatever businesses would let her display it. And every flyer would be printed with her logo and phone number.

The phone rang. It was Jen again. "Guess who's coming to town?" her friend chirped. "Princess Somebody from one of the big oil countries. Along with her retinue. Over fifty people! They need some female drivers."

"How do you know this?"

"From Dumb Ass. I just heard him talking about it with one of the reporters. Apparently the princess decided to drop a few zillion on the Mag Mile instead of Rodeo Drive. Piper, these Middle Eastern royals tip big!"

"I am so on this!" Piper exclaimed.

She reached one of her father's old pals, who gave her the number of the owner of a limo company that worked with visiting VIPs, and landed the job. She wasn't exactly sure how she'd juggle the royals and Cooper Graham, but she'd figure it out.

*

Tuesday morning, she was at O'Hare sitting behind the wheel of a black SUV. She'd never seen herself as a chauffeur, but the job sounded interesting, the pay was decent, and the lure of a big tip at the end made this a no-brainer. She was supposed to meet with Graham that afternoon to talk about the club's Web site, but she had more than enough time before then to get whomever she was driving from the airport to the downtown Peninsula Hotel.

The royal family, she'd learned, had something like fifteen thousand members, either highnesses or royal highnesses depending on whether or not they were in line for the throne. They always traveled with a huge retinue: other family members, military guards, servants, and—it was said—briefcases stuffed with cash. She sincerely hoped some of that would be coming her way in the form of a huge tip when the job was over.

Their private jet turned out to be a 747, and their VIP status let them avoid the lines at passport control. An armada of SUVs and half a dozen cargo vans for luggage waited for them. When the retinue emerged, only the servants were in traditional Islamic dress. The female royals—at least a dozen of them, ranging from teens to late middle age—wore the latest designer fashions. Diamonds glittered, spindly Louboutins clicked on the asphalt, Hermès bags swung at their sides.

The Middle East's most pampered princesses had come to town.

7

Piper opened the back door of the SUV for a beautiful woman in her forties with big designer sunglasses propped on top of a mane of luxurious dark hair. She wore a vibrant purple Chanel jacket, a short black leather skirt, and stilettos that looked like surface-to-air missiles.

They'd barely pulled away before the woman took out her cell and began an intense conversation in Arabic. Piper had a hundred questions she wanted to ask, but she'd been instructed not to address any of the royals, which was a major bummer. The woman didn't once look at her—not that she projected hostility. Piper was simply invisible.

By the time the motorcade arrived at the Peninsula, Piper's jaw ached from the effort of keeping her mouth closed. She'd been given the sixth position in the line of limos, an indication that her passenger wasn't the ranking princess. The woman exited without acknowledging her, but as she disappeared into the hotel, one of the Realm's grim-faced officials ordered Piper to wait.

She waited. Half an hour passed. An hour. The guard barked at her like a dog when she finally got out to run inside and use the hotel restroom. "I ordered you to wait!"

"Be right back." As she bolted through the lobby, she remembered that slavery hadn't been abolished in the Realm until 1962.

When she came out, a servant girl was sitting in the backseat. She was young, with a round face and soulful dark eyes. Unlike the royals, she was traditionally dressed in a plain gray abaya and navy hijab. Piper apologized for keeping her waiting, something that seemed to startle the girl. "Is not a problem."

Piper was happy to hear her speak English, and since she hadn't been given orders not to address the servants, she introduced herself. "I'm Piper."

"I am Faiza," the girl said shyly. "Her Highness, Princess Kefaya, has sent me to get these shoes." She held up a page torn from a glossy French fashion magazine that pictured a pair of T-strap leather stiletto sandals. "You will take me to get them, please."

"Sure. Where do we go?"

"Where they have these shoes."

"Do you know the name of the store?"

"Her Highness did not tell me."

"Can you call her and ask?"

Faiza could not have looked more horrified. "Oh, no. That is not what we do. You will take me to find the shoes, please."

Piper held out her hand for the magazine page. It bore a prominent YSL logo. She pulled out her phone and discovered a Saint Laurent boutique in the Waldorf a couple of blocks away.

"Do you like your work?" she asked the girl as she turned onto Rush.

The question seemed to confuse her. "Work is to work." And then, as if she'd said the wrong thing, she went on nervously, "Her Highness, Princess Kefaya, never strikes me, and I only have to share my bed with one other servant, so it is very good."

But she didn't sound as if it were all that good, and Piper got the message. Speaking about her employment could get Faiza into trouble. Still, Piper couldn't miss the yearning in those dark, soulful eyes as they gazed out at the young girls striding along the city sidewalks with their trendy backpacks and confident gaits.

She'd planned to circle the Waldorf while Faiza made her purchase, but Faiza begged her to come inside. The struggle between the girl's natural timidity and her determination to do her job made it impossible to refuse. Piper reluctantly turned the SUV over to one of the Waldorf's valets and went with her.

The designer boutique with its white marble floors, soaring ceilings, and array of luxury goods bore no resemblance to the DSW where Piper shopped. This place smelled of perfume and privilege. Faiza handed the magazine page back to Piper. "Her Highness needs in every color, please."

"Every color?" While Piper was processing that, a young, beautifully groomed clerk approached. She was clearly drawn more by Faiza's traditional garb than by Piper's chauffeur's uniform—white blouse, dark slacks, and a black blazer she'd found at Goodwill yesterday. The clerk's eagerness suggested word had gotten out that the richest of the world's royals were in Chicago.

But as anxious as the clerk was to help, she could only produce the shoe in two of its five colors, which sent Faiza into so much distress that her hands shook as she opened a zippered pouch and pulled out a thick wad of U.S. currency—a meaty stack of hundred-dollar bills that would be mere pocket change to a family worth more than a trillion dollars.

When the transaction was complete, Faiza returned the leftover cash to her bag, meticulously folding the receipt. She clutched the bag to her chest as they left the boutique, her forehead puckered with worry lines that had no place on such a young face.

Piper got back on her phone and forty-five minutes later helped Faiza purchase a red pair from Barneys. But even that wasn't good enough. "You do not understand." Faiza twisted her fingers around the clasp of her bag. "I cannot fail Her Highness. She must have all the shoes."

Piper blared her horn at an overly aggressive taxi driver. "Don't you think five pairs is a little piggy?"

Faiza didn't understand, which was just as well.

Piper's meeting with Graham wasn't for three hours, which should give her enough time to drive out to a suburban Nordstrom where she'd located the final two pairs, grab them, get Faiza back to the Peninsula, then make it to Spiral. Piper forced a smile. "Let's go."

As they sped west out of the city, Faiza grew less guarded and more like the nineteen-year-old she was. Piper told her a little about her job with Graham and learned Faiza was Pakistani, as well as a devout Muslim who'd gone to the Realm at fourteen to find work and to visit the country's holy cities so she could pray for the parents and sister she'd lost. Instead, she'd ended up enduring brutally long hours and what Piper regarded as a kind of imprisonment, since her passport had been taken from her when she'd first been employed, and she hadn't seen it since.

Faiza repeatedly checked her bag for the receipts. Some of the country's royals had a reputation for abusing their servants, and Piper didn't like to imagine what might happen if the receipts didn't reconcile with the cash Faiza carried.

The Nordstrom that carried the shoes was located in Stars territory in the far western suburbs. The clock was ticking, and the clerk took forever to ring up the purchase. But as long as the traffic gods were kind, Piper could still make it back in time for her meeting.

They weren't. An accident on the Reagan Tollway brought traffic to a standstill, and since Graham had refused to give her his cell number, she couldn't even call him. She could only stew.

The traffic inched forward, then stopped again. Inched and stopped. Before long, Piper's shoulders were so tense her muscles screamed. She took a few deep breaths. Nothing she did would make the traffic go faster. She concentrated on her passenger. "If you could do anything you wanted, Faiza, what would it be?"

Seconds ticked past before she replied. "Dreams are foolish for someone like me."

Piper realized the question had been unintentionally cruel. "I'm sorry. I didn't mean to pry."

Faiza released a long, slow breath of her own. "I would go to Canada and study to be a nurse. One who helps babies born too early, the way my sister was born. But those kinds of dreams are not meant to be." She spoke matter-of-factly. This was no bid for pity.

"Why Canada?"

"My father's sister lives there. She is my only family, but I have not seen her since I was a child."

"Do you stay in contact? Talk to her on the phone?"

"I do not have a telephone. I have not been able to speak with her for almost two years."

"Would you like to use mine?" Piper said impulsively.

She heard Faiza's sharp intake of breath. "You would let me do that?"

"Sure." Piper already had so many money troubles, what did a few more dollars on her cell bill matter? "Do you know her number?"

"Oh, yes. I have memorized it. But if anybody knew . . ."

"They're not going to find out from me." She tossed her cell in the backseat and told Faiza how to use it.

The aunt must have answered, because a joyous, rapid-fire conversation in what Piper assumed was Urdu followed. As the conversation went on, the traffic finally began to move, and by the time Faiza returned her phone, they were back on the Eisenhower.

"My *khala* has been so worried about me." Faiza's voice was choked with tears. "She dreams that I can come to live with her, but I have no money, no way to get there."

Piper's cell rang. She wasn't supposed to take personal calls when she was driving, but she couldn't ignore this one, and she put it on speaker.

"Interesting," a familiar male voice said. "Here I am sitting in my office waiting for a meeting that was supposed to start ten minutes ago, yet I'm still alone."

"I'm stuck in traffic." Before he could upbraid her, she went on the offensive. "If you hadn't refused to give me your cell number, I would have called."

"Stuck in traffic is not an excuse. It's a sign of bad planning."

"I'll send that to Oprah as an inspirational quote."

"I liked it better when you were pretending to be in love with me."

"My meds kicked in."

He snorted.

She gnawed at her bottom lip and looked at the clock on the dashboard. "If I'd had your cell number—"

"I told you. If you need me, call my agent."

"I thought you were being sarcastic."

"I'm never sarcastic."

"Not exactly true, but . . . I'll be there in thirty-five minutes."

"At which time I'll be at the gym." The call went dead.

As Piper disconnected, Faiza spoke up, clearly incredulous. "You were talking to your employer, the American football player? So disrespectfully?"

"He annoyed me."

"But surely you will be punished."

Almost certainly. But not in the way Faiza meant. "Employers here can't do anything but fire you."

"This is a very strange, very wonderful country." Faiza radiated goodness in a way Piper could only admire, and the wistfulness in her voice was heartwrenching.

They finally reached the hotel. Faiza touched Piper's shoulder. "Thank you for what you have done, my friend. I shall pray for you every night."

That seemed a little excessive, but Piper wasn't one to turn down anyone's prayers.

*

"When I said I'd be at the gym, it wasn't an invitation for you to show up." Coop had to shout over the scream of Norwegian black metal blaring through the speakers. A bead of sweat flew from his jaw as he delivered a violent left-right combination to the punching bag. Piper barely stopped herself from pointing out that it was not only bad form, but also counterproductive, to go after the bag with all that force.

Pro Title Gym was the smelly, windowless, hole-in-the-wall mecca of Chicago's most elite athletes—a stripped-down space with cinder block walls, dented black rubber mats, and rusty squat racks lining a wall that held an American flag and a yellowed sign with a quote from *Fight Club* that read LISTEN UP, MAGGOTS. YOU ARE NOT SPECIAL. The place reeked of sweat and rubber. No juice bars or trendy workout clothes. Pro Title was hard-core, expensive, and exclusive.

"How did you get in here?" Coop snarled like a Rottweiler.

"I slept with the dude at the front desk," she retorted over the shrieking, distorted guitars.

"Bull." An uppercut to the bag.

In fact, all she'd had to do was explain that she worked for Coop. Wearing her chauffeur's uniform instead of being dressed like a football groupie gave her credibility, and the guy had let her in. "It's my story, and I'll tell it how I want."

He delivered another punishing jab. "Go away."

That was fine with her. She hadn't expected to conduct their meeting here, merely to show him that she took her job seriously. But she didn't immediately move. She couldn't. Not when the muscles under Coop's sweat-stained T-shirt rippled like wind over water every time he punched. She had to stop this. Right now. Because if she didn't, she might start thinking about growing her fricking hair! She spun toward the door.

"Hold it!" Another Rottweiler bark. "Why are you dressed like that? You look like a mortician."

She calmed herself down enough to tell him who she was driving for. “Only during the daytime,” she shouted over the music. “This is my chauffeur’s uniform.”

“It’s ugly.” Another annihilating punch at the bag.

“So’s your disposition.”

That bounced right off him. “Do you care at all how you look?”

“Not much.”

He stopped punishing the bag and regarded her critically. “You’ve worn the same dress every time you’ve been in the club.”

“Said the man in cowboy boots.”

“It’s my trademark,” he retorted. “Go buy some new clothes. You’re making the place look bad.”

She watched a rivulet of sweat roll down his neck. He smelled like good sweat, the healthy smell of a guy who always wore clean clothes to the gym. Until this moment, she hadn’t realized there was such a thing as a good sweat smell. Now she knew, and she wished she didn’t because thinking about anything that had to do with his body was a distraction she couldn’t afford. “New clothes aren’t in my budget.”

He returned to the bag. “Send me the bill. You need to look like you fit in.”

He had a point, but still . . . “I’m not buying anything uncomfortable.”

“By that, I assume you mean anything that looks decent? Yeah, that’d be a real deal breaker.”

“Try being female for a while. Then you can talk.”

Coop couldn’t get used to it. No conversation was ever straightforward with her. Abandoning the bag, he grabbed a scuffed black iron kettlebell and crouched down, extending the weight in front of him and trying to ignore her. He felt the strain in his delts, the hard pull in his thighs. He'd always liked brutal workouts, but he'd never needed them like he did now, when he was trapped at Spiral night after night.

Not *trapped*. He loved the energy of the club, the challenge of once again proving himself. He just wasn't used to spending so many hours inside.

He fought the urge to switch hands by glaring at Sherlock Holmes. She wasn't so impervious to fashion that she'd done up the top button of her blouse. Too bad she hadn't opened the next one.

His arm began to spasm. A bead of sweat dripped into his eye. He changed hands. "I'm going shopping with you." He yelled it out, but the music blaring from the speaker over his head abruptly ended so that his voice echoed off the cinder block walls. A White Sox pitcher on the next mat looked over at him. So did Piper, staring at him with those big blue eyes that didn't miss a thing. Had he really just volunteered to go clothes shopping with a woman?

"Goody," she said, with a snide expression he'd make damn sure he never saw on her face once he got her naked. "Let's get manis and pedis, while we're at it. And invite our girlfriends."

She killed him with that mouth of hers, but he roped in a smile and matched her sarcasm with cool. "I don't trust your judgment."

"But you trust your own?"

"I know what I like."

"I'm sure you do, but pasties and a G-string don't seem all that appropriate for work."

She was killing him and doing it so gleefully.

He came up with a sneer. "I'm busy until next week. Try to keep it together until then. I'll meet your wise ass at BellaLana. It's on Oak Street."

That got a satisfying rile out of her. "I'm not shopping on Oak Street! Do you have any idea what clothes cost in those stores?"

"Pocket change."

That made her blood boil, as he'd known it would. He lowered the kettlebell. "Get the hell out of here so I can finish my workout." And smack himself in the head a couple of times for letting her get to him.

Still, his offer wasn't entirely irrational. Sherlock had a habit of being everywhere at once when she was in the club, and he liked knowing another set of eyes was looking out for his interests—a set of eyes he could absolutely trust. You could say a lot of negative things about Sherlock—lack of deference to her employer being number one—but that woman was serious about her ethics.

Not that he intended to tell her how valuable she was proving to be. Just as he didn't intend to tell her what he was going to do to her once he got her in bed.

*

The next night, Piper spotted Dell, one of the bouncers, near the bar. He was a blond surfer type with a tat of a jaguar running up the side of his neck. He'd had a short-lived career with the Bears and was especially popular with the female customers—so popular that he seemed oblivious to anything else that might be happening in the club.

She couldn't stand it any longer. She pulled him away from his admirers with the excuse that she wanted to interview him for a Web site profile. Instead, she pointed out a group crowding Coop on the other side of the room. "Those women with Coop are drunk and getting obnoxious. That redhead especially. She's hanging all over him. Maybe you could go over and distract her so he has some room?"

Dell looked down at her as if she were a gnat to be crushed. "You telling me how to do my job?"

"Yeah, she's getting good at that." Jonah had come up behind them, and the two men, all bulging muscle and sour belligerence, formed a wall between her and the rest of the room.

"Look, guys, I'm just suggesting you watch Coop a little more closely."

Jonah smirked. "And I'm suggesting you mind your own fucking business. What is that, anyway? Sending out cute little tweets and posting pretty pictures?"

The bouncers weren't her responsibility, and she should have kept her mouth shut, but when had she ever? "Thanks for the reminder. I've got a sweet one of you making kissy-faces in the mirror."

Yep, she knew how to get along with her coworkers, all right.

Over the next few days, she drove the minor princesses and their servants shopping as part of a five-car, sometimes six-car motorcade that included at least two vans to transport their mountain of purchases back to the hotel, everything paid for in cash. But instead of envy, Piper began to feel pity, especially for the teenage miniprincesses. Sometimes she saw the identical yearning in their eyes that she'd seen in Faiza's, a yearning that couldn't be satisfied with a dozen trips to the Apple store. A yearning to walk unaccompanied along the sidewalk with the same carefree strides as the American girls they watched through the darkened windows of their SUVs.

On the day of her dreaded dress-shopping appointment, Princess K's sister took forever at her facialist, which made Piper ten minutes late arriving at BellaLana, where Coop was leaning against a jewelry case and chatting comfortably with the female staff. If Piper had been prone to hives, one look at the racks of expensive clothes on display would have given them to her.

The black, white, and silver decor gave the place an industrial, op art, fin de siècle vibe—both luxurious and somehow condescending, as if daring its customers not to find it chic. Of all the things she didn't want to be wearing right now, her chauffeur's uniform was at the top of her list, especially since she'd sweated out the armpits under her suit jacket as she'd run from the parking lot.

Coop looked up. His lips formed a smile, but his eyes told her he'd noted the fact that she'd once again kept him waiting. The saleswomen regarded her with various degrees of incredulity, unable to believe someone so odd-looking could be with Chicago's most eligible bachelor.

"Ladies, this is Piper," Coop said. "She's given up her career as a mortician, but she's having a hard time breaking old fashion habits."

Piper reined in a laugh.

"You've come to the right place," an überstylish redhead said. "Working as a mortician must have been super depressing."

"Not so much as you'd think," Piper said. "That's how I met Coop. Burying the ashes of his career."

Coop snorted. The redheaded saleswoman clearly recognized she was in over her head and hustled Piper toward a dressing room.

"Nothing too crazy," Coop called out. "She's got enough of that going on in her head."

The first dress was a drab forest green, but there was nothing drab about the skintight fit or the hemline, which barely cleared her butt. Thankfully, she'd shaved her legs, but still . . . "This isn't exactly my style."

"No fly?" Coop said from the other side of the dressing room door.

Okay, Piper had to laugh at that.

The saleswoman, whose name was Louise, looked mystified. "It's really fashion forward."

Piper winced at her reflection. An eternity stretched between the bottom of the dress and her bare feet. "I think I need to go a few steps fashion backward." Or take a fast trip to H&M, which was where she really belonged.

"Lemme see," Coop said.

The saleswoman pushed the dressing room door open. Coop sat on one of the big square silver-and-black ottomans not far from the mirrors. Piper tried to tug down the hem. "I look like a pine tree."

"With really good legs," Heath Champion said from the front entrance. He wandered into the store and sprawled on the ottoman next to Coop's. "I like it."

"I don't," Coop said, his eyes on her thighs. "Too conservative."

She gaped at him. "In what universe is this conservative?"

He shook his head sadly. "You have to remember you're not a mortician any longer."

Heath grinned.

She gestured toward the sports agent. "What's he doing here, Coop? Not that it isn't a pleasure to see you, Mr. Champion, but why here?"

"Coop told me to show up, and what could I do? I've made millions off the guy."

"I needed another opinion," Coop said. "He's more used to buying women clothes than I am."

Louise appeared with another armload of dresses and hustled Piper back into the dressing room. In the next half hour, Piper modeled a slinky red number missing a middle, a dark blue number missing a front, and a gold thingy that made her look like a Little League trophy. "I'm an investigator," she hissed at both men, "not a pitcher for the Peewee Penguins."

Heath grinned. "I like this woman."

"No mystery why," Coop retorted.

It was a mystery to Piper, but she had something more pressing on her mind. "This is clearly not working," she declared as Louise went off to gather up more dresses Piper didn't want to wear. "I'd freeze to death in every one of these. Not to mention that I can't do my job if I'm worrying the whole time about my . . . my *cooter* hanging out!"

That cracked them both up, clearly signaling that it was time for Piper to take charge. "Louise, you and I need to talk . . ."

8

After much wrangling, Piper ended up with a mulberry knit that had long, tight sleeves and a hem that nearly made it to her knees. The dress was high in the front but had enough dip in the back to be nightclub appropriate. Coop also insisted on a minuscule cobalt-blue bodycon dress that was only saved from sluttery by a longer, sheer black overlay. One glance at the final tab and she got light-headed. "I could have bought fifteen dresses at H&M for what one of these cost."

"Your big mistake was not making him buy a couple more," Heath said as they stepped into the sunny early-October afternoon.

A middle-aged man coming out of Starbucks spotted Coop and called out to him. "Hey, Coop! You're the best!"

Coop waved at the guy.

"Piper's gonna need shoes," Champion said.

"She'll have to put it on my bill, because I can't stand listening to any more of her complaining." Coop acted as if she weren't standing right next to him. "I never met a woman so averse to spending my money."

She sighed. "Unlike you two rich boys, I have to get back to work."

"Don't forget where your real job is," Coop warned. "And next time you're late, I'm docking your pay."

"Yes, *sir*." She peeled off toward the parking garage.

✶

As the two men watched her disappear, Heath shook his head. "She doesn't have a clue, does she?"

"Nope." Coop refused to say more.

They passed a men's boutique featuring plaid pants he wouldn't have been caught dead in. Splashes of fallen leaves brightened a black-and-white store awning. More leaves lay like rusty fifty-dollar bills on the sidewalks.

"She kind of sneaks up on you," Heath said. "It's those legs."

It was the whole damn package. Piper's curves were right where they belonged, with nothing exaggerated, everything strong and efficient. But mostly it was her eyes. And her irreverence. And that crazy kind of decency lying underneath all her attitude.

"She reminds me of Annabelle," Heath said. "The first time I met her."

Coop knew what he meant. Annabelle had the same kind of feistiness. But there was a big difference. "Annabelle's sweet and Piper's a viper."

"Obviously you haven't spent enough time around my wife." Heath glanced toward a bra and panty set in the window of Agent Provocateur.

"Just as long as the two of them never meet," Coop said.

"I think it'd be entertaining."

Coop shuddered. He liked Annabelle, but he didn't like the way she wanted to poke her nose into his relationships. "Make sure it never happens."

"I'm promising nothin', pal. And for the record . . . Why did you really want me here?"

It took a few beats too long for Coop to respond. "Exactly what I said. You have more experience with women's clothes."

Heath hadn't gotten where he was by being stupid, and Coop expected to be called on his bullshit, but Heath merely smiled his python's smile. "And she's never been in *People* magazine," he said. "This gets more and more interesting." He slapped Coop on the shoulder and headed back to the bra and panties at Agent Provocateur.

"Dude!" Two teens who should have been in school dashed across the street to high-five him. Coop welcomed the interruption. Inviting Heath to show up had backfired. He'd been so sure his agent would be bored. Not that Heath would have shown it—he was too slick—but he'd have been texting the whole time, and that's all it would have taken. Seeing Sherlock through his agent's jaded eyes would have restored Coop to sanity. He would have remembered all the women more beautiful, more accomplished, more Coop-like who were part of his world. Instead, Heath's cell had stayed in his pocket. But then Heath liked quirky women. Witness Annabelle. The two of them—the matchmaker and the sports agent—were a love story for the books.

Coop knew exactly what women on the hunt looked like, felt like, smelled like, and Sherlock had none of the characteristics. She refused to come on to him. All she wanted was a job, and once he lost that hold, he'd be no more important to her than those dresses he'd bought.

This would require careful strategy, something he was very good at.

✶

Piper wore the cobalt dress that night—her fourth night on duty at the club—but instead of making her blend in with the trendy crowd, it attracted more attention than she wanted. A couple of guys asked to buy her drinks, and PhairoZ, the club's guest DJ, singled her out during his break.

PhairoZ—real name Jason Schmidt—looked like a tatted-up European soccer star. Coop was a smart businessman. He understood that he was the lure drawing customers in for their first visit, but the club itself had to draw them back, so he hired the best DJs to keep things fresh, as well as a good-looking male staff. Where the women were, the male customers would follow.

"So you want to hang after I get off?" PhairoZ leaned one palm against the wall behind her.

"Thanks, but seriously . . ." She regarded him with earnest eyes and what she hoped was a semi-shy expression. "You're way too hot for me."

"That just means I can warm you up faster."

She resisted her natural tendency for put-downs. "I'm too insecure." She gave his arm a friendly squeeze, ducked under it, and walked away.

That night, she hovered in Spiral's basement behind an industrial-size water heater, the same place she'd waited for the past two nights. Overhead, she heard the staff closing up for the night—or early morning, since it was a little after three. She yawned. She'd broken up a tussle in the ladies' room; tailed Dell, the useless bouncer; and made sure some very drunk women found a cab. But in five hours, she had to be at the Peninsula to take one of the older princesses to her plastic surgeon's office, and she wanted to go to bed.

The sound of footsteps cut through her grogginess. She peered around the water heater and saw a figure wearing stiletto boots and carrying a backpack coming down the stairs. The same backpack Taylor brought to work each evening. Taylor glanced around, then crossed the basement toward the liquor storage room.

The lock had been changed, and there were now only two keys—one for Coop and one for Tony, the club manager, a decent guy who'd already earned Piper's trust. It was his key that, at Piper's request, had spent the past two nights conveniently lying out on his desk.

The lock rattled. Piper raised her camera, quickly adjusted the settings, and clicked away.

✶

Two nights later, Taylor was gone. She and her boyfriend Keith, Spiral's ex-bartender, had been operating a small but profitable black market business selling Spiral's top-shelf brands. Piper had only been working for Cooper Graham for six days, and she'd already earned her salary.

Around eleven o'clock, Deidre Joss entered the club with Noah. Coop must have been looking for her because he appeared right away and led her up to VIP. But Noah Parks had spotted Piper, and he didn't follow.

While Deidre had traded in her black office attire for an amazing beaded black sheath, Noah still wore his conservative businessman's suit and a necktie. "I'm surprised to see you here," he said, taking in Piper's new mulberry dress.

"Coop hired me to do some social media for him."

Noah regarded her stonily. "I'm sure you've told him by now who you were working for."

"I promised confidentiality, and that's what I've delivered," she replied tersely.

"You're saying you didn't tell him?"

"That's exactly what I'm saying. And please remind Deidre of that the next time she needs to hire an investigator."

He took a sip from his glass and regarded her thoughtfully. "Impressive."

Not long after, she spotted Jonah scowling at her from across the floor, a scowl she suspected would get more unpleasant if he learned she intended to get his pal Dell fired. From the beginning, something about Dell's manner had made her suspicious, and her suspicions had paid off earlier tonight when he was managing the door and she'd seen him take a tip in the form of a bag of white powder from a drunk who wanted to get in.

She went upstairs to check out VIP. Noah had joined Deidre and Coop there, but Coop was only paying attention to Deidre. He hadn't said much to Piper about the nightclub franchise he was developing, but she knew him well enough to suspect that Deidre's refusal to make a final decision on financing was driving him crazy—not that he'd let her see that. Another man would be courting other firms, but Deidre had a stellar reputation, and Coop, being Coop, would only want to work with the best.

He laughed and leaned in closer to Deidre. Setting aside business, Coop genuinely liked her. Piper felt a stab of jealousy. Not because he liked her. No, that wasn't it at all. Of course not. Piper was merely jealous because Deidre had it all: a megasuccessful business, a huge bank account, brains, beauty, self-confidence . . . And because Coop so obviously liked her.

She wanted to hit herself in the head. She was jealous! Jealous because she wanted Coop to like her, too. A ridiculous reaction. Coop was her employer, and all that mattered was that he like the way she was doing her job.

Thanks to Duke, she had years of practice scrubbing away feelings that made her uncomfortable, and she buried her self-disgust in a couple of warm bourbon fudge brownies from the kitchen.

Deidre and Noah finally left. Piper made her way through the lounges to the dance floor where the vibrant LED wall showcased the throng of bodies gyrating to DJ PhairoZ's electro beats. Coop wasn't far away, his customary throng crowding him.

An oversize goon in Gucci—she'd caught a glimpse of his logoed belt—was doing his best to back Coop against a wall. He wasn't an ordinary fan. This guy was drunk and belligerent. He was also as tall as Coop and fifty pounds heavier. His arms gesticulated in agitated loops, and the club's laser lights turned his complexion from blue to red to Hulk green. She glanced around for one of the bouncers. As usual, none were in sight. Wishing she'd traded her stilettos for flats, she pushed her way through the dancers just as the goon clenched his fist and leaned in.

Coop put a hand to the guy's chest. The goon didn't like that. His arm shot back, ready to throw a punch. She hurled herself forward and caught his arm before it could land. Shifting her weight, she thrust an elbow to his solar plexus and dropped him to the floor.

The dancers skittered back. Reeking of booze, the goon croaked for air and tried to get up. The side seam on her new mulberry dress ripped as she straddled him. She caught a momentary glimpse of Coop's incredulous face before Jonah and Ernie appeared, blocking her view. They looked down at her, as if she were the one at fault.

"Get him out of here," she ordered. Jonah's expression was murderous, but he and Ernie led the guy away.

One of the female servers rushed over to her. "Are you okay?"

"Of course she's okay," the aggravated voice of her employer retorted. "She's the Man of Steel. Just ask her."

So much for gratitude.

PhairoZ did a quick switch to acid techno. A firm hand hooked her arm and drew her none too gently off the dance floor. As Coop maneuvered her through the crowd, she realized the skirt of her damaged dress had ripped at the side, revealing an unimaginative pair of white hip huggers.

He directed her through the kitchen and out the door that led into the back hallway. Only then did he drop her arm. She knew him well enough to know what was coming, and she wasn't having it, so she got in his face before he could get in hers. "Unlike your bouncers, I won't stand by and watch my employer being assaulted."

His face reddened with massacred ego. "I wasn't being assaulted, and don't you ever try to protect me again."

"Somebody has to do it." She was the professional here, and she struggled for calm. "Your bouncers need to stay closer to you. That drunk was getting ready to throw a punch."

"Which he'd never have landed."

"Maybe. Maybe not."

"I hired you to watch the staff, not me."

They were so close she could smell the laundry detergent from his sweater. "You do understand this is a conversation we wouldn't be having if I was one of the men on your staff."

"You're not. And don't you try to pull the sexist card on me!"

"When the card fits, play it." The way he was looming over her made it nearly impossible to hold her temper. "If one of your bouncers had pulled the guy off you—highly unlikely, since they're way too busy trying to hook up with the female guests—you wouldn't have thought twice about it."

His eyes narrowed—wary—and she thought she had him, but he wasn't giving up so easily. Instead, he moved even closer, so she could feel his body heat right through her torn mulberry dress. "I don't need to be rescued by anybody."

Her professionalism dropped away. Now she was as angry as he. "Really? What if it's two on one? What are you going to do then?"

"Especially then," he said, with something approaching a sneer.

They were nose-to-nose now. Or they would have been if she were a head taller. "How about three to one?"

"I take care of myself."

She refused to back off. "What if somebody has a gun? What are you going to do then?" She expanded her chest, which, unfortunately, brushed the tips of her breasts against him.

He reared even higher, more of him pressing against her. "Better question—what would you do?"

"I'm trained! You're not."

"What you are"—he growled—"is a pain in the ass." And without warning, he crushed her to him, his head descending, and his mouth clamping over hers.

She was so shocked she gasped, parting her lips, which gave him an access he immediately claimed.

His kiss invaded. Took over. Hard and demanding. His hand went to the rip at the side of her dress. He touched the bare skin of her hip, and his fingers were like flames. Every cell in her body came alive. Wide-awake. Cock-of-the-morning, crowing from the roof of the henhouse, sun blazing high in the sky . . . *that* wide-awake.

She bit back a moan. He felt so good. Tasted so good. He reached farther into the slit of her dress. His knee pressed between her legs. She wanted this. Wanted it enough to forget everything and give in. Wanted it—

"No!" She shoved hard against his chest. "Back off!"

She was furious with him, more furious with herself. "You try that again, and you'll end up on the floor . . . like your drunken friend." She spun away and rushed upstairs.

He was sweating as if he'd just finished a full day of speed drills. What the hell had happened? Was he turning into one more thug who thought playing football gave him the right to assault women? He sagged against the wall, sick inside, trying to pull it back together. Women kissed him, not the other way around. They rose up on their toes, looped their perfumed arms around his neck, opened their mouths, and dove right in. He was going crazy. That was the only explanation. People had told him he'd have adjustment issues with retirement, but he'd never expected anything like this. He was twice her size, and no matter how mighty She-ra, Princess of Power, thought she was, he could crush her.

God, she was pissed. She should have given him a hard knee to the nuts.

But she hadn't.

Because she'd been pissed, but not afraid of him. If she'd felt threatened, even the smallest bit, he'd be doubled over right now clutching his crotch.

Or maybe he was looking for an excuse for bad behavior. A way to feel okay about what he'd done. But there was nothing okay about going after a defenseless woman.

Who wasn't defenseless. Not even close. But still . . .

Shit.

He liked having her around. Hated having her around. She was messing with his focus. But she was also doing a great job, and he'd be a total sleaze to fire her over what had just happened, since he was the one at fault.

He'd have to find another way to deal with her—a way that wouldn't get him ejected from the game.

Her cell rang four hours later, summoning her to the Peninsula earlier than she was scheduled to be there. On the way, she blared her horn at anybody who got close to her. Why had Coop kissed her like that? Because she was winning their argument, that's why, and he couldn't stand to lose. A total power play. Much more frustrating was her response. Of course, he'd noticed. Now she'd have to work twice as hard to make certain he didn't get any more of an upper hand than he already had.

One of the male officials greeted her at the Peninsula with the news that Princess Kefaya wanted to meet with her. Piper couldn't imagine why.

An older servant met her in the lobby and guided her to the elevators. When they got off, the servant led Piper through a black marble foyer into a spacious living room suite with large corner windows.

Princess Kefaya entered from one of the adjoining rooms. Even though it was early, she was fashionably dressed in a luxurious fuchsia tunic that fell to midthigh over sleek gray pants. Elegant gold cuffs encircled her wrists, and a ransom in diamond earrings sparkled through her long coal-black hair.

Faiza followed her into the room. Piper had only caught a glimpse of her since that first day, but she'd thought about her frequently. Faiza stayed by the door, her eyes on the carpet. What must it be like to live every day without hope for a better future?

"You are the driver who works for the American football player?" the princess asked.

"Yes."

"My brother, His Highness, Prince Aamuzhir, is in town. He is a fan of American football. You will bring your employer to meet him tonight. His Highness is staying on the eighteenth floor."

"I can't do that."

The princess wasn't used to anyone telling her something couldn't be done, and her eyebrows arched like a cat's spine. "Faiza! You will personally make arrangements with this driver and see this is done."

Faiza nodded, her head still bowed. She led Piper from the suite to the elevator. As soon as the doors closed, Piper threw up her hands. "Faiza, I can't make Coop do anything, let alone this."

"But the princess has ordered it," Faiza said earnestly.

"The princess is going to be disappointed."

Faiza's forehead puckered. "Can you not persuade him?"

"This is the United States," Piper said as gently as she could. "I know it's hard to understand, but we don't care here about what foreign princesses want."

Piper watched the play of expressions on Faiza's face move from despair to fear to resignation. Piper couldn't bear it. "This isn't your fault. I'll go back and explain."

Faiza regarded her sadly. "Do not trouble yourself. This is my difficulty. If I had not mentioned to my friend Habiba that you work for a famous American football player, none of this would have happened. Habiba means no harm, but she likes very much to talk."

"But you'll be the one punished." Piper knew it was true, and the injustice infuriated her. She was further enraged when the elevator doors opened and the bright light of the lobby revealed what she hadn't noticed before. Faiza's dark purple hijab didn't quite hide a bruise on her cheekbone.

Rage boiled through her. A pair of stern-faced guards stood near the elevator. She grabbed Faiza's arm. "I don't feel good. Help me get to the restroom."

Faiza regarded her with concern, but she was accustomed to serving others, and she immediately directed Piper past the disinterested guards and across the lobby to the ladies' room. No one was inside. "Who hit you?" Piper demanded. "Did the princess do this?"

Faiza touched her cheek. "No. It was Aya." The distasteful way she uttered the name spoke volumes. "Aya is in charge of Her Highness's servants. She likes things done quickly, and I was too slow."

"And the princess allows her to hit the other servants?"

"She does not notice."

"She should!" They were alone, but Piper automatically lowered her voice. "Your aunt in Canada . . . Would she let you stay with her if you could get there?"

"Oh, yes. She has told me this. Every time we come to the United States, I dream of going to her, but it is impossible. I have no way of getting there, and even if I did . . . If I was caught . . ." Her dark eyes were as empty as an old woman's looking at her own death.

She shook her head at the futility of such a thing. "I must find my happiness in knowing how deeply my *khala* keeps me in her heart."

"That's not good enough." The royal family was leaving tomorrow night. Piper hesitated. "What if there was a way to . . . get you into Canada?"

This was crazy. Piper had no idea how to get Faiza away from her employers and across the border.

Faiza's face was a playground of emotions, with hope and defeat riding opposite ends of a seesaw. Defeat quickly won out. "I would do anything, but there is no possibility, my dear friend. Your kindness means much to me."

Kindness wasn't enough. All the way home, Piper thought about helping Faiza escape. It wouldn't be easy to get her out of the country. But it might be possible.

All she needed was a little help . . .

9

"You want me to do *what*?" Cooper Graham snatched a cherry lollipop from his mouth.

She'd cornered him in his rooftop garden, where he was nurturing his cucumbers before the first frost could get them. Even though October had arrived, the garden's high brick walls, multiple levels, and comfortable lounging area formed a beautiful oasis. Raised vegetable beds held cool-weather crops of leeks and spinach; beets, turnips, and broccoli. Big glazed pots and stone jardinières displayed mixes of rosemary and zinnia, parsley and dahlia, lemongrass and marigold. She hadn't liked discovering he'd built this garden himself. It upset some of what she wanted to believe about him.

"You're an adrenaline junkie," she pointed out, crumpling some mint leaves in her fingers. "This should be right up your alley."

"You really are taking medication. Crazy pills!" He plopped the lollipop back in his mouth and returned to the cucumbers.

"A deeply offensive comment," she said with a sniff. "But I'll rise above."

"You do that."

As she moved around a pot of pepper plants to get closer, she noticed a potting table tucked behind the wooden lattice that defined the garden's lounging area. Something on top caught her attention. She gave herself time to regroup by going over to investigate. "What's this?" She held up a perfectly rounded ball of hard-packed dirt, one of half a dozen sitting on top of the table.

"Seed bomb. Unlike you, I have no ethics."

"Meaning . . . ?"

"I'm a guerrilla gardener. Some clay, peat moss, and a batch of seeds shaped into a ball. That's all it takes."

She was starting to get the picture. "You're an urban Johnny Appleseed. You toss these into empty lots."

"It's getting too late in the season now. Best times are spring and early fall. With a little luck and some rain at the right time, a hardscrabble plot of dirt starts to bloom." He reached across the cukes to pull off a few yellowed tomato leaves. "Coreopsis, coneflowers, black-eyed Susans. Maybe some prairie grass. Fun to watch."

"How long have you been doing this?"

"Two, three years. I don't know."

"I thought you were laundering drug money."

He grinned for the first time since she'd cornered him. "You did not."

"Well, not really, but . . ." As interesting as this side of him was, she hadn't lost sight of her goal. "Maybe I should start from the beginning."

"Or maybe you shouldn't. You realize, don't you, that you blew your cover at the club last night with your jujitsu moves? Nobody's going to buy you as my social media specialist any longer."

Something she'd already figured out. Church bells chimed in the distance, and she plunged ahead. "Her name is Faiza. She's only nineteen, and she's been working for the family since she was fourteen. She's sweet and smart, and she only wants what we take for granted. A chance to be free."

He scowled at a ragged bean plant.

"She dreams of going to nursing school so she can take care of preemies, but right now, she's little better than a slave."

He ripped up the bean plant and tossed it aside, crunching on what was left of the lollipop. She moved in on him. "Please, Coop. It's Sunday. The club's closed. All you have to do is go to the Peninsula tonight and have a manly chat with the prince. Think of it as a once-in-a-lifetime opportunity to get an insider's look at a different culture."

He tossed the lollipop stick in a compost bin. "I'm happy with the culture I'm already in. Except for my thieving waitstaff . . ."

A tiny red sugar crystal lingered at the corner of his mouth, and the memory of that ridiculous kiss came back to her. She instinctively licked her lips. "Your waitstaff is basically honest. And if everybody felt the way you do, there'd be no hope for international peace and understanding."

"Thank you, Miss Universe."

"I'm merely pointing out that you're being very narrow-minded."

He jabbed a soil-crusted finger at her. "At least I have a mind. And I seriously doubt my spending a night reliving my glory years with a Middle Eastern oil baron is going to do squat for international relations. As for the rest of your plan . . ." He shuddered.

"I've done a few things in my life I'm not proud of, but what you're asking is creepy."

"It's heroic! It's a chance at redemption for the sins of your past." Like that kiss, she thought, but he hadn't brought it up and neither would she. Although he seemed to be thinking about it. How she knew that, she wasn't certain. Maybe she simply felt it. Or maybe it was something else . . . The calculating look in his eyes. A certain wiliness . . . What was he up to?

He dipped his head and brushed the corner of his eyebrow with his thumb. "If I were going to do this . . . which I'm not . . . I'd expect something in return. What are you prepared to offer?"

"What do you want?"

"An interesting question . . ."

He started smoking her with his gaze. Burning right through her lame-ass chauffeur's outfit. Peeling off every ugly piece of it. And taking his time with it. She might not be smart about everything, but she was smart about this, and she rolled her eyes. "Stop messing with me. You can have any movie star you want, and you're only trying to make me squirm. Just like last night. Well, guess what? It's not working."

"Are you sure about that?" The words slid from his lips, all silk and seduction.

"I'm pretty much un-squirmable."

"Is that so." He stroked the side of his jaw, leaving a dirty smear behind. "Did I ever mention what a bad lover I was when I first started out?"

One thing she had to say about Coop Graham: he was unpredictable. For a reason all his own, he'd decided to steer them into dangerous waters. She needed to back off, but she couldn't do that, not with the way she'd responded to him last night. That meant it was kickoff time. "I don't believe you did," she said.

"I got lots of complaints, so I had to work at it. Treat it as a job."

"Put in the extra practice time, right?"

"Precisely. When I think of the mistakes I made . . ."

"Mortifying, I'm sure."

"But I kept my eye on the ball."

"Only one? Curious. Oh, well, I hope your deformity didn't make you too self-conscious. I'm sure you could still—"

"I finally got the hang of it when I was about—"

"Thirty-six?"

"Eighteen. I was a fast learner. All those older women willing to take a young kid like me into their loving arms . . ."

"Blessed are the merciful. But . . ." She smiled her own wily smile. "As entertaining as this is, you don't have any interest in me. Both of us know you are completely out of my league."

At first he seemed to appreciate her acknowledging this indisputable fact, but then his expression clouded over. "Hold on. Last week you told me how you're a real man-eater."

"There are limits. You're an entirely different species from the Officer Hotties of the world. Way above even my head."

He actually seemed miffed. "Now why would you say something like that about yourself? Where's your pride?"

"Firmly entrenched in the real world. You belong in bed with superstars. Look at me. I'm thirty-three years old. At best, I'm average-looking, and—"

"Define average."

"I have ugly feet, I'm at least ten pounds overweight."

"For a cadaver."

"And . . . I don't give a crap about clothes or the way I look."

"Now that part is true. As for the rest . . . You've heard of power blackouts. All I'd have to do is turn off the lights."

He said it with such mustache-twirling, over-the-top villainy that she would have laughed if so much hadn't been on the line. Instead, she advanced on him. "Let's get serious. A woman's life is at stake. I need you to do this. And your better self—assuming you have one—needs for you to do this."

He'd gotten wise to her tactics, and her swipe had no effect. "Try again, Sherlock. That wasn't even a first down."

She'd run out of arguments, and she slumped against the brick terrace wall. "Do you have a better idea?"

"I sure as hell do. Mind your own business."

She took a deep breath, then slowly shook her head. "I can't."

Coop popped one of the small yellow pear tomatoes in his mouth. It didn't go well with the remnants of his cherry sucker, but he needed to stall. She was right. He'd been messing with her. Trying to make that wrongheaded kiss seem as meaningless as it should have been.

He gazed over at her. She looked so damned disappointed in him. Like she'd caught him torturing a kitten. What she wanted was over-the-top and doomed to failure, but he still felt about two feet tall, an emotion he hadn't experienced since his college coach had deservedly called him out for too much partying.

"All I'm asking for is an hour," she said. "Two at the most."

He never let anybody put him on the defensive, yet that was exactly what she'd done. She saw herself as some kind of knight-ess in shining armor, and she expected him to join her crusade. She worked for him, damn it. He was the quarterback, and she didn't get to call the plays. "You're asking for a lot more than that."

She wouldn't give up. "Isn't a young woman's life worth a little of your time?"

He countered her attempt at emotional blackmail with cold logic. "Her life isn't in danger."

She gazed over the wall at a big maple that had turned red. For once, he couldn't tell if she was sincere or playing him. "Being born in this country gives us opportunities most people in the rest of the world don't have," she said. "Where you happen to be born. It's the luck of the draw, isn't it?"

He'd been born dirt poor, but . . . *Shit.* She was going to make him do this. Or maybe it wasn't her. Maybe it was the challenge of what she wanted.

The prince smelled of some bullshit cologne that probably cost a couple of oil wells but made Coop queasy. The guy had dyed black hair and a thin mustache shaped like seagull wings. His eyeglasses were tinted a weird blue at the top but clear at the bottom, and he wore western clothes—a suit custom fit to his small build and cap-toe gray oxfords that might have fit Coop's feet when he was ten. Coop didn't have anything against small guys. It was Prince Aamuzhir's big ego that put him off.

"You must sail with me before I sell my yacht. It's one of the largest in the world, but the pool is in the stern, and I only swim in the sun." The prince spoke flawless English with a British accent. "With a second pool in the bow, I can swim regardless of which direction I'm sailing." A chuckle. "I'm sure you can't understand why this is important enough to me to buy a new boat. Most people can't."

Coop was in a foul mood. He'd met more than his fair share of assholes like the prince—wealthy men who fed their sense of self-importance by rubbing shoulders with jocks and, at the same time, condescending to them. Still, he nodded affably. "Me? I'm only a worn-down football player. Now you . . . You're a man of the world, a real smart guy. I could see that right away."

Sherlock had done her research. *"Some of the Realm's princes are fairly stand-up guys,"* she'd told him. *"Well educated. Businessmen and government ministers. A fighter pilot. Prince Aamuzhir isn't one of the decent ones. He spends most of his time away from the Realm throwing parties with very expensive hookers."*

The prince blew a plume of cigarette smoke that Coop did his best not to inhale. "Invite some of your friends to sail with me," he ordered. "Dean Robillard. Kevin Tucker. I've not had the pleasure of meeting them."

Fat chance. Robillard and Tucker would dangle this douchebag over the rail of his single-swimming-pool yacht and drop his ass straight in the water.

"I'll give 'em a call," Coop said. "See if they can get away." He took a sip of some very old scotch from a heavy crystal tumbler that he doubted even the Peninsula's collection of luxury barware kept on hand. He'd been in this suite a couple of times, but he'd never seen that gold fountain in the corner, those jewel-studded ashtrays, or the embroidered purple silk throw pillows.

The prince had taken the chaise that sat near the grand piano. As he crossed his ankles, he revealed the pristine soles of shoes he apparently wore only once.

"Tell me, old sport . . ." The prince let loose another stream of air pollution. "How do you think you'd have played against Joe Montana or John Elway?" He asked the question as though it had never been asked before, as if rookie sports journalists all over the country hadn't offered up the same query more times than Coop could remember.

Coop pretended to think it over, took another sip of scotch, then gave his customary answer. "Those guys were my idols. I only wish I'd had the opportunity. All I know is, no matter who I played against, I did my best."

The prince recrossed his ankles. "It is my observation that too many quarterbacks are impatient. They don't read the defense properly."

Coop nodded, as if the prince were one of the great football analysts instead of an egotistical jerkoff who didn't know shit.

He gestured toward Coop's hand. "You have worn your Super Bowl Ring."

Super Bowl rings weren't known for their subtlety. The Stars latest was a gaudy, oversize son of a bitch with enough diamonds to outfit a high-society ball. Coop gazed down at his finger. "Beautiful, i'nt it?"

"Exquisite."

Coop could practically see the guy salivating. "I'll tell you what, Your Highness . . . I never let anybody try on my ring. I worked too damned hard to earn it, but for you . . . Aw, hell . . ." He pulled it off his finger. "You're a man who understands the game the way most people don't. See what it feels like to wear one of these."

Coop didn't bother getting up from his chair, but merely held it out, which forced the prince to scramble from the chaise to get his greedy hands on it.

The prince shoved the ring on his stubby finger. It immediately flopped to the side. He twisted it back into place and held it there as if he never intended to let it go. "A superb piece." He took his time admiring it, even wandering toward the glass-topped dinner table where the light was better. Finally, he said, "Some beautiful ladies will be arriving soon. You'll stay and enjoy them with me."

Coop had the opening he'd been both waiting for and dreading. "I can't pass up an invitation like that." He rose from his chair and pulled out his cell. "I have a PR event, but let me see if I can get out of it." He carried his cell to the doors that opened onto the suite's wraparound terrace and dialed Sherlock, who was waiting in his car around the corner.

"Roy, it's Coop," he said when she answered. "Something came up, and I need to get out of that event at the Union League tonight. Fix it for me, will you?"

"Are you still with him?" she asked.

He glanced over to see the prince fingering the ring. "Yeah, I know I signed a contract, but I can't make it."

"I haven't forgotten that you're my first responsibility . . ." She sounded worried. "I knew this could be risky. If you need me to get you out of there, I'll come up right away."

"Hell, no!" That's the last thing he wanted: Piper Dove rushing in with her magic bracelets and golden lasso. "You didn't tell me there was going to be that much press."

"You're the best."

"All right. I'll be there." He disconnected and shoved his cell back into his pocket. "Damn it all to hell. I can't skip out. I gotta leave." He dipped his head regretfully, as if he'd lost the chance of a lifetime. "It's not too often I meet somebody who understands how to live big the way you do." More headshaking on his part. More regret. Now came the tricky part.

He went over to reclaim his ring. "There was something I wanted to talk to you about, but . . . Oh, well . . ." He held out his hand.

The ring stayed where it was. "Please. Tell me what it is."

"This is kind of embarrassing." Mortifying was more like it. "But you and me . . . we're men of the world, right? Discriminating about the finer things. The two of us . . . we know what we want."

"Of course." The prince caressed the ring with his thumb.

"One of the princess's drivers is a friend of mine—knows I enjoy women. Younger ones. I mean, what man doesn't, right? You've got this servant girl . . . Name's Faiza. The driver pointed her out to me."

"Ahh . . ." The prince beamed at him. "You fancy this servant girl?"

"She's my type. Real, real young. Looks about thirteen." He forced the rest out. "My favorite kind of woman."

"Ah, yes."

His skin was crawling. "I was wondering . . . Do you think you could talk the princess into letting the girl come . . . work for me? Permanently?" He'd hit the word *work* extra hard, and he gave the prince a few moments to fill in the degenerate parts for himself. "Heck. I shouldn't have asked." Again, he held out his hand for the ring. "Glad you appreciated my ring. I'll get out of here now and let you enjoy the rest of your evening."

"Wait." The prince moved a few steps away. "It might be possible . . . But of course, I would have to compensate the princess."

"Well, sure. You say the word, and I'll write a check. What do you think the girl is worth? A couple of thousand?"

"Money between friends? No, no. But perhaps, a token of our friendship?"

Sherlock had assumed Coop could simply convince the prince to turn the girl over, but Coop had known better. "By a token, you mean . . . ?"

The prince's thumb caressed the ring. "Whatever you think the girl is worth to you."

"You drive a hard bargain, but . . . You got her papers? Passport? I don't want to lose that ring and then have her skip out on me."

"But of course. One phone call." The prince gave him an oily smile and reached for his phone. Coop pretended to stare out the window during the short, barked conversation in Arabic. He and the prince had struck a deal.

Coop couldn't wait to get away, but he wasn't turning over the ring without the girl, and he knew how to take his time. He finished his drink and sidetracked the prince's story about a particularly repulsive sex game by recounting a story of his own, this one about last season's Giants game. Finally, the two of them were on the elevator riding down to the lobby.

One of the royal henchmen stood at the front desk riffling through a stack of passports he'd apparently retrieved from the hotel safe. Since the United States and Canada had a loose border, Coop had tried to convince Piper that a passport wasn't absolutely necessary, but she'd been her own stubborn self.

"Without a passport, it'll be nearly impossible for her to apply for legal status," she'd argued. "She won't be able to go to school and get health care. They've stolen her identity, Coop. The passport represents what little of it she has left. Promise me you'll at least try."

He hadn't promised anything, but the short time he'd spent with the prince had steeled his resolve.

The henchman handed the passport over to the prince. A diminutive, robed female figure stood off to the side, clutching a small cloth duffel. Her head was down, so Coop couldn't see her face. She had no way of knowing what was happening to her, and she had to be terrified.

The prince didn't spare her a look—she was a mere female—but gave Coop the passport. Coop flipped it open with his thumb. Glanced at the name and the photo. He walked over to the girl and tilted up her chin with his thumb. Just like he was buying a fucking slave.

It was unmistakably her. Dark brows, round cheeks, trembling lips, and deep brown eyes wide with terror, something he couldn't do anything about right now.

He pocketed her passport and turned back to the prince. "You enjoy the ring, Your Highness. And that Lombardi trophy right in the middle? Solid platinum."

But the Lombardi trophy on the real ring, which was locked in his bedroom safe, was picked out in diamonds—genuine ones, not the cubics that crusted the reproduction rings. He'd had half a dozen replicas made to donate to various charity auctions. The bidders all knew they were copies, but they'd still been popular items.

"Come on," he told the girl, hoping she'd cooperate so he wouldn't have to spook her further by touching her.

Her shoulders hunched, as if she were already trying to protect herself from the atrocity she believed was coming, but she followed him.

"Enjoy her," the prince said as they passed.

Coop wondered how many guards would jump him if he punched the son of a bitch in the teeth, but he was too well-disciplined for that kind of indulgence. Without a backward glance, he led the terrified servant from the lobby. One reproduction Super Bowl ring. That's all this girl's life had been worth.

They passed through the hotel's front doors. Only as he led her around the corner toward the street where Piper was waiting in his car did he address her. "Welcome to America, Ms. Jamali."

*

Watching their reunion made the whole ordeal worthwhile. Piper looked as happy as he'd ever seen her, and Faiza was crying. Piper moved to the backseat to be with the girl, and he slid behind the wheel. As he drove, she held Faiza's hands and explained what had happened. Faiza could barely speak, but the joyous way she threw her arms around Piper spoke volumes.

Piper had chosen Berni Berkovitz's condo as the safest place to stash Faiza for the night. Berni, of the brisket and divinity fudge, wore an odd combination of red tights and a man's ragged cardigan. She flapped her arms in greeting. "This is so exciting! So thrilling!"

The Berkovitz apartment was overstuffed, overheated, and smelled vaguely of mothballs, but Coop agreed with Piper that it was safer keeping Faiza here than at the club. "I don't know what Muslims eat," Berni said as she drew them inside. "But I have some chocolate cake. Is that okay with your religion?"

"Oh, yes," Faiza replied. "But I do not think I could eat. So much has happened."

He needed to talk to Sherlock privately, and he stepped in. "Mrs. Berkovitz, why don't you show Faiza where she can put her things while Piper and I make some plans. And I'm sure she's going to want to call her aunt."

Faiza's anxiety resurfaced. "Is there more problems? I do not want to make problems for you after you have done so much for me."

"Everything's fine." He gave her a reassuring smile, but the prince could realize at any time that he'd been duped, and Piper needed to make sure Faiza was on her way before that happened.

"Ms. Jamali . . ." He dipped into the pocket of his suit coat and pulled out her passport. "I believe this is yours."

Faiza walked toward him slowly, her eyes glued to the passport in his hand. She stopped in front of him, not grabbing it, merely touching the green cover with her fingertips.

"Go on," he said gently. "Take it."

She did, holding it as if she couldn't believe it was really hers. She lifted her head, and pressing one hand to her heart, bowed deeply before him. "*Shokran jazeelan,*" she said in a choked voice. "Thank you."

Damn. If he wasn't careful, he'd be bawlin', too. Not Piper, though. He'd swear not even a gallon of pepper spray could make that woman cry.

Faiza no sooner followed Berni into the bedroom than Piper threw herself smack into his arms. If it hadn't been for his quick reflexes, she might have sacked him again. Not that she'd sacked him the first time, but try telling her that.

"You're the best!" she exclaimed. "The absolute best man in the world!"

She curled her arms around his neck, nestled her head under his chin, and he forgot all about sacks. Despite the disparity in their sizes, her body fit perfectly against his. Her breasts flattened against his chest, her hips rested against the front of his thighs. His hands automatically went to the small of her back. She squeezed him hard, and he went hard in return, as randy as a kid copping his first feel.

She looked up at him, big blue eyes all gooey with gratitude and utterly oblivious to the physical effect she was having on him. It took every morsel of his self-discipline not to curve his hands around that ass, but after last night, he knew if he did he'd get a punch in the gut. Or worse.

How had this unnatural power shift happened? She was hugging him as if he was her best buddy. As if that kiss in the hallway hadn't happened. As if she'd frickin' forgotten all about it!

He steeled himself, took her by the arms, and firmly set her a safe distance away, all the while praying she wouldn't look down and see exactly what she'd done to him.

He wanted her to be at least a little hurt by his rejection, but she only registered happiness. "I knew you could do it! Oh, Coop, you've changed her life forever."

He glowered at her. "Stop jumping around and tell me your plan for getting her out of here."

His grouch didn't faze her. "I'll give her a few days to settle in and make plans with her aunt. Then—"

"Not a good idea." He increased the distance between them, which put him next to a dusty silk flower arrangement, and told her about the prince and the ring, making sure she understood how many holes there were in her original plan. "The prince has a big ego and a small army to go with it. It might take him years to figure out he's been tricked, or he might already realize it. Best to get her on the first flight out of the city tomorrow. Better yet, fly her out of Milwaukee. It's not that much farther than O'Hare, and there's no sense in taking unnecessary chances."

"I'm not putting her on a plane."

"You damned sure are. I'm paying."

She brushed him off. "There are no direct flights, and she's been traumatized enough. Thunder Bay is right across the border from the North Shore of Minnesota. I'm driving her."

"Why would you even think of doing that?" he exclaimed.

She looked at him as if he were the lowest worm on the planet.

And there it was again. The feeling that he wasn't man enough to meet some kind of challenge that existed only in her mind.

"Because it's the right thing to do," she said.

He huffed and puffed, feeling more and more like a blustering idiot. Finally, he made himself shut up. "Fine!" he said, exactly like a sulky teenager. "Have it your way."

But even as he stormed out, he knew what he had to do.

10

Her car wouldn't start! Of all the mornings for this to happen, why did it have to be today? Faiza sat in the passenger seat, clutching her precious passport and darting nervous glances at the cars traveling past Piper's old condo building. If it weren't for Coop and his counterfeit Super Bowl ring, Faiza's employers would almost certainly ignore her defection. Still, Piper couldn't fault Coop for what he'd done. She'd imagined his celebrity status would be enough to get the prince to hand Faiza over as a gift, but Coop understood wealthy egotists better than she did. A bad miscalculation on her part.

While Faiza gnawed at her bottom lip, Piper poked around under the hood of her Sonata, but it wasn't until she inspected the fuse box that she saw the problem. A couple of the fuses were missing. Who the hell had—?

A car stopped next to her, window down. "Get in."

It was Coop, sitting behind the wheel of a silver Audi sedan and looking like the king of the city. "You did this!" she exclaimed. "Where are my fuses?"

"I'll give 'em back when I'm ready," he drawled.

He got out of his car and opened the passenger door of her Sonata. "Good morning, Ms. Jamali. I'm driving you ladies to Canada today."

"No!" Spending hours in a car with him would take too much work on her part. She didn't want him to be decent. She wanted him to keep on being the self-absorbed, arrogant, entitled jock she'd invented in her head when she'd first started to follow him.

But Faiza was glad to see him and eagerly transferred cars, leaving Piper with no option other than to follow. He overrode Faiza's protests about sitting in the Audi's front passenger seat and relegated Piper to the rear. She snatched up the seat belt. "Not only am I perfectly capable of driving to Minnesota by myself, but I guarantee I'm a better driver than you."

"How do you figure?" he said as he pulled away.

"I've been following you, remember? You're hard on the brakes, you tailgate when you get frustrated, and in general, you're too aggressive. I, on the other hand, am trained in evasive driving, ambush avoidance, and offensive contact driving."

"Impressive, but I don't get speeding tickets. I happen to know you can't say the same."

"Only because there's not a cop in the state of Illinois who's going to give a ticket to the great Cooper Graham. But let's see how the Wisconsin Highway Patrol feels about you when we cross into Packers territory."

"Even there," he said smugly. "When you're a big-name athlete like yours truly, you can get away with just about anything."

"Life is so unfair," she muttered. "And where's your Tesla?"

"In the garage. It has to be recharged about every three hundred miles, so road trips require some planning."

"Whose car is this?"

"Mine."

She forced her teeth to unclench. "How many do you have?"

"Only two. Unless you count my truck."

"Why do you need a truck?"

"Haul stuff. Every man needs a truck."

She sighed and started picking the fuzz off her sweater.

As they drove toward the Wisconsin border, Faiza told them about her conversation with her aunt the previous night. Coop used all the charm he never bothered to expend on Piper to chat with her. Faiza maintained her modesty, not looking directly at him, but she clearly adored him. Only as he ventured into politics did Faiza grow fiery.

"The word *Islam* means 'peace, purity, submission, and obedience,'" she said. "What has terrorism to do with any of those things?"

They talked more about the Middle East, about food and music. Near Madison, they ordered lunch at a Burger King drive-through. Faiza was enchanted with the idea of getting a meal through a window. Coop refused Piper's money, as well as her offer to take over the driving. "If you get any ketchup on my seat covers, I'm leaving you by the side of the road," he said.

Faiza took his threat seriously and promised she'd be very careful. "Not you, Faiza," he said. "Only her."

"You do not like Piper?" Faiza sounded genuinely distressed.

"It's complicated," he said. "You see, Piper's crazy in love with me. I have to keep her at a distance."

Piper snorted.

"Oh, no," Faiza cried. "Piper is not crazy. She is very intelligent."

This launched Coop into an explanation of American slang. By the time they'd cleared the Wisconsin Dells, he'd taught Faiza not to take words like *crazy* or *awesome* literally, as well as explaining the meanings of *cool, chill, hang,* and *What up?*

Faiza's giggles made Piper's heart sing, so she was shocked at how peevish she sounded when she said, "Knowing American slang won't do her much good in Canada."

"They have American television in Canada," he pointed out.

Piper was ashamed of herself. Just because she'd been feeling left out was no reason to be so churlish.

Like most men, Coop hated to stop the car, and she accused him of timing them when she and Faiza ran into a service station restroom.

"Glancing at my watch doesn't mean I was timing you," he said righteously.

She gave him the hairy eyeball. "How long did we take?"

"Six minutes and thirty-two seconds."

As irritating as she sometimes found him, he could still make her laugh.

"Buckle up, ladies," he said. "This spaceship is taking off."

They reached Duluth midafternoon, and he finally let Piper take the wheel—mainly because she was sitting behind it when he reappeared from his own restroom trip. "Five minutes, fifty-two seconds," she said. "You're holding us up."

Faiza giggled from the backseat.

"Four minutes tops. You're lying." But he climbed into the passenger seat without protesting.

The wild beauty of Minnesota's North Shore, with its rocky

bluffs, cobblestone beaches, and breathtaking views of Lake Superior, was a well-kept secret from most of America, but Duke had brought Piper to the North Shore on several camping trips when she was a kid, and she'd always loved the area. The signs they passed for fried walleye, smoked whitefish, and wild rice pancakes made her desperately miss the old chauvinist with all his flaws and all his love. Coop was more taken with the advertisements for homemade pies.

"Pull over!" he ordered as he spotted a road sign for the ominously named town of Castle Danger. She turned into a rustic restaurant facing the highway. He emerged not long after with three slabs of pie. "Caramel apple pecan."

The pie was too hard to eat while she was navigating a twisting, two-lane highway, so she couldn't do more than take in the delicious cinnamon fragrance while Coop made exaggerated moaning sounds and provided a food-porn narrative about flaky crusts and gooey filling. "What do you think, Faiza?" he said. "Best pie you ever tasted?"

"Delicious," she replied, but the closer they got to the Canadian border, the more nervous she'd become, and she only took a few bites.

Grand Marais was the last significant town before the Grand Portage border crossing, and when they were several miles away, Piper asked Faiza if she would consider taking off her head scarf until they went through. "We're an odd-looking group," she said. "Even though all our papers are in order, it would make the crossing easier."

Faiza gnawed her bottom lip and gazed at Coop in the front seat. "I cannot do this, Piper."

"Don't worry about it," Coop said. "Pull over, Sherlock, and I'll show you how it's done."

"Do you have a clue how obnoxious you are?"

"What you call obnoxious, other people see as charming and good-looking."

She grinned and pulled over.

The border guard recognized Mr. Big Shot right away, and after a couple of autographs and some football talk, waved them through.

Faiza's aunt lived in a modest white-framed house on a hilly street that offered a distant view of the Thunder Bay port. She'd been watching for them and dashed out before the car even stopped.

Faiza flung herself into her aunt's arms, both women weeping. Other friends and relatives spilled from the house, many of them congregating around Piper to thank her for what she'd done. The women kissed her; the men hugged Coop. They were offered food and drink. The effusiveness of their praise made her self-conscious. After a final, tearful good-bye from Faiza and promises of prayers from everyone, Piper beat Coop to the driver's seat, and they were on their way.

It had been a long day, and it was beginning to grow dark. She hadn't thought ahead to where they'd stay for the night, but Coop informed her he'd reserved rooms at a place in Two Harbors, a North Shore town a good three hours away. She was drained from the events of the past couple of days, and she'd have preferred someplace closer, but he refused. "I've heard about this place, and I want to check it out."

"How much?"

"More than you can afford. You can pay me back in overtime."

He was being difficult just to be difficult, but then he redeemed himself. "I'll admit I wasn't crazy about getting involved in this, but I'm glad you nagged me into it. You did a good thing back there."

"You, too," she said.

An uncomfortable silence fell over the car. She was glad when he flipped on the radio.

He took over the driving when they stopped for gas. Around ten o'clock, he pulled off the two-lane highway into the town of Two Harbors. There weren't many big hotel chains on the North Shore, but even so, she hadn't expected him to turn into the gravel lane that ran alongside the city's iron ore docks.

The hulking docks were eerie at night, their towering, ribbed-steel skeletons reminding her of a dystopian vision of ruined sky-scrapers in a once great city. A freighter loading ore from the nearby mines was berthed at one of the docks, the glare of giant floodlights making the scene even ghostlier.

Ahead of them, on top of a bluff, the thin beam from a light-house pointed a sweeping finger into the harbor. Coop followed the gravel road right up to the gate of the red brick building. With its narrow windows and chalk-white trim, it would have looked like an old-time schoolhouse if it weren't for the square light tower rising above one corner.

"We're staying here?"

"Some friends told me about it. This is the oldest continuously running lighthouse on Lake Superior. The historical society turned it into a B and B a while back."

She reached for the door handle. "As long as it has two bed-rooms, I'm fine with it."

"Hold it!" He hit the door lock, trapping her in the car and looking pissed for no reason at all. "You don't seriously imagine I'll try to get you into bed?"

His reaction took her by surprise. She came up with an exas-perated sigh. "I wouldn't think so, but there was that odious kiss the other night, and since I seem to be a guy magnet for the most unlikely men, what do I know?"

"You're *not* a guy magnet."

"Really? Then what was that kiss about?"

"It was about saving your stupid life." He pointed one long, sturdy finger at her. "Let's get something straight, Sherlock. I have no sexual interest in you. None. Zip. Zero. The only reason I kissed you was as a distraction from what I really wanted to do, which was *strangle* you. Now this conversation is over."

He unlocked the doors and ejected from the car.

What is with him? She obviously needed sleep because she was a tiny bit peeved about his dismissal of her sex appeal, a jab that wouldn't have bothered her if it had come from anyone else. More than a tiny bit. She was peeved enough to want to challenge him, but a middle-aged woman who introduced herself as Marilyn had appeared at the door. "Mr. Smith? Welcome."

Mr. Smith? That was the best he could come up with?

He'd flipped the trunk and pulled out a small duffel. Piper retrieved her backpack and followed him into an old-fashioned kitchen with a rag rug to wipe feet, a porcelain sink, and an antique gas stove. White lace curtains draped the bottom halves of the narrow windows, and a coffee mill perched on one of the sills. Beneath it, an American flag folded into a triangle rested on top of a wooden hope chest.

The kitchen smelled of fresh-baked goodness from the two wedges of chocolate cake sitting out on china plates. Through one doorway, she saw a set of stairs, through the other, a turn-of-the-century dining room complete with a steam radiator, dark floral rug, oak dining table, and sideboard displaying china figurines. These were the old lighthouse keeper's quarters.

Coop introduced her as Ingrid, his massage therapist.

"Piper Dove," she said. "I'm actually Mr. Smith's sobriety coach."

"Well, God bless you," Marilyn said with a cheery smile. "There's no shame in admitting you need help, Mr. Smith."

Piper patted his arm. "Exactly what I've been telling him."

The bad mood that had prompted his little outburst in the car seemed to have faded because he didn't call her out. She, on the other hand, was still miffed by his put-down. This was a new side of herself she didn't like.

Marilyn led them into a back hallway, up three steps to a landing, then another three steps—another landing—and into a square hallway with five doors—three to the bedrooms, one to a bathroom, and another into the light tower.

"You're the only guests tonight, so you won't have to share the bathroom."

One of "Mr. Smith's" eyebrows went up. It hadn't occurred to him that he might have to share a bathroom with the hoi polloi. She, on the other hand, would have appreciated another set of guests for company.

The rooms were homey—wooden headboards, pretty quilts, old-fashioned glass globe lamps, and more lace curtains. Framed black-and-white photographs of ore boats gone-by hung on the walls.

Their hostess, who'd been giving them a minihistory of the lighthouse, pointed out the flashlights in each room for guests who wanted to explore the light tower. "There's a lighthouse ghost, but most guests don't see him." She moved out into the hallway. "If you wouldn't mind, lock the front door after I leave."

She was leaving? Piper wasn't exactly sure why that bothered her. Well, she *was* sure, but . . . Even with the town only a few blocks away, the lighthouse felt isolated, like a deserted island. With no grown-up around to chaperone.

"I'll be back in the morning," Marilyn said. "Breakfast is at eight thirty." She disappeared down the steps, and a few moments later, the front door shut behind her.

Mom! Don't you know you shouldn't leave us kids alone?

He'd set down his duffel, a simple action that burned up all the air in the bedroom. Because of her maddening reaction to what he'd said in the car, she needed to get out of here right away.

"You're skittish," he said as she turned to the door.

She whipped back around. "I am not. I'm hungry."

He dropped his eyelids to half-mast. "Don't expect me to do anything about that. I already told you. I'm not interested."

"For cake! I'm hungry for that chocolate cake she left us. Jeez, what is wrong with you?" She bristled with scorn, even as she resisted a compulsion to whip her sweater over her head, rip off her bra, and see how disinterested he'd be in *that.*

She headed downstairs and retrieved her piece of cake from the kitchen. As she ate, she passed through the dining room into a living room that looked as though it belonged to someone's cozy great-grandmother. The wing chair and blue damask couch had white doily antimacassars across their backs. An old stereopticon and a pot of African violets sat on top of a glass-front bookcase. There was even a spider plant hanging in the window. She imagined the lighthouse keeper and his wife sitting here at night in a time before electronic distractions. They'd be reading, maybe sewing, talking about the next day's weather. Then mounting the stairs to their bedroom . . .

She grabbed the ship's log from the coffee table and flipped it open. The log invited guests to assume the duties of the lighthouse keeper during their stay: raising and lowering the flag in the morning and evening, entering the names of the ships that came into the harbor, and checking the beacon twice a day.

Coop's cake still sat on the kitchen counter. She set her empty dish in the sink and went upstairs to her room. She changed into her black plaid pajama bottoms and Chicago Bears T-shirt, but she wasn't ready for bed. As long as she was here, why not get into the spirit of the place? She fetched her flashlight from the top of the bureau, thrust her feet into flip-flops, and crossed the hallway to play lighthouse keeper.

It was icy cold and dark inside the tower, with not even a trickle of illumination from the big lens above penetrating the thick blackness. She flicked on her flashlight, sending eerie shadows looming up the plastered walls. A narrow staircase with treads painted a dark maroon led to the lantern room high above. A small window on the landing pointed toward the harbor, but fog had crept in since they'd arrived, and she could make out only the dimmest structural outline of the iron ore docks.

She began to climb the stairs. The chill penetrated her T-shirt and pajama bottoms. She curled her toes to keep her flip-flops from slapping the wooden stair treads. The creepy shadows, the darkness, the isolation . . . It was deliciously sinister. She felt as if she'd slipped into one of the mysteries she'd devoured as a kid. *Piper Dove and the Secret of the Lighthouse Murders.*

She reached another tiny landing, this one with a round porthole. Still no light visible from the big lens above. She flipped off her flashlight to gaze through the porthole out toward the lake, but the fog was too thick to see anything.

She heard a noise below.

The click of a door opening. The stealthy sound of a foot hitting the bottom tread.

The lighthouse murderer had followed her here.

She knew his identity. He knew she knew his identity. He couldn't afford to let her leave here alive.

No one to help.

Only herself to depend on.

Alone in a deserted lighthouse with a demented villain who had killed . . . and intended to kill again.

Life didn't get any better than this!

She flattened herself into the corner, not making a sound, the dead flashlight hanging at her side. He moved with the stealth of a panther. But then, he would.

His footsteps came closer. Closer. Closer still.

He hit the landing.

She sprang out. Shrieked. *"Yeeeeeeeeeeoooooooo!"*

He yelped. Dropped his flashlight. Crashed back against the wall.

He was actually clutching his chest. As she turned on her own flashlight, she realized she'd perhaps gone a wee bit too far. "Um . . . Hey, what's up?" she said.

"What the *fuck* are you doing?" he yelled.

"Just . . . having some fun witcha. I might have gotten a little carried away."

A low growl rumbled in his throat. He lunged for her. Caught her by the shoulders. Gave her a hard shake. And then he kissed her. Again.

She felt his anger in the force of his lips, the coiled tension in his body. He dragged her against him, making her seem small and defenseless, even though she was neither.

"I have no sexual interest in you. None. Zip. Zero."

She'd see about that.

She dropped her own flashlight and pressed against him.

He was already hard.

He wasn't the only one who loved a challenge, and instead of withdrawing, she looped her arms around his neck. *Cooper Graham, you are so full of crap.* She tilted her head. Parted her lips. He thought he was so tough. Lord and master over all women. Well, not this woman. She slipped off one flip-flop and stepped up on his shoe to make herself taller and deepen their kiss. Making certain he got the point.

Which he did. His lips softened, opened. Their tongues met. She plowed her fingers into his hair. His big hands cupped her bottom. She wrapped her other leg around his as the warmth of his broad palms spread through the thin cotton pajama fabric to her skin. *How do you like me now?*

Very much, it seemed. Their tongues battled. And . . .

She was melting inside. Melting and burning all at the same time. Her knees grew soggy, forcing her back to arch, ringing alarm clocks of urgency inside her. Buzzing, chiming, flashing alarms of urgency.

She was burning from the inside out. His big, athletic hands lifted her off the floor. Braced her against the wall as if she weighed nothing at all. Their kiss turned into a wild thing all its own. Her hands were under his T-shirt, her fingers sinking into the hard flesh of his back.

He pulled away abruptly. Grabbed her by the shoulder and directed her ahead of him down the stairs. They emerged into the light of the hallway. She spun toward him. Opened her mouth to speak.

"Shut up," he said before she could utter a word. "I don't like this any better than you."

It was the best thing he could have said. They were no longer Piper and Coop. They were simply two bodies in need of release. Depersonalized. Sex at its most primitive.

They were in his bedroom. He made a dash for his duffel. Fumbled around inside it. She could have sworn his hands were shaking, but she was pulling her Bears T-shirt over her head, and that blocked her view. She stood, bare-breasted, in only her pajama bottoms, as he peeled out of his clothes, and, oh, but he was a glorious sight to behold. Fierce muscle and supple tendons, tanned skin and pale scars. She wanted to bite every one of them, but she needed to feel anonymous, and she flipped off the overhead light, sealing them in the darkness.

She heard the last of his clothes disappear, and the next thing she knew she was flat on the bed, still in her pajama bottoms, pressed underneath his body. His legs trapped her own as he turned his single-minded focus on her breasts.

She thrashed beneath the pull of his fingers, the lash of his tongue. She shoved him in the chest hard enough to push him off balance and wedge out from under him so she could climb on top. His washboard abs gave him more than enough muscle to angle up his torso, bring his mouth to her breasts, and continue his black magic. She threw back her head and rode him. He groaned, and she was on her back again, with those big hands yanking off her pajama bottoms.

Once again, his mouth crushed hers, and she arched to meet him. In the thick darkness, he couldn't see, but he could feel, and he did.

It hurt a little as he opened her with his fingers, but only for a moment, and then it didn't hurt at all . . . and she was moving against his hand, mind shut down, crazed, only a body—swimming, surging, no breath—falling apart.

He gave her a moment. Reached for her again. Tortured her. She still hadn't touched him. Not the way she wanted to.

She hated the dark. Needed to see. He twisted. Reached for something. The condom.

She had to touch him. Muscle and skin. She closed her hand around him.

He gave a hoarse cry. And it was over.

Before it had even begun.

11

Coop sprang from the bed. He couldn't believe what had happened. It was a nightmare. Worse than a nightmare. Total humiliation. A sexual apocalypse.

He stalked out of the bedroom and across the hallway. The last time he'd gone off like that, he'd been sixteen. And of all the women he had to relapse with . . . Piper Dove!

He closed himself in the bathroom. The *shared* bathroom. Thank God it wasn't shared now, because he had to be alone.

The foghorn sounded its mournful wail. He flipped on the light, but he couldn't look at himself. Staying at this place had been a terrible idea.

The bathroom was as old-fashioned as everything else, with a radiator under the window and a claw-foot tub surrounded by a white shower curtain. He turned on the water in the tub and somehow maneuvered himself inside. The shower nozzle barely came to his chest, and the curtain kept sticking to him until he felt like he was being attacked by a monster squid.

"You're getting water everywhere," said a grouchy voice from the other side of the curtain.

"Get out of here!"

"I have to pee. Don't look."

"Like I'd want to."

The toilet flushed, and scalding water cascaded down his chest. He jumped back and bumped into the end of the tub. The wet curtain wrapped its tentacles tighter around him. He heard a snort from the other side.

This was what happened when you abandoned your game plan. You got beat. And that's what she'd done. She'd beat him at his own game.

The shower had just returned to its normal temperature when she turned on the sink, and another blast of scalding water assaulted him. Once again, he jumped back.

Premature ejaculation. Just thinking the words made him wince. He was an endurance athlete. The marathon man. The distance swimmer. Stamina was a point of pride with him. She'd messed up his whole life, disrupted everything. But he'd never expected her to disrupt this.

He flipped the shower water to cold. Let the icy blast force his brain to work again. If he started thinking like a loser, he'd turn into one, and nobody bested Cooper Graham. He had to come up with a logical reason for what had happened, something to save face. Maybe he'd tell her he had a medical problem. An encroaching case of the flu. An old injury acting up. Or he could be a dickwad and blame her. Say she'd been—what?—too damn sexy? This was no time for honesty.

He grabbed a towel. One thing was certain. He had to face her. Maybe he could use grief as an excuse. That might work. He'd tell her he'd just gotten the news that his grandfather had died. She had no way of knowing that mean son of a bitch had died twenty years ago. The perfect excuse.

She wasn't in his bedroom, and her own door was shut. He pulled on his jeans and knocked. When she didn't respond, he tried the knob, but it was locked.

He was overcome with grief. Definitely the way to go. The loss of his beloved grandfather. "Open up!"

"Don't worry about it," she said from the other side. "It can happen to anybody."

She was gracious in victory. Oh, so fucking gracious. If women like her were let loose to rule the world, men would become obsolete. "I'm not worried," he heard himself say. "It happens all the time."

Where the hell had that come from?

"Seriously?" she said. "To you?"

He plunged on. "Hell, yes." So much for his dead grandfather.

She threw open the door, eyes blazing. "And you're proud of it?"

"I don't think much about it one way or the other."

Her legs were bare, but she'd pulled her detestable Bears T-shirt back on. "You're a total asshat. You know that, right?"

He propped himself against the doorjamb and fulfilled her low expectations. "The thing you've got to remember, Sherlock, is— when you're me, life is basically a female smorgasbord. I can do what I want, when I want."

Her lips were still puffy from his kisses, and her blueberry Pop-Tart eyes smoldered with outrage. "Are you for real, or are you a comic book character I made up in my nightmares?"

He'd unwittingly stumbled onto the perfect defense, and he went with it. "Most women don't mind, and if they do . . ." He shrugged.

She slammed a hand on her hip. "There are more damselfish in the sea? Is that the way it is?"

He yawned and stretched. "Yeah, I should probably be ashamed of myself."

"But you're not?"

"All they have to do is say no."

"Which they never do."

"Who understands women?"

She was too smart for his own good, and her outrage had begun to shift into something that was beginning to look like amusement. He didn't like that at all, so he called an audible. "Refresh my memory, Sherlock. Did I miss hearing you say no?"

She set her jaw. "You did not hear me say no. I already told you I've been known to use men."

"You also told me you were off them."

"But I didn't say for how long." Just before she shut the door in his face, she fired her final salvo. "Good night, Rocket Man."

*

Piper woke to the sound of a halyard slapping the metal flagpole outside her window. During the night, a deep sense of disappointment had burrowed inside her, and she did her best to shake it off. His failure to execute might have been humiliating for him, but it was a gift to her. Things had gone far enough—much too far—without that final intimacy.

What had she been thinking? She hadn't been thinking. That was the problem. Something about Cooper Graham made her disengage her brain. One thing was blindingly clear: despite their banter, despite the attraction he undeniably held for her, she wasn't going down that path with him again, no matter how good it had been. Almost fantastic. The hard tension of his body under her palms. Those skillful hands that knew just where to go. She shivered.

They barely spoke over a breakfast of strawberry muffins and a delicious ham and cheese frittata she could only pick at. Piper dreaded the hours she'd be locked in the car alone with him, and as they set off from Two Harbors, she was as tightly wound as an ignition coil.

Instead of berating herself about what had happened, she should be happy that she'd made the great Cooper Graham lose control. But she didn't feel happy. She could only hope he wouldn't bring up last night because if he did, she'd have to play all her smart-ass cards, and she wasn't sure how many she had left.

They'd barely cleared the iron ore docks before he released a diabolical chuckle. "Face it, Sherlock. You're easy pickin's. All I have to do is take off my shirt, and you're pretty much a lost cause."

And here they went again. Off to the wisecrack races.

"That's true," she said. "Male chests have always been my weakness. Seriously, Coop, if you get any more muscular, you'll be scratching your armpits and wolfing down bananas."

"You let me worry about that while you figure out how you're going to help me with my little problem."

"Excellent idea. Shut up for the next four hundred miles so I can ponder it."

Another chuckle, which was fine with her, as long as they didn't talk.

*

He should have tossed her right back on the bed and screwed her brains out until she begged him to get to the finish line. Instead, he'd been too mortified to think straight, and he'd dueled with her. Winning was in his blood, and he hated feeling like a loser. Hated even more knowing she had to be seeing him that way. He couldn't pull off to the side of the road and throw her in the backseat like he wanted, but the silence in the car was getting to him. Somehow he had to show her he was still the quarterback of their team.

"I've been thinking about our conversation last night," he said, "and you might have a point."

"I usually do."

She'd loosened her seat belt enough to tuck a leg under her. If she'd been wearing shorts instead of jeans, he'd have had a clear view of the inside of her thigh. A thigh, he now knew, that was firm, smooth, and fine. He hurried on. "What if I'm missing out by not taking a little more time in the sack with my lady friends?"

She pulled a face. "It's so sad. All those traumatized women believing your problem is their fault. I should open a counseling office."

He would not laugh. "Yep. The more I think about it, the more I think you're right. I might have a sex problem."

"Fortunately, there are a lot of books on the subject."

"Hell, I'm not much of a reader. Too many words to sound out."

"Interesting. I've found all kinds of books in the apartment."

"Cleaning people musta left 'em." He kept dishing out the bull, exactly the way it had to be between them. "Since you're the one who pointed out my problem, it's only fair that you help me work through it. Only as a sex partner, you understand. This has nothing to do with our professional relationship."

She glanced over at him, all full of fake regret. "Don't take this wrong, but I've kind of lost interest."

No way a woman who'd responded the way she had last night wasn't still interested, but he only nodded. "I understand."

*

They were quiet for a while. To relieve the tension, Piper called Jada to find out how her killing spree was progressing. Very well, as it turned out. She'd offed five more of her classmates. Eventually, they made a stop for fast food, and Piper took over the driving. By the time they reached the Illinois border, the effort to appear relaxed had left her shoulders screaming. She struggled to find a topic of conversation that would take them through the last leg of this unending trip. "I happen to know you're a real softy. And I mean that in a nonsexual way. Although . . ."

He choked on his Coke.

She smiled to herself. "These hospital visits you make to Lurie . . ."

"No idea what you're talking about."

He knew, all right. Even though he managed to sneak in and out of Lurie Children's Hospital without attracting the attention of the press, she'd uncovered the interesting fact that he spent a lot of time visiting sick children. "I can't picture you around kids." Another lie. From what she'd seen, he was as relaxed with children as he was around beautiful women. "You can tell me. It's the hot nurses, right?"

"Now you're embarrassin' me."

"But there's one mystery I can't figure out. Not even with my amazing detecting skills."

"Shocker."

"When I was following you, you'd sometimes hang out on the mean streets with various scurvy-looking characters. What's that about?"

He polished off his Coke. "Shootin' the bull, that's all."

"I don't believe you. Tell me. I'm like a priest."

"You're not anything like a priest. You're—"

"Stop stalling."

He shifted in his seat, suddenly uncomfortable. "I don't know. It's . . . I'm not going to do anything about it, so there's no point discussing it."

But something told her he wanted to talk, and she welcomed any topic that didn't lead back to the bedroom. She waited.

He gazed out the passenger window. "I had this idea . . . But it takes too much time and too much effort, with no guarantee of a payoff." He turned back to her. "All those empty city lots are a waste. Nothing but weeds and trash."

She was starting to get the picture. "You'd like to do something more about that than throw seed bombs."

He shrugged. "There are too many people with no jobs and no prospects. All those empty plots of land. Seems like an opportunity for somebody."

"But not for you."

"Hell, no. All I'm interested in now is business." He pulled out his cell and called Tony.

She listened to them talk about the new bouncer Tony had hired to replace Dell, who'd been fired four days ago. She wondered if Coop had figured out yet that she'd finished her job for him.

After six nights on the floor, she'd done as much as she could. His staff was clean, and she and Tony had put together new procedures that should keep things relatively honest. Her salary from

Coop, along with the pay from her chauffeur job, would hold her over for a while. How long depended on what was in the tip envelope the limo owner was collecting for her and how much further she could stretch out her job at Spiral. Her job that was over.

She told herself to think more like a shark and less like a Girl Scout. The salary Coop paid was her lifeline, and she needed to hold on to her job. Except there was no more she could do for him.

If only Duke hadn't taught her about integrity—along with how to shoot, fish, and feel bad about being female. As much as she needed to bleed Coop a little longer, she couldn't do it. As he ended his conversation with Tony, she gripped the wheel a little tighter. "I've done everything I can for you."

He set his cell in the empty cup holder and practically leered at her. "Not quite everything . . ."

"I'm talking about my job," she said quickly. "I've done what you hired me for. Your biggest problem right now is your lamebrained refusal to keep a bouncer near you."

"I don't need a babysitter."

"It's interesting that every other big-name jock who comes into the club brings along all kinds of hired muscle, but you're too tough."

"I can take care of myself." He couldn't have sounded more belligerent. "Are you really telling me you're thinking about quitting?"

"It's not quitting. Spiral's clean. All that's left is for you to hire a female bouncer. It's not smart to have your men touching any of your women customers, no matter how drunk they are. You could end up with a big fat lawsuit for sexual assault."

"Good point. You're hired."

She should have anticipated this, and for a moment, she let herself consider it. But she couldn't work until early morning four nights a week and keep building her business, not long term. Before she knew it, she'd be a nightclub bouncer instead of a detective, and she hadn't come this far to throw away her dream.

"No, thanks. I'm an investigator. You'll have to find someone else."

"This is about last night, isn't it? You're quitting because you—"

"Because I slept with the boss?" The other reason she couldn't stay on.

He glared across the seat at her. "That is completely unethical on your part! As unethical as it would be if I fired you."

"Report me to the EEOC," she snapped.

"Stop being a smart-ass. You know exactly what I mean."

She struggled to sound professional. "Coop, I want to end this on a positive note. I hope you agree that I've done a good job for you, and I'd appreciate it if you'd recommend me to your friends."

"Yeah, I'll do that, all right." He snapped down his sun visor and grabbed his cell.

Coop tried to tell himself this was a good thing. She'd done her job—done it well—and he'd been waiting for the time when she'd no longer be working for him so they could launch a full-out affair. But now that time had come, and he was no longer confident that she'd cooperate.

He pretended to check ESPN on his phone. Spending a few weeks naked with her had become more important than it should. Maybe it had something to do with his retirement, with making certain the space between who he used to be and who he was now hadn't changed.

She was new territory for him. Unsentimental and unpredictable. A woman who didn't take him seriously—who didn't care how many games he'd won, how rich he was, how famous. A woman who didn't find him frickin' irresistible!

It galled him. Compared to his usual women, she was a *guy,* for god's sake. A guy packaged in an incredibly sexy, incredibly appealing, incredibly tough little body. Which basically contradicted everything he'd been trying to tell himself about her.

And that was the reason he couldn't let Piper Dove waltz out of his life. Because he wanted her, and she refused to want him back. She didn't flatter him or flirt with him, and she definitely hadn't fallen for him.

He needed her to do that. Not fall in love for real. He'd hate that. Just *fall* for him.

"I want an exit interview," he said when they'd pulled up behind her car in the city. "Tomorrow night at the club." He handed over the fuses he'd taken from her Sonata without offering to put them back in. She'd know how to do that herself. Of course she would. She was the leading edge of a new civilization, one that rendered the traditional male skills of ex-jocks obsolete.

He left her with her head buried under the hood of her car, rump thrust out, and headed home. His garage door opened soundlessly. He parked next to his Tesla, grabbed his duffel, and let himself out through the side door. The floodlights on the back of the garage had burned out, and the path was dark. He heard a rustle. With no more warning than that, a man leaped from the shrubs and swung something that looked like a tire iron at Coop's head. Coop spun and jerked. His adrenaline kicked in. He drove his shoulder into the man's chest and grabbed his arm.

The guy grunted but didn't fall. He tried to swing the tire iron again but Coop had his arm. He twisted it. The man kicked out, hitting Coop in his bad knee and throwing him off balance. Coop took a hard shot that would have sent him down if his reflexes hadn't been so sharp. The guy was big. Hulking. Coop ignored the shooting pain in his knee to go after him.

The fight was short but brutal, and the thug had finally had enough. He tore away from Coop's grasp, screamed something at him, and took off into the alley. Coop started after him, but his knee buckled, and by the time he got his balance again, the thug was gone.

His jaw throbbed. His knee hurt like hell, and his knuckles were bleeding. But instead of calling the cops . . . instead of going inside to grab some ice for his face . . . he limped back into the garage and climbed into his car.

✶

"Oh my god! What happened to you?" Piper grabbed the edge of the door, her eyes wide with alarm. She was wearing a fucking Bears jersey again. How many of those sons of bitches did she have?

He pushed past her into the apartment. "You're the hotshot investigator. You tell me!"

Instead of calling him on his bullshit, she slammed the door and came after him, her mouth set in hard lines. "Who did this to you?"

She had vengeance written all over her. As if she personally intended to go after the perpetrator. Which, he realized, she did.

He headed for the refrigerator, her fierceness beginning to settle him down. "A thug ambushed me as I was coming out of my garage." He grabbed a dish towel and some ice.

It didn't seem to occur to her to play Nurse Nancy, unlike the time she'd shoved him down in the alley. She snatched up a notepad. "Start at the beginning and tell me exactly what happened."

"I got mugged, that's what." He pressed the ice pack to his face.

"Tell me what the guy looked like."

"Big. That's all I know. It was dark."

"What was he wearing?"

"A Brooks Brothers suit! How the hell do I know? I told you, it was dark."

"What about security cameras? Lights?"

He shook his head, then wished he hadn't. "They'd burned out."

"How convenient."

She made him start at the beginning and go over it, detail by detail. There wasn't much to tell, and he regretted coming here. Wasn't sure why he had.

She looked up from her notepad. "You said he yelled something as he was running away. What was it?"

"I don't remember."

"Think."

He raked his fingers through his hair. "Hell, I don't know. Some kind of threat. 'I'll get you.' Something like that."

"'I'll get you.' That's what he said?"

"Yeah, I think that's what it was." He shifted the ice pack.

"That doesn't sound like your garden-variety mugger. And why didn't he have a gun? They're as easy to come by as candy bars in this town and more convenient than a tire iron."

"You've seen too many TV shows."

She persisted. "If he'd been after your wallet, he would have had a gun. It's like he was after you personally. But why?"

He glared at her jersey. "Because he's a Bears fan."

"Not funny." She stabbed her pen in the air. "You need to get to the ER."

"A bruised jaw. Some sore ribs. I'll take care of it. And before you say anything, I'm not reporting this to the cops."

He was surprised when she didn't argue. Maybe she understood that if he reported this, the story would hit national news, the press would be all over him, and without surveillance video, the police wouldn't be able to do squat. All he'd end up with was publicity he didn't want.

She shoved the pencil behind her ear. "Something's not right about this, and I don't want you going back home yet. You're sleeping here tonight."

He regarded her incredulously. She had to be kidding. He tossed down the ice pack. "It'll be a cold day in hell before I hide behind a woman's skirts. Or, in your case, an ugly T-shirt." He made it outside the building before she could yell at him about sexism and all that other crap.

He got home without a problem. His jaw hurt like a bitch, and he needed to get cleaned up, but before he did that, he crossed through the kitchen and went out into his garden.

As always, the good scent of dirt and green growing things did their work. He loved this place.

The illumination from a pair of headlights shone over the wall from the alley behind the building. The same headlights that had followed him home. With a sense of resignation, he pulled out his cell and hit the contact button. "Go get some sleep, Sherlock. I'm not going anywhere."

12

Piper woke Dell up the next morning. Spiral's recently fired bouncer glared at her from his open apartment door. Scrubby blond stubble covered his jaw, his eyes were sleep crusted, and he wore only a pair of boxers. "What the hell do you want?"

She'd already seen what she'd come here for, although not what she'd expected. Dell looked like he'd had a hard night, but he wasn't bruised or cut. He bore none of the signs of injury Coop had inflicted on his unknown assailant last night. Whatever else Dell had done, he wasn't the culprit behind the ambush.

"Verifying your address," she said. "Tony wanted to make sure you got your severance check."

"Tell Tony to go fuck himself."

"I'll do that."

As she began to turn away, he stepped into the hallway, his belligerence replaced by the smarmy come-on tone he used with the swishy-hairs. "Hey, you wanna hang for a while?"

"Not so much, but thanks for thinking of me."

One suspect eliminated. Now she had to find Keith and Taylor. As for the possibility that Prince Aamuzhir had discovered he was the owner of a phony Super Bowl ring and wanted revenge . . . That was going to be much more complicated.

On her way to Lincoln Park, she contemplated the e-mail she'd gotten from the limo owner that morning about her tip from the royals, from which she'd learned she'd received only half of what the male drivers had been given. She'd worked harder than most of them, but in the world of the royals, gender trumped everything. She should have seen it coming, but the injustice still made her livid.

The woman who answered the door of Heath Champion's luxurious Lincoln Park home was several inches shorter than Piper, with curly auburn hair and a friendly smile. Nothing about her well-scrubbed, girl-next-door appearance matched Piper's preconceived notion about what the wife of a megasuccessful sports agent would look like.

"You're Piper," she said. "I've heard all about you. I'm Annabelle."

"And so the warriors meet," a male voice said from inside the house.

Annabelle laughed, stepped aside to let Piper enter, and took Piper's black bomber jacket.

The luxurious hallway of the house, with its tumbled marble floors, modernistic bronze chandelier, and S-shaped staircase, would have been intimidating if it weren't for a purple stuffed puppy, discarded marker pens, an unidentifiable Lego structure, and the array of sneakers scattered around. "Thanks for letting me charge in so early," Piper said.

Heath appeared from around the corner, a curly-haired toddler wearing a pink tutu and a blue flannel pajama top at his side. "What's up? You sounded mysterious on the phone."

Piper shot Annabelle an apologetic look and sidestepped a black-and-gold *Star Wars* figure. "Maybe we should talk in private."

Heath retrieved his cell phone from the toddler. "Annabelle would just worm it out of me after you leave."

"That's true," Annabelle said with a self-satisfied smile.

Heath grinned. "My wife has built her business on keeping other people's secrets. She's a matchmaker. Perfect for You. You might have heard of it."

"Of course." Piper had done some research on Heath since their first meeting and unearthed a very interesting story about the way he'd met Annabelle Granger Champion.

They settled at a lacquered kitchen table in front of long windows looking out on a fall garden. As the toddler, whose name was Lila, consumed a bowl of raspberries, Piper told Heath and Annabelle about last night's attack on Coop. Both were understandably concerned. "Are you sure he's okay?" Annabelle said.

"He refused to go to the ER, but I think so." She handed a wayward berry back to the toddler, who gave her a gooey, raspberry-flecked smile. "He thinks it was a random mugging, but I'm not so sure. I thought you might be more cooperative about telling me who his enemies are than he's going to be."

"He doesn't have a lot of them," Heath said. "A couple of players might hold a few grudges, but that's part of the game. There's a sports reporter who hates his guts because Coop publicly called him out for stupidity. Complete moron, but I don't see why he'd wait so long to retaliate."

"What about women?"

Heath looked at Annabelle, who took over the conversation. "You mean his Hollywood lineup? The breakups were painful for a couple of them, but he was never a jerk, and I don't believe any of them are out for revenge."

"There've been some crazies, though," Heath said.

"Any recent ones?" Piper inquired. *Besides me.*

"You'd have to ask him," Heath said.

"Coop's my new pro bono project," Annabelle declared with a grin.

"Which he doesn't know," Heath said, in case Piper missed the point. "What about the trouble he was having at the club with the bartender he fired?"

"I'm looking into that."

A mini version of Heath wandered into the kitchen and regarded her curiously. "Who're you?"

"This is Piper," Heath said. "She's a detective. And, Piper, this is Trev. He's five."

"Five and a half," the boy said. "You got a badge?"

She could tell a lot about the kid by the glint in his eyes, which were the same shade of money-green as his father's. "No badge," she said, "but a couple of useful superpowers."

He regarded her with a combination of anticipation and skepticism. "Flying?"

"Sure."

"X-ray vision?"

"I couldn't do my job without it."

Trevor threw down the gauntlet. "Telekinesis?"

A big word for a little kid. Piper eyed his father, who shrugged. "Trev gets his brains from his mother."

"Telekinesis is tricky," Piper said. "I'm still working on that one."

"That's what I figured," he said wisely. "What about invisibility?"

"Did you notice me here when you were eating breakfast?"

"No."

"Well, then."

Heath laughed. "Come on, pal. Get your backpack. It's time to leave for school."

As Piper began to rise from the table, Annabelle stopped her. "Keep me company while I finish my coffee."

"And here we go," Heath murmured.

Annabelle shot him a glare. "Do you have something to say?"

"Not a word." He gave her a quick kiss, planted another on the top of his daughter's head, and grabbed his son.

As her husband and child disappeared, Annabelle gave Piper a long, assessing look followed by a bright smile. "So . . . tell me all about yourself . . ."

✶

Piper left the Champion house feeling as though she'd made a new friend, but since Annabelle Champion lived among the city's movers and shakers, while Piper lived above a Dumpster, it was a questionable assumption.

She didn't want to show up at Coop's before he'd had his second cup of coffee, so she headed for Lincoln Square. Berni had called her late last night to check on Piper's progress finding Howard, and hearing that Piper had run a computer check through the major search engines hadn't satisfied her. Berni wanted more.

"I've been reading up, Piper. There are these whatchacall databases where you can register missing persons. I want you to do that."

"Those databases are for people who aren't legally dead," she said as gently as she could.

"A technicality."

Hardly a technicality when Piper had watched Howard's urn being lowered into the ground at Westlawn Cemetery.

"I never saw the body," Berni said. "You remember that."

"Yes, ma'am."

Piper outmaneuvered a blue Mazda to snag one of the diagonal parking places on Lincoln Avenue. The morning was cloudy and chilly, hinting at rain, but a few hardy souls sat on the benches. A motorcycle shot past, and she took an unoccupied bench.

She tucked her hands in the pockets of her bomber jacket. On the bricks near her feet, someone had made an elaborate chalk drawing of a pelican. It felt good to sit still for a moment. Between working at Spiral at night, chauffeuring during the day, and planning Faiza's escape, she'd barely had a chance to breathe.

Eventually, she got chilled and began walking back to her car, indulging in a little window-shopping along the way. Her phone pinged. A text from Eric Vargas.

See U tonight?

As she pondered her response, she saw an elderly man cross Lincoln Avenue toward Leland. Potbelly, pants pulled too high at the waist, bright white sneakers, and a wedge of yellow foam rubber on top of his head.

She began to run. A CTA bus cut in front of her. She dodged it, avoided a UPS truck and a bicyclist, but by the time she'd reached

Leland, the man was gone. She searched the area, ducking into alleys and side streets, but the man with the Green Bay Packers cheesehead was nowhere in sight.

Piper reminded herself that she hadn't gotten a good look at his face. But Howard had the identical potbelly and the same penchant for wearing white sneakers and hitching his pants too high. The height had also seemed right.

The theme from *Buffy* interrupted her thoughts. It was Jen. "Berni wants me to use my media contacts to get the public to look for Howard. And she's guilted Amber into helping her put up missing person flyers. Everybody's going to think she's crazy."

Piper gazed out at the brick buildings lining the square. "Maybe not quite as crazy as you think."

She arranged to meet Jen and Amber at Big Shoulders Coffee on Friday. They'd all have preferred one of the neighborhood bars, but Amber had to sing later that night.

On her way to Lakeview, Piper planned her strategy for dealing with Coop. "Let me up," she said, when he finally answered his intercom.

"You got food with you?"

"No food, but I make a great omelet."

"You can cook?"

"Sure, I can cook." No need to tell him she hated doing it, but Duke had expected her to cook and take care of the house right along with acting like his son instead of his daughter. Nobody knew more about growing up with mixed messages than she did.

"Okay, you can come up. But you can't ask me any more questions that I can't answer. Got it?"

"Absolutely. No questions." He knew she was lying, so she didn't feel bad about it.

When she stepped off the elevator into his condo, she found him sprawled on his couch holding an ice pack to his shoulder. He hadn't shaved, and his burnt-toast hair was a delicious rumple. Despite the bruise on his jaw, he was just so . . . *everything.* All that battered, lived-in masculinity would wake up any woman. Even the dead ones. Rugged men like him were born to win ball games and sire warrior children.

Children? She had to get more sleep. As much as she liked kids, she didn't want her own and wasn't in the habit of thinking about them.

He came off the couch. He was shirtless, and he wore gray sweatpants like other men wore Hugo Boss. They slipped low on his hips, revealing a flat, muscled abdomen and a thin line of dark hair pointing straight toward . . .

Toward her stupid *downfall.*

She was furious with herself. This had to stop. She was calling Eric. She was going to get this . . . this urgency out of her system even if she had to seduce Hottie in the back of his squad car.

"I'd ask how you're feeling," she managed to say, "but some things are self-evident."

"I've been through worse."

"Shouldn't you bandage up your chest?" *Right this second. Wrap up all that muscle so I can't see it.*

"They don't do that anymore," he said. "Constricts your breathing."

So what was her excuse? Because she could barely fill her lungs.

Just as she found herself praying he'd put on more clothes, he grabbed a zippered navy sweatshirt from the back of the couch and shoved his arms through the sleeves. But he didn't zip it. "You mentioned something about an omelet?" he said. "Let me see what I've still got growing."

Sweatshirt falling open to reveal one of Mother Nature's masterpieces, he went out to his rooftop garden. Instead of using his absence to regain her equilibrium, she followed him.

He was pulling up something she at first thought was an onion but then realized was a leek. He looked so much more at home here than he did working the crowd at Spiral. Utterly relaxed. It struck her how much digging in the dirt with those big, competent hands suited him.

"It doesn't feel right," she said. "Somebody like you owning a nightclub."

"I don't know why you'd say that."

"Because Farmer Coop was born to plow the fields."

"That's Rancher Coop to you. I'm from Oklahoma, remember? And I've never been so glad to get out of a place."

Despite the chilly weather, he was barefoot and still hadn't zipped his sweatshirt, but the cold didn't seem to bother him. She glanced over at the cozy nook not far from the French doors: round, slate-topped table; a cushioned chaise wide enough for two.

"Your bio doesn't say much about your childhood," she observed. "Only that you grew up on a ranch and lost your mother when you were young." The same as she had. "It's as though you barely existed before you started playing for Oklahoma State."

He'd composted most of the tomato plants, but a few remained, and he pulled off a couple of small tomatoes, popping one into his mouth. "We were tenant ranchers. Just my dad and me. Sixty acres, not all of it good. Some cattle and pigs. Feed corn. He was a Vietnam vet before anybody understood much about PTSD. Sometimes he was okay. Other times, he wasn't."

She sensed what was coming next—the alcoholism, the physical abuse. She wished she hadn't brought up the subject.

But he surprised her. "Dad was a gentle guy—one reason the war was so hard on him. A lot of the time, he couldn't function—could barely get out of bed—so I had to take over." He pulled the cover off a pot of herbs he'd been guarding from frost. "I was around seven the first time I drove the truck. I remember sitting on a pile of feed sacks and riggin' up some blocks so I could reach the pedals." He laughed, but she didn't find it all that funny. "There were a couple of winters where I swear I missed more school than I attended."

"That's not right."

He shrugged and gathered up his harvest. "Animals have to be fed and watered, and Dad couldn't always leave the house."

"A hard life for a kid."

"I didn't know any different."

She followed him inside. He set what he'd picked next to the sink and turned on the faucet. His sweatpants had fallen so low on his hips, she was glad his back was turned to her. "The first big city I ever visited was Norman," he said. "I was sixteen, and I thought I'd walked into paradise. Once Dad died, I never looked back."

She dropped her jacket over the back of a counter stool. "There must be something about rural life you miss, or you wouldn't have created that amazing garden."

"I like growing things. Always have." He tossed some spinach into a stainless-steel colander. "I started out at Oklahoma State with a major in plant and soil science, but then I discovered I'd actually have to go to class. 'Student athlete'—now there's an oxymoron." He splashed water on the spinach and shook the colander. "I love the pace of city life, and as much as I like animals, I didn't like raising them. Especially pigs." He cleaned a handful of herbs and laid them on a paper towel. "I can't tell you how many times those bastards managed to get out of their pen and tear up my vegetable garden. Pigs are the only animal I hate."

She thought of Oinky. "Pigs are sweet!"

"That's right. You sleep with one."

"I don't sleep with—"

He looked at her over his shoulder. "See how sweet you'd think they are, city girl, if you'd been six years old and had those two-hundred-pound porkers charge you whenever you went into their pen. One slip, and you're lunch. They'll eat anything."

"Well, we eat them, so . . ."

"I'm not saying there isn't some kind of divine justice at work, but kids and pigs don't belong together." He pulled out a chef's knife. "I still have nightmares about them."

"Let me get this straight. You, Cooper Graham, five-time first team All-Pro, two-time NFL MVP, are afraid of pigs?"

"Yep." The blade hit the cutting board.

She laughed, then remembered she wasn't here to be entertained. "I went to see Dell this morning. Not a single bruise on him."

"Are you back to this again?"

"Did you know your close pal Keith and his girlfriend Taylor moved out of their place without leaving a forwarding address?"

He pointed the tip of the knife in her general direction. "For the last time. It was a mugging, not some preplanned attack."

"I'm sure you'd like to think so. Help me sort through it, will you, so I can stop obsessing about it?"

He scraped the back of his hand over the beard scruff on his jaw. "Keith's a hothead, but the two of us already had it out."

"That was before Taylor got fired, right?" She located the eggs.

"Staging an ambush isn't his style."

"You have more faith in your old pal than I do." She rummaged for some cheese and found a chunk of imported cheddar.

"While you're sorting things out . . ." He gazed across the counter at her. She wished he'd pull up his pants. Or zip his sweatshirt. Or go bald. Except he'd still look great.

"Aren't you overlooking a couple of more obvious villains in your imaginary scenario?" He carried the leeks over to a chopping board. "Starting with that mysterious client who hired you to follow me?"

"If I had any doubts about my former client, don't you think I would have acted on them?" She located a skillet and cheese grater. "I promise you, my mystery client isn't a threat."

"Exactly. Nobody is. It was a random crime. Some thug who was lurking in the alley looking for easy prey."

She wasn't getting any more out of him now, and she temporarily backed off. "How are things with Deidre coming along?"

"Slower than I'd like, but she'll come through."

"You're sure about that."

"She'd be crazy not to. I have a great concept and the right connections to carry it off."

She didn't miss the determined set of his jaw. In Coop's mind, once he'd decided on something, it was as good as done.

After that, they worked together without saying much other than "Stop hogging the sink" and "Where's the sriracha?" She sautéed the vegetables in a little olive oil, tossed in the eggs she'd beaten, and topped them with the herbs he'd chopped along with a generous handful of grated cheddar. He took plain white plates from the cupboard and extracted the bread he'd put in the toaster.

By the time everything was ready, the domesticity of the scene had started making her itchy. She wished she didn't like him so much, but how could she not? Coop was the man she'd have wanted to be if she'd been male. Setting aside his money and fame, he was smart, he understood hard work, and, except for being stubborn and dictatorial, he was rock-bottom decent.

"Let's eat outside," she said as he poured them coffee. "But only if you zip your sweatshirt first." She needed a good reason other than the real one. "Those bruises aren't exactly appetizing."

"Your sympathy for human suffering warms my heart."

"I'm a giver, all right."

The corners of his eyes crinkled.

Even on a chilly October morning, the nook he'd created in the corner of the garden was inviting. Its vine-covered latticework made a natural windbreak, and the purple canvas chair cushions were thick and comfortable. It had been a long time since she'd had anything as tasty as the fluffy omelet she'd made with the ingredients he'd gathered. She was almost . . . happy.

Coop watched her across the table. Pipe didn't believe in picking at her food, and even though she took small bites, she managed to consume the omelet in record time. When she remembered to eat, she gave it all she had, the same way she did everything. How could someone so tough, so determined, and so ballsy be so intrinsically female?

It was too damp and overcast for comfortable outdoor dining, but he'd been so conscious of the inviting bed above their heads that he hadn't protested moving out here. It was a good place to cool off. Except all he'd done so far was heat up.

Pipe set her fork on her plate. He'd noticed before how dainty her hands were and made a mental note never to use that word to her face.

Earlier, he'd seen her staring at his chest. He'd initially assumed she was checking out his bruises, but then he remembered her attraction for that particular part of his body and decided something more interesting was going on in her head. But leaving his sweatshirt open on purpose was one of the biggest cheeseball moves he'd ever made. Still, anything that gave him an edge was fair game.

"Annabelle Champion doesn't seem to think you have any crazed ex-girlfriends lurking around," she said.

"Now what were you doing talking to Annabelle?"

"Satisfying my curiosity."

"Well, stop it. You quit, remember? And I'm not hiring you back."

"Who else do you trust enough to investigate what happened? She also said there'd been a couple of crazies."

"Most recently? A loony named Esmerelda Crocker."

"Totally harmless."

"Are you?" He leaned back in his chair and took her in. Her face was so full of life. Those bright eyes had a whole world going on behind them. And that wide mouth . . . So much he wanted to do with that mouth. So much he wanted that mouth to do to him.

She took too long to look away. He smiled to himself. She wasn't as detached as she liked to pretend.

She reached for that ratty messenger bag she carried around and pulled out a notebook. "You've been in the public eye for years. You have to have gotten your fair share of hate mail."

"The Stars office still screens my mail. If they'd gotten anything they thought was serious, they'd have let me know."

"Who do I talk to there?"

"You don't talk to anybody. And put that notebook away. This was a random attack, and you're trolling for a job."

"A job that needs doing."

"Really? Then why haven't you brought up the most obvious suspect? My pal, the Prince of Darkness."

She toyed with the edge of her notebook. "I'm getting there."

"Very slowly. And I know why."

She nodded. "Because I feel responsible."

"You aren't, but I like your guilt." He appreciated the way she stepped up to the plate with none of the pretend ignorance so many people hid behind. Pipe was a straight shooter. Except when she chose not to be.

She balled up her napkin. "How was I supposed to know you were going to give Prince Aamuzhir a phony Super Bowl ring? And he's in London now. Yes, I checked. Not that it means anything. And, yes again, I'm worried. It's one thing dealing with a disgruntled former employee or a Broncos fan who's still holding a grudge over that Hail Mary you threw against them on fourth-and-ten. It's another thing entirely to deal with a foreign dignitary—and I use that word loosely. He could easily have hired that thug."

"Look, Pipe. I know your heart's in the right place, but the bottom line is that you're an investigator without a job, and you're trying to manufacture one."

As soon as he'd said it, he wanted to take it back. Her eyes darkened, and her wide mouth collapsed at the corners, if only for a moment. She'd always been impervious, even amused, by the insults he'd enjoyed tossing at her—insults about the way she dressed, her ballsy attitude—but he'd insulted her integrity, and her hurt was painful to watch.

She rose from her chair, back straight. "I gotta go."

He got up and blocked her way. "Hold on. That didn't come out the way I meant."

"I think it came out exactly the way you meant," she said quietly.

"No, it didn't." He cupped her shoulders. She didn't pull away. Instead, she lifted her head and stared him down, daring him to insult her again.

Her shoulders nestled in his palms. Her personality was so big that he sometimes forgot how small she was compared to him. "Pipe, you love what you do, and all I'm saying is—that could be impairing your judgment."

She actually seemed to think it over. Finally, she shook her head. "No. But apology accepted."

He hadn't really apologized.

"And you're the one with the impaired judgment. You want to believe the attack was random, so you've closed your mind to any other possibility."

Her motives were pure, if wrongheaded. "I wish I'd had you on my offensive line when I was playing. Nobody would have been able to touch me."

She smiled—open and genuine. Sulking wasn't in her nature.

He wasn't exactly sure when their eyes locked, only that he still had his hands on her shoulders and that his aches and pains seemed to have faded. She lifted her arm, and her fingers brushed his bruised jaw in a caress so gentle he could barely feel it. The breeze blew a strand of dark hair across her cheek. He wasn't used to looking at anyone like this. Gazing so deeply. Seeing nothing but big eyes and a soft, inviting mouth. Kissing her felt like the most natural thing in the world.

She could have stopped him simply by turning her head, but she didn't. She opened her lips and slipped her hands under his sweatshirt to touch his bare back.

Their kiss gathered heat, and their bodies melded. A hot rush of blood ripped through him. All he wanted was to be inside her. To satisfy her in a way no one ever had. He wanted to hear her moan. Have her beg him. Want him as much as he wanted her.

She had his sweatshirt off. He pulled her top over her head. She wore a black bra beneath. He drew her toward the big chaise.

The purple cushions were soft, but he landed on his bad side and winced.

She jerked back from him as if she'd burned him. "We can't. You're—"

He stopped her words with his mouth and rolled to his good side, taking her with him. He cupped her bottom through her jeans. He had to get them off her. Strip everything away. He heard a buzzing in his head as he slipped his finger under her bra strap. His lips went to her shoulder. The buzzing grew louder. Pushing him on. Louder still. More demanding.

She shoved herself away from him so abruptly he nearly fell off the chaise.

She reached for something.

The buzz . . . it wasn't coming from inside his sex-obsessed brain. It was coming from above them.

A silver X-shaped drone hovered in the air overhead. He let out a blistering curse. The drone made a small circle just above the garden. Circled again.

And then it exploded.

Shards of fiberglass, plastic, and metal flew everywhere.

Piper stood in the middle of his garden, dressed only in her jeans and a black bra, her arm raised. And in her hand, the hand that had, only moments before, been caressing him, she held a semi-automatic pistol.

One shot. That's all it had taken for her to bring down the drone. One perfect shot.

He sagged against the brick terrace wall. Nothing like a woman with a gun to spoil the mood.

13

The street below the terrace wall was quiet, with only a dog walker and a female jogger in sight. "You stay here," Piper ordered as she pulled her T-shirt back over her head and bolted toward the French doors.

"Like hell!"

They spent the next hour scouring the neighborhood together. It would have been more efficient to split up, but Piper wanted to keep him in her sight. No one on the street had seen anyone operating a drone, but all of them wanted to talk to Coop about his career.

On the elevator back up to his condo, he finally got around to the question he'd been waiting to ask. "Are you always packing?"

"Not in the club, if that's what you're wondering."

He had been. The image of Piper turning into a one-woman SWAT team to protect him from whatever she defined as a threat wasn't anything he cared to contemplate. "No more guns," he said, after she'd gone to the terrace to bag up the pieces of the drone.

"You grew up on a ranch," she protested.

"And I can shoot. But that doesn't mean I want 'em around me in the city."

She looked up at him and grinned. "Admit it. That was one hell of a shot."

A shot he doubted he could have made. "Respectable."

She laughed and picked up her jacket from the kitchen barstool. "Good news. I've decided to take that bouncer job you offered me."

He should have anticipated this. "Forget it. The offer's off the table."

"And why's that?"

"You only want the job now because you've decided I need a bodyguard. In my own club!"

"Nonsense. You can take care of yourself."

She said it with an absolute sincerity that didn't mean a thing. He was caught in a dilemma. He needed her, wanted her, but on his terms, so he poked his finger toward her forehead. "If I hire you, you're a bouncer—only there to take care of the women."

"Of course."

"No bodyguard needed. *None.*"

"Understood. Completely understood."

"Okay. You can have the job."

"Great."

As she walked back into the kitchen, all he could think was—shit, now he had a bodyguard.

She grabbed her jacket and turned back into the Woman of Steel. "There won't be any more physical contact between us. Not while I'm working for you. Agreed?"

She wasn't the only one who could dish out crap. He rested his shoulder against the refrigerator door and gave her his laziest drawl. "Now, sweetheart . . . Do you really think you can keep your hands off me?"

Then he kicked her out.

Piper fingered the broken wing of the drone. She'd pieced together enough to make out the model and manufacturer, but an online check and a couple of phone calls revealed that the company had sold thousands of these. The creepiest part was knowing this particular model offered live-streaming video. Whoever had sent it up had seen her heavy make-out session with Coop.

She gazed morosely out her office window into the parking lot. What had almost happened between them this morning was, in a way, worse than what had happened at the lighthouse, because she should have been prepared. She knew the effect he had on her, yet she'd been stupid all over again. No more. His body was forbidden. She drove the point home by giving herself a sharp slap on the cheek.

Faiza called, interrupting Piper's self-flagellation. She was giddy with her newfound freedom, and full of stories that made Piper smile. They'd just ended their call when her phone chimed with a text from Eric.

Get my message? Dinner tonight?

Eric was her sexual savior, and she started thinking about where they'd go to do the deed. She didn't like the idea of the ever-vigilant Jada seeing a man disappear inside her apartment. But Eric also had a roommate, and Piper was past the age of having sex while a bro played *Call of Duty* on the other side of the bedroom wall.

She went back to work. A routine online check to see if anything new had shown up about Spiral revealed a recent post on a local club life message board left there by somebody who called himself Homeboy7777.

> *Spiral is the best place in Chicago to score all kinds of good shit without getting stabbed or shot.*

She'd stake her reputation on the fact that nobody was scoring much of anything at Spiral, now that Dell was gone. Registering herself as Wastoid69, she posted an appropriately obscene response, denouncing Homeboy7777 as a troll and Spiral as a "fucking drug wasteland only good for picking up the hottest chicks in the city."

*

At five on Friday evening, Piper met Jen and Amber at Big Shoulders. It was one of their favorite places, with good coffee, friendly baristas, and Carl Sandburg's poetry painted on the wall.

> *Hog Butcher for the World,*
> *Tool Maker, Stacker of Wheat . . .*

Piper hadn't seen her friends for two weeks, and she'd been looking forward to this all day, but Jen was uncharacteristically glum. "Dumb Ass called me into his office and asked me how I felt about getting a face-lift."

Amber Kwan smacked the flat of her hand on the table hard enough to rattle her cup of house-blended tea. "Your face is perfect," she exclaimed. "Ask him how he feels about a sexual discrimination lawsuit!"

Hearing the soft-spoken opera singer speak so vehemently made Piper laugh, and even Jen smiled, but only for a moment. "I'm trapped," she said. "I don't want to leave the city, and what other local station is going to hire a forty-two-year-old meteorologist?"

The early October days were getting shorter, and a streetlight came on outside the window. "Maybe you need to remind him how many over-forty women are watching the news," Piper said. "How does he think they'll react if they hear about the kind of discrimination you're facing?"

"Yeah, that'd work, all right," Jen scoffed. "He'd twist the story against me while he replaced me with someone younger, prettier, and cheaper. After that, I'm sure every male-owned station in town would jump at the opportunity to hire a known whistle-blower."

She had a point.

Amber distracted Jen with the latest gossip from the Lyric. Without Berni shooting her threatening looks, Amber was funny and relaxed. Piper made up her mind to talk to Berni about her attitude, whether Amber wanted her to or not. Then she dropped the bombshell about what she'd seen in Lincoln Square.

Amber and Jen peppered her with questions, none of which she could answer because, two days ago, she'd let an overweight senior wearing a foam cheesehead get away from her.

Buffy interrupted. It was Coop, and she excused herself to take the call. "What's up, boss?" *Boss,* not lover.

"Logan Stray."

"The teen pop star?"

"He's not a teen any longer. He's coming to the club tonight to celebrate his twenty-first birthday, and you're on guard duty."

"I'm not a bodyguard, remember?"

"Tonight you are. Nothing's going to happen to that little putz's ninety-million-dollar body on my turf."

"Doesn't he have his own security?"

"Pop star bodyguards aren't good at saying 'no' to the kid who signs their paychecks. I want someone around who reports to me. The club doesn't need bad publicity."

"You're already getting some." She filled him in on the message board post she'd uncovered that afternoon.

He wasn't happy. "Stay on top of it. I don't want to give Deidre any excuse to walk away from this deal."

"I understand. The post probably came from somebody who got turned away at the door, but I'll keep a close eye out."

"Real close."

A blender whirred on a few feet away. She stuck her finger in her ear so she could hear the rest of what he was saying. "Wear that blue dress tonight, and try to look sexy. As far as Logan and his crew are concerned, you're a special hostess."

"That makes me sound like a hooker."

"As soon as he sees you, he'll know you aren't."

She couldn't decide if that was a compliment.

*

Logan Stray and his posse showed up just after midnight. The pop star was barely Piper's height but looked even smaller next to his hulking bodyguards. His black knit cap revealed a fringe of dirty-blond hair complemented by a scraggly soul patch. His dark-framed sunglasses were unnecessary in the dim light of the VIP lounge, and she stifled a grin as he bumped into a table. He might be cool, but he definitely wasn't smart.

The three women who clung to his entourage wore tatters of spandex that made Piper's short, cobalt-blue dress seem demure. The group settled in a gargantuan booth overlooking the main club floor. Piper introduced herself to the closest of his bodyguards as the club's VIP coordinator because it sounded better than "special hostess." She greeted Logan, who gave her the once-over.

Before long, the group had ordered a couple of magnums of Armand de Brignac, two liters of Grey Goose, some Gran Patrón Platinum, and lots of Red Bull. Coop took his time coming to greet the pop star. Logan hopped up and gave him a couple of manly slaps on the back. Only a few days had passed since Coop had been attacked, and she noticed his nearly imperceptible wince. But as she stepped forward to intervene, he gave her a back-off glare.

She was growing increasingly frustrated by all the inventive ways Coop kept her from sticking close to him. This was her third night as the club's sole female bouncer, and her attempts to get the other bouncers to step in had only increased their hostility. They'd disliked her before, but even more now that they'd been informed that Coop had originally hired her as a watchdog. She couldn't shake her uneasiness about his safety. She'd have felt better if she'd been able to track down Keith and his girlfriend's new address.

Word had gotten out that Logan Stray was in the club, and the crowd had reached capacity. Coop sat with the group for a while, drinking club soda and hating every minute, although he acted as genial as ever, so maybe she was imagining it. But turning himself into a nightclub impresario didn't seem to be what Coop should be doing with his life.

Piper stopped him as he excused himself. "You're hurting," she whispered. "Take that ridiculous body of yours home and bury your head in one of those books you pretend not to read."

He repaid her with his calculated heart-melter of a drawl. "You seem to be spending a lot of time thinking about my body. Too bad I haven't made up my mind whether you'll get to see any more of it."

She swallowed. "That's okay. I'm starting a relationship with . . ." For a fraction of a second she forgot his name. "With Eric. Our cop pal. We're thinking about taking it to the next level." And maybe they would, if she ever got around to returning his texts.

Coop seemed to tense up, or maybe not, because he sounded as laid-back as ever. "He's a player."

"I know, right? We're a perfect match."

He scowled at her and walked away.

Not long after, Jonah approached. If he'd had hair, it would have been bristling. "I heard you were on my boys again, telling them how they're supposed to do their job."

She did her best imitation of a reasonable professional. "The club's packed tonight, and you know Coop got hurt a couple of days ago." Coop had explained his injuries away as a sparring accident. "I'm sure he'd appreciate you keeping the crowd from bear-hugging him."

He moved so close she could see his nose hairs. "I'm in charge of the bouncers, and that includes you. Now how about you tuck your balls back between your legs and mind your own business."

"Stop being a jerk."

That infuriated him. "Ever since you came here, you've been trying to take over. It's no mystery that you're the one who got Dell fired."

She reared back on her ridiculous high heels and craned her neck to look up at him. "Dell was a dishonest turd, but then you probably knew that."

He jutted his jaw. "You're riding high right now, but once the boss stops boning you, he won't even remember your name."

A fireball exploded in her head, and she dug her finger into the middle of his chest. "Meet me in the alley after closing, you scumbag. Then we'll see who has the biggest set of balls."

She'd finally pierced his swagger. "Are you serious? You want to fight me?"

Not exactly. But just because he was big didn't mean he was quick, and maybe she'd get lucky. Probably not, but maybe. She curled her lip at him. "Why not?"

He puffed out his chest. "I'm not fighting a chick."

"Afraid I'll get you pregnant?"

He stepped back, as if she were contagious. "You're a lunatic, you know that?"

She grimaced as he stalked off. He was quite possibly right.

The three original women in the booth with Logan Stray had been joined by two more, all of them young and beautiful. Since Logan had seemed oblivious to her earlier, she was surprised when he gestured for her to scramble over them and sit next to him, but her heels were killing her, so she didn't object.

"How old are you?" he said as she slid in. He'd begun to slur his words, not surprising, considering the amount of liquor being consumed at the table.

"Thirty-three, chronologically."

"What does that mean?"

She slipped off her shoes under the table and took note of the tiny pimple lurking next to his soul patch. "I don't always act my age."

"Older or younger?" He asked as if he were genuinely interested.

"It depends on the situation."

"What about now?"

"Um . . . forty-two."

"Seriously?" He grinned. "That's sick. I dig older women." His breath held the overly sweet stench of the Red Bull he'd been mixing with Grey Goose, and he seemed to be having trouble focusing. "People think everythin's a big party for me, but it's not. I got all this business to handle. Lotta people to take care of."

For a moment he looked like a lonely fifteen-year-old, and she felt a flash of pity for him. She'd been lucky enough to celebrate her own twenty-first birthday at a bar in Boystown with a rowdy group of friends—people who liked her for herself. Maybe Logan knew that without his fame and money, none of these people would be here.

He swallowed the last of his current drink. "I wanna dance."

Celebs frequently left VIP to go down to the floor, but there was a weird energy in the club tonight that she didn't like. Too many people, everything louder than normal, guests bumping into each other, servers dropping trays, glasses shattering. A fight had already broken out, and although Ernie and Bryan had intervened so quickly that hardly anyone had noticed, she didn't want there to be another.

"Let's talk instead," she said. "It's a real crush down there to-night."

"Tha's what makes it fun." He grabbed her arm. "Come on."

The girls in the booth didn't like seeing him leave with her instead of one of them, but Piper needed to stay close. Also, Jen would love hearing about this.

Spiral's patrons were older than Logan's core group of tween fans, but he was still a celeb, and people began to press in on him. His bodyguards made a phalanx through the crowd. The DJ segued into "Not Witch U Now," his last hit.

She was a decent dancer, but, drunk or sober, Logan was a great dancer, and she didn't try to compete but simply surrendered to the beat. He gave her a drunken grin. More people came on the floor, trying to get closer. Logan moved to the edge, grabbed the drink one of his drunken posse members handed him, and downed it.

The music grew louder. Three willowy hair-swishers cut Piper out. As they began grinding on Logan, she pictured a trio of beautiful sharks devouring a very small herring. One looped her arms around his neck, another around his waist. Even drunk, Logan started to look nervous. His security, along with Jonah and Bryan, began to move in, but something about the women's determination made Piper certain there'd be trouble if the men touched them. She wedged herself in front of the closest woman, but there was only one of her, three of them . . .

And one of Coop Graham . . .

"Ladies . . ." He tapped two of the outliers on their shoulders, at the same time giving Piper the signal to close back in on Logan. "I'm getting lonely here."

The women moved in for the bigger prize.

Logan, in the meantime, lost his balance. Whether someone pushed him or he was too drunk to stand, Piper couldn't tell, but he staggered, then fell to the dance floor. His sunglasses flew off and crunched under one of the dancers' feet.

A couple of his drunken bodyguards rushed in, pushing everyone who stood in their way, and knocking over two of the male guests. One of them landed on Logan, but that didn't stop his security from trying to charge through a cluster of women who were blocking their path. Piper spun on them both. "*Back off! Now!*"

Miraculously, they stopped. Coop helped the male guests up, patting them on the back and inviting them to VIP for a drink. The three shark women pushed their way through the dancers, trying to return to their pop idol herring. Coop stepped in front of them, ready to pile on the charm, even though all the jostling had to be hurting him. Logan's bodyguards began to shove into the crowd again as Piper got Logan to his feet.

"Tell your posse to back off," she shouted into his ear, "and I'll make your wildest dreams come true."

He gave her a drunken leer. "For real?"

"A one-way ticket to paradise."

As he complied, she grabbed his arm, pulled him to the edge of the floor, and steered him into the kitchen.

A massive tray of bourbon brownies nested in square paper liners sat on the counter. She'd barely eaten all day, and she grabbed a couple of them, warm and oozing chocolate. "Private party," she told Logan.

Using a combination of strength and stealth, she managed to maneuver him up the stairs and into her apartment. "Wha's this," he slurred.

"The Garden of Eden," she said dryly.

He gave her a lopsided grin. His eyes without his sunglasses were small, brown, and unremarkable. "Whadda you got to drink?" he asked as he tried to prop himself against the counter that divided the living area and kitchen.

All she had were a couple of juice boxes and some beer. She kicked off her shoes and held up the two squished bourbon brownies. "I've got something even better."

"Pot brownies!" He would have grabbed them both if she hadn't sequestered one at the end of the counter for herself.

A knock sounded at her apartment door. She padded barefoot across the room. "Who is it?"

"Cops. Open up before I break down the door."

"Very funny." She opened the door and gave Eric a weary smile.

"I just got off duty," he said, letting himself in. "I saw your light on."

Something he could only have observed if he'd driven down the alley.

He sank into the couch, as if he intended to stay for a while. Logan, in the meantime, saw only a uniformed police officer and began stuffing both brownies in his mouth as fast as he could. As he supported himself on the edge of the counter, he held up his empty, chocolate-smeared hands and spoke to Eric through the globs. "Chuz bwahnee, mon. Noshin een 'em," which she interpreted as, "Just brownies, man. Nothing in them."

Eric looked at her. She shrugged. The door opened, and Coop came in without knocking.

He took in the scene—Office Hottie looking right at home on her couch, herself barefoot in a designer dress, and a drunken, ninety-million-dollar tween idol with chocolate on his face.

A vaguely bemused expression crossed his face. "I pay you for this, right?"

"Not enough."

"Coop! Great to see you, man." Eric hopped up for a backslap that had to be painful.

Coop slapped him back a little harder than necessary. "You, too."

With all the backslapping going on, none of them noticed that Logan had slipped out into the hallway. Not until they heard a shuffle, followed by the loud voice of a teenage girl.

"You're dead!"

And here they went again . . .

14

Eric drew his gun as Coop charged ahead into the hallway. Piper followed and peered over Coop's shoulder to see Logan curled on the floor, eyes closed, not moving. Jada stood in her apartment doorway, hair tangled, one leg of her checked pajamas hung up on her calf, and an orange-and-blue Nerf gun at her side.

"I killed him." She moaned.

Footsteps sounded in the hallway below, and Tony shouted up from the bottom of the stairs. "Coop! Can you get down here? Somebody called immigration. They've herded the staff in the kitchen to check green cards."

Coop threw up his big hands. "Great. This is just great! Can you deal with boy singer while I take care of INS?" He shot a quick glance between Eric and Piper, then looked back at Eric. "You want to come with me? I might need a character witness."

"Great idea," Piper said. With a uniformed cop at his side, nobody would mess with Coop. She was doubly glad that Tony checked green cards before he hired, but that made her wonder: exactly who had called INS?

Eric holstered his gun, bent down to pick up a Nerf bullet, and looked over at Jada. "I'd better run this through ballistics."

Jada's eyes widened in horror. He grinned and tossed her the bullet. Piper smiled. Maybe she *would* sleep with him.

As Coop and Eric disappeared downstairs, Logan stirred and looked up at Piper. "You wanna go fer a ride in mah plane?"

"Sorry, flyboy, I have to work."

"Tha's okay." He dropped his head back to the floor and closed his eyes.

"Ohmygod," Jada squealed. "That's Logan Stray!"

"If only you'd figured that out before you fired," Piper said. "It's the middle of the night!"

"Something woke me up, and the Pius Assassins are very resourceful." She went to her knees on the floor beside Logan. "Ohmygod, I can't believe it's Logan Stray. I, like, used to love him."

Her mother appeared in the doorway. Glossy, sleep-tousled hair tumbled around her shoulders, and the unfastened top buttons of her pajamas revealed a column of warm caramel skin. Karah, with her scrubbed face and womanly body, looked more alluring than a dozen overly made-up hair-swingers. Piper was glad Coop had gone downstairs.

"Jada, what are you doing out here?" Karah exclaimed.

Piper saw no need to rat out the teenager. "Sorry about that. We were making too much noise and woke her up."

Jada carefully slipped the Nerf gun behind her leg where her mother couldn't see.

Piper gazed down at Logan. "As long as you two are awake, would you help me move him?"

"I will!" Jada exclaimed.

They maneuvered Logan back into the apartment and onto Piper's couch. She fetched a bucket from under the kitchen sink and put it next to him, just in case.

Jada hovered over him. "Ohmygod, if he, like, gets sick, somebody should be watching him. Can I do it? Please, Piper! I'll sleep in the chair. Can I, Mom? Please?"

"Absolutely not."

Piper remembered how much Jada wanted to fit in at her new school and thought about the cred this would give her with her classmates. "It's okay with me, Karah," she said. "I'll watch out for her. And this'll be a once-in-a-lifetime opportunity for Jada to observe firsthand the perils of fame."

Karah hesitated, then conceded, maybe because she'd arrived at the same conclusion as Piper. "If there are any problems, send her home right away."

Problems? How could there be any problems? Piper thought, but didn't say.

She wouldn't let Jada sleep in the same room as Logan, even if he was comatose, and she sent the teenager to the bedroom. The club was closing, so she didn't have to go back downstairs. After she'd washed her face and exchanged her dress for sweats, she curled up in the living room chair.

It seemed as though she'd barely fallen asleep before a thin shaft of sunlight followed by a rap on the door awakened her. She peeled open her eyelids. Across the room, Logan Stray lay on his stomach, a hand and foot dangling over the edge of the couch onto the carpet. In the bedroom, Jada was still asleep.

Her neck was stiff, and it cracked as she pulled herself out of the chair. Cursing whoever was on the other side, she stumbled across the carpet.

Two bright-eyed women with cheery smiles pasted on their faces barged in. One held a cardboard tray of coffee, the other a box of doughnuts. Piper gripped the doorknob to support herself. "You are going to die."

"And good morning to you."

"How'd you get in?" Piper growled.

"Cleaning crew." Jen set the doughnut box on the counter, and Amber did the same with the coffee.

"Go away."

"Can't," Jen said. "Dumb Ass asked me out."

Amber puffed up with outrage. "She's thinking about going, and you know he'll tell her she has to have sex with him to keep her job."

"Probably." Jen ripped open the doughnut lid and pulled out a Bismarck.

Piper yawned. "Timezit?"

"Eight o'clock," Amber said, "and you're always awake at this time."

"Not when I've been up most of the night!"

Just then, Logan rolled over, and the part of him that wasn't already on the floor slid there. But he still didn't wake up.

"That's Logan Stray!" Jen exclaimed. And then, after a long pause, "Is he alive?"

Piper slouched back into the chair. "I guess."

"If you killed him, we'll help you hide the body."

"I know who Logan Stray is!" Amber sounded as if she'd come up with the answer to Final Jeopardy.

Someone else knocked on the door.

"Will everybody leave me the hell alone?" Piper shouted.

But Jen had already opened the door, and Berni stormed in. Her short hair erupted in an orange geyser around her face, and a pair of pink sweatpants poked out from under another of Howard's old cardigans. "I knew it! You all came here so you could talk about me behind my back!" She spotted Logan on the floor. "Isn't he a little young for you, Piper?"

Piper buried her face in her hands. "Will somebody please kill me?"

Berni rounded on Amber. "You're behind this secret meeting. You think I'm too old to know what I saw with my own eyes. Next thing you'll try to get me hauled off to a nursing home."

Piper lunged for the coffee.

"Calm down, Berni," Jen said. "Stop being so mean to Amber."

"Me?! Why don't you tell her to stop being so hateful to me?"

Maybe it was the coffee or the sugar from the doughnuts, but Amber, like Tosca about to hurl herself from the battlement, reared up to her full height and advanced. "I have never been hateful to you, but from the day we met, you've either acted as if I didn't exist or been outright—"

"You called me *Mrs. Berkovitz*!"

"—or you've been outright rude. I was brought up to be respectful of my elders, but—"

"There!" Berni pointed an accusing finger at all of them. "Did you hear what she said? Did you hear what she called me?"

Mild-mannered Amber's anger was a sight to behold. "Regardless of your age, there's no excuse for racial prejudice!"

Berni puffed up. "What racial prejudice? Stop trying to change the subject. And how can you talk about respect after the way you've treated me?"

Jen was still looking dumbfounded, but Piper was starting to get the drift.

"I've treated you with nothing but respect!" Amber exclaimed.

"Like I'm in my coffin. You call that respectful? Jumping in front of me to open doors . . . running out to get my newspaper in the winter because you think I'm too old and weak to get it for myself . . . You think I don't see what you do, but I still have eyes. Piper doesn't behave like that. Neither does Jen. Is that respectful?"

Amber's mouth closed on its way to its next sentence. Jen laughed.

Somebody had to be the grown-up here, and Piper figured she was it. "Amber," she said with forced patience. "Berni doesn't hate your guts because you're Korean . . ."

Berni protested. "What does Korean have to do with anything?"

"She hates you because you were brought up to be respectful of your elders," Piper said. "Which she *is*."

"That was unnecessary," Berni sniffed. "And I don't *hate* her."

Piper gave Berni a sickeningly sweet smile. "Berni is too *old* to change her ways, and too *inarticulate* to have explained what's been bothering her, so from now on, don't do another considerate thing for her. Matter of fact, treat her like crap. Then maybe she'll appreciate you the same way Jen and I do."

"I don't know why you're saying all this," Berni grumbled. "Amber's a smart girl. She knows."

"I didn't know!" Amber exclaimed. "How could I?"

Berni's mouth arranged itself in something approaching a pout. "I don't like feeling old."

"Good," Piper said, "because you're acting like a five-year-old."

Amber's proper Korean upbringing once again reared itself. "Piper, you shouldn't say—" She caught herself and took a deep breath. "Berni, from now on, you can get your own newspaper."

Coop sauntered through the open door. He glanced from the women to the body on the floor. "Is he still alive?"

"No idea," Piper said, and then, "Don't you ever sleep?"

"Did you check his pulse?"

"I don't care enough." Piper looked around her. There were now four uninvited adult people jammed into her tiny living room, one teenager still asleep in her bed, and a comatose pop idol on her floor. "Everybody get the hell out of here!"

"Grouchy," Coop observed.

Berni bustled toward his side. "Cooper! Mr. Graham! I was hoping I might see you. I have a pound of homemade divinity in my car. I was going to leave it with Piper, but now I can give it to you personally."

Logan chose that moment to roll over, look up at all of them, and gag.

Jen was the closest, but she was too late with the bucket.

Long seconds ticked by before Coop looked over at Piper. "Yeah . . ." he said slowly. "I should probably give you a raise."

Berni pressed both hands to her cheeks in delight. "Oh, Piper! I just love your life."

*

That afternoon, Piper tracked down a friend of Taylor's and learned she'd left Chicago for Vegas to take a casino job. The friend didn't know where Keith was, only that Taylor had broken up with him because "he was a loser." Piper intended to check out the story, but it rang true, and Taylor moved toward the bottom of her list of suspects.

At the club that night, she tossed out two members of a rowdy bachelorette party snorting bumps of cocaine off a credit card in the ladies' room. More lies about the club had shown up online, and she didn't need Coop's reminder that Spiral's reputation had to be spotless. Jonah stopped her as she came back inside from tossing the women out. "Where were you last night?"

With everything that had happened, she'd forgotten all about her ill-advised challenge to meet him in the alley. "I was a little busy babysitting our visiting pop star."

He smirked. "It's okay. I won't tell anybody you chickened out."

"Amazing. I've time-traveled back to fifth grade recess."

He regarded her blankly. She thought about explaining, but it was too much trouble, and she made herself take the higher path. "I concede. You're bigger and stronger."

"I sure as hell am."

That smirk was more than she could take. "But I'm smarter and faster."

"Bullshit, you are."

"I guess we'll have to find out then, won't we?" She hated this about herself. Why couldn't she walk away? No. Not her. She was incapable of turning the other cheek. "I'm not ripping another dress, so give me a few minutes to change after the club closes."

"Take all the time you want."

He didn't believe she'd show up, but he was wrong. She'd be there, and knowing that depressed her. Not because she was afraid to face him. That would either go well or it wouldn't. But because she still had this compulsion to prove she was the better man. Even to a cretin like Jonah. *Thanks, Duke.*

Blaming her insecurities on a father who'd loved her, even as he'd forbidden her to show any weakness and suffocated her with his overprotection, made her feel worse. When was she going to grow up enough not to regard everything in life as a test she had to pass to prove her own worth? Unfortunately, today wasn't that day because she'd backed herself into a corner—again—and she was emotionally incapable of not seeing this through.

After the club closed, she changed into jeans and sneakers, pulled on a Bears jersey, and, full of self-disgust, headed back downstairs. She peeked into the alley to make sure Coop's car was gone, then stepped outside.

Jonah was already there, standing next to the Dumpster, smoking a cigar with Ernie and Bryan, his best bouncer buddies. She waved at them. "Hey, Jonah. I see you brought backup."

He hadn't expected her to appear, and his cigar twitched at the corner of his mouth. His buddies snorted.

"I'm not surprised you didn't want to face me alone." She sounded exactly like the eleven-year-old who'd once fought Dugan Finke for pulling up her T-shirt. Dugan had been twice her size and beat the crap out of her, but he'd never touched her or her T-shirt again.

Jonah was in a conundrum. Because she was female, he couldn't swing at her the way he wanted. All he could do was drop his cigar and look threatening.

She believed in fair play, and she took pity on him. She walked closer and, with a smile on her face, shoved the heels of her hands against his chest, hooked out her leg, and sent him down.

Cursing, he was back on his feet in a flash, temper on fire, poised to launch. She braced herself, but before he could get to her, his pals sprang forward and grabbed his arms.

"Don't do it, J."

"You can't hit her!"

Jonah struggled to get free. "Let me go! I'm going to take her head off!"

"Try it!" she countered.

He screamed more invective, and since he couldn't get to her, it wasn't honorable to keep taunting him, so she joined him in ordering his boys to let him go. They were so engrossed in yelling at each other that none of them noticed Coop's Tesla squealing into the alley.

Just as Jonah managed to work himself free, Coop threw himself between them. "*What the* hell *is going on here?*"

He didn't wait for an answer. Instead, he swung hard, catching Jonah in the side of his jaw and sending him bouncing against the Dumpster. "You're fired, you son of a bitch. I don't ever want to see your face around here again."

"She started it!" Jonah cried, cradling his jaw.

The adrenaline that had been driving her began to ooze away, leaving her tired and dispirited. "I kind of did," she said.

Coop swiveled around and stared at her. When he finally spoke, each word was a surface-to-air missile. "You *kind of* did?"

"I hit him first."

Ernie and Bryan nodded. "She did, boss."

"I'm not good at self-restraint," she said, as if that weren't blindingly clear. "And I'd appreciate it if you didn't fire Jonah."

Coop's dangerous eyebrow went up.

"You would?" Jonah said, clearly dumbfounded.

"Not because of me, anyway," she said.

Coop was furious. "Maybe I should fire you instead? Because clearly you can't be left unsupervised."

"If I could respectfully disagree . . ." Ernie said. "She's been making our job a lot easier."

To her shock, Jonah spoke up, even as he continued to cradle his jaw. "That bachelorette party tonight. A couple of 'em were causing trouble, and she took care of it."

Coop looked ready to explode. "Everybody get the *hell* out of here!"

She was more than willing to do that.

"Except *you.*" His finger aimed at her temple. "Stay right where you are."

He kept her waiting until all three men had hastily driven away, and then he grabbed her arm and started dragging her toward his car.

She tried to dig in her heels. "It would probably be better if I went to my apartment now."

"You're going to my place." He planted his hand on top of her head as if he were a cop and shoved her into the Tesla's passenger seat. "I don't want Jada and Karah to hear you scream."

Not good at all.

He took off down the alley, tires spitting gravel. Even when he was calm, he was an aggressive driver, and since he wasn't calm now, he was hell on wheels. As she breathed in the scent of his brown suede jacket, she ticked off all the ways she'd failed them both. She'd been juvenile, unprofessional, and hotheaded—dangerous qualities in an investigator. And all because she hadn't been enough of a grown woman to put her leftover childhood insecurities behind her. Coop had every right to be furious with her.

The area around his garage was mercifully free of predators, except for him. When she didn't get out of the car quickly enough—and why should she hurry?—he extracted her. As soon as her feet hit the cement, he pressed her against the car and ran his hands over her body, touching pretty much whatever he wanted to touch, his jaw set like tempered steel. "Not armed?"

"I wanted to teach him a lesson, not kill him."

His hands slid up the insides of her thighs, then moved from her butt to her waist. When he was satisfied, he led her from the garage. "Let's go."

"Look, Coop . . . I understand you're pissed, and I don't blame—"

"Oh, no. I'm not pissed. I'm way beyond pissed." He clasped her upper arm again, not hurting her, but holding her in a lock she'd have trouble breaking.

They were inside his condo much too soon, but now that he had her there, he didn't seem certain what to do with her. A perfect time to make a dash toward the kitchen. "Hungry? I'll fix you an omelet."

"I'm not hungry," he said thoughtfully. "I'm trying to decide whether I want to do this rough or easy."

She held up her hand. "I vote for easy."

"You don't have a vote." He tossed his suede jacket over the back of the couch. "So I'm clear . . . You started the fight, right?"

"Technically."

"Technically?"

"We have a history, but—"

"And you decided the best way to handle that history was to go after a former Clemson linebacker in the alley? Do I have that right?"

"If you give a bully an inch . . ."

"That's only true when you're *twelve*!"

Before she could concede his point, he stalked toward her. "If you had problems with Jonah, you should have come to me."

Suddenly, she was as hot as he. "I handle my own problems."

"By damn, not any longer. I'm either going to fire your ass or . . . or . . ." He seemed to be having difficulty coming up with something more dire, even though getting fired was at the top of her personal dire list. "Or . . . spank it."

"You're not serious."

He actually seemed to ponder. "Yeah," he said thoughtfully. "I guess I am." One of his long arms whipped out, snaked her waist, lifted her off her feet, and dragged her to the couch. Seconds later, he turned her upside down over his lap.

She blinked.

His palm came down hard on the fleshiest part of her rear. All the blood rushed to her head. "*Ow!* Oh, my god! You are *kidding* me!"

Another smack. "Does this feel like I'm kidding?" *Whack.*

"It feels like you've *lost your mind.*"

"Never felt saner." *Whack. Whack.*

"This is wrong in so many ways. I don't even know where to start. *Ouch!* Yes, I do know! I'm calling my lawyer."

"You don't have a lawyer." Another smack. "Besides, don't you read? Rough sex is the rage these days."

"Only between consenting adults! *Stop it!* Do I look like I'm consenting?"

"If you weren't, I'd be on my ass right now."

True. She was hardly helpless. She let another smack land, then gritted her teeth. "I don't want to hurt you."

"You worry about yourself."

Another whap. And then his hand stalled. His palm curled around the sting. Lingered. Rubbed.

"Cooper Graham! You are feeling me up."

"I'm sure I'm not." His hand slid between her legs, cupping her through the denim, and his voice held a husky edge that made her weak with lust. First she'd engaged in playground behavior, and now she'd let herself be turned on by caveman theatrics. She was hopeless. And, despite all the lectures she'd given herself, she didn't care. "My mistake," she said, her voice as raspy as his.

He slipped his hand under her Bears jersey and traced his thumb up the bumps of her spine. He stalled at her bra. "You have too many clothes on . . ."

She didn't know whether he helped her or she levered herself up, but within seconds, she was on his lap, straddling him, her knees sinking into the couch cushions on either side of his thighs.

He clasped her waist. She slipped her hands around the back of his neck and gazed into that granite-carved face. "Are we really going to do this?"

His forehead creased. "It seems like it."

It seemed that way to her, too. "What about your scruples? I'm still the hired help."

He leaned forward and nibbled on her bottom lip. "You're not the help. You're the obstacle."

She nuzzled the cleft in his chin. "To what?"

"My peace of mind."

That was something she definitely understood.

He brushed his lips across hers. "What about your scruples?"

"Temporary leave of absence," she murmured.

He found the corner of her mouth. "I never spanked a woman in my life. Never even thought about it. Damn, it felt good."

She resisted the urge to rub her tingling bottom. "It didn't hurt one bit."

He drew back so that she was looking straight into those tarnished golden-brown eyes. "I'm still furious with you," he said.

"Understood." She met his gaze straight on. "If it's any consolation, I'm even more furious with me."

Maybe that satisfied him because he brought his lips to her neck. "Promise you won't fight any more of my men?"

She tilted her head to give him more room. "I promise." *Unless they're not watching out for you.*

He dumped her off his lap. "Okay. Let's get this over with."

She was done for. Hopeless and reckless. She reached for the bottom of his sweater and pulled it over his head.

It didn't take long before they were both naked and back on the couch. Even a short interruption while he protected them didn't dampen her desire. She wanted this—wanted dirty, no-holds-barred sex with this man. And maybe, maybe, she wanted to make him lose control the same way he'd done last time.

But he wasn't playing her game. "Keep your hands to yourself, lady," he said as she reached for him.

"You, too," she replied. "No. Wait. You can put your hands anywhere you like."

And he did.

She straddled him, the position opening her to the intimate abrasion of his fingers. His eyes were darker now, burnished with desire, but their gazes were no longer locked. That was an intimacy neither of them wanted.

She lowered her mouth to his, delivering a deep kiss, a kiss that began to feel as if it held too much of her. A hand tunneled into her hair, keeping her there. Mouths, teeth, tongues merged and battled. She lowered her hand to clasp him, but he was having none of it. He pushed her back into the cushions and pressed open her thighs. He gazed at all he'd exposed, and then claimed what she so willingly offered.

The press of his thumbs into her thighs, the sweet laceration of his mouth, the teasing, the torment . . . And then the abandonment. The cruel, callous, abandonment . . . until he shifted his weight.

This time there was no mistaking that hard thrust—sweetly painful. Her fingers dug into his back, slick now with sweat. The delicious burden of his body pressed down on her. Into her. Deep and deeper still, this tight, powerful breaching.

A crazy fracas broke out behind her eyelids. Inky swirls orbiting into a whirling vortex that spun faster and faster until it erupted into a perfect supernova.

He thrust on, full press. Her head thrashed. She cried out. His hips drove deeper. Stilled.

Finally . . . The silent howl of his arched neck. Muscles convulsing. The long shudder of his body.

And then the quiet.

They calmed. When she could breathe, she maneuvered for a more comfortable position only to send them both to the floor.

They lay there for a few moments, on their sides, wedged between the couch and his flying saucer coffee table. His finger circled the breast he'd neglected while he'd been busy with other parts. "You felt like a virgin."

"It's been a while." She rested her head in the crook of his arm and gave in to the inevitable. "This can't interfere with work."

"Absolutely not," he said, even more vehemently than she had.

"Because if it's going to . . ."

"It won't. We're too smart for that. And we both know this had to happen. Now we're going to see it through."

"Lovers when we're naked," she said. "Business associates when we're not."

"I couldn't have phrased it better." He wedged up on one elbow. "Have I mentioned how much I like you? When I don't feel like killing you."

She smiled. "I like you, too. Most of the time, anyway, and that's rare. I'm much too critical of your sex."

He tweaked her nipple. "From the way you were screaming, I think my sex did pretty damn well for itself."

"Definitely better than last time."

"You aren't going to let me forget, are you?"

"I'm not that decent." She tugged hard on a piece of his hair. "You'd better not try that spanking thing again, because you won't get away with it twice."

"I'll treasure the memory."

She traced her fingers down the hard slope of his arm. "You should know I'm not usually so selfish. I believe in giving as well as taking."

"You'll have to prove that." He nuzzled her neck. "Let's hop in the shower so I can see if you're all talk."

"So soon?"

"I'm a highly trained athlete. I have powers far beyond those of mortal men."

She definitely couldn't argue with that. He helped her off the floor, and they headed for the open staircase, but before they got to the top, she had to make sure they were clear. "We agree, right? No games. We'll do this until we get bored with each other or until another ravishingly beautiful movie star decides she needs some quarterback arm candy."

He grinned and squeezed her rear. "It's a deal. And no screwing around with your cop boyfriend."

"Not until I'm done with you."

His walk-in shower was bigger than four of her bathrooms. Its tumbled marble walls, multiple nozzles, and movable showerheads became a sexual playground for an inventive couple. Which they were.

"You're definitely not selfish," Coop muttered sometime later as he leaned against the wall to catch his breath.

Not selfish, but maybe stupid, she thought. She pushed the idea aside. She finally knew what she was doing. She'd set her boundaries and been up front about her needs. Most important, she was aware of her limitations when it came to having a relationship with a wealthy celebrity sex god, a man so far out of her realm of experience that the two of them barely occupied the same planet. She wasn't beautiful or sophisticated. Didn't care about clothes or makeup, and wouldn't know how to swish her hair even if it were a foot longer. He was attracted to her out of novelty. And novelty was, by definition, temporary.

She gave them two weeks max before it fell apart. And she was okay with that. Two weeks of mind-blowing sex was perfect. But as she wrapped herself in an oversize bath towel, a shadow fell over one corner of her heart, a premonition that, when the sex stopped, she'd have lost a friend. One of the best friends she'd ever had.

15

On Monday morning, she got a call from the owner of a neighborhood minimart who'd seen her flyer. He wanted her to investigate what he believed was a fraudulent injury claim from one of his former employees, a guy named Wylie Hill. She headed south to check him out.

Pilsen was a predominantly Mexican-American Chicago neighborhood, rich with art and immigrant tradition. Two men leaned against a mural of the Virgin of Guadalupe and watched a couple of hipsters walk by. An old woman in bedroom slippers came up the steps from her basement apartment to sweep the sidewalk.

Wylie eventually appeared and sat smoking on the stoop of the row house where he'd rented a room. She was happy to have a new client, but stakeouts were her least favorite part of the job. First, because they were boring, and second, because they gave her too much time to think, especially today.

She and Coop had spent most of yesterday in bed, and not once had she been plagued by the emptiness that had always come over her when she was with a man—the panicky disconnect that made her look for excuses to get away. With Coop, there'd been nearly as much talking as there'd been sex. She'd described a couple of Duke's more interesting investigations. He'd talked about ranch life and urban gardening. They'd exchanged surprisingly similar opinions about politics and religion. He'd even pried out some stories about her schizophrenic upbringing—stories she now regretted sharing. Too much talking. Too many places inside her she didn't want him to see. From now on, she was leaving his place as soon as he put his clothes back on.

Wylie Hill had either genuinely hurt his back unloading boxes or was the laziest man alive, because he didn't do much except sit on his stoop. By late the next afternoon, when she couldn't stand the boredom any longer, she made a quick trip to her office and did some work on her Web site. As she was getting ready to lock back up and return to her stakeout, Coop appeared, bringing an influx of testosterone along with him. He gazed around, taking in the framed posters of pulp detective magazine covers. "You really do have an office."

"A little humbler than yours, but it'll work until my luxury suite in the Hancock opens up." She surreptitiously turned the notepad she'd been writing on facedown. "What are you doing here?"

"Curious to see how the other half lives." He reached across her desk and flipped over the notepad she'd tried to conceal. "Your shrink?"

She'd intended to keep what she'd learned to herself until she had more information, but she couldn't do that now. "I finally tracked down your ex-bartender. He's working in a Bridgeport dive bar."

"You weren't planning to tell me about it?"

"After I talked to him. That's what you pay me to do, remember?"

"Right." He skirted the borders of the rug to poke at the soil of her windowsill orchid, a gift from Amber. "When are you going to see him?"

"Tonight. He goes on duty at nine. I'll call you in the morning."

"No need. I'm going with you. And you're overwatering that orchid."

"Thanks for the info, and you'll only complicate things. Now, go away. I have some surveillance work to do for a new client." *And simply breathing your oxygen is fogging my brain.*

"Great. I'll come along. It'll be interesting to get a glimpse into the seedier side of your life."

"Surveillance is way too boring for you."

"I can handle it."

At first he did. But after a few hours, he grew restless and stared rummaging around in her backseat. "Got anything to eat in here?"

"Fresh out."

"What's this?" He held up her pink Tinkle Belle.

"Ice cream scoop."

"Weird-looking ice cream scoop." He began to pull it from its plastic bag.

"Leave it alone." She hadn't needed to use it recently, but still . . .

Enlightenment struck. He gazed through the plastic bag at the Tinkle Belle, then at her. "I always wondered how women—"

"Now you know. Put it back."

She'd parked catty-corner from the beat-up Pilsen row house where Hill lived. As Tejano music blared from a vintage clothing shop next door, Coop flipped open her glove box and rooted around. When he got tired of that, he poked at a loose panel on her dashboard. She willed him to be still so she could try to forget he was there. As if that were possible.

"How do you know your guy's inside?" he asked.

She pointed toward the top floor. "He's passed by that corner window a couple of times."

"Maybe he's in for the night."

"Could be."

"What if he really did throw out his back on the job?"

"Then he deserves his money."

A lowrider shot past. Coop draped his arm across the seat, his fingers brushing her shoulder. "You don't always have to be the toughest Viking in the longboat, you know."

She should never have told him about Duke's child-rearing habits. She had to retrench. "I'm not a romantic, if that's what you mean. I don't dream of a hubby and house full of mini-me's. I had more than enough of domesticity taking care of my father when I was growing up." Along with never whining, crying, or admitting uncertainty.

"It's understandable that your father was overprotective, considering what happened to your mother, but it was dead wrong of him to leave everything to your stepmother."

Piper shrugged, as if it were no big deal. "What was your mother like?"

"She was adventurous. Funny. Not very domestic. Pretty much the opposite of my old man. A little like you. Except sweet."

She smiled. The front door of the row house opened, and a nervous-looking guy with a bony face and untidy shoulder-length hair emerged. Piper straightened. "That's him."

Hill sat on the lighted stoop and lit a cigarette. Coop watched him smoke for a while, then looked at the time on his phone. "This is like watching paint dry, and it's barely seven o'clock."

"You didn't have to come with me."

"I was hoping for a high-speed chase."

So was she.

Wylie stood and stretched. Piper picked up her Nikon, adjusted the focus, and took a couple of shots.

"Not exactly proof of anything," he said.

"Employers like to know you're on the job."

Wylie was finishing his third cigarette when he pulled out his cell and held it to his ear, as if he'd just gotten a call. He said a few words, pitched the cigarette butt into the gutter, and took off down the street, moving a little fast for a guy with an injured back. He climbed behind the wheel of an old gray Corolla. Piper stuck the camera out the window and took another shot as he pulled away.

"Now can we have a high-speed chase?" Coop asked.

"Maybe next time."

✶

Piper was a good driver, alert and agile behind the wheel. He'd noticed that on their drive to Canada. She kept well back from the Corolla as it headed north a few blocks, turned onto Racine, and again onto Eighteenth. Eventually Wylie eased the car down a street partially closed for road construction. Coop could see a liquor store and taco place, but not much else. Pipe pulled into a loading zone, set aside her Nikon, and grabbed her cell instead. "Stay here," she said as she opened the car door. "I mean it, Coop. You're too conspicuous."

He hated that she was right, but it was a mild evening, and there were enough people on the street to make it certain he'd be recognized. Still, it was a tough neighborhood, and he hated the idea of her going off alone.

He glanced at his watch as she disappeared around the construction barricades. He'd been with her for a couple of hours, and he still hadn't told her what had happened earlier today. He needed to get it over with instead of putting it off, but he could already predict her reaction.

He drummed his fingers on his knees and gazed toward the corner where she'd disappeared. He knew how competent she was. She could take care of herself. She probably had that Glock stuck in her jacket pocket. But he felt like a pussy sitting here while she was out there by herself.

More minutes ticked by until he couldn't stand it any longer. He checked the backseat again for a ball cap or anything he could use to mask his identity, but found only a pair of purple sunglasses. *Screw it.* He got out of the car.

Just then, she came around the corner. He slipped back inside, but not before she'd seen him. "Leg cramp," he said as she climbed back in.

She rolled her eyes at him and started the car. "It looks like Wylie's back problem is all better." She passed over her cell.

He flipped to her photos and saw a pawnshop next to the taco place. Hill was coming out of it carrying a television with maybe a thirty-inch screen. Even in the dim evening light, she'd captured it all. The way he balanced the weight of the set in his arms. How he propped it on the rear fender while he opened the trunk. And, most damning, how he managed to maneuvered it into the trunk without any extraordinary effort.

"The pawnbroker came out to hold the door for him," she said. "I heard them talking. Wylie had put out the word that he wanted a new TV, and the broker called to tell him the ticket on that one had expired."

"Case solved."

"Yeah." She didn't look all that happy about it. "I was hoping it would last another couple of days."

"The price you pay for being good at what you do." He set down her cell. "It would have been a lot more interesting if you'd had to shoot him."

"Life can be cruel that way."

When they reached Hill's apartment, she took more photos of him unloading the set. It was nearly time for Keith to start work, but Coop made her stop at a Taco Bell where he had a couple of 7-Layer Burritos and she ate half of a steak gordita. Even with the windows down, the car smelled of chili powder, cumin, and lust.

She'd been up front. She'd told him she used men for sex, but she was hardly the picture of a man-eater with those blueberry eyes that looked straight at him. His own scruples about sleeping with an employee had conveniently vanished. Piper was no ordinary employee. Half the time he felt as if he worked for her.

She wiped a dab of sauce from her chin. "This was Duke's idea of fine dining. Taco Bell and a Big Gulp. You would have liked him."

That was debatable. Overprotecting a daughter with such an adventurous nature while he also bullied her had been an epic fail on Duke Dove's part. Coop returned his empty food wrapper to the bag. "Not his taste in football teams."

She gave him her wicked look. "The Bears are a man's team—the monsters of the Midway as opposed to you pansy-assed glamour boys from the 'burbs."

"Despite our winning stats."

"Duke's opinions weren't always supported by facts."

"Just like yours. I swear, if I see you in that Bears jersey one more time, I'm going to rip it off you."

The words hung in the air between them. He couldn't stand it a moment longer, and he reached across the seat. She leaned against him, but only for a second before she pulled away. "Don't make me cuff you."

She was such a punk. Such a stubborn, sexy, driven, funny little punk.

She tried to talk him into going home, but he wasn't having it, and she eventually gave up. "The bar is on the fringes of Bridgeport," she told him as they headed south on Halstead. "Right by Bubbly Creek."

"Bubbly Creek?"

"Don't tell me you've lived in Chicago this long and never heard of it."

"I've been a little busy."

"It's the South Fork of the Chicago River, but nobody calls it that. A hundred years ago, all the meatpacking companies around the Union Stock Yards dumped their waste in it. I did a term paper for a college biology class." She paused and glanced over at him. "Term papers are the things all of us who actually went to class had to do."

He gave her his cowboy drawl. "Wouldn't know about that. I was too busy cruisin' around town in the shiny red Corvette the alums bought me."

She shot him her withering look, which was so damned cute he would have kissed her nose if she'd been another kind of woman. "So, Bubbly Creek?" he said.

"The slaughterhouses threw their carcasses in the water—guts, blood, hair—every putrid thing you could think of, then tossed in all the processing chemicals, too. After a while the creek started to bubble from the decomposition. That's how it got its name. Sometimes the sludge got so thick that people could walk on it. The government's poured millions into cleanup, but it can still bubble on a hot day."

"Mother Nature takes a long time to get over being pissed off."

"Women are like that." She pulled into a crumbling parking lot next to a squat, aluminum-framed building with an Old Style sign hanging above the front door. "Keith's come down in the world," she said.

He needed to get this over with. "Before we go in, you should know . . . I was doing some paperwork at the club today, and when I came out, somebody had slashed my tires."

"What?!"

He'd known she'd go ballistic, and she didn't prove him wrong. "Why didn't you tell me this right away?"

Because he hated to admit she was right about these incidents not being arbitrary. Worse than that, he hated knowing somebody was getting the best of him. "It could have been random," he said.

"Don't even start with me about that."

She began peppering him with questions, as he'd known she would. When had it happened? Who might have witnessed it? Had he seen anyone hanging around the alley?

He told her everything he knew, which was exactly nothing. Tony and the cleaning staff had been inside the club. None of them had seen anything. He hadn't reported it to the police.

She set her jaw in that way she had. "Let's see what your pal Keith has to say about this."

A notice next to the front door read: PROTECTED WITH LOADED GUNS. He suspected the sign wasn't meant to be ironic.

The place smelled of stale beer and cigarette smoke left over from the eighties. A long bar, square tables, a yellowed linoleum floor, and random wall art served as decor, while the Bee Gees singing "How Deep Is Your Love" on the jukebox provided questionable ambience.

None of the array of beaten-down locals looked up as they walked in. Keith was behind the bar, his back to the door. Piper took a seat at the end of the bar. Keith turned and saw them both. The rag he'd been using stalled in his hand.

Pipe proved her familiarity with dive bars. "Two PBRs."

Coop hadn't had a Pabst since he was fourteen, but this wasn't the kind of place where you ordered the latest IPA.

Keith brought over their beers. He needed a haircut, and he hunched his left shoulder, the same way he always did when he wanted to look tough. The same thing he'd done when Coop had fired him.

"Come here to laugh at the corpse?" Keith set the beers in front of them with a hard thud that sent a splash of suds over the rims.

"You did it to yourself, pal." Coop still hadn't gotten past the sting of betrayal.

"I'm buying this place as soon as I get the cash together," Keith said belligerently. "Make it into something."

"Good luck."

Keith took a couple of swipes at the bar with his rag. "There was a time you'd have helped me."

"Yeah, well, that train pulled out of the station a while back."

Keith had never had much of a poker face, and the corners of his mouth dipped. He looked over at Piper. "What are you doing with her?"

"I'm his new girlfriend," she retorted. "He upgraded."

Considering the accomplished women in his past, that wasn't exactly true. But in another way, it was.

Keith dismissed her and returned his attention to Coop. "You know what I miss?"

"What's that?"

"Sitting around shootin' the shit. That's what I miss."

Coop shrugged.

"For what it's worth," Keith said, "it was Taylor who came up with the idea. Stupid bitch. She moved out on me right after I got this job."

Coop took a sip of beer. "All you had to do was tell her no."

Keith gave a bitter laugh. "You're the one with character, remember? I'm the one who always screwed the pooch."

Piper set down her mug. "So, Keith, while you're all full of regret . . . Last week, somebody jumped your ex-pal here. Know anything about that?"

Keith looked genuinely shocked. Ignoring Piper, he stared at Coop. "She serious?"

Coop nodded.

Keith's left shoulder went up. "You think it was me?"

Coop considered it. "Not really."

"But I have a more suspicious nature," Piper said. "I heard you took a swing at Coop when he fired your ass, so it's not beyond the realm of possibility."

Keith's face flushed with anger. "I've done a lot of shitty crap in my life, but I'd never do that."

Piper bore in—drilling him on where he'd been that night. At the bar working, as it turned out. Where he'd been this afternoon—asleep with no alibi. But Coop stopped paying attention. Whatever else Keith had done, he hadn't been behind any of this.

While Pipe continued her interrogation, Coop took a pull on his beer and contemplated hidden enemies. He hated this. He wanted his enemies where he could see them, right across the line of scrimmage.

✶

Soccer wasn't Coop's game, but Deidre Joss had invited him to Toyota Park to see the Chicago Fire play D.C. United, and he wouldn't turn her down. He liked everything about Deidre, from her personality to her reputation, everything except how long it was taking her to commit to his operation.

He glanced across the stadium's executive viewing suite at Piper. She managed to look both cute and sexy in a loopy orange sweater and a pair of jeans that actually fit. Her predictable dark tousle of a hairstyle wouldn't work on another woman but somehow fit her perfectly. Pipe was the least needy female he'd ever been involved with, and their relationship was working out even better than he'd hoped.

He'd invited her to come with him right after they'd returned from last night's confrontation with Keith. She'd launched into a predictable refusal—they weren't dating, and this sounded like a date—then immediately reversed herself and accepted. He knew why. She wanted to keep him in her sights. Totally maddening and completely unnecessary. He'd nearly withdrawn the invitation, but then he hadn't. He respected perseverance, no matter how misguided.

When he'd picked her up, she'd dropped a bombshell on him. A flood of online complaints about Spiral had popped up, complaints about everything from rude serving staff to dirty glasses to bad music—none of which was true. The reviews looked as though they'd been planted, and she'd already started the process of trying to get them taken down, but she'd warned him it would take time.

He was furious, and not even her reminder that she had years of experience handling problems like this had mollified him. She didn't understand. She couldn't. He had a new life, and failure wasn't an option.

Deidre stepped away from the group she'd been talking to and caught his eye. He hoped like hell she hadn't caught wind of the bad reviews. Forcing a smile, he went over to join her.

✶

Piper gazed out onto the soccer field from the sweeping windows of Deidre Joss's viewing suite, but the action on the field was secondary to the puzzle pieces that refused to fit together in her brain. She didn't get it. The mugging, the drone, and the tire slashing were active acts. But the online sabotage and the false tip to the INS seemed more cerebral. How did it all come together?

Behind her, she heard Deidre laugh at something Coop was saying. The two of them looked as though they belonged together. Deidre, tall and poised as a ballerina, and Coop, all rangy self-confidence. A pair of good-looking high-achievers completely at home with the luxuries their hard work had brought them. Deidre was obviously taken with Coop, but she wasn't pushy about it.

"Enjoying the game?" Noah Parks said as he came up beside her.

All afternoon she'd watched him take care of Deidre. He didn't crowd her, but if Deidre needed a fresh drink, he was there. If she seemed to tire of a conversation, he stepped in to deflect it. Piper could use a Noah Parks in her life.

"It's not like watching the Bears, but yes, I am," she said. On the field, the Fire successfully tipped away a shot at the goal. "These are really nice digs."

"Deidre has a skybox at Soldier Field, too, and one at the Midwest Sports Complex."

Where the Stars played. "A girl can't have too many skyboxes."

He laughed. "She uses them for business entertainment." He gazed through the glass down at the field. "Interesting that you've become part of Coop's inner circle, considering the way you two started out."

He was probably fishing for information, but he wasn't getting anything from her. "He's bored, and I'm a novelty."

The Fire scored their first goal, and she excused herself to get a hot dog from the buffet.

Everybody in the suite wanted to talk to Coop, and it wasn't until the second half that he approached her. "I just learned that Deidre Joss is the person who hired you to follow me."

Piper straightened. "Why do you think that?"

"Because she told me."

"*Really?*" She'd spoken too loudly, and some of the people in the skybox turned to stare, but Piper was outraged. After swearing Piper to secrecy and nearly destroying her career in the process, Deidre Joss had just blurted it out to Mr. Golden Eyes?

It was a good thing her cell vibrated right then. She pulled it out of her jeans pocket and glanced at the screen. Why was Tony calling her?

"Coop turned off his phone again," Tony said when she answered. "Is he with you?"

"Yes. You want to talk to him?"

"No. Tell him we've got a big problem, and he needs to get over here right away."

✶

The kitchen was infested with cockroaches. Coop had never seen so many. Hundreds of them scattered from the light he'd just turned on. They scampered across the floor, the counters, along the stovetop. A pale-faced Tony was huddled in the hallway, right outside the door. "An exterminator's on his way. We're going to have to close down for at least a week."

Wonder Woman took one look at the insect bedlam and headed for the hallway, too. "I am so out of here." She spun back. "If any of those get up in my apartment, you're a dead man."

✶

Coop barged into her apartment a few hours later. She was sitting on her couch, curled over her laptop. The exterminator was already at work downstairs, but Tony had been right. They'd be closed at least a week. Exactly seven days too long.

"You'd better have shaken out your clothes before you came in here," she said.

He stalked across the room. "You're one hell of a bodyguard."

"I'm not your bodyguard, remember? And I've been doing what I had to do."

"Hiding from a few bugs?"

She shuddered. "I'm not proud of myself."

There it was again. That refusal to defend herself over anything she perceived as a personal weakness.

"I've been doing some research," she said as he started to pace. "You can buy cockroaches by the hundreds on the Internet. Did you know their severed heads can survive if they're refrigerated? Only for a few hours, but still."

"I didn't know that. And I wish I didn't know it now."

"I'll start tracking down dealers tomorrow, but finding out who placed the order is a long shot. They even sell them on Amazon."

But his mind wasn't on Amazon, and neither was hers. "With Keith out of the picture," she said, "we both know who the next most logical suspect is."

He didn't ask who she meant. He knew.

She closed the lid on her laptop, stared at it for a moment, then rubbed her eyes. "He's in Miami."

16

South Beach was a twenty-four-hour carnival of swaying palms; Latin rock music; Easter-egg-colored art deco buildings; and shapely, long-haired women strolling along Ocean Drive with hoop earrings the size of bracelets and colorful thongs showing through tight white shorts. She and Coop arrived early the next afternoon at the Setai hotel, a Collins Avenue sepulcher serving the very wealthy, where Coop had booked a suite with a nightly room rate that could have bought her a set of tires and a new laptop.

Prince Aamuzhir had left London three days earlier for Miami and his five-hundred-foot yacht. Piper had wanted to go see him alone, but Coop had loudly vetoed the idea, pointing out that she couldn't get to Aamuzhir without him. She'd attempted to dissuade him, but he wasn't a man to hide from his enemies, and she couldn't put her heart into it.

Coop had no trouble wrangling an invitation to the yacht, and exactly one month from the day he'd caught her spying on him at the club, they were back in his old stomping grounds. Everyone from the skycaps to the food truck vendors selling empanadas greeted him as a returning hero. She did her best to stay in the background and was disheartened to realize that some part of her wanted to tell the world he was her lover.

While he worked out in the hotel gym, she took in the ocean view through the massive wall of bedroom windows and changed from her travel clothes into one of the outfits she'd picked up in a rush shopping trip. They were meeting some of his former teammates for dinner, an invitation she'd tried to get out of.

"I'm only pretending to be your girlfriend when we're on the yacht tomorrow," she'd reminded him. "Tonight you'll be with your old teammates. You don't need a fake girlfriend."

For some reason, that had irritated him. "You're a little more than a fake. We're sleeping together."

"A technicality."

"You're going with me," he'd retorted.

She came out of the suite's luxury bathroom as Coop returned from the gym. The guilt that had been dogging her once again nipped at her heels. If she hadn't talked him into helping Faiza escape, he wouldn't be in this situation.

He stopped inside the door of the suite and stared at her. "Where the hell did you get that?"

She gazed down at her short hot-pink A-line jersey dress. "What's wrong with it?" The spaghetti straps that crossed in the back hadn't come undone, and the stack of silver bangles encircled her wrist in the proper place. She'd put on makeup and traded the sneakers she'd worn on the plane for barely-there sandals. She'd even pieced out her hair with what was left of an old jar of hair gel. So what if she'd bought her dress at H&M instead of one of his ridiculously overpriced boutiques?

"Nothing's wrong with it," he said, circling her. "That's why the world as I know it has come to an end. You look female."

He was in rare form for a man willing to put his life in danger by meeting up with a powerful prince who could be holding a big grudge, but every time she tried to apologize for getting him into such a dangerous situation, he became more annoyed, so she gave him the once-over instead. "More than anyone, you should know I look very female."

"Not with your clothes on. At least not most of the time."

She appreciated his insight. "I know how to put clothes together, the same way I know how to cook. I just prefer not to."

"Thanks to Duke Dove."

"What do you mean by that?"

"Out of curiosity, did he ever mention that you're pretty?"

"Why would he?" She didn't like the way he was studying her, as if he saw something she couldn't. "I have to look at least a little like I could be one of your playmates. It's a stretch, I know, but—"

"Not that much of a stretch."

The conversation was making her jittery. "These are strictly work clothes, and I expensed everything, so it's all yours when the job's done. Except for my sandals. And the bracelets are from an old boyfriend who didn't know me nearly well enough."

"Obviously not." He sniffed the air as if he'd smelled something odious. "Are you wearing perfume?"

"Magazine sample."

"Leave it between the pages. You smell great without it."

And so did he, even after his workout. Male sweat on a clean body. She wanted to strip that sweaty T-shirt right off him and drag him into the bedroom.

He looked thoughtful. "If I own that dress, that means I can rip it off you anytime I want, right?"

"I suppose so. Although I'd appreciate it if you'd wait until the job is over."

"That," he said, "is going to be hard."

She dipped her gaze. "So I see."

He smiled, but the guilt she was carrying dampened her own amusement. She should have come up with a way to help Faiza without involving him.

His irritation returned. "Stop it, Pipe. You didn't make me do anything I wasn't willing to do."

"I know that," she said, way too vehemently.

He arched a brow at her, reading her mind in a way no one else had ever been able to.

She picked up his cell. "One of the prince's people called while you were gone. About a launch to take us out to his yacht tomorrow."

He stripped off his T-shirt. "Unacceptable. There's no way I'm letting that jerk control when we get on and off that boat."

"Exactly. I've already hired our own launch."

"Of course you have." He lifted her off the floor so her sandaled toes dangled over the top of his sneakers. His long, deep kiss destroyed most of her makeup, and her hot-pink dress soon landed in a puddle on the floor. He wanted to take her into the shower, but she dragged him into the bedroom instead.

They made love—no, not love. And—although she wasn't averse to using the well-placed *F*-word—what they were doing wasn't that either. Instead, they . . . had sex—lots of sex—in a bed with a sweeping ocean view that transformed the room into an aerie over the sea. She wanted to stay naked for the rest of the night. Apparently, he did, too, because she had to kick him out of bed.

If his teammates were surprised to see Coop with a woman who'd never been on TMZ, they didn't show it. He openly introduced her as an investigator he'd met when he'd hired her to look into employee misconduct.

It was an entertaining group. She was comfortable with men like this, and the women, who were openly curious about her, made an effort to draw her into their conversations. Since most of them were mothers, the talk centered on their children, but Piper enjoyed seeing the cute kid photos on their cells. At the same time, she was more than grateful that she didn't have any photos of her own to pass around. When maternal genes had been distributed, she'd been hanging out at the bar.

Coop touched her frequently, looping his arm around her shoulders, touching her earlobe. She liked it too much. It made her wonder . . . when this affair ended, was maintaining their friendship completely outside the realm of possibility? Maybe they could meet up for Mexican food sometime or catch a Blackhawks game. She knew she'd miss the best sex she'd ever had, but what if she missed the friendship even more?

Too depressing to think about.

*

The launch she'd hired picked them up the next afternoon and took them out to the prince's yacht. With four decks, a helipad, and a Darth Vader–black hull, it was an ocean-bound fortress, and the closer they got, the more nervous she became. Coop, however, was hard-eyed and focused. "I wouldn't miss this for the world."

A steward, who introduced himself as Malik, greeted them with cardamom-scented coffee and dates. "Let me show you to your stateroom. You can change into swimwear there, if you'd like. His Highness will arrive soon."

On the way to their stateroom on the second deck, Malik pointed out the direction to the pool, movie theater, and gym where, he assured them, guests would find a complete array of shoes and work-out clothes. As they passed through the main salon, he indicated the grand staircase that eventually led to the owner's private quarters on the top deck and also mentioned the saunas, hair salon, and massage room.

Their stateroom had picture windows looking out at the sea and enough gilt for a cathedral. "Even you're not rich enough to buy one of these little boats," she said with undisguised glee. And then, "Are you?"

"Hard to say." He looked around with distaste. "It's fine for a couple of days, but I like dirt under my feet."

"And coming out of your mouth."

Their bedroom romp had been a deliciously erotic verbal smut fest, and he grazed his knuckles over the top of her breast.

After she'd changed into her suit, she wrapped a zebra-striped scarf she'd retrieved from her bag of disguises around her waist. His gaze moved from everything she hadn't covered up to the bright yellow tote she wasn't letting out of her sight. "What all do you have in there?" he asked suspiciously.

"The latest issue of *Cosmo* and an eyelash curler—what do you think?"

He gave her his deadeye look. "I *think* you'd better keep your cool."

"You worry about yourself."

"If only it were that simple," he muttered.

They headed down one deck to the pool. Half a dozen pristine sail-shaped canopies protected the white couches and cushy chaises from the sun. Tables held platters of tropical fruit, cheeses, flatbreads, roasted nuts, and exotic-looking dips, while the full-length bar displayed every variety of liquor forbidden in the Realm. Malik appeared to see what they would like to drink. Coop ordered a beer, but Piper opted for iced tea.

Coop looked disgustingly amazing in dark green board shorts that turned his eyes into pirate's doubloons. As he headed toward the pool, he tossed aside his T-shirt, revealing the chest she adored, not only for its impressive muscles, but also for its sprinkling of hair—just enough so he looked like a real man instead of an oiled-up male centerfold.

She regarded him enviously as he performed a semigraceful dive off the board. Her new black swimsuit was technically a one-piece, but with two diagonal cutouts—one a big sideways V under the bandeau top, and the other above the low bottom—it didn't feel dependable enough to risk a dive. She'd have preferred something more functional, but she couldn't imagine any of Coop's girlfriends worrying about practicality. And that's what she was passing herself off as. One of Coop's girlfriends.

Uneasiness crept along the pit of her stomach. Being a girlfriend implied a relationship, with maybe some kind of potential. But that wasn't how they were. She was his sex partner, his investigator, his bodyguard, whether he wanted to acknowledge it or not. A bogus girlfriend.

Coop hauled himself back up on the pool deck, rivulets of water running down every taut muscle. She wanted to lick him. Instead, she slipped her sunglasses to the top of her head and curled her lip. "That dive was a six-point-three at best."

"Let's see you do better."

That's the way it was between them. Challenges and competition. Neither willing to give the other an inch.

A helicopter buzzed overhead. Soon, a jet-black Airbus landed on the helipad in the bow.

The prince joined them half an hour later, along with three young—very young—beauties in the most minuscule of string bikinis. The girl-women retired to the couches on the other side of the pool, not speaking to him or to each other.

She'd seen photos of the prince, but his dyed black hair and weird mustache made him even less appetizing in person. A gaudy gold crest decorated the pocket of his white sports shirt, and his navy Bermudas revealed pigeon legs. From twenty feet away, she could smell the overpowering musk of his cologne.

He greeted Coop effusively, which could mean either that he hadn't yet figured out Coop had dumped a fake ring on him or that he was simply a good actor. Coop slapped him on the back a tad too hard but offset it with a cornpone grin and an Oklahoma drawl. "It sure is good to see you again, Yer Highness. This is a real nice dinghy you got."

The prince regarded him through creepy glasses tinted at the top but clear at the bottom. "As you can see, it's no longer new."

"Sure looks good to me."

"You could not bring your friends with you?"

"Naw. Robillard's just had another kid, and Tucker's off doing something with his wife." Coop's derisive tone telegraphed his disgust for any man who'd put a woman's needs ahead of his own.

"Unforgivable." And then the prince chuckled. "Tell me, my friend. How did you find that little gift I gave you? Was she as sweet as you hoped?"

It took Coop a moment to understand what he meant, and then his jaw set in a most unpleasant way. She shot forward before he erupted. "Your Highness," she gushed. "I'm so honored to meet you." She fingered her zebra-striped sarong in a semicurtsy that would almost surely have amused Coop if he weren't so pissed off.

The prince addressed her with a degree of arrogance that signaled he was doing her a favor by speaking to her at all. "Madam. I hope you're finding my ship comfortable."

"Oh, yes. It's really, really super awesome."

He returned his attention to Coop, already forgetting her existence. "Coop, sit with me. Our last visit was too short. Do you remember the Titans game where you fumbled on third-and-four? I was looking at the film, and it's clear to me what you did wrong."

Piper wanted to take his head off, but her iron-willed lover had himself back under control, so she went over to join the girl-women.

They were all legs and breasts, lithe and perfect, even without their heavy eye makeup, belly chains, and the elaborate manicures that left their hands as useless as the feet of aristocratic women had once been in China. They didn't seem interested in talking to each other, but they responded to Piper's conversational gambits.

Two were from Miami and the third was Puerto Rican. One had recently graduated from high school, another was working on her GED, and the third had dropped out of college freshman year. They hadn't known each other until three days ago, when one of the prince's aides had spotted them on the beach and invited them to be the prince's "guests" for the week, promising them each a thousand dollars a day for their time. All three cast envious gazes toward Coop. She could see their curiosity about how someone who was neither lithe nor perfect had managed to attract his attention.

"We both like sports," Piper said, as if that explained it.

"I like sports," the one named Cierra offered wistfully.

"I thought it would be exciting being with a real prince," the Puerto Rican beauty said, "but it's kind of boring."

"He can't get it up without porn," the recent high school graduate and only brunette whispered.

Piper didn't want to hear the details of the odious prince's sex life, and she decided to test the waters. "Coop seems to like him," she lied. "He even gave him his Super Bowl ring."

The recent high school graduate rolled her eyes. "We know. He brags about it."

"Really?" Did that mean he hadn't yet discovered it was a fake? Piper pretended to adjust her sunglasses. "He's not wearing it. I guess it's too heavy."

The girl shrugged.

"He's got small hands," Cierra said.

"Small everything," the other blonde said.

They laughed, as worldly wise as the most practiced courtesans.

"He put it on my big toe," Cierra announced. "Last night."

"I'll bet it fit better than on his skinny finger," the brunette said.

"He told me he's going to have it sized." Cierra yawned. "Like I care."

Piper pretended to adjust her swimsuit straps. So, the Prince didn't know it wasn't the real thing. But the jeweler would as soon as he saw it, and he would certainly pass on that information.

The girls had fallen silent again, and Piper tried to sort out her thoughts. If the prince thought the ring was genuine, he couldn't be the person threatening Coop. But the fake ring was still a ticking time bomb. Coop should have bribed the guy some other way, but no. Coop believed he was invincible.

She rose from the chaise. Wrapping her makeshift sarong around her waist, she wandered over to the men. She took pleasure in interrupting the prince's lecture on how quarterbacks gave away the play by staring down the pass receiver, a mistake Coop had undoubtedly corrected before he'd left high school.

Coop had his game face on. Just barely. She touched his shoulder. "I'm going to take advantage of the gym. I'll see you later."

He regarded her suspiciously, but with lunch being laid in front of him, he couldn't easily excuse himself to go with her.

As soon as she was out of sight, she bypassed the gym and slipped up the steps. At the top, she ran into a uniformed crew member. She smiled, one more guest exploring the ship. "I can't believe you get to work here. Everything is so beautiful."

"Yes, madam."

"Is there really a nightclub on the ship? That's so amazing. I'd love to see it."

"On the third deck. I'll show you the elevator."

"Oh, no. I can find it myself. I want to see the salon first. Who knows if I'll get a chance to visit a ship like this again?"

"As you wish." He gestured toward the stern.

In the main salon, another crew member was vacuuming the largest Persian rug Piper had ever seen, spoiling any chance Piper had to sneak up the main staircase to the prince's private quarters on the top deck. The man turned off the vacuum and nodded politely. Piper babbled about how fantastic the ship was, speculated on how much it must have cost, and finally moved toward the elevator. There was no button for the top deck, so she hit the one for the third.

It opened onto a triangular room with a small dance floor, a disco ball, and ocean views. A door on one side of the bar took her into a longer corridor, where she discovered a service door that connected the decks for the crew.

As her foot hit the first tread, she heard someone enter the stairwell below. She rushed to the top, moving as soundlessly as she could, and slipped out into a mercifully empty service corridor for the fourth deck.

A door at the end opened into a small kitchen. She passed through it into a dining room and through that into a room dominated by a giant television screen. Behind her, she heard voices. She dashed through the closest door and found herself in the prince's bedroom.

It was almost comically overdecorated, but the ceiling mirror above the bed curtailed any amusement. Behind her, the voices were coming closer, speaking a language she couldn't understand. She dove for what she hoped was the closet.

It turned out to be little more than a shallow niche holding racks of shoes. She squeezed into the tiny space between the racks and the door. The darkness was thick and claustrophobic, smelling too strongly of musk, leather, and something overly sweet.

The voices were in the bedroom now. The edges of the shelves dug into her spine. If they opened the shoe closet door, they'd see her right away, and if that happened, she could very well end up dead in the ocean.

Coop would be beyond pissed.

*

Coop waved away the cigar Aamuzhir offered. Where the hell was Piper? Not in the gym, that was for damned sure. Her workouts mainly consisted of some halfhearted push-ups and a couple of laps around the block.

This trip had been a colossal waste of time. Aamuzhir had actually bragged to him about the good deal he'd made trading an insignificant servant girl for the championship ring. Whatever other sleazy things Aamuzhir had done, he wasn't the one after Coop.

The prince pulled a cigar from the jeweled box on the table and pointed it directly at the three women by the pool, as if they were inanimate objects. "Feel free to enjoy yourself, my friend. They're not as young as you might wish, but they're very pliable."

Coop had to steady himself. Those girls barely looked eighteen. But as satisfying as it would be to beat the crap out of this degenerate, he needed to wipe him from his life forever or Pipe would never get off his back about that ring. "Afraid my days of horn-doggin' it are over," he said. "I'm about to be a married man."

"You Americans," Aamuzhir said with lofty amusement. "So provincial."

"You sound like my buddy Pete. Nothing could ever make that guy settle down. He doesn't think anybody else should, either."

"That's not an option for most of us," the prince said on a thin trail of cigar smoke.

Coop felt pity for Aamuzhir's wives. "Yeah, Pete's a real character. I guess you could technically say he's a mercenary."

"Mercenary?" That piqued the prince's interest.

"He's fought in Africa, the Middle East. Who knows where else? He has a real talent for explosives. The bigger the target, the better." He leaned closer. "Do you know, he once blew a boat about this size straight out of the Gulf of Aden?" He forced a chuckle. "That's the kind of guy who's a good friend to have on your side. If anybody ever tried to screw me over, Pete would take care of them long before I could. Dude's crazy, but you gotta love his loyalty."

While Aamuzhir listened, Coop went on, extolling the nonexistent Pete's destructive skills, right along with his personal loyalty. Aamuzhir wasn't into subtlety, and Coop laid it on thick, wanting to make sure he'd recall this conversation if he figured out Coop had dumped a fake ring on him. When Coop felt he'd gone far enough, he pushed back his chair. "Now if you'll excuse me, I'm gonna make sure my fiancée didn't get lost."

The prince was not happy about losing Coop's attention, but Coop had done his job and didn't care. He nodded at the women who were watching him from their chaises just as Piper appeared. Her cheeks were flushed, and she was breathing faster than normal. He didn't like it.

"There you are, sweetheart." He pulled out his phone and sent a quick text to the launch owner. "I know you're having a great time, but we need to be heading back soon."

"Do we have to?" The way she turned it into a whine told him she was as ready as he to get off this ship of fools.

"We have a meeting with our wedding planner," he said. "Remember?"

Other than a slight narrowing around her eyes, she didn't flinch. "I was all for eloping to city hall," she said. "You're the one who has to have pink doves and flower girls."

He couldn't help but grin. He'd had enough contact with Aamuzhir to last him forever, and he dragged her to the pool, where he intended to keep them both until the launch arrived.

*

They couldn't talk privately on the launch, but as soon as they reached the Setai, Pipe tried to make a getaway. "I need some exercise. I'm taking a beach walk. See you later." She peeled off from him, her dress swishing around her thighs.

He had her arm before she could reach the sidewalk. "A walk sounds good. I'll come with you."

"No need," she said brightly. "Why don't you call some of your friends?"

"Why don't I not?"

"Fine. I didn't feel like walking anyway."

"Good. Because you're not going anywhere." He led her into the hotel, but on his way to the elevator bank, he changed direction. Once he got her near that bed, she'd make him forget they needed to talk, so instead, he steered her to a seating niche.

✶

The Setai's Asian-inspired courtyard was an oasis of luxurious, lemongrass-scented calm with low couches that seemed to float on the shallow water of the central serenity pool. Except for the manicured palms and the single orange centered on each side table, the space was a composition of every shade of gray, from charcoal to pearl. The only sounds came from the distant murmur of voices and the calming trickle of running water, but not even the peace of their surroundings could convince Piper this would go well.

Coop folded himself next to her on the couch. "Considering how useless this trip was, I don't see what you're trying to avoid, so spit it out. What don't you want to tell me?"

"Not entirely useless," she replied carefully. "We've eliminated one more suspect. Since the prince is still showing off your ring, he has no motive to attack you."

"Yet you disappeared."

"I wanted to look around."

"Look around where?"

She'd done what she thought she had to, but he wouldn't see it that way, and she was having misgivings. "Aamuzhir's bedroom. It gave me the creeps."

He snapped to attention. "You were in his bedroom? Where anyone could have walked in on you?"

She shrugged. By the time she got out of that claustrophobic shoe closet, she had ridges in her back from the shelf edges. Fortunately, she'd found what she was looking for before the crew members returned. "He has some disgusting things in that room."

"Stop hedging."

She reached into her tote for the zebra-striped scarf she'd used as a sarong. He watched as she carefully unfolded it. Inside was his reproduction ring.

He sat up straighter. "What are you doing with that?"

The courtyard was no longer so peaceful, but she reminded herself she'd done what was best. "One of his girlfriends told me he was getting ready to have it sized to fit his finger. Any jeweler would know right away that it's not genuine and pass on the news. So I took it. Aamuzhir might be a weasel, but he's a weasel with unlimited funds, and you can't have this hanging over your head for the rest of your life."

He was staring at her as though she'd stepped in from another planet. "You stole the ring?"

"I had to."

He looked more horrified than angry. "You realize if he doesn't figure out you're responsible, he'll blame one of those girls or someone on his crew. Do you have any idea what he might do to them?"

"He won't do anything."

"You don't know that."

"I kind of do." She made herself meet his eyes. "I . . . left a substitute."

"I'm not following you."

"The real thing," she said in a rush.

He cocked his head. "You couldn't have. The real ring is in my bedroom safe."

She didn't say anything. Just sat there and waited for him to figure it out.

"Piper . . ." His voice was a slow tsunami relentlessly rolling toward the shore.

"I had to put an end to this. He had to be neutralized."

"So you . . ."

She took a deep breath. "I took the fake and gave him the real thing."

The tsunami hit the shore. "You cracked my safe!"

"Not technically." Duke had introduced her to the world of locks—the way the tumblers, drive cams, and wheel flies worked. She'd celebrated her fifteenth birthday by cracking his safe, but breaking into Coop's had required only a little trial and error. His combination had turned out to be his high school, college, and pro jersey numbers. She'd been in and out of the safe before he'd made coffee. "Your combination was easy," she said.

"You got into my safe and stole my Super Bowl ring." Disbelief etched every word. "Then you took it to that bastard's yacht, sneaked into his bedroom, and exchanged the copy for the real thing?"

"You never wear it," she said, more unsure by the second of the wisdom of what she'd done. "I'll make it right, Coop. I don't know how, but I will. This had to stop for your own good."

"I'd already handled it!" He shot up from the couch, took a step away, then came right back at her. "While you were breaking and entering, I neutralized the son of a bitch. And I did it *without* handing over my ring!"

"What do you mean you neutralized him?"

He told her. Spitting out the words. Telling her about his nonexistent mercenary friend and the implied threat he'd delivered. Growing more and more furious with each word. "You stepped so far across the line you're in another universe."

"Coop, I—"

He leaned forward. In her face. "You have no idea what I went through to earn that ring. The drills, the two-a-days. The surgeries. Watching tape at four in the morning before anybody else saw it. Beating the coaches to the office. I studied fucking *thermodynamics*!"

"I didn't—"

"I earned that ring with blood and brains and more pain than you can imagine." The ferocity he unleashed had built his legend, but she'd never imagined it unleashed on her. "I've played in hundred-degree heat, in weather so cold my hands were numb. Do you know what I did to get ready to play when it was that cold? I held my hands in ice water—kept them there—just so I could get used to the feeling. And I smiled while I did it, and do you know why? Because I wanted to win. Because I wanted to make my life mean something!"

She came to her feet, her heart in her throat. "I'm—"

He stormed off, leaving her alone in the middle of a tranquil courtyard that smelled of oranges and lemongrass.

17

The drinks in the sports bar were cheap, the tourists few, and the locals uninterested in a woman sitting in the corner staring blindly at a televised soccer game being played somewhere in the world. It was two in the morning. A few men had approached her, but Piper had turned such blank eyes on them that they'd quickly left her alone.

She was lower than low, and now she was doing what all messed-up detectives did when they were lost. She was getting drunk.

She should never have taken his ring. She wouldn't have if she'd been smart enough to come up with another plan. But she hadn't been smart enough—not as smart as he'd been. Some detective she was turning out to be. And now here she sat, drowning her ineptitude in liquor.

She polished off her third drink. Ordered a fourth. She was

swilling old-fashioneds, but with no cherry, no orange, straight bourbon whiskey, extra hard on the bitters.

Duke Dove would never have done anything so half-brained. But then, Duke had been a pro, while she was still an amateur.

Her fresh drink arrived. She thought she might be getting double vision, but she sipped it anyway. The ice cubes clinked against the side of her glass as the chair next to her squeaked on the wooden floor. She didn't look up. "Get lost."

A familiar hand—a familiar, ringless hand—plunked a bottle of Sam Adams on the table. Another mistake on her part—asking the hotel doorman for directions to the nearest cheap bar. She'd never thought Coop would follow her.

She stared up at the soccer game. "I'm not a team player," she finally said, her speech only slightly slurred.

"I've noticed." The words crackled with hostility.

Her fresh glass sported a waxy lipstick imprint that hadn't come from her. She took a sip from the other side. "I don' know how to be."

"You against the world, right?"

"Tha's the way it's always been." She stuck her index finger in her drink and shifted around the ice cubes. "Today I hit the downside."

"Way down."

"I'm not looking for a pass, if tha's what you're thinking. I did something stupid because I din't have a better idea. I'll figure out how to pay you back."

He scraped his thumbnail down the middle of the beer label, ripping it in two. "Like you said. Not a team player."

She couldn't take it any longer, and she began to stand so she could escape to the ladies' room. When she wobbled, he caught her arm and steered her back into her chair.

"Do not be nice to me," she said fiercely. "I screwed up, and I know it."

"Yeah, you did." His jaw set in that way he had when he was furious. "Here's the most challenging part of being a leader. Understanding you may not always know what's best for the team."

"Right now, all I know is I have a client—or I used to have one—who's being threatened, and I don' have any idea who's behind it."

That wasn't a great way to try to salvage her job—a job she didn't deserve to hold on to—and he didn't reassure her. Instead, he pushed back his chair. "You're going back to the hotel."

✶

He had to get rid of her. Coop knew exactly how it felt to call an audible and have it backfire, but Pipe had thrown out the whole damned playbook, and that meant she was out.

The wheels of the 747 hit the tarmac at O'Hare, but she slept through it. She was impulsive, but she wasn't stupid, and she had to know what was coming—had to know he couldn't keep her around. He had no room for a blue-eyed badass who went off half-cocked doing whatever she damn well pleased.

Yet, despite the fact that he couldn't trust her judgment, he also trusted her more than anyone he'd ever known. No person he'd ever worked with had cared more about his welfare. Sure, his teammates and coaches had cared, but they'd had ulterior motives. Piper, on the other hand, would protect him in her own screwball way even if he weren't paying her a dime. Because that's the way she was made. Loyal to the end. And that's what this was. The end.

The plane pulled up to the gate, and she began to stir. Being her lover made this more complicated than it should be. He'd known the affair was a mistake, but he'd gone ahead and done it anyway. Now he had to break it off and fire her.

He'd made tough calls before, but none as tough as this.

*

WHAT'S BUGGING COOPER GRAHAM?

Cockroaches! Thousands of them are swarming the former Stars quarterback's hot new nightspot, Spiral. "They're everywhere," an associate who asked to remain anonymous says. "I've never seen anything like it."

The club is closed while exterminators try to eradicate the vermin, but whether the party crowd will return is the big question. Maybe Spiral should be renamed Death Spiral?

The news was all over the Internet. Piper sat at her office desk and buried her still-throbbing head in her hands. She only vaguely remembered collapsing on the hotel room couch last night, but she definitely remembered the strain between them at the airport. They'd barely spoken.

She wished he'd fired her on the plane so they could get it over with, but he hadn't. Since they'd been lovers, he'd do it more carefully. He'd probably tell her she could keep the apartment for a while. He'd almost surely offer her a generous severance. The thought of his magnanimity made her want to choke.

She smacked herself in the cheek—a really bad idea, considering her jackhammer of a hangover. Until he fired her, she had a job, and she'd keep doing it right to the bitter end. She owed him that much and more.

The online smears, a mugging, a tire slashing, and a drone. It didn't jibe. And who'd called INS—or was that even relevant? As for the cockroaches . . . Tony had told Spiral's employees the club had to be closed for repairs to the cooling system, so the leak about the infestation hadn't come from the staff. Coop had moved Karah and Jada to a hotel while the fumigation was going on. They knew the truth, but they also knew to keep it to themselves. Someone from the exterminating company could easily have blabbed, but Piper found it more likely that the same person who'd dumped the bugs had made sure the word got out.

She'd hit a dead end, and she had no idea where to go next, other than to make certain the club had a better video security system. She called Tony to talk about it. If it had been last week, she'd have talked to Coop directly, but it wasn't last week.

The rest of Saturday and Sunday passed without word from Coop. She couldn't go back to her apartment until the fumigation was done, so she slept on her office couch, not just because she didn't want to impose on Jen or Amber, but also because she was too depressed to be around people.

The flyers she'd distributed netted a Monday-morning phone call from a suspicious wife, and by the next day, Piper had the unpleasant task of confirming the woman's suspicions. Duke had been right. Once a wife got around to hiring a detective, she pretty much already knew the truth.

Helping others was supposed to be at least a partial cure for depression, so she tried to come up with someone she could help whose initials weren't C.G. She thought of Jen's problems with Dumb Ass and poked around the darker corners of the Internet for a few hours but didn't come up with anything interesting.

Wednesday arrived, and the owner of an air duct cleaning service called. He'd heard Piper was good at handling rat-ass employees who claimed to have been hurt on the job but were goddam liars. The guy sounded like a jerk, but Piper drove to Rogers Park to meet him anyway. On the way back, Tony called to tell her the club was reopening that night, and he needed her back on duty.

"Did you check with Coop about that?" she asked.

"About what?"

"About me coming back."

"Why wouldn't you come back?"

"Never mind. I'll talk to him."

She ran Coop to ground in his office at Spiral that evening. She hadn't seen the point in changing into her nighttime work clothes, and she was still wearing jeans along with a bulky gunmetal-gray sweater that was the closest thing she had to armor.

He was sitting at the desk with his ankles propped on top and idly tossing a softball back and forth. All the lights were off except the desk lamp, which cast the side of his face in shadow. He looked up as she came in, then returned his attention to the softball.

She gathered her courage. "Stop being such a chickenshit and get it over with. You know you have to fire me, and I'd appreciate it if you'd do it now so I can stop thinking about it."

He pitched the ball from his right hand to his left.

She curled her fingers around the cuffs of her sweater. "I know it's a lot to ask, but I'd like to keep the apartment a little longer. I promise, you'll never see me."

He tossed the ball back.

"I'll give my files to whoever you hire to take my place," she said. "And you'd better hire someone, Coop, because this isn't over." She'd stay on the case even after he fired her. She owed him answers. And a Super Bowl ring . . .

He dropped his feet to the floor, but whatever he was about to say was lost as Jada burst into the office, her Nerf gun nowhere in sight. "Mom was in an accident!" she cried. "She's in the hospital!"

Coop shot up from his desk. "Where is she? What happened?"

"I don't know." Jada began to sob. "A nurse called me from the emergency room. What if she dies?"

Coop grabbed his jacket. "Let's go."

*

They had to take her Sonata because Coop had lent out his Audi for the evening. To Karah.

They found her hooked up to an IV and a monitor. Her curly dark hair spilled out in a lopsided corona around the gauze bandage wrapping her head, and more bandaging protected her left wrist and arm. Two police officers stood at the side of her bed.

Jada ran to her mother. Karah winced as she drew her daughter to her breast. "It's okay, baby. It's okay." Over the top of Jada's head, Karah saw Coop, and her face collapsed. "I wrecked your car, Coop. After everything you've done for me."

"Don't worry about the car," Coop said. "As long as you're okay."

Karah slipped her hand into Jada's hair. "I should never have taken it. I thought I was being so careful."

"Cars can be replaced," Coop said. "You can't."

The officers were doing their best to keep their professional cool with Cooper Graham in the room. The taller of the two turned to him. "She said you gave her permission to take your car?"

Coop nodded. "Hers wouldn't start, and I was going to be at my club all night, so I didn't need it."

"My professor invited some of us to her house up in Wadsworth,"

Karah said, "and I really wanted to go. If only I'd stayed home." She gazed at Coop again. "I'm sorry."

"No more apologies. This is why I have insurance."

"Tell us again what you remember," the second officer said.

"The road was dark, and there wasn't much traffic." Karah looked over at Coop. "I wasn't speeding. I swear."

"I've seen you drive," Coop said with a forced smile. "I believe you."

"I saw headlights behind me, but I didn't pay much attention. It happened so fast. The headlights came closer, and I slowed down so the driver could pass. He pulled out, and— He must have turned off his lights because everything went dark. His car swerved and hit the side of the Audi. Hit hard. I . . . I lost control. I skidded and hit something. What did I hit?"

"A utility pole," the taller cop said.

Karah's hand went to her cheek. "Whoever hit me didn't even stop to see if I was okay."

Piper and Coop exchanged glances, then Piper moved closer to the bed. "You said 'he.' Did you get a look at the driver?"

"No. I don't know for sure it was a man. That's a country road, and there aren't any streetlights. It was too dark to see anything."

Piper glanced over at Coop, who threw her a keep-your-mouth shut glare in return. The police needed to know about the attacks on him, but she was smarter now than she'd been a few days ago, and she'd talk to him first.

The police continued to question Karah, but other than a vague sense that the car was large—maybe even a truck—she didn't know more.

She wouldn't be released from the hospital until the next day, and Piper told her she'd sleep at their place tonight to be with Jada.

Coop had to get back to the club for the reopening, and Piper followed him out into the hallway. The ding of call buttons and beep of monitors, the smell of antiseptic and sickness brought back those awful weeks before Duke had died.

"I want you on the floor tomorrow night," he said.

She shook off the memories. "I . . . still have a job?"

"You're the only female bouncer I have," he said grimly.

That wasn't what she was asking, and he knew it. She dodged a food cart. "I'm taking your advice about being a team player," she said more firmly.

He headed toward the elevator bank. "Glad to hear it."

"I'm giving you a chance to tell me why I shouldn't talk to the police about the attacks on you before I go ahead and do it."

He jammed his finger at the elevator button. "That sounds more like an ultimatum than being a team player."

"Baby steps."

A long exhale. "I've had enough bad publicity with the bug infestation. I don't want this splashed all over the papers, too."

"I understand. But the Audi has tinted windows. The road was dark. We both know what happened tonight was intended for you."

His jaw set. "I should have anticipated something like this. Instead, I lent her my car. If I'd thought for a minute . . ." The elevator doors opened. "Leave the police out of this. That's an order."

The doors slid shut between them.

Piper got Jada off to school the next morning, then called Eric. He still hadn't caught on to the fact that she wasn't interested in dating him, and he agreed to take her to the lot where the Audi had been towed. As she photographed the streaks of black paint the mystery vehicle had left behind, she knew that Karah's accident was all that had kept Coop from firing her. As it was, she didn't know whether he only intended her to work as a bouncer. Not that it made any difference. Nothing could make her give up now.

Eric propped his elbow on the Audi's undamaged roof, the morning sun glinting off the lenses of his aviators. "There's this new Italian place I like on Clark. How about it?"

He was a nice guy, and she needed to be honest. "I can't date you, Eric."

"Whoa . . ."

"I'm an idiot, okay? Instead of being attracted to a solid, gorgeous guy like you, I got myself involved with a—a—" *A solid, gorgeous guy like Cooper Graham* . . . ". . . with someone else. It's over, but I need some space. As I said, I'm an idiot."

He squinted against the morning sun. "Cooper Graham. I knew it."

She swallowed. "Do you seriously think he'd be interested in me?"

"Why not?"

This didn't seem the time to talk about men being attracted to her merely because she was one of the guys. "I'll fix you up with someone."

That was one too many blows to his ego. "I don't need anybody fixing me up."

"Not even with Jennifer MacLeish? Chicago's favorite meteorologist?"

"You know her?"

"Yep." She'd have to persuade Jen, but they just might hit it off. "We can still help each other out now and then, though. Don't you agree?"

"How do you mean?"

She hoped she'd read his ambitious nature correctly. "I'm an ordinary citizen. I can legally go places a police officer can't, and that might be useful to you someday."

He was listening. "Maybe."

"And I'd like to be able to call on you occasionally. This accident, for example . . . I'm concerned about Coop."

Eric wasn't all good looks. He also had a brain. "You think whoever did this was after Coop?"

"I'm keeping an open mind." Not so very open.

"Intriguing." He stuck his thumb in his belt. "About this date with Jennifer MacLeish . . ."

*

The former air duct cleaning employee she was supposed to be investigating lived with his girlfriend and baby in her parents' home. Piper followed the family to Brown's Chicken, but as they went inside, she started worrying about Coop. He should be at the gym now, right on schedule. A schedule anyone with half a brain could figure out. Her anxiety got the best of her, and she hurried back to her car.

His Tesla was in the gym lot. She took a broken-down baby stroller somebody had put out at the curb from her trunk and pushed it, wobbly wheel and all, across the street. When Coop finally came out, she watched his reflection in a music store window. The stroller had done the trick, and he didn't spare her a look.

She trailed him to Heath's house, not caring if he spotted her. Once he was safely inside, she returned to her South Side stakeout and found the family in a hardscrabble neighborhood park.

She settled on a bench and watched them. Only the mother

picked up their toddler, but that might only prove Piper's target was a tuned-out father. Still, her gut told her the guy's injury was real, and sure enough, when the toddler took a tumble, he swooped up the baby, then clutched his back.

The owner of the air duct cleaning company was as much of a jerk as she'd originally suspected, and he wasn't happy with either her report or the single photo she'd managed to take. She could easily have stretched out the job by playing on his suspicions, but instead, like the great businesswoman she wasn't, she convinced him he'd be wasting his money.

✶

A few hours later, she picked up Karah from the hospital and drove her home where she fixed them all dinner. A couple of Band-Aids had replaced the bandage around her head, and her arm was sprained, but not broken. She could have been hurt so much worse.

As they ate, Jada talked about a report she was doing on child sex trafficking. Karah wasn't happy to learn that the curriculum at her daughter's parochial school included the seamiest side of street life, but Jada kept going. "Do you know there are, like, girls younger than me right here in the United States that are—"

Karah reached out to brush a lock of hair from Jada's cheek. "Let's talk about this when we're not eating dinner."

"But, Mom . . ." Jada's amber eyes flashed with outrage. "Some of these girls are, like, being raped a bunch of times every day by these old guys, but when the police show up, they arrest the girls for prostitution. Girls my age!"

Piper had done some reading about child sex trafficking and found the subject so disturbing that she'd pushed it into her mental back closet. But witnessing a fifteen-year-old's outrage made her ashamed of her apathy.

Jada stopped eating. "They're victims of this horrible sex abuse, and it's so not right for them to get arrested. We're going to write letters to Congress."

"Good for you," Piper said.

Karah squeezed her daughter's hand. "I'll write a letter, too."

After dinner, Piper changed for work. She dreaded going back to Spiral, dreaded anything that would put her near Coop and closer to getting permanently fired. As she deserved . . .

The house was packed. Coop and Tony had pulled out all the stops to overcome the bad publicity from the cockroach invasion—specials on top-shelf drinks and lots of celebrities scheduled to show up all week: football players, actors, and a beautiful country singer.

Jonah greeted Piper with a grunt and a rough slap on the back, his simian version of an olive branch. She gave him an elbow to the gut but was glad she didn't put any force behind it because at least one of the bouncers stayed close to Coop all evening, something Coop didn't look pleased about.

Deidre Joss showed up again, this time alone. She and Coop disappeared. When half an hour passed and he hadn't returned, Piper started to worry.

She checked the alley first. New security cameras had been installed as she'd recommended, and Coop's Tesla sat there unharmed. He must be in his office. But what if Deidre were still with him? Piper couldn't imagine anything worse than walking in on the two of them doing whatever they might be doing, and she knocked loudly on the door. When it swung open, Coop looked irritated. "You need something?"

"Security check. I wanted to make sure no one was in here who shouldn't be."

"Is that Piper?" Deidre said from inside the room.

Coop opened the door wider. Behind him, Piper could see Deidre standing near the couch, her hair a perfect waterfall, her dancer's carriage upright, her stilettos arranged in third position. She even wore a softly draped ballerina-pink dress.

Deidre was exactly the kind of high-achieving woman Coop was most attracted to, and it wasn't hard to imagine the two of them married. In between board meetings, Deidre would bear him three beautiful children, and on weekends, she'd prepare gourmet meals. Piper wondered if Coop would someday look back on his fling with her and wonder how he could have been so crazy.

"I've been looking for a chance to talk to you," Deidre said. "Come in."

Piper reluctantly did as she was told.

"According to Noah, I owe you an apology," Deidre said. "He told me in no uncertain terms that I made life difficult for you by not letting you tell Cooper I was the one who'd hired you."

His name is Coop, Piper thought, even as she plastered on a smile. "No harm done."

"Other than my threatening to sue her," Coop said.

"Oh, no! You didn't." Deidre looked horrified. "I am sorry, Piper. I didn't know that."

She was so damned nice. And smart. And successful.

Piper hated her.

Deidre directed her attention back to Coop. "I have to be up early, so I need to get home. Good talk." She extended her arm to shake his hand, when what she really wanted to do was give him a long, deep good-bye kiss. Or maybe Piper was projecting.

One thing she did know: Coop genuinely liked Deidre. And why wouldn't he?

"See that Deidre gets to her car safely, will you, Piper?" He squeezed Deidre's hand. "Apologies, Deidre, but I have to get back on the floor."

Deidre smiled. "One of the things I most admire about you."

Along with his abs, his smile, that incredible mouth . . . *Which I've sampled, and you haven't.*

Piper's self-disgust hit a new high . . . or low, depending on how she looked at it.

She escorted Deidre from the club to the lot across the street where she'd left her BMW. "You really didn't need to walk me to my car," Deidre said.

"It's nice to get some fresh air."

"Did you know that Noah's become a big fan of yours?"

"Really?"

Deidre stopped and smiled. "You're the first woman he's shown any interest in since his divorce."

Piper made a noncommittal murmur.

"Girlfriend to girlfriend . . . He's solid. Ambitious. I don't know what I'd have done without him after Sam's death. He can be a little intense, I'll give you that, but maybe you should let him take you out to dinner and you can see if you hit it off."

"I don't really have any time to date now."

She tilted her head. "Because of Cooper? I heard a rumor that the two of you have more than a professional relationship."

Piper hadn't seen this coming. "Fascinating what people will say."

"Is it true?"

"You don't believe in subtlety, do you?"

"Not since I lost my husband. Hell of a way to learn how short life can be." She shifted her clutch to her other hand and waited, regarding Piper in an open, patient manner. "Well?"

Piper began walking toward the BMW. "I think you probably know by now that I never comment on my clients."

"I respect that." The locks on her car clicked. She opened the driver's door, then turned back to Piper. "But if it is true . . . I like him a lot, and I'm going to give you a run for your money." She didn't say it in a bitchy way, more as a straight-up point of information. "And if it's not true, tell him I'm low maintenance and fabulous."

Piper laughed. Whether from surprise or amusement, she didn't know. What she did know was that Deidre Joss was a force of nature.

Deidre pulled out of the parking lot. Piper crossed the street back to the club, barely avoiding a Lexus whose driver thought he owned the right-of-way. It felt good to have a target for her frustration, and she flipped him the bird.

*

The next night was a Friday, and the club was even busier. She helped Ernie toss out some men who were making themselves obnoxious, ordered the servers to cut off a couple of overzealous dancers, and broke up a fight heading for the alley. She was proving to be an excellent bouncer. If only she were as good an investigator.

By the time she entered her apartment, she was dead on her feet. She peeled off her dress, tugged on her Bears T-shirt, and brushed her teeth. As she came out of the bathroom, she heard her door open. She peeked into the living room.

Coop had makeup smears on his sweater sleeve and lipstick on the side of his neck. He looked tired, disheveled, and irritable. "I'm too tired to drive home."

He'd been everywhere tonight, and she knew how tired he was, but she hardened her heart. "You can't stay here."

"Sure I can. It's my apartment."

He began emptying his pockets on the counter between the kitchen and living room, and she was temporarily distracted by what emerged: his cell, key fob, and a tampon wrapper with something written on it, probably a phone number.

Somebody had spilled a drink on him, and he smelled like liquor. "Coop, I'm serious. We're . . . over." She faltered on the word, but it had to be said. Their relationship was a train wreck. "Lovers need to be on equal footing, and we're not."

He took in her sleepwear. "Do you ever wash that T-shirt?"

"Frequently. I have more than one."

"Of course you do." He jerked his sweater over his head, filling the room with the scent of a dozen different perfumes. She spotted another lipstick mark on the opposite side of his neck. It was hard being Cooper Graham.

He would have already fired her if Karah hadn't been run off the road. He probably still would. "Did you hear me?"

"I'm taking a shower, then I'm going to bed." He headed for the bathroom. "Try your best not to jump me."

18

Piper settled into bed, turned out the light, and tucked the sheet around her. Her life was a mess. She was sleeping with her boss, or maybe her ex-boss, who might or might not also be her ex-lover, but then why was he here, and why was she letting him decide this anyway? She was too miserable about her life to have a good answer to anything. She had no financial security. She was virtually homeless. And, in the only case she had that mattered, she was proving to be a shitty investigator.

The shower stopped running, the door squeaked open, and the mattress sagged. She moved as far away from him as she could, but he made no attempt to touch her. She was both offended and comforted.

She awoke in the middle of a blazingly erotic dream to find him inside her. She was wet and yielding, her body thrumming. His weight pressed down heavy, as if he were still half-asleep, both of them more animal than human. By the end, they were awake, not speaking, moving apart and finally falling back to sleep in the mess of what had happened.

*

When Coop awakened the next morning, he was alone and hungover. He dragged his arm across his eyes. For the first time since the club had opened, he'd gotten drunk. It had started a few hours before closing when he'd had a couple of drinks, then a couple more, a few more after that, until he didn't trust himself to drive home. He'd never been a big drinker, preferring pot in his younger days and, as he'd gotten older, happy with a couple of beers. But last night, as he'd watched Piper moving around the club, things had gotten away from him.

She was everywhere at once—keeping an eye on the guests, the servers, and on him. She'd gotten her way with the bouncers, and one of them was always nearby. It was easier not having to watch his back, but he objected to the principle. Just because he was no longer in the game didn't mean he couldn't watch out for himself. He'd growled at Jonah to call off his boys, but the son of a bitch was more afraid of her than of him, and nothing changed.

He wished he could kick her out of this apartment. He needed the place for nights like this. He needed his life back, the way it had been before she'd barged into it.

Something twisted in his gut, the thing he didn't want to look at. The thing that every day kept pushing closer to the surface. And for no reason. He had everything he wanted. Money. Reputation. He felt physically better than he had in years. As for Spiral . . . The club had been at capacity since they'd reopened three nights ago. And best of all, Deidre had invited him to her farm next Monday.

The playful way she'd delivered the invitation suggested his waiting was about to be over. Everything was going his way.

And yet . . . He wasn't happy.

It was because of Piper.

She had a dream—the same way he did. A single-minded focus that got her out of bed every morning and drove her through the day. A passion. So why did he feel as if his life had become a cloudy reflection in the mirror of hers?

She appeared in the doorway wearing jeans and a snarl. Her hair was still damp, so she must have showered, although he hadn't heard her. She stood there looking at him. "I can't do this anymore, Coop."

He pushed himself up from the pillows. "Could you let me wake up first?"

"I don't sleep with men who don't respect me."

That infuriated him. "Who says I don't respect you?"

"How could you after the way I screwed up?"

"You sure as hell did." He jumped naked out of bed and stormed into the bathroom, where he threw himself into the shower again. He hated being backed into a corner, and that's what she was doing.

He hadn't been able to fire her because he trusted her—not with his ring, that was for sure—but with his life. Somehow, she'd become the juice that made things worthwhile. Maybe that explained why he was so unhappy.

All his clean clothes were in his office, and he came out in a towel. She, of course, was waiting for him.

"I apologize," she said.

"You should. Sometimes I think you live to give me a hard time."

"I'm not apologizing for that. I'm apologizing for trying to have a straightforward conversation with you before you've had your coffee." She held out a steaming mug.

As he took it from her, he realized she was staring at something. Him. It was his chest again. She was a sucker for his chest. And he was only wearing a towel. He took a long swig from the mug and let her look.

She dragged her eyes back to his face. "I don't understand why you haven't fired me, and I don't like feeling that maybe you're keeping me on because I'm putting out."

She might as well have slapped him. "That's bullshit! What kind of scum do you think I am?"

"I don't think you're scum at all."

"Then why would you say something like that?"

"Because I can't think of any other reason."

"How about this? You're the best bouncer I have."

Even as the words came out, he knew it was the wrong thing to say. She stared at him with the saddest face he'd ever seen, then she turned and walked away.

He stopped her as she snatched up her messenger bag to leave. "You are, Piper. But that's not why I didn't fire you." Hot coffee splashed on the back of his hand and he sucked it off. "I meant to fire you," he said, setting down his mug. "You made a big mistake, and I've been pissed. But the thing is . . . You're the underdog who's willing to work twice as hard as anybody else. And those have always been the kinds of players I like best on my team."

Until that moment, he hadn't been able to articulate it, even to himself, but now that he'd said it, he felt better.

She looked a little starry-eyed, which he liked, and then troubled, which he didn't like. "I appreciate that," she said. "But the brutal fact is that I'm no closer to getting to the bottom of this than I was when you hired me. And I have no idea what to do next."

"You'll figure it out."

"How can you say that?"

"Because that's what you do."

Coop's faith put a knot in her throat the size of a football. She carried it with her all weekend. She couldn't fail him. She couldn't. But then she wondered if her determination to prove herself to Coop was all that different from her never-ending battle to win Duke's approval. No, it was different. Duke's misguided fear for her safety had kept him from giving her the opportunity she'd craved—the opportunity he'd raised her to take on. Unlike her father, Coop had given her the chance Duke had withheld, and she couldn't disappoint him.

Monday morning found her in the main office building at the Stars Complex Headquarters in DuPage County. The team logo of three interlocking gold stars in a sky-blue circle was etched into the glass wall of the PR office—the wall that overlooked the building's main lobby where lighted niches protected by bulletproof glass displayed the team's major trophies and where visitors signed in at an impressive, crescent-shaped ivory granite reception desk.

With the football season in full swing, the PR office was humming with activity—phones ringing, computer screens glowing, people hurrying in and out. Coop had finally cleared the way for her to go through the mail that had accumulated for him, and a young publicist with cat's-eye makeup and an earnest manner showed her to the room's only empty desk and explained the procedure.

"We take care of most of Coop's fan mail. We mail out autograph cards, his FAQ, and we have a special package for kids who write him. We work with his agent on appearance requests. Even though he's retired, he still gets a lot of mail."

"Any of it hostile?"

"Not much. He got some his first season with the Stars after a couple of bad games. 'Go back to Miami.' That kind of thing. The fans didn't know he was playing with a broken finger."

"What about women?"

"Thongs, nude photos. We've pretty much seen it all. And I do mean all." She gestured toward the desk. "Go ahead. Take your time and let me know if you need anything else."

"Thanks."

Piper settled behind the pile of paper—both snail mail and e-mail printouts. The majority were requests for autographs and photos. Some of it was really sweet. Kids who idolized him. Fans who'd followed his career from the very beginning. One was from a man who'd lost his son in a car accident and found relief from his grief in remembering how his son had idolized Coop. Piper pulled that one out as something she thought Coop should personally respond to. There were also a number of notes from parents of athletically talented offspring looking for advice.

And the women. Photos accompanied letters that listed the sender's credentials to be Coop's next girlfriend: an athletic nature, a modeling career, a college degree in sports management, a super-special expertise in fellatio.

As Piper pondered that, she became aware of a subtle shift in the atmosphere of the room. She looked up.

In the doorway stood Phoebe Somerville Calebow, the owner of the Chicago Stars, the wife of the former head coach and current

Stars president Dan Calebow, the mother of four, and the single most powerful woman in the NFL, if not the universe.

Piper jumped to her feet as the Stars owner approached the very desk where Piper was sitting. "Mrs. . . . uh . . . Mrs. Calebow."

Phoebe Somerville Calebow took her in. "So you're Coop's detective."

The fact that Phoebe Calebow knew of her existence was so dumbfoundingly dumbfounding that Piper couldn't muster anything more than a shaky nod.

"My quarterbacks do tend to get involved with unusual women," she said.

Those involvements had been well publicized, and like everyone else in Chicago, Piper knew the history. Cal Bonner had married a world-renowned physicist. Kevin Tucker was married to a prize-winning children's book author. An eccentric artist had made an unlikely match with Dean Robillard. And it wasn't only the quarterbacks. The team's legendary wide receiver, Bobby Tom Denton, was married to the current mayor of Telarosa, Texas.

Mrs. Calebow gestured Piper back into her chair, then perched on the side of the desk. Middle age hadn't diminished her curvy, blond beauty, and not even her tortoiseshell smart-girl glasses could dilute her aura of ripe sexuality. "So what are your intentions toward my guy?"

Piper wasn't used to anyone intimidating her, but being in the presence of Phoebe Calebow was being in the presence of greatness. She swallowed. "I don't think I have any intentions."

Mrs. Calebow arched one beautifully shaped and very skeptical eyebrow.

"We're . . . That part is over," Piper said. "It's all professional now. I have a job to do. And . . . How did you know about me?"

"I keep track of my men," Mrs. Calebow said with a wry smile. "Do you read?"

"Read?"

"Books."

"Of course. Thrillers. Mysteries. Police procedurals. At least I did until the past month, when I started working so late." She babbled on. "I like biographies and autobiographies, too. But only about women. Which, I know, is sexist, but those are the stories that resonate with me. Oh, and cookbooks. I hate cooking but I like reading about it. And technology." She forced herself to shut up.

"Interesting." Mrs. Calebow uncoiled her legs from the desk corner, legs that could still have found a place in the Rockettes chorus line. "Nice meeting you, Ms. Dove."

She swept from the office, leaving Piper to wonder what had just happened.

*

Piper didn't leave the Stars headquarters until midafternoon, by which time she'd dug through all Coop's PR records. On her way to her car, she experienced her familiar frustration. Nothing she'd read had raised a red flag. As she eased onto the two-lane road marked STARS DRIVE, she once again tried to figure out what she was missing and once again came up empty.

Instead of heading east toward the city, she took the Reagan Tollway west. She hadn't seen Coop since their sleepover three nights ago, but she'd called him yesterday morning to make sure he wasn't planning to throw himself into any big crowds or take off on a solitary hike. "I'm going over to Heath and Annabelle's to watch the Stars game," he'd said.

She'd asked Coop why he didn't go to see the games in person. He'd pointed out how unfair it would be to the Stars' new quarterback having TV cameras track Coop's reaction to every play.

"Deidre's invited us both to an overnight house party at her farm on Monday night," he'd announced.

"That should make you happy."

"What will make me happy is getting a financial commitment from her."

"You're going ahead with it, then?" she'd said. "Building your empire."

"Of course I am. Why would you even ask?"

Because running a chain of nightclubs didn't seem right for Coop, but she'd held her tongue. She also hadn't mentioned that he could easily get a more personal commitment from Deidre. But he probably already knew that.

"I like Deidre," she'd said carefully. "Even though she fired me."

"I like her, too. A lot."

And why wouldn't he?

Piper got off at the Farnsworth exit and headed north. She didn't want to go to Deidre's overnight house party, but she also didn't want Coop out of her sight for two days, so she'd agreed to meet him there.

St. Charles was a pretty town on the Fox River about forty miles west of the Loop. The Joss family farm lay to the northwest, its entrance marked by stone pillars and a white rail fence. Burnished leaves from the trees lining the drive drifted over the hood of her car as she made her way to the large, two-story white house. She parked her car between Coop's Tesla and a red Lexus. This looked like a working farm, with a stable, barn, and paddock. The fields had been cleared for next year's planting.

Her only familiarity with country house parties came from reading English novels, but the farmhouse was distinctly American with its wide front porch and arrangements of multicolored pumpkins, corn sheaves, mums, and pots of ornamental kale at the top of the steps. A set of wooden rocking chairs with orange and brown cushions sat on each side of a hunter-green front door where a natural wreath of leaves, seedpods, and small gourds hung. It all belonged on a magazine cover.

A middle-aged housekeeper in jeans and a white T-shirt rescued her from an unfamiliar sense of yearning. "Everyone is out riding now," the housekeeper said as she showed Piper her room, "but they should be back soon. Feel free to explore."

Since she'd been sitting most of the day, she was happy to poke around the barn and the outbuildings. The housekeeper had told her that the farm grew corn, soybeans, and some wheat, but there was also a sizable vegetable garden where a few pumpkins remained on the vines, along with some cabbage, broccoli, and Swiss chard, a vegetable she wouldn't have recognized if Coop hadn't pointed it out in his garden. In the stable, three empty stalls filled with fresh beds of straw waited for their occupants to return.

She saw them before they saw her. Deidre rode a lively roan mare between Noah and Coop, who was on a dappled gray. With her upright carriage, dark hair knotted at the nape of her neck, riding hat, and breeches, she looked ready for a horse show. As for Coop . . . Piper had never seen him more comfortable. His body moved in perfect synchronicity with his mount, and she once again pondered how someone who so clearly belonged in the country was so at home in the big city.

As Piper stood inside the doorway, the stable hand who'd been listening to Lil Wayne in the corner got up to go to work. Coop dismounted as gracefully as he dodged defensive ends. Piper watched the way the denim tightened around his thighs and then made herself not watch.

After Deidre dismounted, Coop looped an arm across her shoulders. He looked like a man in love. Rumpled hair. Easy laugh. A dirty bomb exploded in Piper's heart.

He finally spotted her and released the arm he'd thrown around Deidre—not out of guilt but to pass the reins over to the stable hand. "You should have gotten here earlier, Pipe. We had a great ride."

"You're a natural, Cooper." Deidre's praise was straightforward, without a hint of girlishness. "I can tell you spent a lot of time on horseback when you were a kid."

"I never learned to ride pretty," he said, "but I got the job done."

Deidre gave him an open smile. "I think you ride very pretty."

Piper wanted to barf.

For the first time, she noticed Noah. His high-end suede jacket and ironed denim shirt suggested he'd have been much happier behind a desk.

It quickly became apparent that Deidre had planned a very small house party—only the four of them. Piper didn't need her detective skills to figure out that Deidre was playing matchmaker. Maybe she simply enjoyed fixing people up, or maybe she was hoping that Piper and Noah would hit it off so she'd have a clear path to Coop. But a relationship between Piper and Noah Parks would never happen. He was intelligent, and his squared-off profile wasn't unattractive, but he didn't seem to possess a shred of humor.

Coop gestured toward the field behind the garden. "How did your wheat do with all the rain this summer, Deidre?"

"I'm embarrassed to say that I don't know. We have a tenant who farms the place. When my husband was alive, he knew everything that happened here, but I only ride and relax."

"Sam loved the farm," Noah said. "It was in his family for three generations."

As they left the stable behind, Deidre talked about how she and her late husband had torn down the old farmhouse to build the new one. She spoke of Sam matter-of-factly. Deidre Joss was a woman who held her emotions close to her chest.

Noah fell in step next to Piper, and she did some not-so-subtle probing. "It has to be hard for Deidre. Losing her husband at such a young age. Snowmobile accident, right?"

"Driving too fast."

"What was he like?"

"Sam? Easygoing, fun to be around. A little irresponsible. Everybody liked him. Hard not to. They were only married five years."

"A good marriage?"

She expected Noah to freeze her out, but he didn't. "They were crazy about each other, but she was the one who had to do the heavy lifting."

They'd reached the house, and Deidre announced cocktails in an hour on the patio. "Coop, let me show you your room."

Which wouldn't be anyplace near Piper's.

She washed her face and put on a little makeup but didn't change from the slacks and sweater she'd worn to the Stars Complex. As she reached for her messenger bag to check her phone, she remembered she'd left it in her car and went downstairs to get it.

A light breeze ruffled the tree branches near the house. The smell of fall was hard in the air, a smell she loved. It was nearly dark, and the floodlights mounted on the corner of the barn shone on her Sonata, Coop's Tesla, and the Lexus. As she walked toward the cars, she noted the Lexus's license plate. ARARAT.

Overhead, an owl hooted and swooped toward a stand of trees beyond the barn. A wisp of memory tantalized her but wouldn't take shape. She reclaimed her bag and texted Jen to find out if she'd returned Eric's call. Then she made her way to the back of the house.

The three of them were seated around a blazing, stone fire pit. The patio had an outdoor kitchen with a built-in grill, a sink, and a tiled countertop. Garden torches illuminated the perimeter and cast a faint light over a swimming pool covered for the season. Noah was cross-examining Coop. ". . . and you've also gotten too much bad publicity. Forgive me for being blunt, but that's a sign of bad management."

"It's a sign of bad luck," Coop countered.

"You know I've been opposed to this from the beginning," Noah said. "I've never liked the idea of trusting this large an investment to the whims of professional athletes who already have more money than they can spend. Yourself excluded, of course."

"If that's what the plan was, you'd be right, Noah. But you keep missing the point. Athletes retire young. Sure, some of them are more than happy to spend their time going through their money, but those aren't the guys I'm after. I want the ones who are smart, ambitious, and out for a new challenge but not willing to bankroll themselves. There are a lot of them."

Deidre stayed silent, taking in both Coop's answers and Noah's questions. "It's too risky an investment for us," Noah said. "We don't know the industry, and we don't understand the market."

"Did you understand China's market for water-purification systems when you made that investment?" Coop turned to Deidre.

"Taking a few well-calculated risks makes business more interesting, doesn't it?"

Deidre spoke for the first time. "I like the idea of diversifying into the so-called sin industries, even though Noah has raised some good points. The fact that he's not often wrong has been my only hesitation."

"This time he's wrong," Coop countered. "And, Deidre, as much as I'm enjoying your hospitality . . . and as much as I'd like to work with you, it's time to make up your mind. I'll give you another couple of days. Then I'll have to move on."

Coop didn't want to move on. Piper knew that Deidre was the only partner he wanted.

Far from being rattled, Deidre smiled. "I don't think we'll need that long."

"Piper!" Noah came to his feet. "Let me get you something to drink. Cocktail? Wine?"

"I'll have a beer." She walked out into the torchlight. "Whatever Coop's drinking."

"You and Coop appear to have a lot of the same tastes. It's no surprise you like working together." Noah moved to the outdoor bar. "That's another question I have. You seem to be Coop's confidante . . ."

Was it her imagination, or did he veil that last word with all kinds of hidden meanings?

He pulled a frosted mug from the small built-in refrigerator. "We know he was a great quarterback, but is he a great businessman?"

Deidre showed her first sign of impatience. "How do you expect her to answer that?"

"In her normal straightforward fashion," Noah said. "Piper knows him better than either of us, and I've developed a healthy respect for her opinion. So tell us, Piper. Do you see Coop as a captain of industry?"

"I see Coop as being successful at whatever he sets his mind to," Piper said carefully.

Noah walked toward her with a frosted beer mug. "But is running nightclubs what he should be setting his mind to? Tell us what your gut says."

No. Absolutely not. Coop lifted an eyebrow at her, once again reading her mind. She took the mug. "I'm not going to second-guess Coop's hopes and dreams, but I will say that you couldn't pick anyone to do business with who's more honest or hardworking."

The housekeeper interrupted, looking flustered. The reason was immediately apparent as a pair of uniformed police officers followed her out onto the patio. "Deidre, these men are from the St. Charles police department."

Piper came to her feet. Deidre merely looked curious. "What can I help you with?"

They ignored her to focus on Coop. "Mr. Graham, you'll have to come with us. We have a warrant for your arrest."

Noah stepped forward. "That's ludicrous. On what charge?"

The officer regarded Coop grimly. "Sexual assault."

19

The warrant had come from the city of Chicago. A woman had accused Coop of sexually assaulting her at the club last Wednesday night.

Deidre was regarding him with something like repulsion.

"Don't be stupid," Piper said harshly. "He didn't assault anybody. He's been set up."

Coop gazed over at her, his expression unreadable.

The officers led him away in handcuffs, which would have devastated Piper if she weren't so furious. She had his attorney on the phone before the squad car pulled out of the driveway.

Deidre's hand shook as she poured herself a fresh drink. "I—I can't imagine him doing anything like that."

"Professional athletes always believe they're above the law." Noah seemed almost smug. "The more I learn about the world of Cooper Graham, the less I like it."

And that's when Piper remembered.

ARARAT.

*

Coop was arrested in the suburbs instead of the city, so it would take hours for him to post bail and get released, but Piper wouldn't be at the police station waiting for him. Instead, she'd pulled a black hoodie over her head and was breaking into Noah Parks's house in the city.

The lock was relatively simple to pick, but the renovated Streeterville greystone had an alarm system, and its banshee screeches gave her only a few minutes to search before the police showed up.

The interior smelled of fresh paint. Timer lights in the hallway and the living room gave her enough illumination to see where she was going.

ARARAT.

She'd spotted that license plate on Thursday night when Deidre had visited Spiral and Piper had walked her to her car. On Piper's way back to the club, a red Lexus had sped past her so recklessly that she'd shot the car the bird. That red Lexus had the license plate ARARAT. The mountain where the ark had come to rest.

Noah's ark.

Noah Parks had followed Deidre to the club that night. Maybe he'd been worried about her safety, but Deidre was more than capable of taking care of herself. More likely, he hadn't wanted her out of his sight. And after watching him with her earlier and seeing his barely concealed dislike of Coop, Piper thought she knew why.

The minutes raced by too quickly. His laptop wasn't in his office at the rear of the house. She raced upstairs and poked her head into the bedrooms. Parks was too much of a workaholic not to have a computer in his house, but where was it? And what was on it?

She'd pickpocketed Noah's cell phone right after the police had left and hidden away with it in the first-floor powder room. Like a lot of busy people who are always on their phones, he'd neglected to bother with a password, and she'd quickly found and memorized one interesting piece of information. But she needed more, and she could stay in Deidre's powder room for only so long. Leaving the phone on the patio where he'd think he'd dropped it, she'd excused herself from spending the night, rushed back to the city, and now here she was, undertaking her first break-in.

She ran back downstairs again, the scream of the alarm system frying her nerves. She couldn't afford to stay any longer. One more sweep. She cut through the living room, the den. Nothing. She had to get out before the police arrived. Now. She passed through the kitchen again. And there it was. On the granite counter. She grabbed it, ran out through the rear and down the alley to her car.

Once she got back to her office and stopped shaking, she made a pot of strong coffee to keep herself alert. Then she settled behind her desk and began the work of cloning the laptop's hard drive.

An hour later, she was in.

*

Her cell rang. She jerked her head up from her desk and fumbled to pick it up. Eight A.M. She'd fallen asleep less than an hour ago. "'Lo," she croaked.

"Nice to know how much you care." The uncharacteristically sulky note in Coop's voice reassured her as nothing else could have.

"Yeah, well, I had things to do, and I called your attorney, didn't I?" She grabbed her mug, took a slug of cold coffee, and shuddered.

"Aren't you going to ask me?"

She rubbed her eyes. "About what?"

"I've been accused of a sex crime!" he exclaimed. "I'm currently out of jail on bond!"

"Oh, that."

"You think this is some kind of a joke?"

"Don't even go there." The anger she'd barely been able to suppress boiled to the surface. "Thousands of women won't report they've been raped because they're afraid they'll be called liars. And then there's this. It's too much, Coop. I swear I am going to nail whoever accused you."

There was such a long pause she thought he'd hung up. But then she heard him clear his throat. His voice sounded strange. Tight. "Thanks."

"You're welcome."

"What have you been up to?" He didn't say it in a casual, *What's up?* way. More of an *I want a full report* way.

"I've got things to do. I'll call you later." She disconnected and shut down her cell. So much for teamwork.

As she tried to release the crick in her neck, she turned her attention back to her computer, where news bulletins were already broadcasting word of Coop's arrest. The injustice brought her fully awake.

In the trash folder on Noah's laptop, she'd found an e-mail from Bendah's Bug Farm. *Thank you for your order . . .* As satisfying as that had been, it paled in comparison to what else she'd discovered. When she'd swiped Noah's cell, she'd found a phone number he called at night, sometimes as late as two in the morning. The number had shown up so frequently that she'd ignored every ethical principle she believed in and broken into his house to steal the computer she hoped would be there, a computer that would give her even more information about the secret life of Noah Parks.

A few hours of cyber-digging had given her what she wanted—a link between the number and a name—Rochelle Mauvais, née Ellen Englley. There'd been no photos on his phone but there were plenty on the computer she'd stolen. A young, very pretty blonde. A couple of photos showed her with Noah, but most of them were of Ellen/Rochelle alone . . . and undressed. Then, at dawn, she'd hit the mother lode. A mysterious ten-thousand-dollar bank transfer made two days ago.

The remnants of the adrenaline buzz still hadn't faded. Nothing since she'd taken over the agency had been as satisfying as the work she'd just done with her fingers and a keyboard. But that sense of accomplishment couldn't erase the knowledge that Noah Parks wasn't the only criminal around.

She gazed across the office at her framed *True Detective* posters. She'd never imagined herself as a lawbreaker, yet that's what she was. She'd turned her back on her own principles and ignored the law, as if it had been written for other people. When this was over, she needed to take a long, unwelcome look at what she was becoming.

"I'm not asking you to give me her name," she told Eric as she spoke to him on the phone a few minutes later. "All I'm asking is for you to see if the name I gave you matches the name of the woman who accused Coop. A simple yes or no."

He called her back ten minutes later. "How did you get this information?"

Instead of answering his question, she gave him Ellen/Rochelle's address and told him to meet her there in half an hour.

The interview with Ellen was short and brutal. Ellen, it turned out, had started working as an escort to pay off her college loans but quickly discovered escort work was a more lucrative way to earn a living than the jobs she could get with her bachelor's degree in communications. Noah had been an early client. Although Piper had no proof that the ten thousand dollars he'd transferred from his bank had ended up in Ellen's account, she had enough details to act as though she did, and Ellen crumbled, admitting she'd lied about Coop.

This, she thought as Eric led Noah's mistress to the police station, *is for all the women who told the truth but nobody believed them.*

Deidre had returned to the city from the farm. Piper called her office and made an appointment for three o'clock. That gave her just enough time to shower and change. As she left her office, she imagined the phalanx of reporters camped outside Coop's condo and wished she could throw herself between him and every one of them.

Her urge to protect him was ferocious enough to scare her. She tried to plan out her upcoming meeting with Deidre, but she was so muzzy from lack of sleep that she took an automatic detour through Lincoln Square. And there, sitting by the fountain, was an elderly man wearing a horned Viking's helmet.

A horned, *Minnesota Vikings* fan helmet.

She couldn't deal with this now, but instead of driving away, she wheeled into a NO PARKING space, jumped out of her car, and strode toward him. He didn't spot her until she was about thirty feet away, and then he sprang up and began to run. She dashed in front of him. "*Police!*"

Depressing how hard it was to go straight once you started stepping over the line.

As soon as she cornered him, she saw he wasn't Howard Berkovitz. His face was thinner, his hair grayer. But they were the same height, the same build, about the same age, and there was a strong resemblance.

"I didn't do anything wrong," he said, with the familiar accent of someone born and raised in Chicago.

"I know you didn't." She tried to look friendly so he'd see she wasn't dangerous. "And I'm not really a police officer."

"Then why was you running after me? I saw you before. You're the one who was chasing me a coupla weeks back."

"It's a long story. I'm harmless, I swear. Could you do me a huge favor and let me buy you a cup of coffee so I can explain?"

"I don't like to talk to people."

"I'll do the talking. Please. I've barely slept, and I've had a horrible few days, and I'd really appreciate it."

His eyes narrowed, drawing his fuzzy gray eyebrows closer together. "Okay, but no funny stuff."

"Promise."

They were soon settled at one of the tables in a Western Avenue coffee shop with purple walls and weathered hardwood floors. She didn't ask any questions, not even his name, and definitely not why he chose to walk around Lincoln Square wearing sports fan headgear. Instead, she told him about Berni.

"And this woman thought I was her dead husband?" he said when she was done. "She sounds like a cuckoo to me."

"Berni's eccentric, but she's not crazy. She just misses her husband."

He rubbed his chin, dislodging the Vikings helmet enough to make the horns crooked. "I guess I can understand. I lost my wife last year."

"I'm sorry to hear that."

"I should have appreciated her more."

Piper kept her expression neutral. Time was ticking away. She needed to finish this quickly if she hoped to get a shower before she showed up in Deidre's office. She confronted the elephant in the coffee shop. "You must be a real football fan."

"More baseball. I love the Sox. You can take the kid outta the South Side, but you can't take the South Side outta the kid."

"I see." She didn't, and she nodded toward his headgear.

"Oh, I gotcha. You're talking about this?" He pulled off the horned Vikings helmet and set it on the table between them. "I wear stuff like this to keep people from bothering me. Since Ellie died, I don't like to talk to anybody."

Piper was starting to get the picture. "The Vikings helmet, the cheesehead—they keep people away."

He gave a satisfied nod. "Because they think I'm crazy."

"Like you think Berni's crazy?"

He thought it over. "I'm a fair guy. That's a good point."

"Would you be willing to talk to Berni? The three of us could meet here."

"I don't like to talk to people," he repeated, in case she'd missed the point the other two times he'd mentioned it.

"That's okay. Berni loves to talk. And all you'd have to do is nod. I think she needs to see you so she can let go of Howard."

He stared into his coffee mug. "It's hard to let go."

"I can imagine it is."

"I gotta say it sounds interesting. Most things are boring these days. Now when I was working, it was different . . ."

Although he said he didn't like to talk, once he got started, he didn't want to stop. His name was Willie Mahoney. He was a Chicago native who'd worked for the gas company until his retirement. His wife of forty-eight years had been a "spark plug." His kids were grown and lived out of state. He was lonely. By the time he wound down, Piper had a parking ticket, and she'd lost her chance to shower.

She drove directly to Lakeview and picked up Coop in the alley four doors down from his condo. The image of him being led away in handcuffs was still seared on her brain, and she had to clutch the steering wheel to keep from hugging him. Fortunately, he was in a sour mood. "I don't enjoy sneaking out of my own house."

"You'd rather join that media convention in your front yard?"

He grunted something and folded his big frame into the Sonata's passenger seat. "What's this about, and where are we going?"

She dodged both questions. "Thanks for trusting me."

"Where did you get that idea?"

"You're here, aren't you?"

Barely. His eyes were bloodshot and his jaw scruffy. She wanted to comfort him—reassure him—but he wouldn't appreciate it. "I hope you looked better when they took your mug shot."

He almost smiled. "You have no pity."

The last thing he wanted from her, she knew.

"And you're not exactly looking you're best," he said. "As a matter of fact—"

"It's been a long couple of days." She flipped on KISS FM and turned up the volume to end the conversation.

She waited until she was ready to pull into the parking lot behind the building that housed Joss Investments to explain. "We're meeting Deidre."

"So I see." He rubbed his eyes. "I don't want to meet Deidre."

"Teamwork."

"There isn't any teamwork happening here. I have no idea what you're doing, and you haven't enlightened me."

She took in all his weary gorgeousness. "This is the last time I'll ask you to trust me. I promise."

He shoved open the car door. "Why the hell not? What's another miserable day?"

She collected the laptop from the trunk. He must have thought it was hers because he didn't ask about it. The laptop, however, was the first thing Noah spotted as Deidre's secretary let them into her office. He came to his feet from the side table where he and Deidre had been going over some files.

Deidre greeted Coop with a cool nod, her previous warmth gone, and moved toward her desk, as if she wanted a barrier between them. "You didn't tell me Cooper was coming, Piper. You led me to believe we'd only be meeting with you."

"Is that what you thought? My mistake."

Coop positioned himself between the door and an oil painting of Deidre's father. Crossing his arms over his chest, he rested one shoulder against the wall, letting Piper take the lead. She wanted so badly to do this for him, to lay it out at his feet like a Super Bowl trophy. She handed the laptop over to Noah. "I think this belongs to you. It's the oddest thing. Somebody left it on my doorstep last night. And don't worry. I backed it up."

Noah's lower lip thinned as the corners of his mouth contracted, but he couldn't directly accuse her of stealing without casting suspicion on himself.

Deidre steepled her fingers on the desktop. "What's this about, Piper?"

"It's about your right-hand man here. He's a criminal. I'm guessing you didn't know that?"

Noah turned vicious. "Get out of here."

Deidre's bewildered expression looked strange on the face of a woman accustomed to being in control. Piper confronted Noah. "Does the name Ellen Englley ring a bell?"

Noah stalked toward Deidre's desk. "I'm calling security."

"You know her better as Rochelle Mauvais," Piper said. "It's a great hooker name."

The color drained from his face. "I don't know what you're talking about."

Deidre had come to her feet, her hands braced on the desktop.

"Ellen is Noah's longtime . . . girlfriend," Piper explained. "She's also the woman who accused Coop of rape. Interesting, right?"

Coop straightened from his position against the wall.

Noah leaned over and hit the intercom on Deidre's desk. "Get security up here!"

"Ellen told me all about it," Piper said.

Deidre looked dazed. "Noah, is this true?"

"No! Of course, it's not true."

"She's with the police right now," Piper said. "Along with a copy of your computer's hard drive."

Noah bolted for the door. But Coop was too quick for him. He threw a block that sent Noah staggering backward. Before he could fall, Coop grabbed him and shoved him down on the office couch. "Let's hear what Piper has to say."

Piper had a lot to say. "Noah paid Ms. Englley ten thousand dollars to accuse Coop of rape. Noah wanted to destroy him. Get him out of your life. He even used a drone to spy on him." Noah slumped forward on the couch, his head in his hands. Deidre stood frozen as Piper went on. "The police are going to find that hard drive very interesting. You really should empty your e-mail trash folder, although dumping the cockroaches at the club is small potatoes compared to the rest."

"You stole it," he said into his hands.

"Why, Noah?" Deidre cried. "Why would you do something like this?"

He set his jaw, refusing to speak, so Piper answered for him. "He wants to be the most important man in your life. He got used to the way you relied on him after your husband died. Maybe he hoped to be the next Mr. Joss, but whether he wanted that or not, he had to make sure he stayed the most important man in your life. Your personal interest in Coop was threatening that. He wanted both Coop and Spiral out of the picture."

Coop witnessed it all, saying nothing.

Deidre sank back into her chair. She put her head in her hands, then slowly lifted it. "How could you do this?"

"What else was I supposed to do?" Noah's face twisted bitterly. "I couldn't stop you from marrying Sam, even though anybody could see he wasn't good enough for you. I wasn't going to lose you to Graham, too."

"I trusted you more than I trusted anyone."

"I needed more time!" he exclaimed. "I love you. I've always loved you."

Loved Joss Investments was more like it.

The door shot open and two security guards charged in.

Deidre came up from the chair, in full command. "Put him in his office and keep him there until the police get here." As they led him away, she went to Coop. "I don't know how I can ever make this up to you."

Piper had a few ideas, and she hated every one of them.

*

Coop got behind the wheel of Piper's Sonata himself and headed toward Spiral. "How did you get his computer?"

Piper rested her head and shut her eyes. Words were pressing at her lips, emotions churning—thoughts and feelings so contradictory, so painful, she couldn't let them escape. "I can't talk to you until I get some sleep."

"I need answers."

"I'm serious, Coop. I haven't slept since Sunday night, and I need to go to bed."

"Fine. I'll be with my lawyers most of tomorrow, but I'll pick you up for dinner at five o'clock."

She opened her eyes. "What are you? Eighty years old? Who goes out to dinner that early?"

"You're bitchy when you don't sleep."

"Got it. Old Country Buffet at five o'clock."

"Five o'clock because I want plenty of time to get you drunk."

"In that case . . ." She shut her eyes again.

By the time Piper awoke the next day, the police had issued a statement saying Coop had been falsely accused. They didn't name Noah but merely referred to "a person with a grudge against the former Stars quarterback." By noon, the local channels were showing footage of Ellen Englley with a hoodie pulled over her head trying to duck the news cameras. Piper gazed at the screen in disgust. Noah's mistress would probably end up with a reality show.

Coop's attorney held a short press conference at three o'clock where, among other things, Piper learned that Coop was a longstanding member of the NFL's task force on sexual violence. His attorney read a statement from Coop about the serious impact false accusations have on real rape victims. How could Piper not want to protect someone like that?

Eric called with the unwelcome news that Noah Parks had an airtight alibi for both the night Coop had been attacked outside his condo and the night Karah had been forced off the road. Piper assumed Noah had hired someone to carry out the first attack, but she'd been counting on him being behind the wheel of the mystery vehicle that had gone after the Tesla. Unless the police found another connection, Noah could get off with a slap on the wrist.

She made herself focus on the long-sleeved, bittersweet-orange knit dress she'd unearthed from the back of the closet. She'd last worn it at a college friend's wedding a couple of years ago. The boatneck framed her long neck, something she generally didn't think about, but for tonight, she wanted to feel at least halfway pretty.

Coop had traded in his jeans and boots for an open-collar white dress shirt, gray pants, and a darker gray sports coat that fit his body as if he'd grown it there. Appreciation glinted in his eyes. "Damn, Pipe, you really do know how to look like a girl."

"I told you I could," she said. "Where are we going to dinner?"

"Drinks first. This great new place I've heard about."

"You're going to be mobbed."

"All taken care of."

He was right. The great new place turned out to be right below them, which explained their early date time.

Even though Spiral wouldn't open for another four hours, soft light glowed from inside the cube-shaped cocktail tables, and the suspended rods glimmered like golden stalactites above the bar. The leather banquettes were welcoming, and music played quietly in the background. No one was around.

Coop stepped behind the bar. "We have three hours until the staff shows up," he said. "The place is locked tight for now, and I gave strict orders that nobody can get in until eight."

"Not much prep time before the club opens."

"They'll cope." He uncorked a very expensive cabernet and filled two goblets.

"I'm sorry I couldn't be a team player," she said as she slid up onto a barstool. "But you weren't exactly available for consultation."

"You're forgiven."

She held up the wine goblet he gave her. "Here's to being innocent."

"Not in that dress."

The dress's wide neckline extended all the way to her collarbones, but the rest of it hugged her body. "I was talking about you."

"I know." He smiled. "How did you figure it out?"

She told him about Noah's license plate.

"Not much to go on."

"And intuition. He hovered around Deidre, and there was something about his attitude toward you that felt more personal than professional."

He rested his hand on the bar and gave her one of his brain-piercing looks. "How did you get his computer?"

He'd brought up the thing she most didn't want to look at. "Not legally." She stared into her wineglass. "I'm turning into somebody I don't respect. One of those people so focused on the end goal that they don't care how they reach it."

"It's called passion."

She had another word for it. *Unethical.*

✶

Coop watched her sip her wine. She wasn't happy, and he wanted her to be. She should be.

He took a platter of meats, cheeses, olives, and summer rolls from the refrigerator under the bar and carried it to the closest banquette. She followed him with their wine goblets, steady as can be on those stilettos she detested. She hadn't believed he'd assaulted anybody. Not for a moment. She'd been impatient when he'd pressed her about it—as if he were wasting her time by bringing it up. No one had ever had such blind faith in him. What the hell was a man supposed to do with a woman like this?

She slid into the banquette, her skirt riding up on her thighs enough for him to lose his train of thought. Even without tonight's mascara, her eyelashes were long and thick, and her glossy cinnamon mouth was an invitation. He loved her face best scrubbed clean, but he also loved knowing that she'd bothered fixing herself up just for him.

"This feels ceremonial," she said.

"It is. A celebration." She'd put her investigator's license in jeopardy doing whatever it was she'd done, and that bothered him even more than knowing he'd needed someone else to solve his problems.

"You don't look happy," she said.

"I'm very happy."

"Then why are you frowning?"

"Because I'm trying not to act like the animal I am by picturing what's under your dress. I'm not proud of myself."

She smiled.

He set down his drink. "Let's dance."

"Really?"

"Why not?"

She took his hand and slid out of the banquette. He led her to the floor. It was odd to realize this was the first time he'd been able to dance in his own club strictly for pleasure.

And pleasure it was. The sweet fit of her body against his own was almost painful, although he wished when he'd programmed the music, he'd avoided this off-the-charts sentimental Ed Sheeran ballad. On the other hand, it suited his mood.

"This is just weird," she said, resting the top of her head against the side of his jaw and leaning even closer into him.

"If only you weren't such a romantic."

She laughed. Why did he keep worrying about leading her on when she had her feet so firmly planted on the ground and her head so far below the clouds?

They danced in silence, their hands clasped, their bodies swaying, breathing in each other's air. The Sheeran song ended and Etta James began to sing "At Last." He drew her back to the banquette.

She nibbled at the appetizers, taking those dainty bites that always threw him off. He needed to tell her what her trust meant to him. Instead, he asked her to take him through everything she'd done from the time the police had carted him away to their meeting with Deidre.

"I'll give you the best first." She told him about finding the man Mrs. Berkovitz thought was her dead husband.

"Incredible," he said as she finished. "And how much did Mrs. B. pay you to do this job for her?"

"A hundred dollars. I was planning to take her out to dinner, but now I'm hoping I can take them both out."

"You have a good heart, Piper Dove."

She speared a cheese cube. "And flexible ethics."

He rose to fetch the bottle of cabernet from the bar. "Go ahead. Get it all out."

"I don't want to."

"That bad?"

"Depends on how you feel about breaking and entering, not to mention burglary. I also lied to your accuser about the money transfer, but I don't feel bad about that. Then there's your ring . . ."

He set the bottle on the table. "Don't you think you're being a little hard on yourself?"

"The end justifies the means? I'd like to believe that, but I can't."

"You're a high achiever, Pipe. It's the way you're made." The way Duke Dove had made her.

She gave him a bright, phony smile. "No more depressing talk. Tell me about jail. Did anybody try to make you his bitch?"

"I was held in a conference room filled with cops who wanted a replay of last year's Super Bowl. So that would be a no."

"Disappointing."

He shoved an olive in her mouth.

The music picked up tempo, and they went back to the dance floor. Before long, she'd kicked off her heels, and he got rid of his suit coat. As the tunes grew more erotic, so did their dancing. Pharrell to Rihanna; Bowie to Beyoncé. Piper on her toes. Pressing that sweet butt hard against him. Rotating, then spinning around to face him, her face flushed, her lids heavy. Rotating again. Butt pressing . . . If she didn't stop, he'd have a repeat performance of their first time, so he grabbed her by the arms and pressed her against the wall.

He kissed her. Open mouth. Kissed her and kissed her and kissed her again—mouth, neck, back to her mouth. Long, deep explorations. The two of them making out as if this were as far as they could go. Devouring each other. Clothes sticking to their skin. One song after another.

Marvin Gaye . . . "Let's get it on . . ."

Missy Elliott . . . "Let me work it . . ."

And still they kissed. A make-out session for the ages.

Do it all night . . . All night . . .

The skirt of her dress was in his fists. Shoved to her waist. His belt opening under her palms.

How does it feel . . . It feels . . .

Underpants. Zipper. Wool and nylon scattering on the dance floor.

Up against the wall. In the hall . . . Hot against the wall.

Freefall . . .

Her legs around his hips. Butt in his hands. Wet beneath his fingers. Inside her.

Work it. Work it, work it.

Inside.

Like that. And that.

And that . . .

*

Her knit dress had survived the thrilling abuse, but her underpants hadn't, and since it felt weird to wear a bra without underpants, she abandoned lingerie altogether and pulled her dress back on over her bare skin. She touched her lips. They felt puffy. She'd be sore tomorrow, and not only her lips.

Her teeth started to chatter, and her legs weren't working right. She sank down on the ladies' room couch.

The worst thing in the world had happened to her.

20

She loved him. She had stupidly, recklessly fallen in love with Cooper Graham. She'd had plenty of warning—the buzz she'd experience whenever he appeared, the delight she took in making him laugh, the rules she'd broken for him. How could she not have correctly identified that intense wash of emotion engulfing her at the most unexpected times?

She was so dizzy she put her head between her knees, which only made it worse. All the signs had been there, but she'd refused to pay heed to any of them. She'd believed she was immune to falling in love. And maybe she had been. Immune to falling in love with anyone other than Cooper Graham. But watching him being led away in handcuffs had broken open the steel trap that had caged her heart for so long she'd been unaware of its existence. Until now.

She made herself sit back up. She didn't do love. She had no resources to handle it. How could she walk out this door and act as if everything were normal? He was so perceptive, so good at reading her mind. He'd see her feelings on her face. And if he did see . . . He'd be so kind. So fricking kind.

The minutes ticked by. Any second now he'd barge in to check on her. She wanted to hide in here forever, but she couldn't do that, and she made herself stand up. There was only one way she could save herself. Only one way to avoid his pity, his kindness.

She had to get out there and finish this.

He emerged from the kitchen with his shirtsleeves rolled up. His lips looked as swollen as hers. Had she bitten him? He'd arranged the silverware haphazardly on their banquette table, along with two neatly plated arugula and apple salads he almost certainly hadn't made himself.

"Lobster risotto." He set down the bowls he'd been carrying. "Direct from the kitchen warming drawer. Extra creamy." His half-lidded gaze slid over her. "Like you."

The erotic jolt that zipped through her proved exactly how vulnerable she was. She sank into the banquette.

Forcing herself to eat was even more difficult than pretending nothing had changed. "You're an amazing cook," she said.

She knew, and he knew she knew, that he hadn't prepared any of this, but he played along. "Got my finger cut up a little bit going after the claw meat."

"Injuries happen to all great chefs."

He grinned. She relentlessly attacked the risotto. It was creamy, just as he'd noted. Cheesy, with succulent chunks of buttery lobster that threatened to stick in her throat. They talked, or mainly he did, going back over what had happened with Parks. She finally told him how she'd gotten Noah's computer, but even that wasn't as difficult as what she had to say, and she finally gave up her attempt to eat.

"No good?" he said.

"Pregnancy screws up your appetite."

He dropped his fork, and his stark horror testified that she was trying too hard to act normally. "I'm kidding."

"Not funny!" he practically roared.

"You know I turn into a wiseass when I'm stressed."

"I don't care how stressed you are. Don't ever joke about— What are you stressed about?"

Maybe she could put this off for a few days. A few weeks . . . The possibility was as seductive as the serpent in the Garden of Eden and as destructive. She had to do this quickly. Perfectly. Be as ruthless with herself as Duke used to be when she'd cried over a broken balloon or a scuffed knee. She was her father's daughter, and she made herself look him square in the eye. "Breaking up with you."

"Yeah, right."

Lay it out logically. Men understand logic. "My job's over. I finally have a little money in the bank. I even have another place to stay."

"You already have a place to stay."

"A better place. Amber's leaving in a couple of days for a tour with her choral group, and she isn't coming back to the Lyric until December, so I'm going to stay at her place." She hadn't talked to Amber. Hadn't even thought about staying there until this very minute.

His frown deepened. "Completely unnecessary."

"I've done what you hired me to do."

"Which doesn't have anything to do with the two of us."

She swallowed the lump in her throat. "Sure it does. The job's over, and so are we."

His hand curled into a fist on the table. "What are you talking about? We're both having a good time. Great sex. You're the woman I want to be with."

"The woman you want to be with right now."

"What's wrong with that?"

Another piece of her heart crumbled. "For you, nothing. But there's a lot wrong with it for me." She could only nudge at the corners of the truth. "I can't keep hanging around all your razzle-dazzle. That's not my world. I'm a homegrown Chicago girl. You're . . . the stars." She managed a creaky smile. "'Star light, star bright,' and all that."

"That doesn't half make sense." His hand opened. Pointed. "You've told me how you see things, so I know you're not looking for an engagement ring."

The way he said it was a knife through her heart. She wasn't a romantic. She *wasn't.* She didn't want rings and bridal veils. That wasn't her. But his casual dismissal of any kind of future made her throat close up.

She had to be tough. That's who she was, and that's what he expected. She pulled in a thread of air. "A woman's never dumped you, has she?"

"We're not talking about dumping."

"In other words, no. You're the one who does the dumping. You don't know how to deal with any other scenario. Don't you see? This isn't about me or about our relationship. It's about your need to win." It was the truth and maybe he knew it, too, because he grew hostile.

"I don't need you psychoanalyzing me."

"It's for your own good, and, yes, I really am breaking up with you."

His lips thinned. "You're a quitter, Piper Dove. I never thought I'd say that about you, but you're running away from the two of us like a scared teenager."

So true. With her emotional survival at stake, what else could she do? "I'm not running away. I'm being pragmatic. We're two different worlds, Coop. It's time I go back to mine and you go on with yours."

"Is that what you really want?"

"Yes. Yes, it is."

He came to his feet and threw down his napkin, his expression as cold as she'd ever seen it. "The hell with you then."

✶

Coop stalked upstairs to his office. Where did she get off? Tonight was supposed to have been a celebration. He'd planned to surprise her by asking her to move in with him, an invitation he'd never offered any other woman. And what had she done? She'd spoiled the whole thing.

Leave it to Piper Dove to take something straightforward and turn it into a mess. They had fun together. They saw life the same way. What was so hard to understand about that? But instead of appreciating what they had, she had to screw it up.

She was right about one thing, though. He didn't like to lose. Especially when there was no need for it. He made up his mind. He'd ignore her for a couple of days, give her some time to miss what they had. Get tough with her. Because toughness was something Piper Dove understood.

✶

Her final four nights working at the club were hell, but she'd promised Tony she'd stay till the end of the week, and she couldn't leave him in the lurch. The story of Coop and his false accuser had played big in the media, and the club was packed every night. Whenever she turned around, there was Coop.

Saturday finally came. Her last night. With all the publicity, any lingering debate about leaving Coop alone on the floor was over. Jonah had organized the bouncers so one of them was always at his side. Until tonight, Piper had been able to beg off "Coop duty" because, as the only female bouncer, she already had too much territory to cover. But on Saturday Ernie called in sick, and she had to take her turn.

Coop had made it easy for her to keep her distance by acting as if she didn't exist. He was proving what she already knew about him—how much he hated to lose. She missed their closeness so much that she ached—those intimate glances they'd exchanged, their shared amusement over some inanity only they found hilarious. All of it gone.

It was also her last night sleeping above the club. Amber was happy to have an apartment-sitter, and tomorrow Piper was moving in. By tomorrow this chapter in her life would be over. The worst chapter.

The best chapter.

As she watched one of the hair-swishers pressing in on him close enough to leave another makeup smear on his shirt, Jonah tapped her on the shoulder. "Time for you to take over with Coop." He glanced toward their employer. "What's with you two, anyway? I haven't seen you guys talk all week."

She was leaving, and Coop was staying. She had to do the right thing. "Coop dumped me. In the nicest possible way, of course. He's the perfect gentleman."

"No shit? I figured you guys were gonna last a little longer."

"S'okay. It had to happen. Better sooner than later."

Jonah gave her a clumsy pat on the back. Even though he was a cretin, she'd developed a reluctant fondness for him.

Within a few minutes of Jonah's departure, the crowd again started pressing in on Coop, and she had her work cut out for her. "Let the man have some room."

Most people didn't give her trouble, and the few who did were drunk and easy to handle. It was a good thing nobody was getting in her face, because she needed a target for every raw, painful emotion swirling inside her. Only a few more hours . . .

A bro in a fedora and V-neck sweater wedged in on Coop. She grew increasingly furious as she listened to the moron relive every snap Coop had fumbled and every ball he'd thrown late. Coop was used to this kind of bull, and he was handling it fine. But she wasn't. As the bro started in on Coop's lousy leadership skills, all the horrible feelings churning inside her found their target, and her temper exploded. She shoved between a couple of his pals, reared up on her stilettos, and grabbed the guy's shirtfront. "Back off, asshole, or I will rip your fucking head off. Do you understand me?"

Coop's eyebrows shot up. The guy blinked, then jutted out his jaw with false bravado. "Yeah? Who are you?"

"She's my bodyguard," Coop said evenly. "Best not to mess with her."

The guy began edging away. "Who needs this shithole club?"

Bryan quickly separated the jerk from the crowd. Coop looked down at her with displeasure. "Real smooth."

"He irritated me."

"Cut it out."

She couldn't handle this any longer, and she walked away. One more hour, and her job would be over.

She checked the ladies' room and VIP. All well. When she finally came back downstairs, she ran into a group of men surrounding Coop near the mezzanine stairs. An especially loud, gel-haired jock type had positioned himself as close as he could and was gesturing toward him with his beer. "You and me, Coop. We know what it's like. I had a bitch try to nail me once. Just like what happened to you."

"You don't say." Coop turned away.

But the guy wasn't done. "Bitch was asking for it. She wanted it. Anybody could see that."

And then the idiot made the mistake of grabbing Coop's arm. Coop spun and, with no more warning than that, drew back his fist and punched the guy, sending him bouncing into the crowd.

Crap. Piper shot forward. The guy hit the floor and rolled to his knees, cradling his jaw. She knelt next to him and gazed up at her ex-lover. "Real smooth, Coop."

Coop glared down and threw her words right back at her. "He irritated me."

Despite his ferocious expression, she nearly hugged him. *This is for all the women who told the truth but nobody believed them.*

✶

Three o'clock finally came. She slipped off her heels and dragged herself upstairs to spend her last night in the apartment. Tomorrow, she'd be sleeping in Amber's double bed underneath an *Aida* poster.

She got undressed and pulled a plain brown T-shirt over her

underpants. She gazed down at the alley from her back window. Coop had left, the spot where he parked his car was empty. As empty as she felt inside.

She crawled into her too-big bed and stared up at the ceiling. She'd done the right thing. She might not believe she could hurt any more than she did now, but staying with him longer—hiding how much she cared—would only make their inevitable breakup more agonizing.

She finally fell into a restless sleep only to be plagued by nightmare figures with clown faces, jackboots, and selfie sticks. They chased her into a crimson jungle where dead women hung head down from telephone poles. She had to scream. But she couldn't find the air. She had to find air. She struggled to find a scream somewhere. Anywhere.

She jolted awake. It was still dark. Her T-shirt stuck to her skin, and she'd drooled on the pillow. Her heart was racing. Only a dream . . . Only a dream . . .

Somebody stood in the doorway. A dark, silent silhouette. Her voice came out in a grateful croak. "Coop?"

He rushed toward the bed.

It happened so fast. One moment she was trapped in a nightmare, and the next moment, a man was grabbing her. A man who was not Coop.

She screamed.

"Shut up!" He had her by the arm. Shook her. She tried to fight, but the sheet trapped her. His hard shake wrenched her neck. She freed an arm and clawed at his face. He slapped her. Her ears rang. The struggle was frantic, the only sounds her gasps. And then even those stopped as his fingers closed around her neck and his thumbs pressed her windpipe.

The overhead light blazed on.

The pressure on her throat stopped as the man jerked up and spun around. She rolled off the opposite side of the bed, fighting to free herself from the sheet as she fell. She hit the floor. Seconds later, she was on her knees, eyes blinking against the sudden light.

Jada stood in the doorway, her Nerf gun at her side, staring at the attacker, a man Piper had never seen. Jada's voice wobbled. "Hank?"

He had a shaved head and a gun. A silver-barreled, nine-millimeter Beretta. Pointed straight at Jada.

And then right back at Piper.

He scowled. He was big, muscular. He might once have been a decent-looking guy, but the ugliness of hate had transformed his long face into a mask of malevolence. "What the fuck . . . Where's Karah? Why isn't Karah here?"

Jada whimpered from the doorway. He backed toward the far wall so he could keep them both within easy range of his gun. He had the wrong apartment. He was looking for Karah. Piper choked out the words. "She's—she's not here. I'm staying with Jada."

He turned the gun toward Jada. "Where is she?"

Piper prayed Jada wouldn't tell him her mother was asleep in the next apartment.

"I—I don't know," Jada sobbed.

"You lying little bitch."

"She's . . . at an overnight seminar," Piper managed to say. "For a class she's taking. Now get the hell out of here!"

"You're lying." He was sweating, flushed, maybe high on meth. "She's with Graham. Whoring around with that bastard."

He jabbed the gun at Piper. "Get over there with her."

Piper moved carefully toward Jada, who stood frozen, the useless

Nerf gun slipping to the floor. She wrapped an arm around the girl's shoulders and prayed Karah wouldn't wake up. "Karah's not here. Now get out. Leave us alone."

"She's gonna pay for being a whore. She's gotta pay."

"Nobody has to pay," she said carefully. "Just go."

"Yeah, you'd all like to make me disappear. Make me forget what she did to me."

"That's in the past. Let it go."

He moved closer to them. The gun steady. His attention on Jada. "And her little baby doll. Not so little anymore."

Tentacles of dread slithered through her body. And then she heard it. The click of the apartment door opening. *Karah.* He would kill her. And maybe Jada, too.

She'd never felt more helpless. Her Glock was locked in the trunk of her car, and all the self-defense moves in the world were useless as long as he had that gun trained on Jada.

But it wasn't Karah whose voice echoed from the living room. It was Coop, and her dread turned to ice. "I couldn't sleep," he said.

Hank grabbed Jada, jammed the gun against her temple, and jerked his head at Piper, gesturing her through the bedroom door ahead of him.

Coop froze as he saw them emerging. Piper first, then Jada and Hank. "Coop . . ." Jada sobbed, terrified.

"He's looking for Karah." Piper tried to take a step forward only to have Hank shift the gun from Jada's head to her own.

"Stay right where you are or I'll blow your head off!"

The gun barrel pressed into Piper's skull. She tried to block out Jada's sobs, fought a terror so stark it threatened to paralyze her. She glued her eyes to Coop's.

Teamwork.

"Put that gun away." Coop's voice was low and ugly.

"You come here looking for your whore?" Hank sneered.

"He's talking about Karah," Piper said. "Not me."

Coop didn't ask any questions. He was a pressure player, and it was fourth-and-goal with seconds left on the clock. "Drop the gun," he said, his lips barely moving.

"Why should I?" The gun jabbed deeper into Piper's temple. "I'm going to punish her. She left me and came running to you with her skirt over her head."

"You got a dirty mind," Coop said. "Karah's nothing to me."

"You're a liar! Just like she is."

"I've got no reason to lie to you." Coop was cool, easy, except for the intense watchfulness in his eyes and the muscle ticking at the corner of his jaw.

With no warning, the pressure on Piper's head disappeared, and Hank jammed the gun back into Jada's temple. Jada whimpered as he dug the barrel deeper. "I was gonna blow Karah's head off, but that's not bad enough. I'm gonna hurt her where it'll hurt the most." He threw the back of his arm over Jada's throat. "I'm gonna blow her kid's head off first."

Jada gagged. Her body convulsed.

A trickle of perspiration slithered between Piper's breasts. Her skin was clammy, her heart pounding. "Why do you think Coop and Karah were lovers?" She needed to talk. Say something. Anything. "Coop's my lover. Coop and I have been lovers forever. We're more than lovers. We're in love." She talked on. Stalling for time. Distracting him from the gun digging into Jada's head. "He doesn't even like Karah. He laughs about her behind her back."

"You liar."

Out of the corner of her eye, she saw Coop move. Slowly. A

quarter step to the left. She kept talking. "You know what a loser she is. You know that more than anybody. She doesn't even take care of Jada. Her own daughter. That's why I stay with her. Because Karah hates her own daughter." Coop took another step. *Teamwork. Teamwork.* "How could you still care about a woman like that? She said she never wanted to be a mother. That Jada's holding her back. Keeping her from being free."

A strangled, howling sob came from the bottom of Jada's soul. Hank jerked, and Coop went airborne. That long, lean body extended. He dove. And threw the greatest man-to-man block of his career. A crushing, illegal block that hit at the knees and shook the room.

Piper grabbed Jada and fell on top of her, shielding the girl with her own body as the gun went off.

21

Piper folded her body over Jada's to keep her safe. She was afraid to raise her head and expose any part of Jada to harm. The nightmare seconds dragged by. Was Coop dead? Let it be Hank who'd taken the bullet. Or the wall. Or the floor. Anything but Coop. He had to stay alive. He had to stay alive because she loved him—loved him with all her heart—and because she had to protect Jada and because he had to finish the job she couldn't.

Coop, be alive.

A garbled woman's scream. Not her own. Not Jada's. Karah.

"You bitch!" Hank's howl of outrage chilled Piper to the bone.

A fierce obscenity from Coop.

He was alive.

Jada's body heaved beneath Piper. Where was the gun? Piper had to get the gun. She turned her head.

Coop had Hank trapped on the floor. There was blood.

Piper reared off Jada and dove for the gun. As she came to her knees with the weapon in both hands, she saw Karah standing just inside the door, her mouth an oval of horror. Piper shouted at her to call the police.

What happened next was short and brutal. Coop hauled Hank up by the throat and slammed him into the wall. He beat him until Hank collapsed unconscious to the floor.

Jada grabbed her Nerf gun. With sobs racking her body, she rushed toward Hank and fired at his crumpled figure. One foam bullet after another.

Piper saw the blood smear on the wall first and then, seconds later, she saw something far worse. A crimson rose blooming through the wool of Coop's jacket.

The EMTs had to block her from climbing into the ambulance with him. She jumped in her car and followed, not thinking about speed limits but only about what parts of him that bullet might have hit. When they reached the ER, she refused to leave him alone for even a moment.

He'd been shot in the side. Both an entry and exit wound, so that was good. No vital organs hit. That was good, too. Except he'd been hurt, and that was horrible. Unthinkable.

She stood guard by his bed, cross-examining every doctor, nurse, technician, and orderly who came in to check on him. She even tried to go into the X-ray lab with him, but they threatened to call security.

Coop was fully conscious through all this, but he made no attempt to settle her down. Instead, he watched her with a kind of bemusement.

While Coop was in X-ray, Piper began putting it all together. She'd assumed he had only one enemy—Noah Parks. But she'd been wrong. Noah was behind the attempts to sabotage the club, the drone, and the false accusation. But Karah's pathologically jealous ex-boyfriend was responsible for the rest. Hank believed Coop and Karah were lovers. He was the one who'd attacked Coop the night they'd come back from taking Faiza to Canada. He was the one who'd slashed Coop's tires. She also suspected he'd known exactly who was behind the wheel of the Audi the night he'd run it off the road. If he couldn't have Karah for himself, he wanted to make certain no other man could have her.

She told the police all of it and tried not to imagine what would have happened to Karah and Jada if Hank hadn't gotten the apartments confused. Or what would have happened to all of them if Coop hadn't shown up.

She waited until eight in the morning to call Heath, who came running into the emergency room barely half an hour later, his face as pale as a hospital sheet. His questions were terse but thorough, and as soon as he understood that Coop was going to be all right, he reverted to his normal manner with a nod toward his client stretched out on the hospital bed. "Nice nightie."

"Leave him alone," Piper snarled.

Coop and Heath exchanged looks she ignored. She didn't want anyone harassing Coop about anything right now.

Later that morning, Piper talked to both Karah and Jada on the phone. Hank was in jail for attempted murder, along with a slew of other charges. Karah blamed herself for everything. "He was really sweet when we started dating, and by the time I realized how sick he was, it was too late. That's why I left St. Louis. To get away from him. I never thought he'd follow me."

Piper tried to comfort her and then spoke with Jada. Their conversation was reassuring. "Mom is going to make me see a counselor for a while to make sure I don't, like, go psycho or anything because of what happened, but I'm pretty sure I won't. And guess what else? After the police left, Mom said she'd take me out for pancakes, and with everything that happened, I wasn't paying attention, and Clara shot me. I'm officially dead."

"Oh, no. I'm really sorry."

"I know. I thought I'd be more depressed, but it's kind of okay because it was Clara who shot me, and her and I are kind of getting to be friends."

"Still, after everything that happened today, that's rotten timing."

"Yeah, but I could tell she, like, felt really bad about it, and she needs the money even worse than I do, so I told her it was okay, and we're going to hang out tomorrow and work on our project about child sex trafficking. The good thing is that I don't have to carry around those stupid Nerf guns anymore."

The doctors overrode Coop's protests and insisted on keeping him overnight. Coop had already kicked Heath out, but he seemed to expect Piper to hang around, not that she would have left.

The orderly assigned to transport Coop from the ER to his private room looked like a nice kid, but Piper stayed by the wheelchair as they traveled up an elevator and down several long corridors. Coop fumed the whole time, not from pain, but because the medical staff wouldn't let him walk.

There were too many people hanging around outside his room, and Piper wasn't having it. "If you're not his doctor or nurse, you shouldn't be here. Move on."

Mr. Nice Guy raised his hand from the wheelchair and gave his cocky grin. "Appreciate your concern."

The adrenaline she'd been riding on had faded, leaving her exhausted and heartsick. All she wanted to do was get away, but she couldn't leave him in a hospital full of people looking for excuses to come into his room. He needed someone stationed outside his door until he was discharged, and while a nurse took his vitals, she got Jonah on the phone and told him what had happened.

Coop had been given the hospital's version of the penthouse—a large room with a city view. He had the head of the bed in an upright position as she came back into the room from talking to Jonah. "You should be lying down," she said.

He looked at her oddly, as if she were a stranger he was trying to identify, but then he reverted back to his normal self. "Get serious. I had worse injuries in high school. I can't believe they're not letting me out until tomorrow."

"It's for your own good." She turned her back on him and went to the window.

"Thanks, by the way," he said. "I appreciate you watching out for me."

He didn't sound begrudging, and she pondered what it must have cost him to say those words. How could she have done this to herself? How could she have fallen in love with someone so different? "I'm the one who's grateful," she said. "If you hadn't come back to the apartment . . ." She turned to him from the window. "Why did you?"

He dropped his head back onto the pillow. "I wanted to talk to you."

"It couldn't wait until morning?" She wrapped her arms around her chest, hugging herself.

"It was important," he said.

She regarded him quizzically.

His jaw set in that obstinate way she'd come to know. "I was hoping you'd calmed down enough to realize this whole breaking-up thing makes no sense. Instead of that, we need to ratchet it up. That's what I'd been planning to talk to you about at dinner on Wednesday night before you had your freak-out. Moving in together. My place, not yours."

The knife twisted in her chest. "Why would I move in with you?"

His eyes narrowed. "It's a good thing I have an oversize ego because if I didn't, you'd have destroyed it." She swallowed the constriction in her throat as he went on. "You're being stubborn about this for no reason. It's common sense."

Could he really have convinced himself of something so fundamentally wrong? "I don't know why you'd say that."

"I've done a lot of thinking about the two of us this week." The color was coming back to his face. "You look me in the eye and tell me this isn't the best relationship you've ever had, because I know it's the best one for me."

That brought her to a full stop, and she quashed a dangerous spark of hope. "Really? If this is your best relationship, you are in serious need of therapy."

She watched his stubbornness take over. The stubbornness that refused to accept a loss. The quality that made him a champion, but also made her so wary of him. She had to do something quickly. Something definitive. She knew exactly what it was, but she wasn't certain she could go through with it. She took a deep breath. She had to do this for no other reason than that she loved him enough to want the best for him . . . even if it broke her heart.

"Here's the thing, Coop . . ." She took a shaky breath. "As soon as the dust settles, you need to call Deidre."

He tilted the bed back a few inches. "I've lost the desire to do business with her."

"What happened with Noah wasn't her fault, and I'm not talking about business. I'm talking about your personal relationship." She pushed the words through her throat. "She's better than Hollywood. The two of you are perfect for each other. And she's already half in love with you. If we learned anything last night, we learned how short life can be. If you keep dallying around with another woman—namely me—you're going to screw up your chance to find your perfect woman."

He looked at her as though she'd developed a hole in her brain, and the bed came back up. "Deidre Joss is not my perfect woman."

How could he not see what was so clear? "She is! She's smart, successful, beautiful—the kind of woman who'll always have your back. And she's crazy about you. She's also nice. A decent human being."

"It's official," he declared. "You are out of your mind."

"You're thirty-seven years old. It's time."

"Let me get this straight. You're trying to break up with me *and* fix me up with another woman, both at the same time? Do I have that right?"

"Not any woman. You and Deidre are a matched set. I've seen the way you act when you're together. You could easily fall in love with her if you'd give it half a chance. It might not be clear to you what you should be doing with your life, but it's clear to me."

"Go ahead," he said with something close to a sneer. "Tell me. I know you're dying to."

"All right. You need to get out of the nightclub business. It's wrong for you. Buy some land. Plant it. Grow crap. And settle down . . . with the right woman. Someone who's as . . . as dazzling as you are. You need someone spectacular. Someone brainy and gorgeous and successful, but grounded, too. Like you."

He spoke with almost a sense of wonder. "This is so mind-numbingly fascinating. So tell me . . . What do I do about the fact that I might be maybe"—his gaze wavered ever so slightly—"falling a little bit in love with you?"

A sob threatened to spill right out of her. Somehow she managed to alter it into a harsh, unfunny laugh. "You're not."

"You know that, then."

She did. As surely as she knew anything. *A little bit in love.* As if there were such a thing. She would not cry in front of him. *Never.* "You're a champion. That's in your blood. It's the mind-set that's made you great. But this is life, not a game. And instead of throwing up a smoke screen, think about what I've said. About you. About Deidre. About everything."

This made him furious. "What happens with us, then? After I've hooked up with Deidre, that is."

"Nothing happens with us."

"Don't you want to be *pals*?" The rough sweep of his arm made him wince, but he didn't seem to care. "Get together now and then to have a couple of beers? Go to a strip club? Poker night? Just us *guys*."

She couldn't take any more. "I'll wait in the hall until Jonah gets here."

"You do that," he said.

*

I might be maybe . . . falling a little bit in love with you. Love either was or wasn't. She knew that now. For the first time since she was a kid, she cried. All the way to her apartment—big, blubbery tears that sloshed down her cheeks and dripped on her jacket. Tears that came from a well with no bottom.

She'd waited too long to fall in love. That was why this was so hard. She should have fallen in love for the first time when she was a teenager, like any normal girl. And a couple more times after that. If she'd done things the normal way, she'd have practice dealing with heartbreak, but she'd had none. That was why her world had fallen apart.

The Sonata's front wheel climbed the curb as she turned into the alley behind Spiral. She had to pack up her things, but she couldn't go inside with her nose running and tears everywhere. She couldn't let anyone see her so broken. She backed up and drove blindly to the lakefront. When she got there, she stumbled across the grass to the lakeshore path.

The wind was sharp off the water. It cut hard through her sweatshirt, but her tears kept running. All the tears she'd never let herself shed over the years were escaping at the same time. Tears for a mother she couldn't remember, a father who had loved and resented her, and an ex-quarterback who'd stolen her heart when she wasn't paying attention.

She started to run. There weren't many joggers on this part of the path, and a few snowflakes scuttled in the wind. November would be here in a couple of days. And then winter. A cold, Chicago winter. She ran faster, trying to outrun her misery.

A woman clad in trendy athletic gear and pushing a jogging stroller was running toward her. As the woman came closer, her pace slowed, and then stopped. "Are you all right?" she asked as her baby slept peacefully in the stroller.

Piper knew how crazed she must look. She slowed long enough to acknowledge the woman's concern. "My . . . dog died."

The woman's ponytail swung. "I'm sorry," she said.

Piper started to run again. She'd told another lie. She'd never been a liar, but now she'd become a pro. All those lies.

"I go by Esme. Lady Esme, actually. Esmerelda is a family name. . . . The fact is . . . I'm your stalker."

She spun around and yelled after the woman. "I broke up with a man I love with all my heart, and he will never, ever love me the same way, and I hurt so bad I don't know what to do with myself."

The only indication that the woman heard was the way she raised her arm from the handle of the jogging stroller and waved.

Piper gazed out at the lake, her hands in fists at her side, her teeth chattering, icy tears on her cheeks. She had to find a new self. A self who was indestructible and who would never, ever again let this happen to her.

A week passed. Piper was gone. It was as though she'd never been there. The cleaning staff had scrubbed his blood off the apartment wall and put the furniture back where it belonged. Coop had walked in there once and couldn't go again.

The image of Piper standing in front of him with a gun shoved to her head was seared on his brain. At that exact moment he'd understood. It was as if a gust of wind had swept away the fog that had obscured the truth he should have recognized long before. But instead of coming out with it right away, he'd screwed up bad at the hospital. He hadn't said the right thing, which was ironic, considering his reputation for working a good sound bite. Years of having microphones shoved in his face had taught him how to divulge exactly what he wanted to, precisely as he intended. But when it came to saying the right words to Piper, he'd fumbled in the worst possible way, and now she wouldn't take his calls.

The wound in his side was healing, but the rest of him was a mess. Someone knocked on his office door. This was the first time in days that anybody had bothered him. He didn't blame them for keeping their distance. He was brusque with the customers, unhappy with the servers, and outright hostile to his bouncers. He'd even gotten into an argument with Tony because Tony insisted there was nothing wrong with the club's HVAC system. But the air was stagnant, not circulating. So heavy with the funk of perfume and liquor it had seeped into Coop's pores.

He twisted from the computer screen he'd been staring at for who knew how long and directed his wrath toward the door. "Go away!"

Jada barged into his office. "You broke up with Piper! How could you do that?"

"Piper broke up with *me.* And how do you know about it?"

"I talked to her on the phone. At first she didn't tell me, but I finally got it out of her."

He leaned back in his chair, trying to be casual, even though he wanted to shake the details out of her. "So . . . what did she say about me?"

"Just that she hadn't seen you since the accident."

"And from this you deduced that I'd broken up with her?"

"She sounded sad." Jada dropped down on the couch. "Why did she break up with you?"

"Because she thinks I didn't take our relationship seriously." He couldn't sit a moment longer. He shot up from his desk, then pretended to adjust the shutter slats on the window behind him.

"Is that what she said?" Jada asked.

"Not in so many words, but . . ." He made himself go over to the small refrigerator next to the bookcases. "She's extremely competitive. She thinks I am, too."

She leaned forward like a minishrink. "Aren't you?"

"Not about her." He pulled out a Coke and held it up. "Want one?"

Jada shook her head. "Are you going to try to get her back?"

"Yeah."

"You don't sound too confident."

"I'm confident."

"You don't sound like it."

She was right. He snapped the Coke's pull-tab, even though he couldn't drink anything right now. "She won't talk to me. She won't answer my texts or pick up her phone." He wasn't exactly sure why he was telling a teenager all this, except that she'd asked, and nobody else had been brave enough.

"You should go to her place and knock on her door," Jada said. "She's staying at her friend Amber's. Or . . . you could wait by her car and then kind of jump out at her and make her listen to you."

"That's okay in the movies, but in real life, it's called stalking. I want to talk to her, not piss—not make her madder."

Another knock sounded on his door. "Get lost!"

The door opened anyway. This time it was Deidre Joss. Now he'd need to be polite, if he still remembered how.

"Bad time?" she asked.

"Sorry, Deidre. I thought it was Tony."

"Poor Tony."

He turned to Jada. "We can talk later."

She hopped up from the couch. "Okay, but don't tell Mom I yelled at you. She doesn't like anything that upsets you."

"Too bad everybody doesn't feel that way," he muttered.

Deidre closed the door after her. He realized he still had the Coke can and held it out. "Want one?"

"No thanks." She looked as cool and sleek as ever in a tidy black suit. No rumpled jeans or Bears T-shirt. No blueberry eyes. Her hair was a smooth, dark curtain instead of a crazy muddle meandering here and there.

"How's the injury?" she said.

"Barely noticeable." Unless he moved too fast. It hurt then, but he wasn't complaining.

"I'm glad to hear it." She came farther into the room. "You haven't returned my calls." She said it without any snark, only sympathy. She was too nice. That's exactly why he could never fall in love with her, and Piper should know him well enough to understand that. "I've heard from Noah's attorney," she said. "He's going to plea-bargain."

Coop got rid of the Coke. "That'll make it simpler."

"I went to see Noah to make sure he understands that once the justice system is done with him, he'll have to find somewhere else to live. Far away from the city. Back to Mommy, is my guess." She slipped her bag from her shoulder and set it on the couch. "I feel like an idiot. I knew he was possessive, but he made my life so much easier after Sam died that I ignored it. I came here to apologize for not being smarter about him and making you go through all this."

"We all have our obtuse times." Especially him. He needed to talk to Piper. He had to explain how he'd felt when he'd seen that gun jammed to her head, but she was making it impossible.

Deidre gave him a bright smile. "You'll be getting a formal offer from us tomorrow. I have complete faith in your vision, and I'm looking forward to financing you. I should have trusted my gut and made this deal weeks ago, but I let Noah get in my head."

The time had come to say it out loud. He tucked his thumb in the pocket of his jeans, then pulled it back out again. "I'm getting out of the business, Deidre. Selling the club." It felt good to finally put his cards on the table.

Her businesswoman's poker face failed her. "But you've been so passionate. Are you sure about this? What's changed?"

"It's been creeping up on me slowly." As slowly as anything could creep up with Piper Dove pushing her misgivings at him like a bulldozer. But Piper was right. All the satisfaction he used to experience when he walked into the club was gone. Spiral was a great place, and he'd enjoyed creating it, but he hadn't enjoyed the day-to-day, and the idea of spending years going from one club to another had lost its allure. "I liked the challenge, liked the idea of building something from scratch, but as it turned out, that was all I liked. I thought nightclubs would be a good business for me—high risk, high reward—but I was wrong."

"Because . . . ?"

He gave her the simplest answer. "I miss the mornings."

She didn't get it, but Piper would understand how tired he was of crowds, of yelling over music, of the smells and flashing strobes. He was sick of living so much of his life at night. He wanted clean air. He wanted more than three hours of sleep before he went out for a morning run. He wanted to do exactly as Piper had said. To "grow crap." He didn't know how he'd work that out, but then he didn't know how he was going to work out a lot of things right now. He only knew he had to make some big changes.

He gazed at his jersey hanging on the wall behind her. "A friend of mine tried to tell me this was the wrong business for me, but it took a while before I figured that out for myself."

"Piper?"

He didn't deny or admit it.

"I called her the other day," Deidre said. "We talked."

It seemed as though everybody was talking to Piper except him.

"Do you know she thinks the two of us should be a couple?" Deidre twisted a silver ring on her finger. "But that's not going to happen, is it?"

He hated hurting women, but he owed her honesty. "I'm afraid not. And I'm sorry about that."

"Not all that sorry." She tucked a lock of hair behind her ear and gave him a rueful smile. "Once I got some perspective, I understood why I'm not the right woman for you. You need someone more . . . unconventional."

Interesting how all these women believed they knew what he needed.

"I'm sorry we won't be doing business together," she said. "If you change your mind, let me know."

"I'll do that," he said, even though he knew he wouldn't.

As soon as Deidre left, he picked up his phone, stared down at it, then sent Piper another text.

I love you. Not a little. With all my heart.

The text went undelivered. She'd finally blocked him.

22

"I don't want to meet him," Berni protested as Piper led her into the coffee shop where they were supposed to meet Willie Mahoney in exactly ten minutes. "He'll think I'm some old lady who's lost her mind."

An apt description for the way Piper felt—old beyond her years and barely able to function. She missed Coop desperately. Getting out of bed in the morning was as much as she could handle, and only a sense of duty was forcing her to fulfill her obligation to Berni.

She played on the older woman's soft heart. "He's a nice man, and he's lonely. You know what it feels like to lose a spouse. You're the perfect person to cheer him up."

"I don't see why it has to be me. He'll think I'm a crackpot."

"He'll think you're interesting, and you need to see him for yourself so you can put this behind you."

Maybe Piper could begin to put Coop behind her if only he'd stop trying to contact her, but he was too competitive to give up without a hard fight. She should have done what he wanted. She should have moved in with him and smothered him with so much affection that she stopped being a challenge. If she'd done that, he would have pushed her out the door as fast as he could. But she hadn't done that because she wasn't tough enough.

She and Berni were ten minutes early, but Willie was already seated at the same back table where he and Piper had talked a week and a half ago. "That's him," she said.

"You didn't tell me he was so good-looking," Berni whispered.

He'd slicked what was left of his hair to his pink scalp. His dress shirt looked as though he'd tried to iron it himself, and he'd accessorized his gray trousers with what appeared to be a new pair of white sneakers. Piper slipped her arm around Berni's waist, grateful for the solid feel of her. "I wanted to surprise you. Let's go."

Berni moved forward as though she were heading for her execution. Willie rose, and Piper introduced them. Berni charged right in. "I know you must think I'm a crazy old lady."

Piper couldn't let that pass. "The first time you saw Willie he was wearing a cheesehead."

"That's true," Willie agreed as they all took their seats. "It keeps people away."

Berni regarded him with concern. "Why would you want to do that? People need other people."

"That's what my kids tell me when they call. Once a week but they can't be bothered to visit."

"You're lucky to have kids. Howard and I couldn't. Howard had a low count, if ya know what I mean."

Willie nodded sagely. "That's too bad. Tough on you both."

Berni dropped her purse to the floor. "I'll say. When Howard—"

Piper jumped up. "I have some calls to make." She didn't, but she was already depressed enough without having to hear about Howard Berkovitz's low sperm count.

Berni waved her off.

Piper camped outside the coffee shop, sitting at one of two metal café tables designed for warmer days instead of the city's typical November gloom. The low-hanging gray clouds obscured any possibility of sunshine. She wondered how long it took the average person to get over a broken heart. Maybe if she tripled that time, she'd have an idea of when she might return to normal again, because right now, she was stumbling through every day feeling as though she had jagged, broken pieces sticking out of her skin.

Her phone rang.

"Piper, it's Annabelle Champion."

Annabelle's cheery voice made her feel marginally better. Annabelle chatted for a few minutes before she got to the point. "I'd like to meet with you about doing some work for me. The company I hired to do background checks has gotten lazy, and I want you to take over the job."

A month ago, Piper would have been ecstatic, but all her edges had grown soft, as if her old self had reached its expiration date. Duke whispered in her ear. *"It's no business for a girl. You shoulda believed me."*

Duke was dead wrong. Her unhappiness had nothing to do with being female and everything to do with her mistaken belief that running Dove Investigations was all she wanted from life.

She rubbed her palm on her jeans. "Can I get back to you? I'm incredibly grateful, but I'm . . . rethinking a few things."

"Do you want to tell me about it?"

Annabelle was so open, so nonjudgmental, that Piper nearly confided in her, but how could a happy woman with a successful business and a husband who loved her understand?

She fell back on a truthful but less revealing response. "It turns out that stakeouts bore me to tears, and I hate telling women their husbands are cheating on them."

"Understandable," Annabelle said.

"I need to reassess."

"That's good for all of us to do occasionally. Get rid of what doesn't work and create something new out of what does."

Great advice, except Piper no longer knew what did or didn't work for her.

After their conversation, Piper went back inside only to have Berni shoo her away with the news that Willie was going to drive her home.

✶

Piper had told him no. And no meant no, right? But Coop couldn't sleep. Kept forgetting to eat. And he'd started staring longingly at the liquor bottles behind the bar. He'd been sure she'd finally pick up one of his phone calls or at least answer a text, but that wasn't happening. He was no closer to speaking with her now than he'd been when she'd walked out of his hospital room one week and one day ago. He couldn't take it any longer, and he drove to Piper's old condo building.

On the way there, he kept remembering what he'd said to Jada about stalking, but trying to have a simple conversation with Piper against her will hardly constituted harassment, did it?

So maybe it was a gray area.

The guys who lived downstairs had buzzed him in before, but

this time they didn't respond, even though he saw movement through their front windows. Next, he tried Jennifer MacLeish but got no answer. He hit the button for Mrs. Berkovitz. "Who's this?" she replied over the intercom.

"It's Cooper Graham, Mrs. B. Can you let me in?"

"Cooper who?"

"Graham. Cooper Graham. Could you hit the buzzer so I can get in?"

"I would," she said hesitantly, "but I . . . I hurt both my hands, and I can't press the button."

A flat-out lie, since she was already using the intercom.

"Try with your elbow," he said with forced patience.

"My arthritis."

He thought for a minute. "If I come up, maybe you could give me some more of that fudge? Best I ever tasted."

A long pause, and then a hoarse whisper. "She won't let me. She warned all of us not to let you in." She stopped whispering. "It's not good to play games with a woman's heart. And that's all I'm going to say about that."

The intercom clicked off. That made him so mad he did the thing he swore he'd never do. He waited by her car, even though it made him feel like he wasn't much better than Karah's ex-boyfriend Hank Marshall. But he had to talk to Piper, and what else was he supposed to do?

He stood in the cold for nearly two hours before she finally appeared. She wore one of the puffy winter coats Chicago women relied on. She'd taken the scissors to her hair again, and it fluttered in soft little feathers.

She saw him right away and came to a dead stop. She shoved

her hands deep into the pockets of her coat. "*Leave me alone!*" She spun around and charged right back into the building.

He was furious with himself. She'd sent a clear message, and he'd ignored it. He felt like he needed a shower.

He drove aimlessly, not knowing what to do now. Eventually he headed for the gym, even though the doctors hadn't cleared him to work out. On the way, a cop stopped him for speeding but predictably refused to give him a ticket until Coop insisted on it. Piper was right. He was a demon behind the wheel, and he needed to be held accountable.

Piper with the gun at her head . . . The image had frozen in his mind like a frame of film stuck in a projector. It was at that moment the mist had finally cleared, and his brain had comprehended what his heart had been trying to tell him for weeks—how much he loved Piper Dove. She was part of him. His laughter, his comfort.

More than that. She was also his conscience and his touchstone. His challenge, too, but not in the way she believed. Being with her challenged him to become his better self, to find a place in the world that no longer depended on a scoreboard victory, to let another person in and trust her to help carry the weight.

But what was he to Piper? Thanks to Duke Dove, he might never find out.

Piper had told him enough about her childhood for him to figure out the rest. Pleasing Duke meant she had to swallow every emotion that displeased him. Her father had punished her tears and rewarded her stoicism. His mission had been to shape her into a warrior strong enough to survive the harsh world that had killed her mother, and he'd built that warrior. But then he'd tried to shut her down by refusing to give her the battlefield that was her birthright.

Coop's own upbringing had been so different. Even as his father had battled his private demons, he'd never shamed Coop for the normal emotions all kids experienced growing up.

"Guys have to cry sometimes, son. It's good to get it out."

Piper hadn't known that kind of emotional acceptance. Pleasing the father she loved meant she could never show weakness, or softness, or vulnerability.

Coop slammed on the brakes so fast he nearly got rear-ended. Of course she was afraid to talk to him. Being forced into a conversation that was guaranteed to be emotional—a conversation where he'd damn well make certain he said what he had to and make her say whatever it was that lay underneath all her bull—wasn't what she'd been trained for.

The sight of that gun . . . The sounds of Jada's sobs . . . And Pipe, standing there so helplessly, her eyes focused on only him, the message as clear as if she'd spoken it aloud.

Teamwork.

✶

The sight of Coop standing by her car yesterday had undone whatever microscopic progress she'd made to move her life forward. Tall and sturdy, those big, capable hands stretched long at his sides, November sunlight striking his cheekbones . . . She'd grown dizzy with a longing so painful it had threatened to bring her to her knees.

She was staring blindly out her office window when Jada called. "You're a detective," the teenager declared. "Clara and I think you should do something about it."

"I'm not exactly in a position to solve the problem of child sex trafficking."

"But you could, like, pretend you were a kid or something on the Internet. And get these guys to maybe meet up with you and arrest them."

"I'm a detective. I can't arrest anybody."

"You could work with the police," Jada insisted. "And talk to important people about how they can't arrest these girls as being, like, prostitutes."

Jada's passion was admirable, but Piper barely knew how to get through the day, let alone solve a problem of this scope.

When their call ended, Piper buried her face in her hands. Annabelle had offered her a job performing background checks, and Deidre Joss had called to talk to her about doing more work for Joss Investments. Dove Investigations was taking off, but she couldn't bring herself to care. Last night's visit to Jen's apartment had been the only bright spot in her week.

"I e-mailed you a YouTube link," she'd told Chicago's finest meteorologist. "Use it as you see fit."

"What do you mean?"

"You'll see."

Piper had finally been able to help Jen by unearthing a video someone had recently posted, a video that had been made during Dumb Ass's college years. Piper had immediately backed it up for posterity. The video showed a younger Dumb Ass on all fours, shirt off, wearing a bra with a pair of women's underpants on his head, as a hairy-chested frat brother rode on his back.

"Oh my god!" Jen had exclaimed. "That pompous ass is mine forever!"

Piper blinked her eyes at the memory. She was doing a lot of that lately.

Her office door clicked open. Her head shot up as Heath Champion walked in. "Long time, no see," the agent said.

She couldn't handle any more trouble. At the same time, she finally had a distraction from her brooding. "What do you want?"

"I'm here to negotiate a deal," he said. "For Coop. He wants you to move in with him."

"*What?* He sent his *agent* to negotiate this?"

"Football players," Heath said in disgust. "A bunch of spoiled brats. They don't know how to do a damned thing for themselves."

She dug her fingernails into her palms. "I don't believe this."

"At least it doesn't involve livestock. I hate it when I have to negotiate livestock."

"Mr. Champion—"

"Heath. I think we know each other well enough by now."

"Heath . . . I am not moving in with your client." Her neck had started to hurt along with her stomach. And she wanted to cry. She dug her fingernails deeper. "Out of curiosity . . . Agents get ten percent when they make a deal for a client, right?"

"The percentage varies, depending on the type of negotiation."

"So if you did negotiate this deal—which you're not going to do—how would you get your cut?"

"Vegetables. Next summer."

"I see."

He leaned back on the heels of his very expensive loafers. "Just to clarify. You don't want to move in with him?"

"That's right." Moving in with him would mean acting as though they were nothing more than sex pals. Before the first day was over, she'd be begging him to fall in love with her. Just the thought made prickles of sweat break out all over her.

"Then make a counteroffer," he said.

"I don't have to make any kind of offer!"

"It's a negotiation. That's part of it."

His exaggerated patience made her want to leap over her desk and throttle him. "My counteroffer is for him to get out of my life."

He had the gall to appear disappointed in her. "That's not a counteroffer. That's an ultimatum. In my experience—and I have a lot of it—these things go better when both parties negotiate in good faith."

She'd stepped smack into the middle of Crazy Town, and ironically, that finally steadied her. She remembered her first meeting with Heath, when Coop had tossed her contract at him and Heath had negotiated more money. For her. These two didn't have a normal agent-client relationship, and they wanted to suck her into their nutso world. Fine. Fight crazy with crazy. This was something she could handle. "A counteroffer? How about this? If he gets out of my life, I promise to send him all my Bears T-shirts."

"I can guarantee he won't accept a few T-shirts in lieu of life in a luxury condo. Surely you can do better."

All she wanted was for the misery to stop, and that wouldn't happen until Coop left her alone. She glared at the Python. "If he gets out of my life, I'll personally fix him up with Deidre Joss."

"You're still not taking this seriously."

She was taking it more seriously than he imagined. Why was Coop putting her through this? She should have talked to him yesterday. She should have stood in the cold and let him say what he had to say without uttering a word in return. But she'd been too big a coward. She still was. "I'll do one free month of IT work for the club. But I'll only work with Tony, and only if Coop forgets I exist."

"Three free months."

"Two months."

"Reasonable." He pulled out his phone. "Let me check with him."

"You do that," she said.

He headed outside into the parking lot. Through the window, she saw him talking on his cell. She watched him pace between her car and his SUV. Finally, he pocketed his phone and came back inside. "No dice. He wants a face-to-face meeting."

She couldn't do it. She couldn't. "No."

"I thought you wanted to get rid of him?"

"More than I've ever wanted anything."

"Then offer him something he can't resist. Other than yourself."

She exploded out of her chair. "When did I get to be so fricking irresistible? Will you tell me that?"

"I'm not the person to answer. Not that I don't find you charming."

She bared her teeth. "I don't want to talk to him!"

"I understand. But this is a negotiation."

It was madness was what it was. "Two free months of IT, and I'll do his employee background checks for a year. One full year!"

"Now you're talking." He slithered out into the parking lot again. She sank behind her desk. They'd made a pact to torture her.

On the other side of the window, Heath was talking. He braced a hand on his hip, pushing back the front edge of his sports coat. Talked some more. Finally, he came back inside.

"He turned you down."

"Of course he did," she said bitterly. "He hates to lose so much he'll do anything to win, no matter how unconscionable."

"Not the kindest assessment coming from a woman in love."

She stared at a point right above his eyebrows. "I'm not in love. And you need to leave."

"I could do that, but . . . it seems Annabelle's stuck her nose in this whole affair, and she's decided you and Coop need some kind of closure. I don't know what it is with women and closure, but there you have it. I should warn you that dealing with me is easier than being forced to deal with my wife. I know she seems decent, but inside, she's a desperado."

"Annabelle wants me to do this?"

"She's real big on that 'closure' thing." He sounded regretful. "If I screw this up, I promised I'd call her, and she'll be over here right away."

Piper collapsed. She could fight the men, but not Annabelle.

A wave of weariness came over her. "I'll meet him, but only in public." She slumped back in her chair. "Big Shoulders Coffee tomorrow afternoon. And only if he gives me his word of honor that he won't try to contact me again afterward."

Somehow she'd pull herself together enough to get through it. The coffee shop was well lit and small enough for conversations to be overheard, so he couldn't get too heated, and she'd be guaranteed to keep her clothes on.

"Hold on." Heath whipped out his cell.

She wanted to scream. Or cry.

This time the Python stayed inside. "Coop, she'll meet you, but only in public—Big Shoulders Coffee tomorrow afternoon—and only if you agree not to contact her again after that." Heath listened, tapped his foot. "Uh-huh . . . Uh-huh . . . All right." He hung up and looked over at her. "It has to be today. And not at Big Shoulders. He has a meeting at city hall, so he'll see you in Daley Plaza right afterward. Two o'clock. It doesn't get much more public than that. I think you should take the deal."

How could winning matter so much? He already had her heart. Now he wanted to stomp it to death.

"Agree?" Heath said.

Her shoulders slumped. "Agree."

"I'll never complain about livestock again," he muttered as he crossed to the door and let himself out.

She shot across the rug, flung the door back open, and yelled into the parking lot. "I hope you choke on your blood vegetables!"

He turned and gave her a thumbs-up, whatever that meant.

23

Piper marched toward the Daley Center as if she were heading to her execution. Anger would have been a more useful emotion than the panic that held her in its grip. She needed to get through this with at least a shred of dignity intact. No matter how much she loved him, how much she'd yearn to fall into his arms, she'd have to hang tough.

An alien-like Picasso sculpture dominated the large plaza in front of the thirty-one-story Daley Center building. Picasso himself had donated the sculpture to the city, and once an artist of his stature handed over such a thing, nobody had the nerve to return it. As Piper approached, the sculpture's two metal eyes glowered at her, and she glowered right back. Glowering was better than running away.

The wind cracked the American flag, and women's long hair blew backward. Her zippered sweater wasn't warm enough for such a cold, damp day. She should have worn her puffy coat, but that would have required thought.

Coop was already there. He stood in the shadow of the Picasso with his head down, unrecognized by the people scurrying past. For a moment, she forgot to breathe.

He saw her, but he didn't approach. Instead, he waited for her to come to him. He wore a dark, formal suit, white shirt, and repp-striped necktie. She stopped a few steps away, far enough to keep from curling into his chest. "You win," she said stonily. "Say whatever it is you want to say, and then leave me alone."

He gazed at her as if he were memorizing her face. She waited for something profound to come out of his mouth, but it didn't. "What have you been up to?" he said.

"Avoiding you. It's been a full-time job."

He nodded, as if he were agreeing with her. He was watching her so intensely, she had to look away. "Get it over with, Coop. Why did you send your shark of an agent after me?"

"I needed to talk to you, and you were making that impossible."

She couldn't soften in front of him. "I'm here. Say whatever it is you want to say."

"You might not like it."

"Then maybe you'd better keep it to yourself."

"I can't do that. It's . . ." He hunched his shoulders against the wind. "It's tough, that's all."

She thought she understood. "You want to end this on your terms, not on mine, so go ahead. Break up with me. You'll feel better if it comes from you, and I can handle it."

"I don't want to break up with you."

"Then what do you want?" she cried. "I won't move in with you!"

"I get that." A pair of pigeons scuttled between them. "I know you're not strong enough to say how you feel about me, so I'm going to tell you how I feel about you."

He was accusing her of being weak. Nobody did that, and she went on the offensive, throwing his words back at him. "You already did. You're maybe a little bit in love with me, remember?"

"I only said it that way to keep from scaring you off."

He'd thrown her off balance.

"You're skittish about us," he said. "You have been from the beginning, and if I'd told you the truth, you would have run. You still might, because I only think I know how you feel about me. I can read your mind about nearly everything, but not about this."

She took a bittersweet morsel of comfort from knowing she'd protected herself, at least a little. "I'm not following this conversation, but when have I been able to follow anything you and your agent doppelgänger do?"

"I love you, Piper. I didn't fall a little bit in love with you. I fell head over heels."

The wind screeched in her ears, and her stomach pitched.

He didn't move. Didn't touch her. A chunk of her hair whipped against her cheek.

"I must have known for a long time," he said quietly, "but I didn't understand what I was feeling until that bastard had his gun on you, and I felt my chest crack open."

She shoved her hands in the pockets of her sweater, not believing, fighting the lure of hope. "An adrenaline rush can make you feel lots of strange things."

"I know all about adrenaline rushes, and they go away. My feelings aren't going to do that."

The bitterness of reality crept up on her. "It hasn't even been two weeks. Give it time."

"Can you really be so cynical?"

She didn't feel cynical. She felt as fragile as spun sugar. She'd pushed his champion's back to the wall, and he was fighting his way out in the only way he knew, by brute force.

"Take a risk, Piper," he said. "I'm not Duke Dove. Tell me how you feel—the truth. Either you love me or you don't. Dig deep. I need to know."

She didn't have to dig deep. But saying it aloud was impossible. Yet, if she didn't, wasn't she taking the coward's way out?

She was hard-core. Hanging tough was how she lived. She shoved her fists deeper in her pockets. "Yes, I love you. Sure, I do. How could I not?" She threw the words in his face. "I love you enough not to let this go any further. We're too different to have a future, so what's the point?"

"The only thing different about us is our bank accounts."

"A big difference."

"Only if you believe money is all that counts."

"And fame. And nightclubs. And Super Bowl rings—"

"Which neither of us has."

"—and Hollywood girlfriends."

"People say opposites attract. The funny thing about that is we're not opposites. We're the same person, different sides of the same coin." A muscle twitched at the corner of his jaw. "Except I'm clearheaded and you're not."

"That isn't—"

"Here's what I don't get: Why is it so hard for you to believe I could love you?"

He was trying to confuse her, and she said the first thing that came into her head. "I'm not beautiful. And you're famous. And I'm not domestic."

He turned belligerent. "Is that all you've got?"

"And your money."

"You already mentioned that."

A group of businessmen had spotted him and began to close in. She spun on them. "Not now!"

For once, Coop didn't try to make up for her brusqueness with a good ol' boy acknowledgment. He didn't even turn.

The men shot her a few dirty looks as they backed away. She didn't care. She'd play bad cop forever to protect him.

"Here's what I know." His intensity was scaring her. "Your father might have meant well, but he screwed with your head so bad that you've lost touch with who you are inside. It's you against the world, and you're scared to death of anything that makes you feel vulnerable."

She had to fight back. "This coming from Mr. Tough Guy himself."

"I'm stubborn and I'm driven, but I've never pretended to be invincible. You're the one with the will of steel."

"That's not true!" she exclaimed. "I fell in love with you, didn't I? And nothing could make me feel less invincible than that."

"Which is exactly why you're so hell-bent on pushing me away."

He was wrong, and there was only one way she could make him understand that and end this forever. She'd have to go through with it. Gut it out until it was blindingly clear to him . . . and to her . . . what an impossible couple they were. She shot up her chin and glared at him. "Okay. I'll do it. I'll move in with you. We'll give it a few weeks and then you'll see."

He drew her to his chest. "Oh, babe . . ."

She closed her eyes. Rested her cheek against his chest. Surrendered.

He clasped her face in his palms and pressed his forehead to hers. Their noses touched. He brushed the tip of his nose gently against hers. "The thing is . . ." he said. "That invitation's off the table."

"*What?*" She reared back. He'd thrown a fake. A classic quarterback fake.

"I'd trust Piper Dove with my life." The tenderness in his eyes cut through her. "But I'm not ready to trust Duke Dove's daughter with my heart."

"Then what do you want?" It was nearly a wail.

"I want a legal document."

"What are you talking about?"

"Marriage."

She pushed herself away from him. "You can't be serious!"

"I didn't plan to bring it up yet. I intended to give you some time to calm down and get used to being loved. But now I see what a mistake that would be. You're so jittery that all you'll be doing is looking for reasons to break us up."

"That's not true!" It was exactly true. The plaza blurred around her, and her ears started to ring.

"You're as stubborn as I am." He brushed his knuckles across her cheek. "The way I see it, as soon as we're legally married, we'll both settle down enough to figure out how to make it work."

"That's crazy! Nobody does that."

"Clearly. But these are extraordinary circumstances, and this is the only scenario I can see working for us."

"It's insane!"

"Probably to most people. But we're different. So I guess you have a decision to make."

"Isn't it enough to say I love you?" Her words were nearly a sob.

"You're the best man I've ever known. Just hearing your voice turns me into mush. But that doesn't mean marriage. I already said I'd live with you, and now you're bullying me!"

"Kind of." He touched her hair with his fingers. "But put yourself in my place. If you were me, what would you do about you?"

"I'd—I'd— That's an impossible question."

"Only because you don't like the answer." He tilted his head toward the building behind them. "I seem to remember there's a marriage license office inside."

Right then she knew. "You planned this, didn't you? That's why you wanted to meet me here. This wasn't some accidentally convenient location."

"I'll admit it occurred to me, but only as an emergency backup plan, and it seems as though that's where we are now." He grasped her elbow and began steering her across the plaza toward the building's glass front. "Don't worry about a thing. It's only a piece of paper. Nothing to be afraid of."

"I'm not . . ."

"Take some deep breaths. That's all you have to do. I'll handle everything else."

That's when she lost her mind. Instead of digging in her heels and pulling away, she went with him. She went right along, as if she had no will of her own. She didn't look at him, didn't talk to him, but she didn't run away, either. She simply gave in to his bullheaded determination.

The marriage license bureau was on the first floor, a spacious glass-fronted area with a long counter holding rows of computers. A barrel-chested clerk standing behind one of those computers spotted Coop seconds after they walked in and rushed them to a private office.

It was all a blur. The clerk asked for her driver's license, and Coop had to take it out of her wallet. When it was time for her signature, he guided her hand to the proper line. And throughout the process, he rubbed her back, as if he were soothing a frightened animal.

With the final paperwork in hand, he led her back outside. When they reached the plaza, he tucked his fingers under her chin. "I know you're upset. Worse than that you're scared, and since fear is something you don't know how to handle, we need to get this out of the way as soon as we can. I'll handle all the arrangements. Invite whoever you want. All you have to do is show up at my place. Six o'clock tomorrow night."

"Tomorrow?" That thin, reedy voice couldn't belong to her.

"Call Heath if you need anything before then. It's best if he deals with you."

"But . . ."

His face grew as grave as she'd ever seen. "I need a solid commitment from you, Pipe. I'm strong about a lot of things, but not about you. So you'll have to take it from here without me pushing you. I've brought us to the goal line. You'll have to carry the ball in."

"But tomorrow? Couldn't we . . . postpone this?"

"For how long? A year? Five years? When would you be comfortable enough to do this?"

She looked down at her feet.

"Exactly. The longer you put it off, the harder it'll be for you."

"But *tomorrow*?"

"I'm not as tough as you are, sweetheart. Better to get it over with and put us both out of our misery."

"I don't think I can do this."

"I hope you're wrong, because I gave you my word of honor. I said if you talked to me today, I wouldn't try to contact you again." His head dipped, and when he looked back up, she saw so much misery in his eyes she felt as if her own raw emotions were staring back at her. "This is all I've got, Pipe," he whispered. "I can't do the last part for you. Either you show up . . . or you don't."

And that was all. He walked away.

✶

Annabelle had great contacts and a talent for working miracles, so Coop dumped all the wedding arrangements on her, but only after she'd made him sit through her lecture. "Marriage is a serious commitment, Coop. Not something you should do impulsively, and this is so rash . . ." On and on she went. He understood how it might look to her, but he'd never done anything less impulsively. Pipe would understand. She had to. And she'd show up, too . . . because if she didn't— He couldn't think about it.

He spent the next day trying to find something to do with himself until six o'clock other than get drunk. The press had gotten word of his appearance at the marriage license bureau yesterday, but he wasn't returning their calls. Instead, he tested his recovery by running a couple of miles, then drank a pot of coffee and ran another mile. He went to the office and stared at his computer. Turned on ESPN. Turned it off. Tried to read.

Around one in the afternoon, Heath called. "I've got your former bouncer here. I gotta say, she's a little high-strung. And loud."

Coop gripped the phone tighter. "Among other things."

Pipe shouted at him in the background. "You can't get married without a prenup, you idiot! And a prenup isn't something you put together in a couple of hours!"

"I'm afraid she's got you there, Champ," Heath said.

"You're worth millions!" she yelled. And then, presumably to Heath, although she was still yelling loud enough for Coop to draw the phone back from his ear. "Do you see what I'm up against? He's an adrenaline junkie."

"She's obviously thought about this," Heath said. "Under the circumstances, I strongly advise you not to go any further without getting your attorneys involved."

"Otherwise, I'll take you for every cent you have!" Even with the phone held away from his ear, he had no trouble hearing that.

"Did you hear?" Heath said.

"Hard not to. You tell her to worry about herself." He hung up.

Annabelle worked her magic. His garden furniture and potting table disappeared from the terrace. Workers delivered chairs, along with outdoor heaters to keep the guests warm against the November night chill and a wooden crate with something that looked suspiciously like a chandelier poking out of the top. As the caterers took over his kitchen, he sealed himself upstairs, growing more anxious by the minute. When he couldn't stand it any longer, he called Heath. "Is she going to show up?"

"Not a clue. I figure you've got a fifty-fifty chance at best."

That wasn't what he wanted to hear.

The minister arrived at four thirty. Or, more properly, the "wedding officiant" arrived. Coop was a wreck.

Shortly after, the guests began to appear. He'd kept the list small, choosing only people Piper knew and would be comfortable with: Tony and the bouncers; Jada and Karah; Mrs. B., who appeared with a sheepish man she introduced as Willie Mahoney, her boyfriend. He wished he could have flown Faiza in, but leaving Canada would make her anxious. Jennifer MacLeish arrived with a happy-looking Eric Vargas on her arm.

Coop pulled her aside. "Have you talked to her?"

Jen looked worried. "Berni and I both knocked on her door, but she told us to go away—except not that politely—and she won't answer her phone. This was not your smartest move."

He was afraid she was right, and he tried to remember why he'd been so sure this would work.

Jonah came up to him. "You want me and the boys to go get her?"

Coop was so tempted, but he shook his head. "She has to do this on her own."

"Risky, boss. Very risky."

Nothing he didn't already know.

Six o'clock arrived. The doomsday hour. Everyone had appeared. Everyone except the bride. He was crazy to have given her an ultimatum. Nobody liked being backed into a corner, but that went triple for Piper Dove.

Another five minutes passed. Then ten more. He'd have to go out on the terrace soon and make the humiliating announcement that the wedding was off.

Just then, the elevator doors opened, and there she was.

She wore a stricken expression and a short lace off-the-shoulder dress that she'd probably bought at H&M and that reminded him of vanilla cake frosting. She'd pulled her hair away from her face with a narrow rhinestone headband that showcased her cheekbones. Every inch of her was perfection. Except for those big blue eyes, which were as close to terrified as he'd ever seen.

He was at her side in three long strides. As she gazed up at him, he saw something he'd never imagined. Something so inconceivable, he thought it was a trick of the light. But it was no trick. Piper Dove's eyes were brimming with tears.

The sight made his own eyes sting, and he clasped her hands. "Babe . . ."

She looked up at him, a single, beautiful tear caught on her bottom lashes. "I'm scared."

He'd never loved her more than at that moment. As crazy as this was, they were doing the right thing. "I know you are." He kissed the corners of her eyes. Tasted the salt. Understood what it cost her to reveal so much.

"You aren't scared?" she said.

"Not now. But a couple of minutes ago . . . You don't want to know."

Her glossy lips trembled. "You were afraid I wouldn't show up."

"Terrified."

"I couldn't do that to you. I love you too much."

The swelling in his throat made his voice husky. "I can see that. Because if you didn't, you wouldn't be here."

She pressed her palms to the lapels of his suit coat. "I don't know anything about being a wife. Are you sure about this?"

"Sixty percent."

That made her smile, the sweetest smile he'd ever seen, a smile so beloved he had to clear his throat before he could speak. "How about this for a plan?" He brushed his thumb against the corner of her mouth. "Once we get through the next couple of hours, we'll pretend tonight never happened. We'll live together, go about our lives, and never mention the word *marriage* again."

She beamed up at him. "You'd do that for me?"

"Absolutely."

"Okay, then."

He took her hand and slipped it through his bent elbow. "Pretend it's a bad dream."

"Not bad at all," he thought he heard her whisper.

He led her across the living room to the terrace door. Together, they stepped out into his fairyland of a rooftop garden.

A softly glimmering crystal chandelier hung from the center of a white canopy swagged with dozens of strands of twinkle lights. Flowers in big gold urns showcased all the colors of fall: plum dahlias, burgundy roses, green hydrangeas, and orange calla lilies. The guests, seated in gilded Chiavari chairs, turned as they entered, and he heard more than one sigh of relief followed by a piercing wolf whistle from Jonah. Piper managed a wobbly smile. He'd flown Amber in on a private plane from Houston as a surprise. She waved at Piper and began to sing "Come Away with Me" in her exquisite coloratura soprano.

Twists of brown and mulberry velvet ribbons marked the makeshift aisle, and the chandelier made her rhinestone headband glitter in her dark hair. She was so caught up in Amber's solo that she didn't notice who waited for them at the front of the aisle, not until the final chorus faded and he began to lead her forward.

Her fingers dug into his arm. "You didn't!" she whispered.

"We needed somebody to marry us," he whispered back.

"But . . ."

The last notes of the song faded away. He cupped his hand over hers as it rested in the crook of his arm and led her the rest of the way down the aisle to the place where Phoebe Somerville Calebow, the owner of the Chicago Stars, waited to marry them.

*

"I warned you from the beginning that I'm a user," Piper told her husband that night as she lay in his arms, all woozy and satiated from their lovemaking.

"How long do you think it'll be before I outlive my usefulness?"

"A very long time." She curled into his chest. She didn't know exactly how she'd pull it off, but she intended to be a superstar wife. "I can't believe we're married." She sighed.

"I thought we weren't going to mention it."

"Only tonight." She flipped to her back. "Now that I've landed a man, I'm thinking about letting myself go. No more dresses, makeup, haircuts . . ."

"You barely get haircuts now," he pointed out, drawing her close once again.

"Dresses are a lot of bother."

"Fine with me, but you're going to miss sneaking looks at yourself in the mirror whenever you get dressed up."

Her smile turned into a frown. "You have to get a prenup. Or a postnup. Honestly, Coop! For someone who's supposed to be a crackerjack businessman, you've been completely irresponsible."

He yawned and curled his hand over her thigh. "You and Heath work it out."

"Is that the way this marriage is going to go? The three of us. You, me, and your agent?"

"That's how it rolls when you marry an overprivileged ex-jock."

She laughed and held up her hand, admiring in the soft bedroom light the ring he'd given her. A spiral of tiny diamonds wrapped a narrow gold band. "You could have afforded a lot bigger."

"True." He kissed the slope of her breast. "But you'd have killed me."

He knew her so well. Not only her jewelry preference, but also her flaws and insecurities, along with every one of her hang-ups. But he loved her all the same.

"I have a ring for you, too," she said, "but you won't get it for a couple of weeks."

He twisted the platinum band she'd bought him by wiping out a big chunk of her savings. "I already have a ring."

"Not that kind of ring."

His head came up off the pillow. "Tell me you didn't—"

"I had to. It was on my conscience. Mrs. Calebow and I had a long conversation after the ceremony, and she and I worked out a trade. A replacement Super Bowl ring in exchange for some computer security work I'll be doing for the Stars this winter."

"Pipe, I don't give a damn about that ring."

"You'd better give a damn!" she exclaimed. "Because now I'll have to give up all my Bears T-shirts for real."

He laughed. "It's a good thing you're tough."

Not so tough. But tough enough. Because once you married a champion, you had to be ready to play at the top of your game.

EPILOGUE

Jada sat cross-legged on the floor of Piper and Coop's house in Lincoln Park and watched eleven-month-old Isabelle Graham and her twin brother, Will, wobble from one piece of furniture to the next looking totally drunk. They were batting around a scruffy pink pig and babbling to each other in a language only they understood, which made them even more adorable. She loved them with all her heart.

She remembered when Piper had found out she was having twins. Jada had been staying with them while her mom was in Lansing meeting Eric's parents for the first time. She'd been a junior in high school, old enough to stay by herself. But she liked spending time with Coop and Piper, so she hadn't bitched about it.

Piper was super nervous when she got pregnant, but that was nothing compared to what happened when she had her first ultrasound. Because Jada was taking biology—and because she'd pleaded with them—Piper and Coop had let her come along for the doctor's appointment. When Piper found out she was having twins, she had a total freak-out. She'd jumped off the table, ultrasound goo still plastered all over her stomach, and charged Coop. "*One!*" she'd yelled. "I said I'd have *one* for you! And you agreed to take care of it! I never said anything about two! Do you have to be an overachiever in *everything*?"

Coop had lifted her off her feet, getting goo all over himself, and said she'd be the best mother of twins ever because of her competitive nature. Then she'd yelled that he was the one with a competitive nature and that she was too emotional to have twins. Coop said it was true she was emotional and asked her if she felt like crying. When she said she did, he'd told her to go ahead. She had, but not for long, and then she'd started hugging him back. The whole time, the medical technician was standing there with the ultrasound thingy in her hand and staring at them like they were both crazy.

Coop had been right about Piper being a great mother, but Coop was a great dad, too. They'd both gone through a lot of changes in the three years since they'd gotten married. Coop had sold Spiral and started an urban gardening program. He already had seven gardens growing in abandoned lots that used to be littered with a bunch of old tires and broken liquor bottles. Coop had former gang members planting and weeding alongside old people and single mothers, everybody working together to feed their communities. In September, Coop was opening a training facility to aid young people in finding jobs in the food industry. Piper said that helping transform neighborhoods was a perfect occupation for a man who loved big challenges.

In Jada's opinion, Piper's work was even more interesting. Dove Investigations now specialized in background checks and fraud investigations for a bunch of companies, and Piper had enough business to hire two employees. But that wasn't the fascinating part. The more Jada had talked to Piper about child sex trafficking, the madder Piper had gotten until she was even more passionate than Jada. Now she used her computer skills to put pimps out of business and find the men who preyed on the girls. Among other things, she posed as a fourteen-year-old in online chat rooms. She also built phony Web sites that the police used to set up stings. Eric, who was a lieutenant now, took over from there. Piper said it was dirty, stomach-churning work, but she'd never felt cleaner.

Jada heard the caterer clanking dishes in the kitchen. Tonight was Coop and Piper's anniversary, and they were throwing a big party to make up for what Coop called their bargain-basement wedding. Piper and Jada didn't think it had been bargain-basement. Piper said it was the most beautiful wedding ever, and Jada loved it because it was the place where her mom had stolen Eric from Piper's friend Jen. That worked out, though, because Jen met a really great guy plus got this big meteorology award. As for Eric . . . He was the coolest stepdad. Jada could talk to him about anything, and he loved her mom. Jada hardly ever thought about what had happened with Hank. Maybe it was bloodthirsty, but she was glad he'd gotten killed in a prison fight.

✶

As the caterers set up a small table in the hallway, Coop stopped inside the living room door. While Jada had watched Isabelle and Will, he and Pipe had gotten dressed for tonight's party. They'd also managed to sneak in a quickie, a luxury since the twins had been born.

He gazed across the living room. Piper had dropped to her knees in the sleek red party dress she'd undoubtedly found on a sales rack somewhere. The twins were throwing themselves at her, one on each side. "Come on, monkeys," Piper said into their necks. "It's bedtime."

He went over to join his family. "I'll put them down," he said. "You relax before the guests get here."

"I'm very relaxed." He sincerely hoped Jada didn't pick up on the mischievous light in her eyes. "I'll take care of them," she said.

"It's okay. I'll handle it."

"No need. You go talk to Jada."

"I already talked to Jada," he said firmly.

Jada laughed. "You guys are ridiculous. You know you'll both end up putting them to bed."

He looked over at her. "You're my witness. You heard what Piper said. Once they came out of the chute, I was supposed to take care of them. Piper and I had an agreement."

"Which I honored," Piper said piously.

"Yeah. At three o'clock in the morning."

Piper smiled the smile that melted his bones. The smile that none of the city and state officials ever got to see when she was battling them in her fight to protect the street girls who had won both her heart and her will. She was the toughest woman he knew. Right up to the moment she walked inside their house.

"Come on, squirts. Bedtime." He swept Isabelle into his arms while Piper picked up Will.

Not long after, he stood between the two cribs as Piper delivered her final bedtime kisses. He was a lucky man. He had good friends, work he believed in, the children of his dreams, and a wife he cherished above all. The doorbell rang, and Piper took his hand. Together, they walked downstairs to greet their friends.

It was a good night to be Cooper Graham. But then every night was.

ACKNOWLEDGMENTS

How can I begin to thank the incredible team at William Morrow and Avon Books for their hard work, as well as the many friendships I've formed over the years: Carrie Feron, my longtime editor, confidante, and life coach; Pamela Spengler-Jaffee, who watches out for me when I'm not making her sip champagne in my shower (long story); Liate Stehlik, the amazing woman I want to be when I grow up; Tavia Kowalchuk, who carries me in her heart when she goes hiking. Thanks to the incomparable Lynn Grady, the superefficient Nicole Fischer and Leora Bernstein, and the enthusiastic Harper sales team: Brian Grogan, Doug Jones, Rachel Levenberg, Carla Parker, Dale Schmidt, and Donna Waitkus. I'm so appreciative of the help I've received from Shawn Nicholls and Angela Craft, as well as the digital marketing support from Tobly McSmith. Virginia Stanley, you've been my cheerleader for more years than I can remember. Elsie Lyons, thank you for my beautiful cover, and Shelly Perron, you are not only my valiant copy editor but the most patient woman on earth.

On the home front, if it weren't for my amazing assistant, Sharon Mitchell, the gap between my books would be much greater. My husband, Bill Phillips, is a man of many talents, including titling this book. My sister Lydia is my lifelong soul mate. I have worked with Steven Axelrod and Lori Antonson at the Axelrod Agency for so long I feel as though they're part of my family.

I am so blessed to have the most wonderful friends. They make me laugh, make me think, cheer me on, and inspire me, especially Nicki Anderson, Robyn Carr, Jennifer Greene, Kristin Hannah, Jayne Ann Krentz, Lindsay Longford, Dawn Struxness, Suzette Van, Julie Wachowski, and Margaret Watson. Andy Kamm and Allison Anderson, thank you for answering my questions. And, Jules, you're my watchdog Down Under.

To my publishers all over the world, you have made me feel so welcome. Special thanks to my dear Marisa Tonnezer at Ediciones B in Barcelona, as well as the remarkable team at Blanvalet in Munich, especially Nicola Bartels, Berit Bohm, Anna-Lisa Hollerbach, and Sebastian Rothfuss. Also my dear Angela Spizig, who is my "voice" in Germany.

To my international readers and bloggers, thank you for introducing my books to so many others. And to all my readers, I love that you demanded another Chicago Stars book. (For those of you not familiar with how Heath and Annabelle became a couple, I think you'll enjoy *Match Me If You Can,* a book also titled by my husband, as he never fails to remind me.) Thanks to all of you who've become my friends on Facebook, Twitter, and Instagram. If you're interested in a list of my books, as well as seeing the titles of the Chicago Stars books in order, please visit my Web site at susanelizabethphillips.com, where you can also sign up for my newsletter.

Happy reading, my friends!
Susan Elizabeth Phillips

ABOUT THE AUTHOR

SUSAN ELIZABETH PHILLIPS soars onto the *New York Times* bestseller list with every new publication. She's the only four-time recipient of the Romance Writers of America's prestigious Favorite Book of the Year Award. A resident of the Chicago suburbs, she is also a wife and the mother of two grown sons.